**"YES, ONE DA[ ]
SUBMIT [   ]T WIFE.**

"Submit. Men don't submit, they rule supreme."

"Yes, I suppose a woman would see things that way."

Granby stepped closer, and Catherine felt trapped.

"Tell me, do I need to apologize for being the son of an earl? Would tossing my rank and privilege to the wind cause those lovely eyes to see me more clearly?"

"Oh, I see you clearly enough, my lord" she replied.

One more step. He was looking down at her, their bodies separated by only a few inches of golden sunlight. "And how do you see me, Miss Hardwick?"

Too close! The lips that had once pressed so confidently down upon hers were only inches away, the eyes that seemed to sear into her very soul were flickering now with a hint of emotion that was easily recognizable. He was going to kiss her again.

HE SAID NO

Patricia Waddell

ZEBRA BOOKS
KENSINGTON PUBLISHING CORP.
http://www.kensingtonbooks.com

One

Summer 1863
Gloucestershire, England

Norton Russell Foxhall, the Earl of Granby, was a man who enjoyed life's many pleasures. Like most gambling men, the earl had a keen eye for cards, horses, and women. He was handsome and charming, always courteous, a gentleman of rank and influence. Yet there was that something about him that caused people to take notice, something impossible to put one's finger on, an elusive quality that hinted of things dangerous and bold.

There were suggestive whispers about him, though nothing for which he could be condemned, being a discreet man and enjoying his pursuits without scandal. He was moderate in his consumption of alcohol, zealous in his love of racing, and untouchable in the area of the heart, or so it was said, since not a single young lady had successfully gotten close to his.

Granby stood apart from the well-dressed crowd, his eyes trained on the horses about to take to the field, his pockets heavy with the day's winnings.

Lady Jane Aldershaw was also attending the steeplechase, which was being held in the heart of the Cotswolds, and the earl wasn't pleased.

He had no aversion to seeing the merry widow in London, but having her follow him into the country was a different matter. Beautiful though she may be, Lady Aldershaw was no exception to the earl's steadfast rule that women weren't to be trusted.

"She's with Gadlett," Viscount Rathbone said as he handed Granby a tankard of ale. "All smiles and doing her best to make you jealous."

Granby's mouth tightened slightly, but he said nothing. Alfred Gadlett was a likable sort, even if he was a bit odd. Of course, he was no match for the ravenous Lady Aldershaw. The earl wasn't worried about being ousted from the woman's bed by a better man. The encounter between himself and Lady Aldershaw had been a brief affair, ended because the earl had found himself bored with the prospect of bedding her again. Few women were able to keep his fires burning for long.

He liked variety too much to be content with a single woman for more than a few months. Lady Aldershaw had begun to try his patience almost immediately, but a widow had her merits—mainly that of knowing marriage wasn't a prerequisite for enjoying oneself, plus a knowledge of the preventive arts that alleviated the worries often associated with less experienced women.

Unfortunately, following Granby to the country ended the discreetness of the affair. It bordered on just plain foolishness, and the earl had no tolerance for fools, no matter their gender.

"I overheard the lady telling one of the locals that she's come to take the waters," Rathbone went on. Though Cheltenham's medicinal spring had been drawing patrons since King George III had visited the town in the previous century, his tone held a hint of cynicism.

Cheltenham was a charming village, nestled in the

uplands of Gloucestershire. The focal point of the town's medicinal wonders could be found at the Pittville Pump Room, a grand establishment that served up crystal goblets of the spring's healing water.

It wasn't unusual to find the foundation of British society visiting Cheltenham throughout the summer season: stylish matrons responsible for sending gossip from one end of the empire to the other; their honorable husbands, who spoke in the House of Lords; and lesser gentry, who enjoyed the races along with the soothing waters. Like Hyde Park, the spas of Cheltenham were a showplace of aristocratic importance where people gathered to be seen.

"If you're not careful, she'll be knocking on your door at the Stretton, claiming you've broken her heart," Rathbone warned.

"I won't be at the Stretton," Granby told him. "See that filly, the black one with a single white stocking?" He pointed to a young thoroughbred that had been bred for endurance, calm temperament, and larger than normal size, the qualities most sought in a good jumper. "While you were fetching ale and eavesdropping on the widow, I was discovering what stable had produced such a fine animal."

"And . . ."

"I intend to visit those stables," the earl announced. "In Winchcombe. Thus leaving Cheltenham and the lovely lady Aldershaw behind. Care to accompany me?"

The viscount shook his head. "Winchcombe is too quaint for me. Besides, Mother's expecting me in Herefordshire next week. Her birthday, you know. Can't very well misplace myself on such a day. Wouldn't be proper."

The very idea of Rathbone doing anything proper was enough to make Granby laugh. Viscount, gambler extraordinaire, skeptic, and friend, Rathbone was a man who saw nothing wrong with enjoying life to its fullest. Having been his friend for years, Granby had learned that when Rathbone was involved, it was wise not to inquire too deeply into the details.

"Give Lady Kendrick my regards," the earl said. "And watch yourself. Her husband may need spectacles to read the *Evening Chronicle*, but he isn't completely blind."

"The risk of getting caught with my pants down is half the fun," Rathbone said laughingly. "Nothing like a challenge to keep a man on his toes."

"Married women are more trouble than virgins," Granby decreed, speaking from the one experience he'd had with the energetic wife of a duke.

The viscount's reply was lost to the roaring cheers of race fans as the next event began. Both men were quickly caught up in the fever of watching the horse they had bet on take the first hurdle, then stretch out to gain speed for the second.

The steeplechase was a rousing run over an obstacle course of stone fences, green hedges, and water jumps. Though not as popular as the track racing to be found at Newmarket or Ascot, it did allow for its own entertainment and profit. In the earl's case, it also permitted him to inspect potential breeding stock for his own stables. A good steeplechase horse could be counted on to add to the betterment of any thoroughbred line.

The race over, Granby walked toward the stabling area, wanting a word with the man who had raced the black filly. He was interrupted along the way by his current nemesis, Lady Aldershaw.

"I thought it was you talking with Rathbone," she said. "How naughty of you not to say hello."

Granby looked at the classic beauty of Jane Aldershaw's face and the womanly curves draped in a gown of blue grosgrain silk. Her raven hair was hidden by a wide-brimmed straw bonnet, bearing a host of unnecessary ribbons. Was it only six days ago that they'd been engaged in a vigorous bout of lovemaking? But that had been then; this was the here and now, and Granby was more interested in horses than the widow's licentious appetites.

Unable to publicly voice his vexation at having her follow him from London, he regarded her with an impassive face. "Here to enjoy the waters?"

Lady Aldershaw lowered her voice to a whisper as she linked her arm through his. The gleam in her eyes was brazenly inviting as she looked up at him. "I'd rather enjoy you."

Granby graciously acknowledged the accolade to his virility with a bland smile. "Have you misplaced Gadlett?"

"You know I can't abide being alone," she said, offering him a perfect pout. "I needed an escort to attend the races. Please don't scold me. Alfred's harmless."

"But I don't mind at all," Granby said, his voice blasé. "I've never been one to begrudge a lady her pleasure."

The war between them didn't show on Granby's face; his expression one of mild interest as he glanced down at her. Realizing the earl had no intention of indulging her mood, the widow quickly changed her approach.

Her current lover was born into fortune and significant family. If he weren't considered such a good catch, she'd give him the tongue-lashing he deserved for deserting her without so much as a by-your-leave, but he was a good catch—an excellent catch and a fabulous lover. After he left her bed, she was forced to sleep from pure exhaustion.

"London has all but shriveled up since Parliament adjourned, and I was loath to travel straightaway to Southampton, so I decided a week or two at the spas would be just the thing."

"Cheltenham can be pleasant."

Jane Aldershaw knew she was being *dismissed*. Discarded as if the last three months had meant nothing to him. It was detestable of Granby to act so, especially in a public place where she dared not censure him for his lack of feeling. Damn the man and his exasperating indifference! He'd pay for treating her so shabbily.

Determined to keep her pride, Lady Aldershaw regarded him with feigned nonchalance. "Perhaps we will see each other at summer's end, at Waltham's regatta party. It's sure to be a crush this year, what with everyone wanting to gain the acquaintance of the new lady Waltham. The marquis has all but kept her a prisoner these past months."

"They're newlyweds," Granby said dryly. "It's to be expected."

Lady Aldershaw was referring to Marshall Bedford, the marquis of Waltham, and his new bride. Granby had feared that the relationship might end in matrimony when Marshall had shown up on his doorstep, determined to drink Evelyn Dennsworth off his mind. Being an understanding friend, Granby had furnished the whiskey.

Unfortunately, two bottles hadn't been enough—the marquis had succumbed to love's lure, wedding the lovely Evelyn shortly after the new year.

After a few awkward moments with Lady Aldershaw clinging to his arm, fate favored the earl with the appearance of Alfred Gadlett, a slender man with pale skin and eyebrows that looked as if they'd been touched up with burnt cork. A baronet with lands and a sizeable income, he was a good-natured chap, who naively expected a lady to be a lady.

"Granby," Gadlett said in greeting. "Good sport to be seen today, don't you agree?"

"Good sport, indeed," the earl replied, casually transferring Lady Aldershaw's gloved hand from his own arm to Alfred Gadlett's. "If you'll excuse me, I have winnings to collect."

Less than an hour later, the earl was in the saddle, riding north. The viscount had decided to ride with him, taking his own course come morning. Their coaches would follow, bringing their valets and luggage. If the weather held, the group would meet later that evening at Cleeve Hill. The hamlet offered a small inn with an accommodating landlord, who prided himself on serving the best ale in Gloucestershire. The following day would see the viscount on his way to Herefordshire, while the earl rode on to Winchcombe.

The two men, both blond and blue-eyed, had been friends since Eton. They were two of the five lords the duke of Morland casually referred to as "the lads."

The lads routinely gathered at Brooks each Wednesday night that Parliament was in session, to play cards with the duke. The game allowed Morland, a crotchety man in his late sixties, to keep an eye on the sons of his late friends. Both Granby and Rathbone could do with a little less overseeing, but their respect for the duke outweighed their occasional inclination to tell the old gent to kindly mind his own business.

"If you insist on continuing this little escapade with Lady Kendrick, be mindful that the old lord and Morland are friends," Granby advised Rathbone as they rode along the tree-shaded road that connected Cheltenham to the smaller towns of Prestbury and Southam.

Rathbone, who had been whistling a gay little tune, ceased and gave Granby a disgruntled look. "Watching me now that Waltham's taken the vow," the viscount remarked. "You'd do well to find a comely lass to replace the voluptuous widow. Celibacy doesn't suit you."

"I suppose I might be forced to attend a few soirees, but time will produce another lady whose lustful immodesties will keep me satisfied for the summer. And I'll be sure not to have the worry of colliding with the woman's husband in the corridor."

"You're turning into a prude," Rathbone grunted. "The next thing I know, I'll be standing by your side at the dreaded altar of sacrifice."

"Perish the thought."

"Then find a woman who isn't interested in marriage. Another widow, or a young woman eager to explore the uncharted territories of passion."

"A woman *not* interested in marriage? A beauty willing to yield to the urgings of unchecked lust? I doubt such a creature exists."

"Perhaps not," Rathbone conceded, "but don't discount the thrill of the chase."

Granby frowned on the inside. That was the problem of late. The chase had ceased to thrill him, probably because there was so little chasing to be done. Women normally gravitated to him like water to the bottom of a downhill slope. His title, his wealth, and his reputation for being a vigorous lover who enjoyed satisfying his partner as much as he satisfied himself, had women competing for his attention.

A woman whose mind wasn't filled with thoughts of marriage. Could such a female exist in the cosseted circle of English society? The earl seriously doubted it. All women silently applauded marriage, no matter their words to the contrary. Even Lady Aldershaw was trying to snag him, and she had no reason to remarry. The widow was well provided for, having inherited a small country estate, a lavish city residence in Marylebone, near Regent's Park, and a hefty allowance that kept her from having to bear the great evil of wearing the same gown twice in one fortnight.

"What has you brooding?" Rathbone asked, after a lengthy silence broken only by the chatter of birds and the rustle of small animals in the underbrush near the road.

"Nothing," Granby replied, not in the mood to discuss his current thoughts. "We should reach the inn shortly after dark. A cold tankard of ale and a hearty meal should serve us well."

"And a willing village lass," the viscount added with a wicked smile.

"You're incorrigible."

"No more than you," Rathbone told him. "The day you're not willing to climb on top of a woman is the day some squint-eyed vicar will be saying saintly words over your grave."

"I certainly hope so," Granby said, smiling. "As much as I distrust the lovely creatures, I can't imagine life without them."

Catherine Hardwick was a beauty, and sure to find a husband her first Season out. *If* that Season ever arrived.

"We've had this conversation before, Aunt Felicity. Society is naught but a labyrinth of silly rules and gossiping tongues. I'm perfectly content here in Winchcombe."

"Don't be tiring, my dear girl," Felicity Forbes-Hammond replied curtly. The elderly lady was an aunt by marriage, and determined to have some matronly influence over her niece's life.

"I was in London with Father only two years ago. It's a noisy place with too many people. The sky was thick with smoke, and the streets in need of a good scrubbing. Winchcombe has sunshine and beautiful country lanes, and I'm free to ride whenever I wish. In London, a lady isn't free to do anything but bat her eyelashes and act as if she doesn't have an ounce more sense than what she was born with."

"You're being stubborn. It's time that you pulled yourself away from this blissful country setting and visited London," Felicity insisted. "Your father relented to your wishes this Season. I daresay you won the argument by sheer persistence. But no longer. I have gained Warren's word that he will not heed your excuses another year. Stop frowning. It's not as if I'm whisking you away this very day. When the time comes, you will travel to London and stay with me, entering society under my watchful eye."

The two women were lingering over breakfast, Catherine's father already having left for the stables and his morning inspection of the horses he loved almost as much as he did his only daughter.

"I have no wish to marry," Catherine stated adamantly.

Felicity Forbes-Hammond was a power to be reckoned with when she made up her mind to accomplish something, and she was of a mind to see her beloved niece married. A stately woman with silver hair and piercing blue eyes, she was nearing seventy, but her heart was still full of fire, and her opinions were firmly stated whether you liked them or not.

Today she sat at the table in a gown of a blue so dark it appeared black, with ecru fichu at the neck, fastened with a brooch of black onyx. Across the table, Catherine could smell an elusive scent of expensive perfume. Her aunt had smooth skin, a well-defined mouth, and the constitution of a warhorse. A beauty in her own time, Felicity had married only once and had no children.

Now, having seen all but one of her nieces to the altar, she was determined to open the doors of society and make a proper job of shoving Catherine through them.

"Marriage is a respectable state," Felicity said, staring unflinchingly at her niece. "And you are being abominably testy about the topic. No one is going to force you to marry. Your father would have you contentedly wed."

"Contentedly wed," Catherine scoffed. A stiffness appeared about her neck and shoulders, a sign that she was going to fight both her aunt and her father every inch of the way. "Veronica Parnell wed two seasons ago, and she is miserable. Her husband is a tyrant. Theirs was said to be a perfect match. But for whom, I ask? Surely not poor Veronica. And what of Sarah Warbeck? Six months after her honeymoon, she found her husband with one of the maids. I'm sure Sarah thought herself happy until that moment. Please do not speak to me of contentment, Aunt Felicity. It does not exist in an arranged marriage."

"No one is arranging anything, my dear. I am simply pointing out that you cannot rusticate forever." She held up a hand to silence Catherine's protest. "Warren has indulged you too much these past few years. He knows the time nears when you will find a man to your liking and marry, no matter how repulsive the idea seems to you now."

"Men aren't to be trusted," Catherine said stridently.

Felicity Forbes-Hammond wasn't easily discouraged. "Soon, you will find that you are not as content as you think yourself to be. You are a woman now, and that maturity will demand things that are best left to marriage."

Catherine had been raised in the country on a small estate that specialized in breeding horses. She didn't blanch at the candid remark, but simply replied, "Knowing what one wants and refusing to be torn from that anchor is another sign of maturity. I'm not going to yield to some man just because he comments on the fairness of my features."

In truth, Catherine's features weren't fair at all, but bold. Her hair was a rich auburn, her eyes a bright, clear hazel. She was tall with an elegant body that was well toned from years of riding and jumping horses. Dressed as she was in a bottle green riding habit with a split skirt that allowed her to ride astride (she refused to have anything to do with a sidesaddle), she was a very impressive young woman. Dressed in satin or silk, she was breathtaking.

"Even a lady of firm intelligence and stout character can find herself catching the lascivious attentions of a man who forgets his manners," Felicity cautioned her. "Your father has witnessed the increasing admiration of the young men of Winchcombe. Realizing that you are fully grown and a woman in your own right, he would offer you the opportunity to meet better than the butcher's son."

"I'd rather have a man without a pence in his pocket than a city gentleman overstuffed with his own importance."

"Wealth is not the issue of which we speak. Nor is title, although you are sure to draw proposals from any number of lords," her aunt remarked. "All your father and I require is that the man be kind of heart and generous in attitude, of good family, and without vices that make him unacceptable as a husband."

"Saints don't populate the ballrooms of London."

"I will not allow you to marry a man who will make you unhappy," Felicity replied with full confidence. "I have a great affection for you, thus my concern that you will wither away if left to your own devices."

"I'm twenty-and-one, hardly withering," Catherine protested with a sinking heart. "Why is it that a woman is looked upon as a pitiful creature if she fails to acquire a husband, while men can remain bachelors their entire lives without their suitability being questioned?"

Felicity laid aside her napkin. "Civilization could hardly carry on if women did not seek marriage and the fulfillment of their natural inclinations, those of being a helpmate and a mother."

Catherine finished her tea, then excused herself from the table. It was obvious that she wasn't going to dissuade Felicity from her current line of thought. She might as well enjoy what she could of the day.

She walked to the stables, stopping along the way to take note of the clear skies. Wind scythed across the open meadows, spinning the leaves as it swept down and set the grass to dancing.

The village of Winchcombe lay south and west of her father's land, a scattering of thatched-roofed cottages and a lane that led the way to Sudeley Castle. It was a quaint little village, though not unknown to travelers.

Sudeley Castle had royal connections; it was steeped in history. Henry VIII had visited Sudeley on more than one occasion, as had more than one of his wives.

The castle now belonged to John Coucher Dent. His wife, Emma, was an enthusiastic lady with varied interests. They had no ties to the royal family, but Mr. Dent's circumstances allowed them to live as though they did. An heir to the wealth of a highly regarded Worcester glove company, the couple were determined to restore the old castle to its former grandeur.

Emma Dent was a collector of all sorts of things; among them were fine lace and embroideries, and theatrical costumes from all over Europe. She corresponded with Florence Nightingale on a regular basis. Like Felicity, Emma was strong in her opinions, dedicated to her family, and very intelligent. Catherine thought her a splendid lady, and often enjoyed afternoon tea at the castle.

Thinking a ride in that direction might help to clear the unpleasantness of the morning's conversation from her mind, Catherine strolled through the open doors of the stable. She was greeted by Jimkins, the stablemaster.

"Good morning to you, miss," he said, lifting his plaid beret. "You'll be wanting one of the boys to saddle your mare."

"I think I'll ride Storm Dancer this morning. He needs a good run."

"Begging your pardon, miss," said Jimkins deferentially, "that stallion's no fit mount for a lady."

"Saddle him anyway." Not being the type of young woman who would allow a frown, or anything else, to prevent her from doing what she wanted, Catherine smiled and said, "A romp will do us both good."

"Your father won't be liking it if you or the horse come limping home."

"Where is Father?"

"Left a while ago, he did. Took the curricle into the village to have a new axle fitted."

"I'll be back before he is," Catherine predicted. "Only a short run along the south lane. I promise."

Jimkins gave her a doubtful look before leading the stallion from his stall. He didn't have any doubts about Catherine's ability to ride the animal. She'd been born to the saddle, taking to her first pony at the age of four and riding every day since. It was a lady riding a man's mount that didn't sit right with him. Never would. Jimkins believed that a young lady shouldn't be gallivanting around the countryside like a cavalry officer, but voicing that opinion would get him nothing but trouble.

She was a feisty one, Hardwick's daughter, full of spirit and not afraid to blast a man's ears if he tried telling her the way of things. Past time she had a husband. Jimkins mumbled that very thing as he saddled Storm Dancer.

Once Storm Dancer was led from the stables, the stallion pawed the graveled courtyard, eager for the run the saddle promised.

"Watch yourself," Jimkins cautioned as Catherine put a booted foot into the stirrup. "He's in high spirits today."

"I'll be careful," she said, accepting the warning because Jimkins had put her on her first pony and led her around the paddock. He could be a crusty old man when he chose, but he was part of the family, at least here at Stonebridge. All the servants were, having taken it upon themselves to help raise Sir Hardwick's daughter after the death of his wife.

Many would think Catherine spoiled and overly pampered, but she wasn't. She was simply confident in the knowledge that she was loved by her father and all those in her household. And she loved them in return.

Giving Jimkins a bright smile, she urged the stallion into a easy trot, holding him back from the run he wanted until they were out of sight of the stables. Once she reached the end of the lane, she crossed the bridge that gave the estate its name, then nudged Storm Dancer forward.

The stallion answered with a burst of speed that left Catherine laughing out loud. She rode with an expertise born of skill and confidence, leaning over the stallion's muscular neck and urging him on with whispered words.

The thoroughbred stretched out his long legs and ate up the ground as if he were racing for the finish line at Epsom. The stallion, eager to run even faster, surged ahead, his muscles straining to devour as much ground as possible with each long stride.

Catherine laughed, enjoying the freedom of the moment, until she rounded the bend and nearly killed a man.

Two

One minute Granby was riding along at a leisurely pace, enjoying the morning sunshine; the next, chaos descended out of a clear blue sky. He reined his mount to the right with a fast, hard jerk. The animal reared up on its hind legs, nearly unseating its rider, but the earl managed to control the horse, avoiding a complete catastrophe.

When he had his mount safely in hand, he turned to find the other rider having more than a bit of difficulty. A woman! And she was riding one of the most magnificent stallions Granby had ever seen.

Catherine took a deep breath, thanking the Almighty that Storm Dancer hadn't put her backside in the dirt. The stallion pranced nervously for several more seconds, then blew out an indignant snort to let her know he'd rather keep running.

"Easy," she said. "Easy, Storm Dancer. Everything's all right."

"I beg to differ with you," came an angry male voice. "Things are far from 'all right.' Blast it woman, you could have killed me, yourself, and two fine horses."

Catherine reined Storm Dancer around, knowing she owed the man an apology. She was about to offer one, but he continued with his tongue-lashing.

"Have you no common sense? One does not ride along a country lane as if the hounds of hell were in pursuit." Steel blue eyes pierced her. "Are they in pursuit?"

"No." She took a quick breath, wanting to explain, but it wasn't quick enough. The man—a gentleman, from the cut of his clothes—continued his lecture.

"What are you doing riding such an animal? A stallion needs to be controlled, not given free rein on a public thoroughfare."

Catherine did her best to accept the scolding, knowing she deserved it. The man was a Londoner; he reeked of good breeding.

She met his angry gaze as he dismounted, then waited as he inspected his horse, stripping off his right glove before moving his hand expertly over the horse's legs and flanks. She should be doing the same with Storm Dancer, but she was eager for the man to be on his way.

Of course, she'd have to apologize first. Good manners demanded it, and she had been in the wrong.

After making sure that his mount hadn't suffered any injury, Granby turned to look at the young woman sitting atop the gray stallion. She was very pretty—not beautiful in the classic way of a lady. Her chin was too stubborn and her lower lip too full. Her hair was red—not the color of a new copper coin, but a spicy shade that made him think of nutmeg. Its rich color accented her hazel eyes. She sat the saddle with ease, her legs hugging the horse's sides. The split skirt of her riding habit covered her legs, stopping midway up her brown, knee-high riding boots.

"I apologize for frightening your horse, and putting your person at risk," she said to him. "This is not a public thoroughfare, but a private lane that is rarely traveled. I was not expecting to encounter anyone. Please forgive the upset, sir. I do wish you a good day."

She was going to ride off and leave him standing in the middle of the lane, despite the cavalier way she'd almost run him to ground. He didn't even know her name, and he did want to know it.

Who was she? Certainly not a village lass. She was too well dressed, and the stallion she was riding wasn't the type of animal to be owned by a local shopkeeper. Whoever she was, her father needed to be told that his daughter was a hellion and sure to get herself killed.

Or perhaps he should speak to her husband.

Granby hoped not—he didn't want the girl to be married. He wanted her to be as wild as she looked, sitting atop the stallion with the wind tugging at her auburn hair and her eyes bright with life. He wanted her to bite and scratch when he kissed her, to hiss before she purred.

And she would purr. He was sure of it.

There was passion in her. It showed in her eyes, slightly slanted and as curious as a cat's.

The thought brought a spontaneous reaction, tightening his body with anticipation. Despite the sexual spark, Granby was determined to put the fear of God into the girl. The thought of her lying in the dirt, trampled by the stallion's hooves—an event that could have easily resulted from her reckless riding—darkened his temper.

"A good day! I think not," he said, reaching out and taking hold of the stallion's bridle. "Get down."

"I will not."

"I would see that the horse isn't injured. Dismount."

Catherine hesitated. Everything about the man warned her away. He was tall and handsome and all too sure of himself. His countenance was stern, and she had no doubt she'd have to suffer another stinging lecture before he let her go her way.

"Down," Granby said, glaring at her. "This minute, or I shall see the deed done myself."

Catherine didn't doubt it. The challenge was implicit in every word he spoke. She left the saddle, but remained by Storm Dancer's side.

Granby didn't hesitate to give her another looking over. Up close, she was even more stunning. Her skin possessed the healthy color of a woman who enjoyed sunshine and fresh air. He found himself staring at her mouth and thinking what it would be like to take her full bottom lip between his teeth. He glanced at her hands. No sign of a ring showed beneath her snug-fitting gloves.

"I am quite capable of seeing to my own horse."

Catherine's gaze shifted to the stallion, then back to the man. He was not a shy lad from the village, nor one of the local farmers who would abide her unusual ways out of respect for her father. Not this man.

He was everything she disliked about proper gentlemen, and he was standing entirely too close. Catherine could see the gray flecks in his blue eyes and the firm set of his jaw. His face was cleanly shaved. The contrast of tanned skin, blue eyes, and silver-blond hair was striking.

He was a strong man. It showed in the way he moved, the set of his shoulders, and the strength of his hands as he controlled the stallion with no more than a grip on the bridle. Looking at him, Catherine couldn't help but think of Lucifer, the fallen angel who was said to be as beautiful as he was sinful.

Oh, yes, this man was the very reason she loathed the idea of a formal Season. He was a man like the one poor Veronica had married, all good looks and smooth words, words that held little truth when spoken by his sort; flattery came as naturally to them as good manners and polished boots.

"Storm Dancer is fine. If he were injured I would have known it immediately."

She wanted to be on her way, and rid of the *gentleman*.

The man ignored the remark, running a strong hand over Storm Dancer's front flanks. The stallion flicked his tail, but made no other sign of rejecting his touch. Catherine didn't like it. The stallion was notoriously skittish of strangers.

Storm Dancer. The name suited the animal, Granby thought as he continued inspecting the stallion, no longer looking for injuries so much as admiring the animal's superb configuration and temperament. At the same time, he had to admit that the girl was an excellent rider. A lot of men would have found themselves lacking when it came to controlling a speeding thoroughbred that suddenly had nowhere to go but over or around another horse and rider, yet the girl had managed it.

A thought took shape in Granby's mind. After a late breakfast at the White Lion Inn, a coaching establishment in the center of Winchcombe, he had asked the innkeeper for directions to Stonebridge Stables. Knowing he was on the right road, seeing the stallion, and judging the young lady's riding abilities and the quality of her clothing, Granby easily reached the conclusion that she was somehow related to Sir Warren Hardwick.

"Our introduction has been postponed," he said, giving her a bold look. "I am Lord Granby. And you are . . ."

Catherine knew when a man had less than gentlemanly intentions toward her. And this man's intentions were as plain as the aristocratic nose on his face. He was stripping her naked with his eyes and enjoying it.

Well, she wasn't. In fact, she'd be within her rights to slap him. Instead of giving in to her temper, Catherine gave him a placid smile, then thanked him for seeing to her horse. "If you're seeking Sudeley Castle, I'd be glad to direct you."

"I know the way to Sudeley," Granby said. "It's Stonebridge Stables I seek."

"Stonebridge." Catherine quickly concluded that the man must be in the market for one of her father's racers. But if he found the stables, he'd relay the experience of their meeting to Jimkins, and her father was sure to hear of it.

"You haven't given me your name," Granby reminded her, certain that it would be Hardwick.

"My name is of little importance," Catherine said, hoping to bring their meeting to a close. She needed to walk Storm Dancer, to cool him down before returning home. But how was she going to do that without meeting Lord Granby a second time in one day?

"I think not," he said. "Our meeting came close to being a disastrous one. I will escort you home."

He was still holding on to Storm Dancer's bridle, his own horse munching lazily at the grass near the roadside. Both animals were fully recovered from the episode that had occurred only minutes earlier.

"I can manage, but thank you for the courtesy."

"I fear it's a necessity," Granby said. "And I must insist on your name."

"There is no necessity, my lord. I was born here. I know my way home."

"But I would learn the way myself," he said calmly. "Considering your recent recklessness, it would be negligent of me not to see you safely home."

"I am not reckless. I can ride as well as any man," Catherine said, disliking his tone. "Had you not been on the lane, I would have encountered no difficulties."

He stood in front of her, cast in gold by the gleaming sunlight. She held his gaze, her eyes challenging and defiant.

"But I was on the lane. I still am," he said, smiling at her.

It was a handsome smile, guaranteed to set a woman's heart to fluttering—but not Catherine's. She was determined not to be influenced by a man's appearance, for she well knew it could hide a black heart, and she'd wager that this man's heart was as black as they came.

"I have already apologized for the incident, my lord. If you please, I will be on my way."

"But I don't please," Granby replied, sensing her nervousness.

It served her right. A few moments of remorse might make her think twice before galloping across the countryside again. She was obviously too wild to be constrained by the unspoken rules of polite society. The thought of taming that wildness, of bringing it under control—his control—sent a shaft of desire through Granby's body.

Catherine quickly calculated how successful she'd be if she attempted to mount Storm Dancer and leave the man to eat the stallion's dust. Not very, considering that he was still holding the stallion by the bridle. Nonetheless, she had to try. If he was the gentleman he claimed to be, he wouldn't physically detain her.

"If you please," she said again, hating the words because they made her sound weak and shy, and she was neither. "My horse."

"*Your* horse?" he said sarcastically. "I think not, Miss Hardwick."

It was a cutting remark that made Catherine grit her teeth. The man was no gentleman. And why had he demanded she tell him her name when he already knew who she was? Of course, if he was on the road to Stonebridge, then he knew that Sir Warren Hardwick owned the property. It had been a lucky guess, nothing more.

"Storm Dancer belongs to my father," she said, forced to correct herself. Her eyes flashed with anger. "Which makes him more mine than yours. Now, kindly step aside."

She moved around him, reaching for the saddle and raising her foot to the stirrup. It was as far as she got.

The next moment, she was being hauled back by an arm around her waist.

"Not so fast, Miss Hardwick."

Catherine's efforts to disengage herself from his grasp were joined by sputters and a billowing of words no real lady would dare to speak. She took a deep breath after calling him a compost heap, then tried kicking him in the shins.

Granby laughed, controlling her easily enough, although she was proving to be a handful—a handful of lush, tempting woman.

"Contain yourself," he said sharply. "Surely you can see that the pleasure of my company is not to be avoided."

"Pleasure! Let me go this very instant."

He was stronger than she'd first imagined. His arm felt like a steel band around her middle, and his thighs even harder. Her backside was pressed against him, and she was locked in place, unable to do more than flail her arms and legs in a ridiculous fashion. It was more than humiliating. It was infuriating. Once she was free, she *was* going to slap his face. Hard.

"Only if you promise to behave yourself."

Granby rather hoped she wouldn't. It had been a long time since he'd had to fight a woman to get a kiss out of her, and he was determined to have just that—a kiss. It was the least she could forfeit after nearly riding him into the dirt.

He carefully kept her at his side, not wanting his physical reaction to alarm her. She continued to stammer and stutter and call him all sorts of names, but to no avail. He was not going to release her until she relented to his authority. Why? Even Granby couldn't be certain. Perhaps it was the "thrill of the chase," as Rathbone had so aptly put it. Regardless of the reason, the girl intrigued him.

Finally, Catherine had no more fight left.

"Let me go," she said, her voice soft and apologetic.

Granby released her, then prepared himself to divert the slap he knew was coming. He caught her wrist as she raised her hand, then pulled her close, holding her tightly against his body.

She fit perfectly.

"I've a dilemma," he said, catching her other wrist before she could slap him with her left hand. "I could cut a switch and curb your recklessness with a good thrashing, or I could kiss you. Which shall it be Miss Hardwick?"

"My father will have you horsewhipped."

Granby laughed. God, she was beautiful when she was angry, all flashing eyes and stiff indignation. A true lady rarely showed her real emotions, but this woman—he could read the rage in her eyes. It was refreshing after all the proper young ladies he had met who suffered from such mediocrity of character that they were almost invisible.

"Then it shall be a kiss," he decreed casually. "But you must give it."

"I most certainly will not!"

"But you must," he told her. "If not, I shall have to take it. I fear your apology was lacking in sincerity. A kiss will set things straight."

His gaze moved to her mouth.

Catherine felt her insides begin to quiver. She'd never been kissed before, unless one counted the hasty peck on the cheek David Malbane had given her last year at the May Day dance. But Lord Granby wasn't threatening her with a quick kiss on the cheek. He'd kiss her like a real man kissed a real woman—full on the mouth.

The realization that she wanted just that kind of kiss frightened Catherine into a moment of speechless wonder. She stared into his eyes. They were as blue as the summer sky, flecked with gray, and staring right back at her.

"A simple kiss," she heard herself saying.

"A kiss is never simple."

Her eyes widened, and Granby realized that she was as innocent as he suspected. Gentlemanly manners called for her immediate release and a formal apology, but he wasn't all that much of a gentleman, and he wanted to kiss her. Just once.

It was a pity he couldn't pursue her. She'd make a fine mistress. But young ladies, feisty or not, were meant for marriage.

"Very well," she said in a low voice, relenting. "I will kiss you."

Granby waited. One second. Two. Then three. Surely the girl knew how to kiss a man.

"Allow me," he finally said, realizing she really didn't have the slightest idea how to go about it.

It wasn't the lascivious sort of kiss he was used to giving a woman. He kept his mouth closed and his tongue to himself.

Catherine Hardwick smelled of sunshine and wildflowers freshly touched by a gentle rain. She tasted young and wild and so good it was all Granby could do not to pull her into the woods and ravish her right then and there.

He had every intention of ending the kiss, when she parted her lips and unknowingly invited him inside. He couldn't resist. His tongue dipped into her mouth, and fate took over from there.

Catherine couldn't believe what was happening. She could hear the sound of wind rustling through the treetops, feel the heat of the sun, and at the same time the world was melting away. The odd feeling of being suspended in time was all too real—her body felt remote, but her thoughts were burning bright.

She liked being kissed.

At least she liked being kissed by this man.

It shouldn't be possible. He was everything she hoped to avoid in her life. *No*, she thought. *I can't like it—or him.*

Granby knew the exact moment she regretted the kiss.

He pulled back, but he didn't release her hands. "We should go now," he said matter-of-factly. "I will ride the stallion, and you shall ride Lieutenant."

He led her by the hand to where the gelding was waiting, then helped her to mount.

To Catherine's dismay, Storm Dancer didn't so much as flick his tail when he found Lord Granby atop his back.

"Come, Miss Hardwick," he said. "It's time to go."

The man was acting as if he kissed women on the road every day. Blast him for being such a charmer. Well, he wouldn't charm her again.

She'd agreed to the kiss because she'd been curious. Her curiosity was satisfied. Kissing a man could be very pleasant. But that was all she ever intended to do with this one. She'd gone riding to think, to find a way around her father and Aunt Felicity's plans. Lord Granby had distracted her, but he hadn't changed her mind about marriage or men.

Three

Granby's first glimpse of Stonebridge Stables was that of a long building of pale limestone, with sturdy doors and a pitched roof. A good distance beyond the stables, a large redbrick, Tudor-style house sat on the southern slope of a hill. It was a very nice house, not grand but welcoming, with double chimneys and a wide veranda. It had the air of opulent solidity acquired by a house after being occupied by the same family for many generations.

The grounds surrounding the house were neat and well managed, as were the paddocks at the base of the hill. He could see both horses and grooms at work, but none of the animals Granby saw compared to the stallion he was riding. Storm Dancer was a superb thoroughbred. The earl had made up his mind to make an offer for the animal the moment he'd realized that it belonged to Stonebridge.

A small, wiry man exited the stables. He slipped off a plaid beret and looked with open curiosity at the man and woman riding toward him. When they were within speaking distance, he called out, "Is everything all right, Miss Hardwick?"

Jimkins only addressed her formally when strangers were about. Any other time, she was "Missy."

"I'm fine, Jimkins. This is Lord Granby, recently arrived from London. I met him on the road. Since his destination was Stonebridge, I rode with him."

It wasn't all the truth, but it was all Catherine was willing to reveal.

Jimkins gave Granby a thorough looking over. The earl had met men like the stablemaster before. They were as protective of the families they served as they were of the horses placed in their care.

"May I ask why you be riding Storm Dancer, milord?"

"I admit to being impressed by the animal," Granby replied. "It took a bit of doing, but I convinced Miss Hardwick to allow me the pleasure of riding him, if only for a short distance."

The old man was looking skeptical, and Granby suspected that he knew the young lady hadn't willingly given up anything. He dismounted, handing the reins over to Jimkins before offering a hand in helping Catherine to dismount. Since they were being observed, she accepted it, sliding gracefully from the saddle. The moment her feet touched the ground, she stepped away from him.

"I will leave you in Jimkin's capable hands," she announced. "He's been with my father for years."

"Is your father in residence?" Granby asked, sensing that if she could run up the hill and away from him, she would. But she couldn't, not without letting Jimkins know that their meeting had been anything but casual.

Catherine wasn't overly worried that Lord Granby would say anything to her father, knowing that she could use the kiss against him. Even though she'd agreed to it, it was still highly improper for a gentleman to do what he'd done.

"My father went into the village," she said, "but he's expected back soon."

"Then I shall wait," Granby told her. The remark was

followed by a devilishly beguiling grin that Jimkins couldn't see. He turned to the stablemaster as soon as the expression did the trick and said, "I didn't pass anyone on the lane."

"It's possible Sir Hardwick took the turnoff to Sudeley Castle. He likes to drop by now and then to see how the mare he sold Mrs. Dent is doing."

"I'm sure you won't have to wait long," Catherine said, her tone as neutral as she could make it. "Jimkins will see to your comfort."

Stonebridge often entertained prospective buyers. There was a small cottage used for that very purpose. Her father rarely invited a buyer into the house. Business was business and family was family.

"Would you be looking to buy a racer, your lordship? Or perhaps a new mare? We've a real beauty in the pasture. She'll do any stallion proud."

"The stallion, if he's for sale."

"He isn't," Catherine said firmly. Her father had rejected every offer he'd received for Storm Dancer. The stallion would serve Stonebridge best at stud, siring future champions.

"Pity. Perhaps I can change Sir Hardwick's mind. I can be very persuasive."

Persuasive! Rude and arrogant was a better description.

Well, she'd had enough of Lord Granby for one day. She was going to the house. She'd have a cup of tea, a short nap, and Lord willing, when she woke up the insufferable man would be gone.

God forbid that Aunt Felicity discover him—a dinner invitation would be issued, and she'd be forced to abide "his lordship" for an entire evening.

Jimkins quickly engaged Granby in conversation, leaving Catherine free to walk up the hill toward the house. She forced herself to stroll casually, knowing a faster pace would only serve to affirm the earl's assumption that he had her on the run. As if she'd run from any man. She was her own person. And she'd prove it by living her life as she saw fit.

Granby watched her go, wondering how much information he might discreetly glean from the stablemaster. Catherine Hardwick wasn't married. Was she betrothed, engaged, enamored of some country squire? He hadn't seen her in London, and she was certainly old enough to have had a Season. Nor had he heard her name mentioned by anyone. If she had attended the last gathering of marriage-hungry females, Rathbone would have surely mentioned it; he had a nose for ferreting out beautiful young women.

After a moment's consideration, Granby doubted that Miss Hardwick had ever graced a London ballroom. She didn't even know how to kiss a man properly, and he couldn't fathom a young woman of her appearance in London without someone stealing a kiss.

"Do you confirm that Storm Dancer isn't for sale?" Granby asked of the stablemaster. It wouldn't do to let the old man think he had more than business on his mind.

Jimkins scratched his head before resettling his cap. "Well, now, ain't my place to say for sure. Sir Hardwick plans to use the stallion for stud, after a race or two. Nothing fancy, mind you, just a few local runs to get the attention of buyers."

"He could take the finish line at Ascot," Granby said. "Why not race him there? Or Epsom or Newmarket? Sir Hardwick's sure to get a good price."

"Sir Hardwick ain't much for venturing far from home," Jimkins told him. "'Course, that may change, what with Miss Hardwick being packed off to London next year."

"To enter society?"

"Aye, that be the reason," Jimkins said, as he led Storm Dancer into the stables for a good grooming.

Granby followed with his own horse. The stable was actually two limestone buildings facing each other, but joined with a single roof that provided a wide working area between the two aisles of stalls. The floor was cobbled and had been freshly scrubbed. Like the grounds, the stables were well kept and well organized. There were two large foaling stalls, big enough to allow several grooms to attend a delivering mare. Sir Hardwick knew his business.

"How long has Sir Hardwick operated a breeding stable?"

"Since he came back from service in Her Majesty's Eighth Hussars. The queen knighted him not long after he returned. It's a shame the Crimean didn't serve him as well," Jimkins said. "Took the starch out of him, it did, but Miss Catherine nursed him back to health. He's as fine a man as you'd ever want to meet."

"Lord Ackerman, a close friend, served with the Eighth Hussars. I shall have to ask if they're acquainted."

"Could be." Jimkins shrugged. He unsaddled the stallion, then called for one of the grooms to do the same for the earl's gelding.

Granby turned his mount over to a young man in his early twenties, with wavy red hair and an abundance of freckles. Another groom hurried inside to take over the task of grooming Storm Dancer.

"Let's leave the boys to their work," Jimkins said. "This way, your lordship."

Granby followed the older man to a small cottage. Like the other outbuildings on the estate, it was built of pale limestone. The roof was thatched, the door painted a bold, bright red. The floors were wood, scuffed by the constant traffic of riding boots. A rag rug lay in front of a large, stone fireplace. The furnishings were clean and comfortable. The wall behind the scarred mahogany desk displayed a painting of Sudeley Castle.

From what the earl could see, the cottage served as Sir Hardwick's office and study.

"There's liquor in the cabinet and ale in the keg," Jimkins told him. "We should be seeing the master before too long."

"Join me in an ale," Granby said, shedding his jacket. He'd lost his hat on the lane when Lieutenant had reared up and nearly unseated him. He'd take time to look for it on his way back to the White Lion Inn. He wasn't in any hurry to leave Winchcombe.

"Aye, I'd be glad to," Jimkins said. He hung his beret on a peg near the door before pouring two tankards of ale from a keg resting in a basin of ice. Most of the ice was melted, but the ale was cold enough to quench a man's summer thirst.

Granby make himself comfortable. The chair he chose was large and well cushioned with wide arms and a matching leather ottoman. "Tell me about Stonebridge Stables. I'd never heard of it until recently. Saw one of your horses run the steeplechase at Cheltenham. A black filly with one white stocking."

"Must have been Stepping Pretty. She's a natural jumper."

"She certainly took the hurdles at Cheltenham easily enough."

"If you're looking for a steeple horse, I'll have to tell you that Storm Dancer's better on an open run."

The sport of the steeplechase was taken from the English fondness for fox hunting, the courses built to resemble a run through a wooded area. The horses that ran such courses had to have more than speed, they had to be good jumpers that a rider could control with a touch of his heels. The object wasn't just to reach the finish line first; marks were given or taken away for the cleanness of each jump.

"I'm looking for breeding stock," Granby replied. "I make my home in Berkshire, near Reading. The stallion would suit me well."

"I'm sure he would." Jimkins smiled, showing a row of crooked teeth.

"I was surprised to see Miss Hardwick riding the stallion." It was a risky remark, but Granby chanced it.

The old man drew a deep breath, then let it out slowly. "She sits a saddle well. Put her on her first pony, a little Shetland it was. As for the stallion, it ain't my place to say what she should or shouldn't be doing."

The reply confirmed what Granby had already concluded. Miss Hardwick liked having things her own way. After that, he carefully kept the conversation focused on horses and the current racing season. As curious as he was about the young lady, the stablemaster wasn't the man to ask. Servants didn't gossip about their employer or their employer's family to anyone but other servants.

Granby was close to thinking that he wouldn't be meeting Sir Hardwick when the sound of crunching gravel announced the arrival of the stable's owner. The earl set aside his ale and followed Jimkins outside.

A curricle was parked in the middle of the stable's courtyard while two grooms busied themselves with removing two young bays from their harness. The horses were perfectly matched, their black manes thick and luxurious against dark brown coats that gleamed in the sunlight.

Sir Warren Hardwick was a burly man, growing bald, with a sharp, resourceful face and eyes of remarkable clarity. An imposing fellow with a deep voice and a stiff military posture, he was not a man anyone would dismiss easily. A long scar lay pinkish white against his weathered face. The wound, now long healed, looked to have been inflicted by the tip of a rapier, cutting from the man's temple to the inner corner of his jaw.

"Good day to you, my lord," he said jovially. "Welcome to Stonebridge."

"Thank you," Granby replied. "I'm impressed by what I've seen so far."

"He's got his eye on Storm Dancer," Jimkins said. "Come across Miss Catherine this morning on the lane. Talked her out of the saddle, he did, and come riding in here atop the brute as easy as you please."

Granby hid his amusement at the way Jimkins had explained the what, why, and where of everything in several casually phrased sentences.

"Took out Storm Dancer, did she?" Sir Hardwick mused out loud. "I can't say that I like it. Wouldn't have allowed it had I been here, but the girl's got a mind of her own. Takes after her mother." He looked toward the house for a moment, as if remembering something in the distant past, then blinked and turned to address Granby. "Hadn't thought about selling the stallion. He's the best stud I've got."

"It's what I have in mind. I'm looking to improve my stables."

Hardwick motioned him back to the cottage. "No harm in hearing a man's offer."

Granby found himself liking Sir Hardwick. Catherine's father was in his late fifties, with an easy way about him that belied his military service. After helping himself to an ale and refilling Granby's tankard, Hardwick settled himself behind his desk with a soft grunt of satisfaction.

"Well now, my lord, have you ever visited our little village before? Winchcombe's been my home all my life. Married a local lass. A fine woman, God rest her soul. Came back after my tour with the Hussars. Didn't have much say in the matter." He ran his finger down the length of his scarred face. "A cossack's sword came close to taking my head off. The charge at Balaclava was a bloody day, sir, a bloody day indeed."

Granby couldn't argue. The fateful Charge of the Light Brigade at Balaclava hadn't been England's finest hour, not if you counted the casualties that lay on the battlefield afterward.

"Would you by chance know Lord Ackerman? He would have been Lieutenant Minstead to you."

"Minstead. A good solider, if I recall. Fine man. So he's a lord now, is he?"

"Inherited the title after his brother's death."

The conversation returned to the stallion. Granby offered a fair price, but Hardwick shook his head. "It's a nice amount of coin, but I'll need to think on the matter."

"Good enough," Granby said, coming to his feet. "I'll return tomorrow, if I may?"

"Come back tonight," Hardwick told him. "For supper. Mrs. Gibson sets a fine table, and we've another visitor, Lady Felicity Forbes-Hammond."

"Thank you for the invitation. I accept," Granby replied. "Lady Forbes-Hammond is an aunt to Lady Sterling, is she not?"

The matron wasn't the exclusive leader of society, but she had influence, often giving or withholding her approval in tandem with London's other hostesses. If she was seeing to the lovely Catherine's debut in London, Hardwick's daughter was sure to be accepted.

"Sterling," Hardwick said, looking pensive. "Yes, I believe you're right. Forgive me if I seem hesitant, but I haven't been to London since the queen called me to knighthood. Didn't think I deserved it. Wasn't anymore courageous than anyone else that day, but one doesn't refuse the queen."

"No, one doesn't," Granby agreed. "I shall call again this evening. Is eight o'clock satisfactory?"

"Excellent. The ladies will be pleased."

Granby knew Lady Felicity would be glad to see him. If she was sponsoring Catherine, then she was already preparing a list of candidates. He'd have to be careful,

or his name would be at the top of that list, especially
since Felicity was related to the wife of one of his best
friends. The matron wasn't above using the connection
to her advantage. Still, it might be an enjoyable evening.

The earl's spirits continued to rise as he rode into
the peaceful little village of Winchcombe, with its quaint
shops and church towers. As he tossed the reins to the
boy who worked at the inn, Granby couldn't help but
smile. It had been a very interesting day.

Four

The eventful day was by no means over, or so Catherine discovered when Felicity announced that Lord Granby was to join them for dinner. They were in the small sitting room on the second floor, taking afternoon tea, when the news was delivered.

"I understand you met Lord Granby on the lane this morning," Felicity said in a congenial tone.

Too congenial for Catherine to think she could sway her aunt to a more palatable topic. She had returned to her room that morning, after her ride and the memorable meeting, in considerable irritation that a man—any man—could have such a profound effect on her. Innocent, but not naive, she was aware of the propensity of men such as the earl to charmingly weasel their way into a lady's affection, only to take advantage.

Of course, there had been nothing charming about the Earl of Granby. And, unfortunately, there was nothing about his appearance to make one think of a weasel. Things could easily be put in perspective, if that were the case.

Since it was not, Catherine had eased her guilt over nearly trampling the man into the ground by telling

herself that the kiss had been more than enough rec-
ompense to settle any injury his lordship's system might
have suffered.

"The earl and I had a common destination," she replied to Felicity's inquiry. "I was returning from my ride
while he was bound for Stonebridge. We shared the
lane, little more."

It was a bold lie, but Catherine didn't dare admit that
the earl had been anything less than the most affable of
gentlemen. Admiring her aunt's social resourcefulness
and becoming the victim of it were two different things.
She had no intention of putting a weapon that could be
used against her into Felicity's capable hands.

It had been a kiss, nothing more.

Another lie.

It had been much more than a kiss. It had been her
first *real* kiss, one she wasn't likely to forget if she were
kissed a million times between now and her dotage.
Therein lay the problem. Despite her belief in the practicality of keeping a man at arm's length, she could recall every detail of the outrageously demanded kiss; even
now, she could feel the strength of Granby's arms and
the searing sensation that had accompanied his tongue
when it had filled her mouth.

It had been a wicked kiss.

Totally improper, both in action and motivation, and
yet its very wickedness had made it all the more appealing.

Catherine wondered if all women felt sinful the first
time they pressed their lips against a man's mouth. She
could ask Veronica or Sarah, both had been lifelong
friends and would surely tell her the truth of it, but
Catherine knew she wouldn't seek the answer. What
had passed between herself and the earl would remain
a very personal, very private matter.

"Lord Granby is a good friend of the viscount's,"
Felicity was saying. "Are you listening, my dear?"

"Yes, of course," Catherine replied, realizing she'd been staring at the vase of roses on the small spindle-legged tabled in the corner with a rather dim-witted expression on her face. It wouldn't do to let Felicity think she was brooding over something. "Sterling married your niece, Rebecca Lowery. Father and I received an invitation, at your insistence, I'm sure, but he was recovering from a sprained ankle and we were unable to attend."

"Lovely wedding," Felicity remarked. "They have a son now. Morgan Emanuel. Inherited his mother's eyes. As blue as periwinkles. Another of Granby's closest friends, the Marquis of Waltham, married this winter. I know nothing of the young lady's family, but it seems a good match."

Catherine chose not to comment. Her aunt had skillfully maneuvered the conversation around to marriage and weddings. Silence was her only ally.

"Well, tell me," Felicity said with a huff of impatient air. "What do you think of Granby?"

If only she could say what she really thought. Knowing she couldn't, Catherine studied the matter for a moment, then presented a bland expression. "He seems a gentleman."

Her transparent attempt at diplomacy failed miserably.

Felicity regarded her with perturbation. "Lord Granby's status as a gentleman does not make him an ogre. Really, child, you can be most stubborn at times."

So much for silence.

"You have matchmaking in your eyes," Catherine replied candidly, "and I'll have none of it. At least, not here at Stonebridge. If I must suffer London, then so be it, but I will not have Lord Granby, or any other man, waved under my nose like a bottle of smelling salts to bring me to my senses."

"You speak of marriage as if it were a plague to be avoided at all cost," Felicity countered just as candidly.

Not a woman to bandy words, she continued in a tone that gave Catherine no recourse. "I suppose it is well enough for some women to remain unwed; especially those who are so independent they cannot see the benefit of things. But not you, my dear. You are young and full of life, and most certainly lovely enough to draw and hold a man's attention, as well as his affection. As for Lord Granby, he is a most eligible man. The taking of a wife is a duty, an obligation to his title, and one he must eventually face. Why not you? Knowing Granby, as I do, I think you well suited."

"Well suited!"

"He is a bit of a rogue, always has been, but both Sterling and Waltham have settled in nicely enough and the ladies who won their hearts are no more lovely, or tenacious, than you."

Catherine almost chocked on her buttered bun. "Really, Aunt Felicity, I have explicit faith in your good sense, but to think that Lord Granby and I are suited to each other is a stretch of the imagination. He is a gentleman of rank and privilege, and will be a guest in our house this evening. I will treat him accordingly, but nothing more."

The conversation which Felicity let pass, not because she was convinced that Catherine had no interest in the earl, but because she was an astute woman, thus knowing when to press forward and when to retreat, was the cause of her niece's bad humor for the balance of the day.

As evening drew near and she was forced to dress for a formal dinner—Felicity had so informed Mrs. Gibson, who did double duty as maid and cook, that the best china was to be used—Catherine couldn't nullify the feeling that doom was on the horizon. If only she hadn't had such a daring encounter with the earl that very morning, she might be able to regard him with total indifference come dinner. That, however, was not the case.

They had shared a most robust kiss, one that had caused the most provocative sensations to curl through Catherine's body. That being the case, she had no desire to face the gentleman again, knowing, as he would, that she had agreed to the kiss.

Oh, he would smile cordially, but underneath that smile would be the knowledge that he had bested her.

Catherine felt no better about the impending meal than she had earlier in the day when the mandate had been handed down that she would be on her father's arm when the earl arrived. Since pleading a headache would only raise Felicity's efforts to their highest level, Catherine weighed her sense of trepidation against her duty as her father's daughter, and decided there was no way around it. She'd have to be charmingly polite to the damn man.

It was an infuriating bit of crow Catherine was forced to swallow as she rang for her maid, Agnes.

Agnes, like Mrs. Gibson, carried out more than one set of duties. She doubled as lady's maid and laundress. Mrs. Gibson was the despot who ruled the household, while Agnes was as quiet as a wren during a rainstorm, rarely answering in more than a single word regardless of the question put to her. Not a pretty girl by any stretch of the imagination, she was a good worker and fit into the household without a hitch, being married to one of the grooms.

Aunt Felicity had brought her own maid, a middle-aged woman with a fair complexion and dark hair. It was this maid, not the expected Agnes, who appeared in Catherine's room a few moments later.

"Lady Forbes-Hammond asked me to attend you, miss," Mary replied, when Catherine voiced her surprise. "I've a good hand with hair and such, and she said you wanted to look your best, what with a lord coming to dinner and all."

"Thank you," Catherine said, thinking Felicity might

have suspected that she cared little about her appearance that night. "I shall wear the blue dress. It's last year's fashion, but I'm certain Lord Granby, being a Londoner, will expect those of us who live in the country to be behind the times."

Mary tightened her mouth, then shook her head. "I think the green would suit you better. Your eyes, miss. They're a lovely shade and the dress would do them justice."

Catherine had already decided against wearing the green satin. It was her finest gown, not fashioned for a ball, nothing that extreme, but well cut for an evening of formal entertaining at home, the very reason Veronica had talked her into buying the fabric.

Poor Veronica. The last letter Catherine had received from her childhood friend had hinted that things were still stiffly formal between Veronica and her husband of less than a year. Lord Curtley had undergone a complete metamorphosis of character after the wedding. Once the vows had been spoken, literally transferring Veronica to his ownership, he had ceased being pleasant, turning instead into a demanding husband who belittled and criticized at every turn.

Veronica lacked Catherine's stout constitution; she was a soft-spoken, amicable young lady who had sincerely thought herself in love. Besotted by a show of false charm was more like it. Catherine had not liked Lord Curtley on sight, but no matter how often she had verbalized her suspicions that the man was not what he professed to be, Veronica had ignored her.

Now her friend was forced to tolerate a husband who found nothing at all suitable about her once he'd assumed control of the large acreage of land in north Gloucestershire that was part of Veronica's dowry.

Sarah was faring no better. Silas Travers, Lord Dunvale, was a baronet and a womanizer. His lands were substantial, and Sarah had all she needed—monetarily speaking. What she lacked was not only her husband's true affection, but his respect.

Less than a fortnight ago, Catherine had taken the coach, duly chaperoned by Agnes and her husband, who visited relatives, thus making the trip beneficial to all, to call upon Sarah in her new home near Farmcotte, a small village northeast of Winchcombe. Her husband had been in residence, gravely restricting their privacy, but Sarah had managed enough time alone with Catherine to relate the detestable details of finding her husband coupling with the parlor maid.

The worst, or so Sarah had said, and Catherine had sympathetically agreed, was not discovering her husband's unfaithfulness as much as it was being forced to see the pretty little parlor maid each and every day— Dunvale had refused to dismiss her, firmly stating that Sarah was making far too much of the "incident."

It was one of the rare times when Catherine had wished herself a man, thus the pleasure of calling Lord Dunvale to account for his despicable actions and subsequent indifference to his wife's tender feelings. Her gender did not, however, prove a deterrent when it came to blistering the man's ears.

Before leaving Farmcotte, Catherine had strolled into his lordship's library, shut the door, and delivered a sermon worthy of any minister, calling down God's wrath on the baronet's head should he do any further harm to his wife.

A letter had come by post less than a week later. Sarah was forced to sadly inform Catherine, her dearest and most devoted friend, that her presence would not be welcome should she try and visit again.

Both women were justified in leaving their unprincipled husbands and returning home to the bosoms of their families, but alas, that was not the way of things at present. Once wed, a woman was forced to endure. Lack of endurance was rewarded not with sympathy or compassion, but with cold disdain, for men ruled England, despite the female sovereign currently occupying the throne.

Had Catherine suffered the distress of her two dearest friends, she would not have hesitated to throw convention to the wind, take a buggy whip to the offending husband, and be on her way. But neither Veronica or Sarah were like her. Neither would risk bringing shame upon their families, though Catherine saw no shame in maintaining one's self-respect.

It was not the quality of a woman's heart that mattered to most men, but her ability to be charming in society, tolerant in her private demands, and gracious in her forgiveness. To be anything less was to be unladylike.

And Aunt Felicity thinks I'm being stubborn.

"Self-preserving is more like it," Catherine mumbled as she sucked in her breath and held it while Mary laced her corset. Much too snug for comfort, Catherine chided her, though the maid showed no signs of remorse.

Next came three petticoats, each fuller and stiffer than the one before, but again a necessary discomfort. By the time pearl earrings and a matching choker were added, Catherine looked as beautiful as anyone had ever seen her.

Her cinnamon-colored hair was arranged in a fashionable coiffure, with curls piled thickly at the crown, and more curls dangling down in a flawlessly planned disarray that accentuated her throat and partially bared shoulders. The gown was modestly cut compared to those worn in London, but given its wearer's graceful curves and bold coloring, perfection was easily achieved.

"Will you require the coach, milord?" Peck asked of his employer as the sun cast its evening rays on Winchcombe, gracing the village with a picturesque illumination that any artist would envy.

"It's a pleasant-enough evening to ride," Granby replied. "Tell the coachman to enjoy a tankard or two."

"As you wish," Peck replied, helping his lordship into a dove gray jacket of impeccable cut.

Any gentleman would be distressed by a failure on his valet's part to have foreseen the possibility of a formal occasion on a country jaunt, thereby failing to pack a proper change of clothes. But that was not the case when it came to Peck. Granby had inherited the unfaltering valet along with his earldom.

Peck—Jasper Jeremiah Peckwick, to those who knew him formally, though Granby couldn't fathom who that might be—was as loyal and opinionated an any gentleman's gentleman in all of Christendom. In his mid-sixties, and suffering from gout whenever the weather took an unpleasant turn, Peck had served Granby's father with the same steadfast devotion in which he now served the new earl. He also felt obliged to remind his employer, whenever the occasion arose, that he was not required to remain in service, having received a tidy pension with the old earl's passing, but felt it his duty until such time as the new earl decided to stop living so shamefully and find himself a proper wife.

Rathbone had once remarked that he fared much better with a ruthless mother than Granby did with his unrelenting valet. The earl was forced to agree. This very evening, as a matter of fact, from the moment he'd announced that he was dining with Sir Warren Hardwick and his daughter, Peck had taken up the gauntlet most vigorously, inquiring into the young lady's attributes, and observing that a nice country lass would settle in nicely.

"Make good mothers, these country girls," Peck said. "Even-tempered and loyal, without having to be encouraged with bangles and fripperies."

"Good heavens, I'm having dinner, not proposing to the chit," Granby said contemptuously. "As for children, you will probably live to see the day, knowing your stubbornness on the matter, but it will not be in the foreseeable future. Miss Hardwick is lovely, but not at all the sort of female I would choose for a wife, *when* the time is forced upon me. Until then, I thank you to keep your opinion of country lasses to yourself."

"As you wish, milord," Peck said, both of them knowing full well that the dogmatic valet would continue voicing his opinion whenever, in his advanced judgment, the young earl needed to hear it.

Both also know that the new earl would ignore the older man's guidance in much the same way he ignored everything else the surly servant had to say. To the earl's way of thinking, it was the best way to deal with Peck's reproof. He couldn't fire the man, nor could he force Peck into retirement. The valet had to be tolerated, for the sake of his father's memory, and that was that.

Leaving the White Lion Inn, Granby tossed a coin to the boy who led his horse from the stable. Within minutes he was mounted and on his way, the sunset having faded to a soft twilight that gentled the evening.

As he rode down Vineyard Street, then crossed the bridge that would take him past the entrance to Sudeley Castle, Granby's thoughts settled upon Miss Catherine Hardwick. Despite the short amount of time that had elapsed since they had parted company, Granby admitted to an eagerness to see her again.

He doubted the lady shared his enthusiasm. That in itself was enough to pique Granby's interest.

Catherine Hardwick was the belle of the village, and no doubt approached in supplication by the local lads. Granby was sure that none of the young men had ever accosted her, forcing her acquiescence as he had done that morning.

He smiled, remembering that very little force had

been necessary once he'd mentioned his intentions were to kiss her. Her cooperation could be easily explained by the fact that she was still young, merely learning life as it came, and there was little of importance to learn in the country, especially when it came to the ways of men.

She had been curious; of that much Granby was certain. But even after the kiss, her eyes had shone too brightly with innocence, and there had been a hint of stubbornness about her mouth, as if she were trying to act more hardened than a young lady her age could possibly be.

Thus her attraction—a mystique that intrigued at the same time it warned a man to tread carefully, lest he be ensnared by her country charms. Or lack of them, Granby amended the thought, recalling the assortment of blasphemies she had heaped upon his head when he'd prevented her riding away.

Perhaps that was the fascination, the cause of the nagging thoughts that had remained with him all day: the contradiction of the lady; one moment innocent, the next fighting and feisty.

Granby knew he should have refused Sir Hardwick's invitation. The business of buying livestock didn't require dinner conversation, but he had wanted to see Catherine again. Her striking good looks were enough to compel any man, but it was her manner, her boldness, that attracted him.

Ladies didn't show their temper, but this one did. She was unlike other women and that difference made her dangerous.

He wanted her—a fiery virgin with catlike eyes and a body created for a man's pleasure. But, scoundrel that he was, he was still no spoiler of innocents.

The virgin daughter of a man knighted by the queen was not a lady to be dallied with inconsequentially, which meant he couldn't pursue Catherine Hardwick. He could smile, and most certainly tease, for her behavior demanded it of him, and perhaps steal another kiss, but nothing more.

Having reached that decision, and the fork in the lane that would take him to Stonebridge, the earl turned his thoughts away from the impulsive behavior that had gotten him a kiss that morning and concentrated on how best to convince Sir Hardwick to part with Storm Dancer.

Five

Granby was shown into the drawing room after giving his hat and gloves to the elderly footman who opened the door. He was immediately impressed with the house. It had been built to live in, not to engage compliments and entertain society; a home with cozy corners and comfortable chairs. There was a grand staircase with a wide balustrade, and furniture by Sheraton and Hepplewhite, purchased for its practicality, not its price, and colorful carpets.

The room offered a sofa upholstered in dark green fabric and decorated with plump cushions embellished by large gold tassels. A spindle-legged side table stood under a mirror framed in gilt, flanked by two button-backed chairs. Three tall windows draped with curtains of somber green velvet looked out over a small garden. The drop dial clock on the wall was chiming the hour when Sir Hardwick strolled into the room.

"Aye, Lord Granby, perfect timing. We shall have a drink before the ladies join us. Thought old Gabs might have shown you to the library, but I see Felicity's had her hand in things. Country lad, like myself, doesn't know what's what when it comes to the formalities of greeting a lord of the realm. Mustn't be offended, he's a good man. Well, my lord, what will it be? Brandy, port, or something with more character?"

"I've a fondness for whiskey."

"A man after my own heart."

After requesting their whiskeys, Hardwick indicated one of the armchairs in tacit invitation, while making himself comfortable on the sofa.

"So, you're of a mind to better your stables, are you? Always a good investment, and a pleasure, but then I prefer horses to people, always have," Hardwick said, beginning the conversation.

Granby replied with a smile and a nod of his head as a stiff-legged Gabs brought in the whiskey. Once it had been dispensed, he eased back in his chair and continued the conversation, commenting on the horse he had seen running the steeplechase at Cheltenham. A discussion ensued, centered around the qualifications of a good jumper.

A few minutes later, the door opened and they were joined by the ladies.

Granby stopped mid-sentence and stood up. One look at Hardwick's daughter and his body tightened. Had the windows been open, his good intentions would have taken flight. Catherine was exquisitely beautiful in a gown of dark emerald green that brought out the fire in her eyes and the rich coloring of her auburn hair. The gown was modestly cut, but no amount of cloth could conceal the utter femininity of her body.

Her expression was bland when she turned to him, but Granby sensed a hint of something in her eyes— embarrassment? No. Resolve. She was determined to act as if he'd never kissed her.

Lady Forbes-Hammond immediately took the lead, smiling up at Granby with an outrageous twinkle in her cobalt blue eyes that confirmed his original suspicions. The matron had matchmaking on her mind.

Despite her obvious motives, Granby greeted Felicity with a warm smile. "Lady Forbes-Hammond," he said, bending over her gloved hand. "As always, a pleasure."

He greeted Catherine with the same politeness, smiling inwardly at the flash of anger in her eyes. So, she was determined to treat him like a stranger, was she? Well, the evening wasn't over, and before it was, Granby was just as determined to make sure the young lady had something to occupy her nightly dreams.

It was wrong of him, he knew, but he'd never been a man to turn away from a challenge, and Catherine's attitude *was* challenging.

"I understand you met my niece on the lane this morning," Felicity said.

"Yes, but I wasn't aware that she was your niece," Granby replied, as the ladies sat down on the sofa.

"Not by blood," Felicity said. "Sir Hardwick's wife and I were close friends. I have kept myself in the family since Lucinda's death."

"A fortuitous blessing, I'm sure."

"There are times Catherine would disagree," Felicity replied with her usual candor. "At present, she is being most stubborn about accompanying me to London. She prefers the country."

"As do I," Granby said, pleased that he hadn't been wrong. Catherine Hardwick had never been paraded among the jackals of London. "Once I convince Sir Hardwick to sell me his prize stallion, I will be on my way to Reading and my own country estate."

"Storm Dancer isn't for sale," Catherine announced, speaking for the first time since entering the room. She hadn't said a word when Lord Granby had bowed over her hand, even though his touch had provoked more than a slight reaction. Those same hands had held her rather forcefully only that morning.

"Well, now, don't be stopping the man from making

an offer," Hardwick interjected humorously. "Every horse has his price."

"Not Storm Dancer," Catherine said, turning her eyes to her father. "You know how I feel about him."

Granby couldn't see her expression from where he was sitting, but he was sure it was perfectly pleading, the beloved daughter silently beseeching her father not to sell off the family pet.

"It wasn't well done of you to have the stallion in the lane this morning," her father replied.

The scolding was done with a smile, Granby noted. So Miss Catherine was the apple of her father's eyes, was she? More the reason to make sure, privately, of course, that the little hellion didn't get herself killed riding around the countryside at breakneck speed.

"Don't tell me you were riding that big brute of an animal this morning," Felicity said in a reproving tone. "Have you no fear for your safety?"

"Storm Dancer isn't a brute."

"Still, I shan't like to see you riding him again." Felicity looked toward Catherine's father, as if to confirm that a decree of just that magnitude would be handed down the moment father and daughter were alone.

Granby observed the exchange, agreeing with Felicity, but unable to voice an opinion.

"I'm an excellent rider," Catherine said in her own defense.

Before anything more could be added, a dour-faced Gabs announced that supper was being served. Granby stood, offering his arm to Felicity, but casting a glance at Catherine. She had managed to regain her blank expression, but he could tell that underneath the calm veneer, her temper was ready to explode.

As the guest of honor, Granby was seated on Hardwick's right. Lady Forbes-Hammond was directly across from him, with Catherine to her left. The dining room was in proportion to the house: not overly large, but not small, the table capable of seating a dozen or more people.

Hardwick led the conversation, commenting on a local newspaper's account of Parliament's last session and the liberal views that were currently sweeping the country. "Pure poppycock, if you ask me," he said, his speech unhindered by the presence of ladies. "Hope you're not one of them liberal-minded lords. Didn't think to ask before speaking my mind."

"It depends on the circumstances," Granby replied. "And I admire a man who speaks his mind. Have you considered standing for the Commons?"

"Perish the thought," Hardwick exclaimed. "I'm a country squire now, and content to be one. More than happy to leave the sputtering and speech-giving to those who enjoy it."

"Did you come to Winchcombe directly from London?" Felicity asked as the footman collected the soup bowls. A roasted duck took center stage on the dining table as she put the question to Granby.

"No. I was attending the steeplechase in Cheltenham. A fine jumper, which I later discovered had been bred here at Stonebridge, detoured me from my original plans to travel straight home to Reading."

Lady Forbes-Hammond directed the conversation from that point, focusing on topics more suited to mixed company. All the while Granby was conscious of Catherine's attention—indirectly, of course. The glances were quick, and often disdainful. She said little, commenting when spoken to directly, but otherwise content to do what she had come to the table to do—enjoy a meal.

In reply to her supercilious glances, Granby issued charming smiles that were guaranteed to ruffle her seemingly calm feathers. By the time the meal ended, the young lady's demeanor had gone from indifferent to hostile.

There was nothing coy or casual about the glare she gave him when he helped her away from the table. When he offered to escort her to the salon, she turned her back on him in a manner that was abruptly impolite, seeking her father's arm instead.

Hardwick didn't take note of the deliberate slight, since he was engaged in instructing Gabs that brandy would be taken in the library. Apparently, the old footman was as deaf as he was stiff, forcing Hardwick to all but shout at him.

The cut, however, did not go unnoticed by Felicity, who sent a fierce scowl in Catherine's direction. Granby pretended it had been his intention all along to offer his arm to the older of the two women, thereby avoiding any disruption to the evening.

His turn would come.

And when it did, he meant to make sure Miss Hardwick realized whom she was engaging in a very dangerous game of cat and mouse. The young lady needed a dose of humility, and Granby was just the man to administer it.

If he knew anything, it was women, having been a devoted fan of the gender since his fifteenth birthday, when he'd become intimately acquainted with a local music teacher. Miss Kane had been employed by a neighboring household to instruct their two tone-deaf daughters. Granby had alleviated her summer frustrations by meeting her almost daily in a snug little cottage on his father's estate. From that summer forth, the heir to the Granby earldom had made women his main occupation.

Confident that Catherine Hardwick had ventured well beyond her league, the earl promised himself a fitting retribution before the night was over.

The library was a large room, done in soft browns and reds, a man's domain. Several glass-fronted cases displayed a collection of books, most of them on horses and horse breeding. Once brandy had been poured and

Turkish cigars lit, Granby made Sir Hardwick an offer for the stallion.

"Well, now, that's a fine price indeed," his host replied, "but I'm still not of a mind to sell Storm Dancer."

While Lord Granby was secluded with her father, enjoying the amenities due a gentleman, Catherine was receiving a tongue-lashing from her aunt.

"My dear girl, you cannot go about cutting a gentleman of Granby's position, it simply isn't done, never mind that it was an extreme rudeness. And don't act as if you don't know what I'm talking about," Felicity continued firmly. "One would think the man suffered from the pox, the way you've treated him this evening. And without excuse."

"I don't like him," Catherine replied, hoping a direct approach would put an end to things.

"Whyever not?"

A slight shrug accompanied the not so truthful answer. "He brings Lord Dunvale to mind. I cannot look at him without thinking of poor Sarah's misery."

"Balderdash!" Felicity retorted. "Granby is nothing at all like Dunvale. And I tire of hearing about poor Sarah's misery. She is married to the man, and there is little that can be done about it. Regardless, her situation should not prevent you from thinking of your own future happiness."

"It won't be found with a man like Lord Granby," Catherine said. "I am not so deeply buried in the country that I haven't heard of the man's reputation."

She was bluffing; Catherine knew nothing about the earl, but it stood to reason that he was a womanizer. His smile was too mischievous, his manner too charming, and his gaze too bold for him to be anything else. He was a rogue, no doubt about it. Sinfully handsome and aristocratically arrogant.

A true gentleman would never have done what he had done. No gentleman would have the audacity to accost a young lady on the road, then accept an invitation to dine at her father's table.

"Comparing Lord Granby to someone as distastefully crude as Dunvale does not excuse your bad manners," Felicity scolded her crisply. "Granby is of respectable family, and titled. As for his disposition, it has always been congenial. I regret that I cannot say the same for you."

Catherine's response was stopped by the appearance of her father and Lord Granby. Forcing a smile to her face, she nonchalantly adjusted the folds of her skirt, refusing to look at the man. It was another cut, one Catherine was certain Felicity observed, but once on the path it seemed impossible for her to change course. The earl could save his charm for some dim-witted debutante, she wanted none of it.

"Granby just made me an offer I had a hard time refusing," her father announced. "He's persistent, I'll give him that."

The look Catherine sent his way would have singed the hair off a lesser man, but Granby only smiled.

"I'm determined to have the stallion," her nemesis announced, unperturbed.

Catherine bit back the retort that almost escaped her lips. She wasn't up to another of Felicity's lectures on manners or marriage. As it was, she was going to have to sneak a sip of whiskey to ward off a headache.

Six

Granby had forgotten how lovely a country morning could be. To Peck's surprise, he had insisted on being awakened early for a brisk ride that put him near Stonebridge. The earl had declined giving his valet any explanation other than a stern glance, with instructions that he would breakfast upon his return.

The morning had dawned clear and bright, with no trace of rain. Golden sunshine dappled the ground as Granby made his way along the lane, then cut east toward Sudeley Castle. If the information he had gleaned from the Stonebridge groom who had readied his horse the previous evening was correct, he was headed on a course that would bisect Miss Hardwick's customary morning path.

His pursuit of the lady was admittedly prideful. He wanted to make sure she understood that he wasn't going to be ignored.

Granby knew he was overreacting to her treatment of him the previous evening. It shouldn't matter a tinker's damn what the impertinent Miss Hardwick thought of him, but it did.

Reflecting upon his mood, he was forced to admit

that one of his kisses—and he was very good at kissing—had never prompted such a response before.

Most women were eager for a second. If Catherine were a prim country miss who swooned at the thought of a man touching her, she would have swooned in his arms, not fought and scratched like a she-cat. No. There was definitely something strange going on. As for the lady herself, Granby knew she'd enjoyed the kiss, once she'd gotten past the shock of it.

She'd been curious, nervous, uncertain, but definitely interested. Since the kiss, she'd put on a protective mask, a social front to keep him at a distance. If he hadn't been expecting it, he might not have seen how easily the young lady could switch personalities. But having seen it, Granby now knew what to expect from her in the future.

His mouth hardened into a grim smile as he ducked to avoid a low branch. The real shock wasn't Miss Hardwick's behavior at all, but his own. Never in his adult life had he risen at the crack of dawn to go galloping down a country lane in hopes of meeting a young woman who had made it abundantly clear that she'd consider it a blessing never to lay eyes on him again.

Urging his horse forward into a meadow speckled with wildflowers, Granby wondered at his own daring in confronting a young woman of good family with the intention of teaching her another lesson. He rode on, driven by a strange need to get things over with—whatever things were, for he was still uncertain exactly what he wanted to prove. The lady's reaction would set the stage.

As expected, her reaction was far from cheery. Riding into the meadow from the opposing direction, she reined in her horse, a sleek chestnut mare, the moment she realized they were on a collision course. It wouldn't have been a real collision, not like the one that had precipitated their first meeting, but the meadow wasn't large

and it was impossible to continue across it without encountering him.

Taking the situation in hand, Granby nudged his
mount forward until the two horses were standing nose
to nose.

"Good morning, Miss Hardwick," he said, greeting
her with the best of smiles. Only his eyes, as silver-blue
as the Channel on a winter's day, hinted that he was
anything but pleasantly surprised at seeing her again.

Catherine bristled at the smooth way he spoke her
name. There was an intimate ring to the words, as if he
had used an endearment to address her.

She had fled the house as soon as dawn had brushed
the sky, wanting some time alone. But, while the sun was
shining on her, fate was not. The last person she wanted
to meet was Lord Granby. The wretched man had ruined her previous day and evening, and she had awakened with stout determination to put him out of her
mind this morning. Now he was here, sitting atop his
horse and smiling at her.

It was an expression she had seen before: the predatory look of a wealthy man of the world. The only uncertainty Catherine had at this moment was the method
Lord Granby would use to try and fool her into thinking he was harmless.

Since he'd dined at her home the previous evening,
she anticipated a subtle approach, but his next remark
proved that she had misjudged him once again.

"An attractive young lady such as yourself should not
be out riding without a chaperone, though I must admit
relief at seeing you choose a more suitable mount this
morning. But breeches? How unladylike."

For a moment Catherine's temper flared out of control, but she managed to contain it. She'd lost her composure on the lane, and things had ended with a disastrous
kiss. She'd not make the same mistake twice.

"Good morning," she replied, then nudged the mare forward in an effort to leave the man with only those words.

Granby maneuvered his gelding with an efficient hand, blocking her path. "Really, Miss Hardwick, a gentleman would think his company wasn't welcome."

"Yours is not," she said, with a sting. She added hardheaded to the man's list of faults. If he insisted upon rudeness, then she'd give it to him, along with a piece of her mind.

"You're a very forthright young woman. It's refreshing to meet someone so uncomplicated," Granby replied, taking no offense at her remark, mainly because he had expected nothing less. "Nevertheless, my experience has led me to believe that no female is uncomplicated, especially a lady."

"Has your *experience* also led you to believe that when a lady announces that she wants nothing to do with you, she is actually saying the opposite?" Catherine asked in a cordial voice that belied her rising anger. "If so, then I would say that your experience is lacking, my lord, for I have no interest in exchanging another word with you."

"And why is that, Miss Hardwick? Was our kiss so dreadful?"

"It was worse than dreadful. And I thank you not to mention it again."

It was impossible to tell if he was pleased or offended by her remark; his expression revealed nothing, at least momentarily. The next second, however, he burst into laughter. The rich sound rolled across the meadow, startling a nest of wrens who went flying into the air with loud indignant shrieks, very much like the sound Catherine wanted to make, but didn't.

Granby realized he was having quite a good time of it. Catherine Hardwick was wearing breeches. Old and faded to a muddy brown, they hugged her legs and left little to the imagination. Her riding jacket was a shade darker, obviously a man's coat that had been altered to fit her. A cream-colored shirt and knee-high riding boots completed her morning attire.

Her face glowed with the color the wind had burnished into her cheeks. Her hair, a gleaming rich auburn in the morning light, was worn in casual style, twisted into a single plait that reached to the small of her back. A woman riding astride a horse wasn't a common sight, but it seemed to suit her extraordinary personality.

Another thought darted through his mind; a woman who could ride a horse astride would have no trouble riding a man just as easily.

Controlling his baser instincts, which included pulling her from the saddle and stealing a second kiss, Granby continued their not-so-friendly banter. "Ah, but I fear I must mention it, Miss Hardwick—or may I take the liberty of calling you Catherine? We are, after all, intimately acquainted."

"You may not! You've taken enough liberties, my lord." She had no more patience to waste on the man. "And there is nothing intimate about our relationship. I would sooner suffer the attention of—"

"I have taken no liberties that you did not agree to," Granby reminded her, his insolent gaze raking over her as if he were systemically ridding her of every garment. "I admit some trepidation in accepting your father's invitation for fear that I might find a horsewhip waiting for me. But since I was greeted with cordial country hospitality, I realize that you did not elaborate on the *details* of our first meeting. May I ask why not?"

"My reasons are my own."

"Rather obvious reasons. You knew your father would not approve of you racing about the lanes as if Storm Dancer had wings. Is that perhaps the reason you are riding a docile mare this morning?"

"My mare is not docile. She is of a finer bloodline than the gelding you are riding."

"Perhaps," Granby conceded, realizing the girl knew as much about horses as her father. The mare was a quality animal.

"If that is all you wish to speak of, then I will continue my ride. Alone." She prepared to ride on, and to Catherine's surprise the earl allowed her to do so—but only long enough to turn his horse around and fall in line with her, heading across the meadow toward the stream that separated the grounds of Sudeley Castle from her father's property.

She often rode the path that opened onto the meadow. It was one of the few places her father didn't use for grazing. A serene place, which she visited whenever she was troubled. There was a rocky knoll overlooking the creek where she sometimes sat for hours, thinking private thoughts. It was there she had planned to rid her mind of the last memories of Lord Granby, but that was impossible now. The man had been waiting in ambush, a handsome highwayman poised to steal more of her time.

One thought led to another and Catherine reined in the mare. "What are you doing here?" she asked. "My father declined your offer for Storm Dancer. I would expect you would be on your way to . . . Reading, was it not?"

"Another forthright question," Granby replied. "The answer is simple. I will remain in Winchcombe until such time as your father does accept my offer. I want the stallion."

"And you always get what you want."

"I don't recall any recent defeats."

Catherine believed him. She also believed that he wasn't talking about horses. His gaze was entirely too bold, and his grin downright wicked, as he looked her way. It was very doubtful that anyone ever told him no. He was a nobleman after all, used to wielding command

and receiving obedience. She was sure he had women falling about his feet, each and every one eager to lay claim to his attention. Well, she wasn't one of them. She'd meant what she said when she'd told Felicity that she'd rather have a country lad without a pence to his name than a well-titled lord, who thought of a wife as little more than a social necessity.

Nothing more was said until they reached the stream. It was narrow and shallow at this point, but grew wider and deeper as it approached the Isbourne River. As a child Catherine had played here, while her father, when he was home on furlough, sat under a nearby tree, reading or simply watching her splash.

She had no memories of her mother, beyond those her father had shared with her, but she knew that she had inherited Lucinda Kenwyn's auburn hair and hazel eyes.

There was a portrait of her mother in the morning room. It had been painted by a local artist shortly after she had married, and there was a joy in her face that Catherine hoped she would fully understand one day.

Regardless of her stubbornness on the issue of marriage, she longed to be loved as much as any woman. But for herself, not because Stonebridge would one day pass into her possession, or because she was the most eligible young lady in the parish now that Sarah and Veronica had wed.

The three of them had been inseparable as children, always getting into trouble, most of which Catherine had instigated, being the boldest. She was still the boldest, no doubt the reason her two friends had been issued proposals and she had not, the fact that they had been carted off to London, to be paraded about like dogs on a leash, notwithstanding. It was disgusting, the way proper people selected their mates.

"Something is putting a frown on that very pretty

face," Granby said, noticing her change in mood. There was a melancholy sheen to her eyes as she stared at the babbling brook.

"Nothing that need concern you, my lord," Catherine replied sharply. She'd almost forgotten that she wasn't alone. Watching the water run over and around the smooth rocks in the stream always had a relaxing effect on her senses.

"Are you always this rude, or did Peck forget to mention that I'd grown horns overnight?"

"Peck?" Catherine inquired in a much nicer voice. The earl was being far more tolerant than she expected, but she still didn't trust him. And he could wait until Hell took a holiday before she'd let Storm Dancer fall into his hands. Her father wasn't hard-pressed for money, so she didn't anticipate that he'd sell the stallion, but men, even fatherly ones, could be unpredictable.

"My valet. Not as dour as your Mr. Gabs, by any means, but a nuisance more times than not."

"Why don't you discharge him?"

"Oh, I couldn't possibly do that. He came with the title. Took an oath the day my father died that he wouldn't forsake me until I came to my senses, married, and had an heir squalling in the nursery."

Something in his voice, a tone of genuine affection, surprised Catherine. She hadn't imagined a man like Lord Granby giving a fig about anyone he employed for wages.

"Are you planning to marry?" she asked a moment later. It was an improper question, but, then, she wasn't a proper lady. There was nothing submissive or shy about her. She'd grown up with stable hands and grooms and Jimkins, who could cuss a blue streak when he felt the need.

"No." Granby replied. The question didn't surprise him. All women were interested in a man's matrimonial status, or lack of it.

"Then I suppose you will have to suffer your annoying valet a few years longer," she said, trying her best to ignore the tingling sensation she felt each time he smiled.

"Yes, I suppose I will," Granby replied laughingly. "Have we reached a truce, or are you going to insult me again?"

"Only if you do something that warrants insult."

The man was a charmer.

She shouldn't even be talking to him, but he was very hard to ignore, sitting atop his horse in such stately fashion, his pale hair catching the sunlight, and those eyes. They were stunning eyes, a fierce silver-blue that seemed to take in the world with a private humor, as if he were laughing at the absurdity of it.

She was right to stay on guard around him, ever watchful, lest he work his charms on her as effortlessly as he had worked them on everyone else. Felicity thought him wonderful, and her father had taken to him, as well. But her perspective was quite different, having been in the man's arms.

Just thinking about it was enough to put Catherine on edge, and she wasn't a skittish female.

"I promise my best behavior," the earl said, sounding sincere.

Catherine nodded slightly, thinking privately that the earl's best behavior could most probably be classified as another gentleman's worst.

"Felicity mentioned your reluctance in attending London," he said to her. "May I ask why?"

He dismounted before she could reply, tethering his horse to the branch of a nearby tree, then walking to where she still sat mounted atop her mare. He looked up at her for a moment, then without asking permission or voicing his intentions, lifted her from the saddle as if she weighed no more than a child.

Catherine soon found her feet firmly planted on the ground, while she looked into those incredible eyes. He was still holding onto her, his hands spanning her waist, not tightly, but casually.

"Why doesn't London interest you?"

Catherine forced herself to step back, so as not to be trapped by the sensual web he was weaving about her. Oh, he was charming, all right. Much too charming for her to let down her guard for so much as a moment. And yet it had only taken a moment for him to capture her attention. Fully, undeniably, it was focused on him. Only him.

"Various reasons," she replied to his question, having forgotten it for the intense seconds that had passed since its asking.

"Have you been there?" He led her mare away, tethering it a short distance from where his own mount was lazily munching the bright green grass that flourished on the banks of the stream. "To London?"

"Once, with Father. But Winchcombe suits me better."

Catherine walked downstream from the horses, stopping near a large boulder that was frequently covered by water during the spring rains. Today, it stood high and dry, jutting from the bank of the stream like a granite watchman.

If she were alone, she would scale the rock, and once perched on its summit look over the meadow while her mind wandered from this to that. Normally, she had little to think about, her life being one of ease and contentment—until the arrival of Lord Granby.

Today, her thoughts were riotous. All because a man had kissed her.

Granby turned, approaching her with a smooth stride.

"Most young ladies of your age would be eager to see London. The city does have its pleasures. The theatre, music, parties, parks, and museums. Things of interest to most young ladies."

He was standing close, not crowding her, but making

her acutely aware of his presence. The sensations started again, a strange tightness in her chest, an odd fluttering in her stomach. Catherine dragged in a deep breath, wondering if she should have taken the time to eat before rushing out of the house. Lack of food could explain the light-headedness that was suddenly afflicting her.

"I am not most young ladies," she said, retaining her candidness. "As for interests, mine are simple. I like horses and riding and clean country air."

"Ah, a woman of simple pleasures."

His voice, the way he said the word "pleasures," had intensified the sensations Catherine was struggling to control. It was as if he were equating the word to her.

"And what pleases you, my lord?" She posed the daring question as she stood uncomfortably under his piercing gaze. "The theatre, music, parties, and rides through Hyde Park?"

He laughed, a rich, full sound that made him seem all the more mysterious. "Like most men, I prefer racing and other games of chance."

"But you do attend the theatre and the opera? I'm sure a man of your rank and influence is inundated by invitations during the Season."

"More than I care to count," he replied, his tone turning more serious. "But politics are also an interest, and more of Her Majesty's business is conducted at social gatherings than in the halls of Parliament."

"The life of a lord," she mused, rather sarcastically. "How positively dreary it must be."

"You mock me, Miss Hardwick."

"Yes, I suppose I do. But then, I mock the life of most aristocrats. It seems so superficial, so snobbish and high-handed. One's success has little to do with one's abilities, and everything to do with name and who successfully married whom to beget an heir."

"I can see you have a rather brutal view of things."

"Not brutal. Practical. Shall I tell you what I think of the honorable institute of British marriages?" she challenged, wanting to impress upon him that she was no simpleminded village lass. "The London Season is nothing more than a civilized slave auction. Ladies dance and present their best manners, dressed like dolls in a window, while the man and his family study her from a distance. The final judgment results in a proposal, the lady having been determined fit to produce and rear the next generation. My father judges a horse's pedigree just as thoroughly."

"A keen observation for one so young."

"An honest observation, as you well know, my lord. Why, even you must bow to obligation and take a wife to perpetuate the treasured title. Am I wrong?"

"I must admit some pain at having to join the ranks you have so adeptly described, but you are correct. Life is often blighted by duty, and one day I will be forced to submit and take a wife."

"Submit. Men don't submit, they rule supreme."

"Yes, I suppose a woman would see things that way."

He stepped closer, and Catherine felt trapped. It was a silly feeling, since there was ample room for her to move away from him if she chose. Still, the sense that a stalking predator was moving in for the kill remained with her.

"Tell me, do I need to apologize for being the son of an earl? Would tossing my rank and privilege to the wind cause those lovely eyes to see me more clearly?"

"Oh, I see you clearly enough, my lord" she replied, realizing that he'd woven that magic again, an intangible web that trapped and mesmerized.

One more step. He was looking down at her, their bodies separated by only a few inches of golden sunlight. "And how do you see me, Miss Hardwick?"

Too close! The lips that had once pressed so confidently down upon hers were only inches away, the eyes that seemed to sear into her very soul, flickered now with a hint of emotion that was easily recognizable. He was going to kiss her again.

Catherine held her breath, wanting and not wanting the kiss with a simultaneous unease. Propriety demanded that she put him in his place, but she really wasn't the respectable young lady she should be.

Growing up around a breeding stable, she knew the facts of life. She'd seen the power of a stallion when he was led to one of the mares. She'd witnessed the mares nibbling and snorting, a prelude to the actual mating. It was shameful to admit it, but she did want Granby to kiss her. She wanted to feel the power of his arms, and the mastery of his mouth. She wanted to be swept away into another private, personal moment of pleasure.

Granby lowered his gaze from her catlike eyes, taking a long, leisurely look at her. She was taller than average, but just the right height for a man his size. Her jacket and cream-colored shirt, though cut like a man's, clearly covered the curves of a woman. Her breasts rose and fell with each breath, emphasizing their size. Soft swells that were waiting to be touched, when the time came.

But not today.

He brought his gaze back up, slowly, until he was once again looking into hazel eyes, wide with anticipation. He wanted to kiss her. Oh, how he wanted it, but not yet. Their rendezvous in the meadow had been deliberate on his part; she needed to be taught a lesson.

It was a victory of sorts, albeit a small one, that she was eagerly waiting for him to claim her mouth. He could see the wanting in her eyes. Her pupils were dilated. She was aroused—wanting, needing.

A surge of satisfaction ran through him as he realized how nice it would be to oblige her. She was an unusual woman, and he enjoyed unusual things, but still there was a lesson to be taught.

"Would you like to know what I see?" he said, his tone not qualifying as a whisper, but almost.

"What?"

Where had her composure gone? To hell in a handbasket, that's where! It took the utmost restraint to keep her hands at her sides. They wanted to rise to his shoulders, to feel the lean, muscular strength of his body. Calling upon what good sense the man had not already drained from her, Catherine managed to hold his gaze.

The silent interrogation continued for several moments, his eyes searching, her heart pounding. Was the man ever going to answer?

"I see a lovely young lady who has undoubtedly been spoiled by an overindulgent father. A young woman who thinks nothing of challenging a gentleman at every turn, because she is foolish enough to think that propriety and good manners will protect her. A very foolish thought indeed, were the man to forget those manners and do as he pleased."

Catherine felt anticipation turn to fear. Surely, he was jesting, teasing her because she'd been rude to him, and his male pride, having been bruised, now demanded retribution. The uncertainty lingered long enough for him to reach out and stroke her cheek. It was a light caress, his fingertips gliding down the curve of her face, hesitating at the corner of her mouth. When had he removed his gloves? His touch was warm, and oh, so tempting.

Then his fingertips were tracing her mouth, her bottom lip and then the top. Had she been thinking more clearly, she would have bitten his finger, but she couldn't move—not a muscle.

His touch was magic.

Sensual, soft, hot magic.

Then he stepped back, and the magic faded.

Catherine watched in stunned amazement as he

walked to where his horse was tied, mounted, and then with a tip of his hat, rode away.

Blast and damn the man!

He'd teased her, then dismissed her; the cat not yet ready to pounce, but most certainly having played with the mouse.

Seven

Two days later, Catherine was still stinging from the way Lord Granby had so skillfully paid her back for the rudeness she'd displayed the evening he had come to dinner.

Realistically, she knew she must share the blame. Her dealings with the earl had been disrespectful in the extreme. Under normal circumstances, she would have presented herself with courtesy. But the circumstances hadn't been ordinary, and she couldn't forget the way he had kissed her, then mockingly made her wish for another kiss.

She had behaved badly, and he no better. He had practiced prudence with just the right amount of callousness to prove his point.

She had wanted him to kiss her, to take her mouth under his and recreate the same wonderfully strange sensations she had felt that morning in the lane.

It was shameful, but true.

Thus the difficulty in forgetting him, in assigning him a place of no importance in her thoughts, in wishing him gone forever.

Catherine did want to see him again—one last time

in which she would prove the victor by charming him, then leaving him to ponder what had gone wrong. It was a just revenge, one she hoped to be able to administer sooner rather than later.

Granby hadn't called again; her father would have told her if the earl had stopped by and made another offer for Storm Dancer. But she was certain that his lordship hadn't taken himself way from Winchcombe. He had sounded most adamant when he'd spoken of convincing her father to sell the stallion.

Catherine was just as resolute that he would not get his hands on Storm Dancer. It had become a matter of principle with her since that morning in the meadow. Letting the earl gain possession of Storm Dancer would be akin to admitting that he had defeated her.

The terms of the war between them weren't entirely clear, being masked in the same indefinable emotions that continued to plague her, but a war it was. The man was entirely too sure of himself, thinking money could get him anything. Well, it wasn't going to get him Storm Dancer.

Those were Catherine's thoughts as she dressed for an afternoon at Sudeley Castle. The invitation had arrived yesterday by footman, and, of course, Felicity had accepted. She had yet to meet Emma Dent, the new mistress of the legendary castle, and was looking forward to the occasion with much enthusiasm.

Catherine shared her aunt's enthusiasm, but for another reason. If Emma was giving a tea, then Lord Granby was sure to be there. Winchcombe was too small of a village for Emma not to have heard that the earl had taken rooms at the White Lion Inn.

Taking unusual care with her dress, Catherine chose a bright yellow muslin with white panels. With matching parasol in hand, and wearing a straw bonnet adorned with white silk daisies and a yellow ribbon, she joined her father and Felicity in the carriage.

"I must say, you're looking quite lovely, my dear," Felicity commented, as the well-trained bays executed a sharp turn in front of the house before prancing down the sloped driveway and across the bridge. "I do expect we shall see Lord Granby again."

"I suppose," Catherine replied nonchalantly.

"If so, I would hope that you've regained your manners."

"What's this?" Catherine's father gave her a sharp glance.

Catherine did her best to look remorseful. She didn't want her father upset with her; it was the one thing she did her best to avoid. Not that he possessed a particularly fierce temper. To the contrary, he was the most patient of men. His disposition was genuinely mellow despite his military career. It was for that very reason that she tried to please him when at all possible.

She'd spent so much of her childhood without him, his duties taking him to all corners of the world. Now that he was home for good, she wanted him content.

"The sight of your daughter cutting Lord Granby most directly was missed by you," Felicity said, "but it was a cut, and not well done of her, I must add."

"When did this take place?" Sir Hardwick wanted to know.

"Two evenings past, when his lordship dined under your very roof. I have already delivered the necessary scolding. My concern now is that another not be necessary."

"It won't be," Catherine said. "I forgot my manners. Don't worry, Father, I shan't let it happen again."

"I should hope not," her father hastened to say. "Lord Granby is a fine man, and a titled gentleman." He gave her a pensive look. "Isn't like you to be rude to anyone. Hope you're not taking Granby's offer for Storm Dancer to heart. Buying and selling horses is what Stonebridge is all about. Can't make pets out of them. Wouldn't be sensible, or profitable."

"You aren't going to sell Storm Dancer, please tell me that you're not."

"Really, Catherine, one would think that that stallion has become the focal point of your life. Young ladies should have other things on their minds," Felicity remarked, a bit harshly.

"He's the best stud we have," Catherine defended her obsession. "Father has said it often enough. The colts he sires will be the future of Stonebridge."

"Perhaps, but it is not the topic of conversation one should take to an afternoon tea," her aunt insisted. "The preservation of civilized conduct is nothing to be scoffed at or misused."

Knowing Felicity wasn't to be swayed, Catherine sat back to quietly plot her revenge should Lord Granby be in attendance.

The tea was just getting under way when the earl rode up to the old castle. It was a brilliant summer day, and Emma had chosen to make the most of it. Tables were arranged on the lawn, and carriages and horses queued up in the drive, delivering an assortment of guests. Some had come from as far away as Gretton, any invitation to Sudeley Castle being looked upon with favor by the local gentry.

Handing his horse over to a groom, Granby walked across the lawn to greet his host and hostess, John and Emma Dent. He was wearing a dark blue jacket and trousers, his shirt a pristine white under a waistcoat of silver silk.

After exchanging a few words with the Dents, he made his way to where Catherine was standing with her father and Felicity.

He passed a bow over her hand. "Miss Hardwick."

"Lord Granby," she replied in her most polite voice. "I feared you had left our small hamlet since my father wasn't receptive to your offer."

The earl smiled, quickly catching on that she hadn't mentioned their second meeting to Sir Hardwick.

"I'm a stubborn man, Miss Hardwick. I'll get the stallion yet."

"By Jove, you just might," Sir Hardwick laughed. "I like a man who doesn't give up."

The earl's gaze moved over Catherine, not as possessively as before—he didn't dare with her father nearby—but long enough to reacquaint himself with her appearance. Elegant and looking like a summer flower, she was the envy of every young woman attending the tea. Her auburn hair was arrayed in sophisticated curls, yet her smile was that of a young girl eager to play. It brought an immediate response from Granby's body, but being well versed in the ways of women, he controlled himself.

"May I be so bold as to invite you for a walk in the gardens?"

With an approving nod from her father and a triumphant smile from Felicity, Catherine rested her hand on the earl's arm. There were guests aplenty, milling about the lawns, so a chaperone wasn't necessary. As a couple, they wouldn't be beyond observation.

"If I'm not mistaken, the new fountain is this way," Granby said as he led her away from the tables, toward a flower garden full of red geraniums.

A group of self-consciously noisy young men were standing along the way, but their conversation stopped as the earl walked by with Catherine on his arm. Granby found himself the recipient of a great many resentful looks, due to his apparent familiarity with the lovely Miss Hardwick. It was easy to see that the local lads considered him a poacher.

The harshest look came from a young man with dark chestnut hair and brown eyes. By the looks of him, he was a merchant's son, his clothes well cut but lacking the style of a polished gentleman. His expression was a deep scowl that advertised jealousy of the worst sort.

So the lovely Catherine did have an admirer.

Granby gave the young man a cursory glance, thinking it would be a waste of a good woman to let this oaf get his hands on Hardwick's daughter. She was meant for a man who would appreciate her beauty, rather than be controlled by it. Whoever the young man was, he was no match for the fiery Catherine.

No words passed between the earl and Catherine until they reached the fountain. It was a large piece of sculpture with mermaids hugging water jars to their otherwise bare breasts.

"Aren't you afraid that local gossip will link your name to mine?" he asked as they stopped walking for a brief moment.

"I pay little attention to gossip. If I did, I wouldn't have accepted your invitation to stroll the grounds. However, it may upset *you* to discover your name linked with mine. Aunt Felicity is determined to find me a suitable husband, and I warn you, she considers an earl *most* suitable."

"I'm well aware of Lady Forbes-Hammond's intentions," Granby replied. "But having heard your opinion of marriage and the obligation of a man's title, I don't think I'm in great jeopardy. I'm under the impression that you don't hold marriage in high esteem."

"On the contrary, my lord. I have nothing against marriage, as long as a man's heart is involved."

"Ah, yes, ladies are notoriously preoccupied with matters of the heart."

He liked talking to her, teasing her. As a debate partner, she was one of the finest he'd ever encountered, speaking her mind with little regard as to how her words would be received. A danger should she go to London, though her beauty was sure to draw a dozen proposals.

"And you, my lord, what are your views of marriage? Other than the honored institution being a dutiful blight, of course."

"I'm insulted again," he said, feigning outrage. "Do you think me so callous as to be heartless in matters of love?"

"You would have to believe in love for those words to impress me, my lord. Your actions give me the impression that just the opposite is true. You said you enjoy games of chance. I think you consider love an equally amusing game."

"And if I do?" he queried, with a half smile.

"Then I say you are more honest than most men."

They moved on, walking slowly through a maze of flower beds and neatly trimmed shrubs to a small garden pond.

"You really don't want to go to London, do you?" Granby asked, amazed that he might actually have stumbled upon a woman who wasn't interested in marriage.

"I need no searching examination of my soul to know that marriage is not a condition that I wish to suffer," she told him. "As far as London is concerned, I have no desire to be put on display. It isn't my will at all, but Felicity's. She has made my father promise that he will not allow me to waste away in the country."

"You may change your mind once you're there."

"I doubt it. I'm perfectly content here in Winchcombe, humble though it may be. I have friends and a devoted father—who does not spoil me, regardless of what you may think. I have the freedom to dress in skirts or breeches. I know of no marriage vow that would offer me the same liberty."

"What of children? Most women seem to want them."

"I'm young. There is plenty of time for children, if I ever marry."

"And if you don't?" He turned toward the rose gar-

den, a large array of fragrant blossoms near the eastern
wing of the massive castle.

"I will continue living at Stonebridge, raising horses,
and living my life as I please."

Granby wasn't certain if he believed her or not. A lot
of women were smart enough to know that the best way
to snare a husband was to pretend they weren't hunting
for one, and Catherine Hardwick was a very intelligent
young woman. If she maintained this attitude, she'd
likely end up with half the lords of England fighting for
her hand when she finally submitted to the dreaded
Season Felicity was insisting upon.

On the other hand, there were women who truly
shunned marriage, women who preferred just the type
of freedom Catherine had described. There were widows who, having once been married, had little inclination to repeat the experience. And spinsters, though the
ones Granby had met seemed not to have taken up
their lot in life willingly.

He looked at the lovely young lady on his arm and tried
to imagine her at the age of thirty. He seriously doubted
Catherine would make it to spinsterhood—not if any of
the local lads had anything to say about it.

She was ripe for the picking, which was surely Felicity's
reason for insisting that she be exposed to eligible gentlemen beyond the quaint hamlet of Winchcombe.

Granby tried not to think of what would happen once
Catherine arrived in London, or if she managed not to
go, what villager would end up winning her hand.

His intentions were entirely selfish.

He wanted her for himself.

The problem was he couldn't have her.

Not without completely ruining her, which he was
too much of a gentleman to do, regardless of her current opinion of him. No, his first decision had been the
right one. He could walk with her in the garden, perhaps steal another kiss, but that was all.

The logic did nothing to soothe his current need, which was growing toward aching proportions with every step they took. Damn. He'd accepted Mrs. Dent's invitation thinking the afternoon might present the perfect opportunity to gain that second kiss. He had not, however, planned on a lawn setting which prevented him from sneaking Catherine into a vacant parlor and having his way with her.

"Are you going to make my father another offer?" she asked.

"Yes. I want Storm Dancer almost as much as I want another kiss from the lady who rode him so daringly."

The announcement brought Catherine's head up and around.

"Does that surprise you, Miss Hardwick?"

"No." She might as well be honest.

"Does it shock you?"

"No."

"Then may I assume that it pleases you?"

It was the opportunity she'd been waiting for, the moment when she could lift her chin and walk away, leaving him the same way he'd left her that morning in the meadow—wanting. So, why wasn't she walking away?

Granby used the short silence to continue his suit. "We will have to return to the other guests soon. Refreshments are due to be served. Since there is no suitable place for me to ravish you, no tree big enough to shield us from a horde of watchful eyes, may I suggest a more discreet rendezvous?"

"Where?"

"It's been several years since I visited Sudeley, but if memory serves there is a small parlor on the second floor, near the servants' stairway. Find your way there and wait for me."

The *perfect* opportunity. She could go into the house on some pretense, then exit using one of the many outer doors, leaving the handsome earl pacing the parlor. The longer he waited, the more irate he'd become, and the more delicious her victory. It could be the last chance she'd have to salvage her pride. Catherine took it.

Granby escorted her back to the front lawn where her father and Felicity were waiting. He engaged Sir Hardwick in a discussion centered around the latest winners at Ascot. John Dent joined them, having witnessed the last race, and offering his opinion of the three-year-old filly that had taken the finish line with a flurry of speed, leaving many a man to curse his losses.

Catherine used the time to prepare a plate of fresh fruit and cheese and sugar cakes for herself and Felicity. She chose a seat that allowed her to watch and listen while the earl mixed with the Dents' guests. His charm became even more apparent as he won their favor, complimenting the improvements the couple had made to the old castle, and the quaint ambience of the village, which had enticed him into staying for a few more days.

The vicar, a robust man in his late fifties, whose voice carried a good distance when he got enthusiastic— which was every time he gave a sermon on the wages of sin—was as impressed as anyone. It wasn't every day that a wealthy earl graced their little town, and St. Peter's needed a new roof.

Catherine was certain that Lord Granby would find himself making a donation before the day was over. Nathan Marlowe could be very persuasive when it came to maintaining God's holy structures.

"What did you and the earl talk about for so long?" Felicity asked, holding firm to her get-to-the-heart-of-the-matter attitude.

"Nothing in particular," Catherine replied with a slight shrug. "He's determined to buy Storm Dancer."

"That horse again! Really, Catherine, is that all you can find to talk about?"

"It's the only thing Lord Granby and I have in common," she replied, not wanting to encourage Felicity to think otherwise.

Before her aunt could launch into a list of what one might discuss when strolling through the garden with a lord of the realm, Catherine was rescued by Emma Dent.

A stout woman whose brown hair was beginning to gray, Emma was always a pleasant conversationalist. She invited both Felicity and Catherine inside to see the newest item in her costume collection, a purple monk's robe, lined with white ermine, that was said to have been worn by Louis XIV during a masquerade ball.

Catherine didn't dare glance at the earl as she followed Emma into the depths of the castle, but she sensed that he was watching her. Would he find an excuse to disengage himself from conversation and follow her inside? If so, would she do likewise and make her way to the parlor?

Her perfect opportunity was turning into a dilemma.

Did she meet the man, use her females skills, then depart? Or would she allow him to kiss her—one last time—before she walked away?

Eight

Catherine was not without courage, but as she made her excuses to Emma and Felicity, she was numb with fear. Could she find the small parlor and slip inside without being seen? Would *he* be waiting? And what would happen next?

The room wasn't difficult to locate. It was, as Lord Granby had said, at the end of the second floor's main corridor and only a stone's throw from the servant staircase. The door was ajar, giving her the impression that the earl might already be inside and waiting.

Catherine stood outside the door for a moment, telling herself that she would and could control the planned encounter, thus accomplishing her main goal—making Lord Granby regret his former arrogance. Then, fortified by a deep breath, she pushed the door wide open and stepped into the room.

It was a small parlor, probably used as a sitting room in the winter. The windows faced south, and the fireplace was large in comparison to the area it would be used to heat. The furnishings were, as Catherine had suspected at first glance, old pieces that had been newly upholstered, a small divan and matching chair in close proximity to an Italian drop-leaf table with cabriole legs and clawed feet. The draperies were a soft blue velvet, the carpet faded from age but still showing enough of the pattern to add a touch of gold and red to the room. The wallpaper was a floral display worthy of any spring garden.

She was in the process of scanning the room more thoroughly, thinking the earl might have taken a seat in one of the high-backed chairs that faced the windows, when the door closed with a resounding click.

"Ah, alone at last."

If she had been waiting for the cat to pounce, she didn't have to wait a second longer. She felt his hands upon her, and she was turned—the full skirt of her dress swirling out like the petals of an upturned buttercup—and pulled into the strong arms that had been occupying her thoughts for more than four days. A quick glimpse of steely blue eyes was all she got before the earl covered her mouth.

She might have been able to make a protest if his hands hadn't snaked around her and pulled her close enough to feel every hard plane of his body, and they were all hard.

But there was nothing hard about his mouth.

It softened as it molded to hers, fitting them together as though they were one person, not two. Revenge melted from Catherine's mind as his tongue pressed slowly inside her mouth, tasting and tormenting in the most delicious way.

Her knees went weak, an affliction she couldn't have imagined until this very moment, as one arm wrapped tightly around her waist, pulling her even closer, while the other hand moved suggestively up her rib cage, stopping just short of cupping her breast.

The kiss seemed to go on and on, his tongue dipping and tasting, until she couldn't breathe. Then he was kissing her differently, creating a whole new set of sensations. He turned his head, adjusting the pressure, parting her lips, then sinking his tongue into her mouth again.

The impropriety of it was staggering, the most outrageous thing Catherine had ever experienced. Then he moved, lifting her and carrying her to the divan. She was put on his lap, the hardness of his thighs beneath her, his hands holding her prisoner while his mouth continued its sensual assault.

And it *was* an attack.

A battle was raging within her. A battle to get closer, to feel more, to touch more of him. Her hands were resting on his shoulders—she had no idea how they'd gotten there. She was leaning against him, feeling the heat of his body through the layers of clothing that separated them.

His mouth was slow and hungry, hot and demanding, taking her into a sphere of things unknown. She was just as hungry to find the next horizon, to know what lay beyond these wonderful kisses.

Granby had trouble breathing. He had known Catherine was beautiful, but looking at her now stole his breath. This creature dressed in daffodil colors was more than he had ever imagined. She was a vision. Rich auburn hair piled smoothly atop her head revealed the elegant curves of her throat. Her breasts were high and firm, their supple roundness making his hands ache to caress them. Her skin was flushed with color, and he knew it would be soft to the touch.

He had longed to have her beside him these many nights, and seeing her now sent a stab of desire through his loins. His heart was pounding in his chest as images raced through his mind, visions of her naked upon his bed.

His hand fell to her leg, inching its way up to the hem of her dress, then higher, caressing her calf as it moved, while he kept her anchored on his lap. He touched her knee above the garter and found warm skin. He buried his face in the soft curve of her throat, inhaling the scent of soap and woman. The silkiness of her hair brushed against his cheek as she moved.

The inside of her thigh was as smooth as he'd imagined, warm and soft and yielding as his fingers caressed it. She parted her legs the slightest bit, but whether instinctively or on purpose, he couldn't be sure.

He caught his breath at the trusting beauty of her response, her eyes closed in pleasure, her lips parted and swollen from his kisses, her skin flushed with the heat of first arousal. Everything about her was wild and untamed, yearning to take the step from young lady to woman. He wanted to lay her down on the floor and strip away their clothing, to bury himself in her hot, tight sheath, to ride her into ecstasy.

He hadn't meant for things to go this far. He'd only planned to kiss her, to show that he could have her if he wanted, that she'd willingly surrender to him as so many others had done. But something had changed.

The moment he'd sealed their mouths, he'd felt it. Wild and wicked, deep and inescapable. A feeling. Undefined and beyond his reach, but still there, curling deep inside him, beckoning him to kiss her one more time.

His blood was rushing through his veins, his body tight and hard and ready to do what every male had been born to do instinctively—to mate.

Not just sex, but a deeper joining. More complete than anything he'd ever experienced before.

If was for precisely that reason that he had to let her go. Every rule he'd ever lived by warned him to put as much distance between them as possible. Hell, if he had any sense, he'd take himself back to London, or to Cheltenham where he could bed Lady Aldershaw. A few hours of pounding, senseless sex and he'd be his old self.

But he couldn't let her go.

Not yet.

"Look at me."

Lashes fluttered, then opened, revealing catlike eyes that had turned soft with desire.

Catherine's gaze roamed over his face, the handsome angles and valleys, the sensual, sculpted lips that had molded so expertly to her own. She wanted to push his jacket aside, unbutton his shirt, and feel the heat of his skin. She wanted to explore and learn, to touch and please, to fulfill his every desire.

He let out a harsh breath as she lifted her hand to his cheek and touched him. He flinched. Then, making an incoherent sound, he lowered his head and took her mouth again.

It was a tender kiss, as if he wanted to leave her with a gentle memory. She moaned in encouragement, not wanting it to end, but sensed that he was pulling away from her, if not physically, then emotionally.

"If I weren't a gentleman, we'd finish this once and for all," he said.

After a moment's hesitation, he lifted her off his lap, then stood, holding her against him, her cheek resting against his chest.

Catherine could hear his heart pounding in unison with her own. He kissed her on the forehead, and she smiled. What had once seemed wrong, now seemed so perfectly right. Revenge had given way to desire. The wicked passion of his kisses still had her blood humming, but the security of his embrace was just as wonderful.

If only they could stay this way forever.

"Oh, my God! Felicity!" She wiggled free of him as the ramifications of what she'd allowed him to do came crashing down on her.

"Shush, no one knows, nor will they, as long as you wash the heat from your face and tidy your hair."

"How long?" she asked, feeling almost ill with panic. If Felicity, or Emma, or her father found them . . .

"Only a few minutes," Granby assured her, gradually getting control of himself. If only they had hours—and even then he wasn't sure he'd be satisfied. It could take a man a lifetime to exhaust the passion Catherine inspired.

A lifetime! What the bloody hell was he thinking!
Better yet, what the bloody hell was he doing!

He walked to the window. The drapes were drawn, so he wasn't worried that anyone on the lawn would glance up and see him. Running his fingers through his hair, he tried to get a grip on what had just happened, what *was* happening, between himself and Catherine. Behind him, he could hear the sounds of her straightening her clothing. His hand had been under her dress, only inches away from the very center of her. Inches and seconds away from ruining a virgin!

He needed a drink.

Reminding himself that he was an old hand at seduction, experienced where she was not, he turned around to offer the comfort she was expecting. Despite the passion of her kisses, she was young and naive, full of adolescent dreams that he was about to crush.

He didn't know what Catherine was feeling or thinking, but he had a pretty good idea. Instead of illicit passion, she was thinking of love, of warm feelings that blossomed like spring flowers.

He wanted her, thus the passion.

But love?

He'd only meant to kiss her, to remind her that she wasn't immune to him, but things had gotten out of control. *He* had gotten out of control. It had been so long since he'd felt the hot rush of real passion, he'd forgotten the blindness that came with it, the lack of fear, but most of all he'd forgotten the consequences of playing cat and mouse with a virgin.

"Some cold water on your face and mouth will erase the evidence," he said calmly.

Catherine stared at him for a long moment. His voice sounded too calm, too cold. And his eyes . . . The shimmering heat was gone. Instead of summer silver, they shone like winter ice.

"The evidence?"

Catherine became oblivious to the possibility of being found alone with the earl as the impact of his statement sank into her mind. Only a few moments ago Granby had been kissing her, touching her. She'd felt his hand on her leg, the heat of his exploring fingers. And he'd held her so tenderly, like a man who loved a woman might hold her—close and secure.

Now, he was telling her that she needed to wash away the evidence of their kiss. But his tone implied even more, as if he wanted her to wash away the memory of it all, everything that had happened between them up to this point in time—the kisses and the feelings.

"Should your father or Lady Forbes-Hammond see you in your present state, it would be difficult to ignore the fact that you have been kissed," Granby explained.

They stood on opposite sides of the room looking at each other, saying nothing, each locked in their own private thoughts. Granby was the one who finally broke eye contact and looked away, back to the draped window, but only for a moment.

When he turned around, intending to apologize, Catherine was gone.

The cold water felt good against Catherine's flushed face, but it did nothing for her temper, which had risen to the boiling point when the earl had turned his back on her.

She took her time drying her face and hands, not wanting to look at herself in the mirror that was hanging over the vanity table. She didn't want to see what others couldn't—the regret of knowing she'd made a fool of herself.

Not once. Not twice. But three times!

How could she be so stupid, so utterly witless as to think the illustrious Lord Granby was doing anything but having fun at her expense?

None of this would have happened if the blasted man, the devilishly charming man, hadn't kissed her on the lane. But fate hadn't allowed the right course of events to take place. Instead, it had twisted and turned, taking her along with it, until she was shaking on the inside because she wanted to kill someone—preferably his lordship.

She had never hated a man more, and yet . . .

Catherine gave herself a hard emotional shake. She didn't care a whit about the man. She'd only agreed to meet him in the parlor to demonstrate that very thing. Of course, he hadn't given her a chance. He'd pulled her into his arms and kissed her into an incoherent state.

She didn't want to think about what he'd done after that. The way she'd let him kiss her, and touch her, and she knew, even though she loathed to admit it, that she would have let him do more—anything he'd wanted to do.

He must think her wanton, or worse, stupid and silly. And she had no one to blame but herself, for she should have jerked away and slapped his face. But she hadn't. She returned his kisses, encouraging him, aiding him in his attempt to teach her a lesson.

It was a lesson hard learned, and he'd taught it well.

She'd allowed herself to be beguiled and bewitched by a charming smile.

Pulling her thoughts together, Catherine returned to the lawn party. Felicity and Emma Dent were deep in conversation, so she strolled toward the garden, keeping her eyes on her destination instead of letting them wander in search of Lord Granby. She was nearing the fountain when David Malbane joined her.

The last thing Catherine wanted to do was to converse with anyone, but there was no helping it. She had known David her entire life. His father owned the tobacco shop in the village, a shop David was due to inherit now that Mr. Malbane was getting on in years.

Two years older, and bearing the brashness of most young men, David wasn't unattractive. He was tall—not as tall as the Earl of Granby, but several inches taller than Catherine—with wavy hair and brown eyes. His face was tanned, his posture good, and his smile friendly as he stopped to tell Catherine how pretty she looked dressed in yellow.

"You always look pretty," he added. "I was going to ask you to walk in the garden with me, but then I saw you with that fancy gent. Don't suppose you'd like to take another turn about the roses?"

"That fancy gent is Lord Granby," Catherine told him. "He's interested in purchasing one of my father's horses. Father asked me to be nice to him. The walk was a simple courtesy, nothing more."

She was getting very good at falsehoods, not at all a thing to be proud of.

"I'd rather you not be *too* nice," David said blatantly.

She knew David meant to court her officially one day, if he ever got up the nerve. She also knew she could marry him. It would solve the problem of a London Season if she did, but the thought of becoming Mrs. David Malbane held no appeal for her. Of course, Granby didn't know that.

She looked past David's shoulder to see the earl once again in conversation with John Dent. For the briefest of moments, their eyes locked. Unable to stop herself, because she was still seething over the underhanded way the earl had lured her into the parlor, kissed her until she'd almost swooned in his arms, then acted as if it were all her fault, Catherine decided revenge wasn't totally out of range. It was doubtful that she could inspire jealousy in the sophisticated lord, but she'd never know unless she tried.

If nothing else, she'd show him that his kisses hadn't been half as incapacitating as he imagined them to be.

Taking David's arm, she smiled up at him. "Thank you. I'd love another stroll in the rose garden."

Granby steeled himself against a rage of emotion. So the little vixen was trying to make him jealous, was she? As if a country bumpkin of a lad could get the job done. Well, it wouldn't. In fact, he applauded the turn of events.

The young man escorting Catherine was the same one who had sent a herd of hostile looks his way earlier in the day. Her admirer, whoever the hell he was, was welcome to Miss Hardwick. It removed from Granby's shoulders the burden of thinking that he'd hurt her unnecessarily. If the chit could still smile like an angel, then she was fully recovered from their little escapade.

Pity, he couldn't say the same.

Though his body had cooled, his senses were still aroused. His mind was not on the conversation he was having with John Dent, but rather on what had almost happened between himself and a virgin. He should be shocked—he *was* shocked—but not for the reason most would think.

Marriage had never been on his agenda, other than acknowledging that one day he would be forced to concede and take a wife. That day could very well have happened much sooner than he had ever thought, had he not come to his senses in time. If the young lady had been anyone but Miss Catherine Hardwick, opinionated and outspoken, the earl might be angry.

He wasn't.

Instead he was saddened by the fact that another

man would one day reap the passion he had aroused this afternoon.

"Will you be staying on for the festival?"

The question, spoken by Catherine's father, caught Granby's attention.

"Festival?"

"St. Peter's," John Dent explained. "Vicar Marlowe's been raising money for a new roof. Almost met his quota, I should say. But the festival's an annual event. Not anything like your London fairs, but entertaining. And there's always the pole race, for those who enjoy a good run of the horses."

"A pole race?"

"The unmarried ladies display their bonnets. The poles are set west of the Osbourne Bridge. The first lad to the pole takes his pick of the bonnets and returns to the village square, having earned the honor of the first dance."

"I'll have several horses running," Sir Hardwick interjected. "Some of the lads work for me. Usually let them take their pick of the stable. Earned my first dance with Catherine's mother by plucking her bonnet off the pole, pretty as you please."

"Will the stallion be running?" the earl asked.

"Not unless that lass of mine is riding instead of displaying her bonnet. Don't have a fellow on the place that can handle him, beside Jimkins and myself, and we're both too old to be chasing bonnets."

Granby managed a half smile. "It's been a while since I attended a village fair. I may consider it. If you'll consider my next bid for the stallion."

"The man sounds serious," John Dent remarked laughingly.

"Persistent. I'll give him that," Hardwick said. "Very well, your lordship, I'll consider your next offer, but be forewarned that I'm not planning on parting with the stud. He's a damn fine animal. Best bloodline I've ever bred."

"The very reason I intend to have him."

They were joined by Emma Dent. After taking her husband's arm, and being informed that the earl had announced his intentions to remain in Winchcombe for the upcoming festival to be held in three days, she extended an invitation for him to stay at Sudeley Castle.

"Please accept," she urged him. "It's a huge house, and much more accommodating than the inn."

Granby looked at the couple. John Dent was a tall man with intelligent eyes and a pleasant disposition. His wife was well-known for her refinement of intellect, as well as her unusual hobbies. Since he'd decided to stay in Winchcombe for a few more days, the earl decided he might as well spend them at Sudeley.

By late afternoon most of the guests had left, leaving only the closest neighbors lingering in the warm sunshine. Granby casually scanned the gardens for Catherine. He'd managed to keep her in sight for most of the afternoon without giving away his keen interest in her whereabouts.

He forced back a frown when he saw her, still on the arm of the village lad and still smiling.

"That's David Malbane," Felicity Forbes-Hammond informed him. "Unless I can wrestle Catherine to London, he'll end up being her husband."

Granby told himself he didn't care. If the young lady chose to toss her life away, it was of no concern to him.

"She's young and lovely," he said as neutrally as possible. "I wager she'll have a dozen proposals before the last dance of her first ball."

"What do you think of Harry Puddick?" Felicity asked. "He's due to inherit a sizeable sum, along with his father's title and lands."

Harry Puddick was a weak-headed sap with an over-protective mother. It had been the rule at Eton to keep him separated from the more adventurous schoolboys, lest his fragile health be stimulated beyond endurance. Even worse than imagining Catherine with the man was imagining the man with Catherine. She'd have Puddick wrapped around her finger in a matter of minutes, poor sod. No. Miss Hardwick needed a firmer hand than Harry Puddick possessed.

"You'd be hard-pressed to find a more ill-suited pair," Granby told her. "Puddick. We called him Pudding at Eton. The nickname fit."

Being much taller than Felicity, the earl didn't see the impish smile that came over her face. "Yes, well, just a thought. I'll be responsible for her introduction. Months away, of course, but it doesn't hurt to be prepared." She gave him a placid look, the smile completely gone. "I'm going to ask Rebecca to host a ball for her. Sterling has excellent connections."

Granby knew Sterling's connections firsthand. The two men had been friends for most of their lives. If Rebecca Sterling sponsored Catherine, then it went without saying that he'd be seeing her in London, as she was paraded about on the arm of one man or another. The thought offered even less comfort than the idea of her marrying David Malbane.

Nine

By mid-morning it appeared as if everyone within twenty miles of Winchcombe had arrived to enjoy the festival. The village square, not usually ornate or festive, had undergone a transformation. There were tented stalls with tempting food, as well as other booths crowded with trinkets and the usual festival wares. The shopkeepers had their doors open and were ready for business, while the tavern-keepers were hastily icing down kegs of ale.

Banners of every color and design fluttered in the breeze. It was one of those near-perfect days; even the gargoyles that loomed over the entrance to the fifteenth-century St. Peter's Church seemed to be smiling.

Catherine knew as they neared the village that she was sure to see Lord Granby again. Emma Dent had told her that his lordship had accepted an invitation to stay at Sudeley Castle until after the festival.

The extension of his visit could mean only one thing. The earl was going to make her father an offer he couldn't refuse.

There hadn't been a great deal of concern in her mind that her father would sell Storm Dancer until the previous evening, when she'd overheard a conversation between her father and Felicity that had shone a different light on the subject, one Catherine hadn't considered before.

A London Season could be very expensive, if she was to be turned out properly. While her father was reasonably secure, he was not an excessively rich man.

The thought of the stallion being sold for the purpose of financing a Season she didn't even want had kept Catherine awake most of the night. If Lord Granby increased his offer for the stallion, then her father might indeed relinquish Storm Dancer into his hands. Catherine was certain that was the earl's intent. He certainly hadn't stayed on in Winchcombe for her sake.

It had been three days since the Sudeley lawn party, and she hadn't seen him, not at Stonebridge, nor in the meadow during her morning rides.

The earl was a charming troublemaker, a man who could easily ingratiate himself into a woman's heart, playing on her inexperience while holding his own feelings in reserve.

That's exactly what he'd done to her, Catherine thought, stiffening at the memory at how easily she'd forsaken control with him. She'd give him his due; he had certainly charmed her into acting the complete fool.

Never again.

Three days of brooding was three too many. Today, she would keep her defenses intact, despite the fact that her traitorous senses craved his touch.

"You and Felicity have a good time. I'll join up with you just before the race," Sir Hardwick said as he tossed a coin to a village lad, who promised to see the carriage and horses safely tended until day's end.

Catherine gave her father a smile and a quick kiss on the cheek before joining Felicity. The older woman had indicated her interest in visiting the local millinery shop. Mrs. Birtley's Emporium couldn't match the establishments found in London, but she did make pretty hats.

Once inside, Catherine drew her aunt into conversation. "I heard you speaking with Father last night. Must I have a whole new wardrobe? My dresses aren't that outdated."

"One does not appear in London the same way one appears in the country, my dear. You will need a good many things—slippers and hats, a nice cloak for evening, and a new riding habit."

"I don't like draining Father's pockets. He wants to extend the stables, and the house is in need of some repairs."

Felicity gave her a pensive look. "Your father didn't seem troubled when I mentioned taking you shopping in London. In fact, he asked that I not dress you in pastels, remarking that more vivid colors suit you much better. I agree, of course. Your coloring is part of your beauty and shouldn't be disguised. Speaking of which, I've noticed your preference for green. What do you think of this ribbon? It would go nicely on a parasol."

"He's going to sell Storm Dancer so he can afford the London Season you've convinced him I need," Catherine said, shaking her head at the length of ribbon.

"So that's what's bothering you. I should have known." Felicity moved on to another display, this one of delicate Irish lace. "First, I do not believe your father would risk financial ruin just to see you have a go at London. Second, I think you're as preoccupied with Lord Granby as you are with that horse."

"I am not."

Felicity stopped just short of a laugh. "Very well, if you say so."

"I do say so," Catherine insisted. He's not at all the sort of man who interests me."

"And David Malbane is?"

"I've known David all my life."

"And you're going to put your bonnet on display for him to snatch in a valiant gallop around the poles."

"Yes."

Felicity studied a length of lace before setting it aside and reaching for another, this one more ivory than white. "If I understand the tradition, and I fear I do, then retrieving your bonnet is a prelude to a public announcement of the man's affection. Are you sure you want to encourage him?"

"Taking my bonnet from the pole doesn't mean I'm going to marry David," Catherine replied. "We're friends. I'll dance the first dance with him. That's all anyone will expect of me."

Before Felicity could respond, Mrs. Birtley finished with the lady at the front counter and hurried to the back of the shop where her two newest customers were still standing by the display of Irish lace.

Sadie Birtley was a stout woman in her late forties with blond hair and work-worn hands. She was also the village gossip, though not a malicious one. Sadie simply enjoyed repeating all the bits of news that she gleaned from her customers, passing them on whether you were interested in hearing them or not.

"Good morning," she said with a bright smile. "It's going to be a grand festival. I hear you're putting your bonnet up this year, Miss Catherine. David's sure to be happy about that."

Catherine declined commenting on David's enthusiasm. She introduced Felicity, then said she'd changed her mind and would Sadie be so kind as to cut her a length of the green ribbon.

"Be happy to," the shopkeeper said, drawing a pair of scissors from her apron pocket. "It's a pretty color. Just right for you."

Once the ribbon had been rolled into a little package that would fit neatly into Catherine's reticule, she and Felicity made their way toward the square.

"Even Mrs. Birtley recognizes the significance of what you're about to do," her aunt said, in a lightly scolding tone. "I'm not against a young lady exploring her options, my dear, but I do not believe David Malbane is the sort of young man you want to encourage to come courting."

"I don't want to encourage anyone," Catherine told her, knowing Felicity would hear only what she chose to, ignoring anything that interfered with her well-laid plans. "That's why a trip to London is a waste of time and Father's hard-earned money. I won't be accepting any proposals."

"You'll feel differently once you're actually in London."

"I wish to take my own path, not one set for me by others," Catherine said in a final effort to get her point across, but the effort was a wasted one. Felicity had other plans.

It was two hours later that Catherine saw the earl arrive. He rode next to the Dents' carriage. Dressed in tan riding breeches and a chocolate brown jacket, he looked every inch the aristocrat.

Catherine stared at him like a woman obsessed. Shocked at where her thoughts were going, she cut them off. Thinking about the man was silly, especially since she hated him. Or did she?

His very presence seemed to trigger emotions she couldn't control.

She tried to avoid thinking about their last encounter, but seeing him brought the memory flashing back. A riot of feelings came with it—a turbulent, chaotic gale that swept through her as the earl dismounted and tossed the reins to one of the young boys who worked at the White Lion. A coin followed, tossed through the air to be caught and held in the lad's palm.

"Will yer be riding in the pole race, milord?"

"No," Granby told the boy, who would be due another coin when he fetched the gelding later in the day.

Catherine heard the remark, standing only a few yards away from where the Dents' carriage had come to a halt. She wasn't surprised to hear that Granby would be an observer rather than a participant. Stylish lords didn't chase a lady's bonnet. Only the lady.

She and Felicity stepped forward to greet Emma Dent as their neighbor stepped down from the carriage. They chatted amiably for a few moments. Catherine listened, making the appropriate responses when necessary, her mind elsewhere.

When Emma's husband joined them, followed by Granby, Catherine was forced to acknowledge the earl's greeting. She couldn't seem to stop her errant thoughts when he looked her full in the eye and remarked on how lovely she looked. It was only a flattering comment, one he'd no doubt spoken hundreds of times to hundreds of ladies. Catherine accepted it as such, not allowing herself to think beyond the words or what they might imply.

Reminding herself that no one could possibly know how she felt about the man—or why—she excused herself, leaving Emma and Felicity to chat while she went in search of something cool to drink.

David would be working in the tobacco shop until the afternoon race. Once the race was finished, the other entertainment would begin—music and dancing until the church bell struck midnight.

Catherine wasn't aware that the earl had followed her until she stopped in front of a booth that was selling lemonade by the glass.

"Two," he said to the young girl who took orders while her mother cut and squeezed more lemons.

Catherine bristled at the sound of his voice. He'd come up behind her so quietly. She did not turn around to look at him, but accepted the glass of lemonade from the girl and stepped aside so the earl could do the same.

"Shall we find a place to sit and enjoy it?" he asked.

"I'd enjoy the lemonade and the day much better were I not forced to abide your company," she said with a smile that belied the tartness of her words.

"I'll admit being due the rudeness," Granby replied, "but it would seem strange for us to turn from acquaintances into mortal enemies. Felicity is sure to notice. Or do you have an explanation in mind that will satisfy her?"

Catherine relented. "Very well, for appearance' sake. I suppose we could sit in the gazebo."

The gazebo stood near the northern corner of the church green, across the cobblestone street from the lemonade booth. It was empty and would remain so until the musicians took up their positions for the evening entertainment.

The church lawn was just the opposite, being crowded with tables and chairs and more than enough people to act as unofficial chaperones while a young lady sipped lemonade and conversed with a gentleman.

Keeping her eyes on their destination, Catherine made her way to the gazebo, walked up the white wooden steps, and took a seat on the bench.

"I'll be leaving Winchcombe tomorrow," Granby announced, raising a polished boot and resting it on the bench. "I wanted to say good-bye."

Catherine's heart skipped several beats, but she refused to let him see how his decision affected her. She should be relieved, but she wasn't. She had been waiting for three days to look him in the eye and bid him a cold and well-deserved farewell, but now that the moment was at hand, she was plagued with panic and a strange sense of regret. Taking a breath, she waited for him to say something besides good-bye.

Her silence prompted Granby to wonder if she'd miss him. He hadn't been able to get her out of his mind. An uneasy suspicion pounded inside his head; he was becoming genuinely fond of the young lady.

He took a sip of lemonade, thinking he'd rather have something stronger. A man of his caliber did not become *fond* of a young woman of marriageable age.

"Are you going to make my father one last offer for Storm Dancer?" Catherine asked, unable to bear the silence a moment longer.

The earl's nearness and the uncomfortable feelings that were growing between them were a disturbing reminder of everything that had happened in the Sudeley parlor.

He smiled at her then, and she watched the emotions in his eyes flare to full flame. He was remembering, just as she was, how it had been. From that first kiss on the lane to the more shameful ones in the parlor, each time he touched her the fire had burned brighter than the time before.

"Will you hate me for buying the stallion?" A flicker of humor shone in his eyes, but his voice sounded sincere, as if her answer might actually have an affect on his actions.

"No. Because you aren't going to get Storm Dancer," she declared, as a plan formed in her mind. It was a rotten trick to play on anyone, especially an earl, but she was due her revenge. The man had come close to breaking her heart.

"I can be a very persuasive man, or have you forgotten?"

"I haven't forgotten," Catherine retorted. "Though you should be ashamed of yourself for bragging about it."

Her response sobered him. She was right, he had been bragging.

"You left the parlor before I could apologize," he said, suffering only a small twinge of conscience as he remembered how it had been that day. Being with her again sent a charge of energy through his body, heightening his already-aroused state, and reminding him that the experience wasn't one that could be repeated without dire consequences. "When I invited you to meet me, I didn't intend for things to go beyond a simple kiss."

There was an awkward pause, during which Catherine considered leaving the gazebo before she poured her lemonade over the earl's head. "Should I be flattered, my lord, or remind you of your own words? A kiss is never simple."

The chit's right on target. There certainly hasn't been anything simple about the kisses we've shared so far. Pity there can't be more.

"Will you accept my apology?" he asked, lowering his voice to the seductive whisper that was part of the reason he was apologizing in the first place.

"On one condition," she said, hoping her plan worked. If it didn't, she'd end up losing Storm Dancer along with the final remnants of her pride.

"And what would that be?"

"In offering an apology, you admit wrongdoing. If that's the case, I would rather have your promise that you'll forget about Storm Dancer. That's an apology I *will* accept."

Granby laughed at her ingenuity. "I daresay the stallion is worth more than a few kisses, no matter how delightful those kisses turned out to be."

Catherine frowned as she smoothed the skirt of her dress. "I suppose I could accept an apology for kissing me so outrageously, if you'll consider an alternative to buying Storm Dancer."

Seeing her sitting, half in sunlight, half in shadows, Granby was once again taken by her near-ethereal beauty. They weren't alone—the entire village was milling about the green—but given the emotions running rampant between them and the inescapable memory of their strange relationship, his curiosity was piqued. Could she be offering him the alternative he wanted?

"I'm listening," he said.

"If you won't consider leaving Winchcombe without making a final bid for Storm Dancer, then may I suggest a wager?"

"A lady who wears breeches and gambles. You are full of surprises, Miss Hardwick."

"A race, not a gamble," Catherine said, giving him a straight look. "If you win, you get to make your offer, although there's no guarantee that my father will accept it. If I win, you leave Winchcombe *without* making a final offer for Storm Dancer, and everything that has happened between us is forgotten."

"Your mare is no match for my gelding, and my gelding is no match for the stallion. It wouldn't be a fair race."

"We will ride horses that are equally matched," she told him. "My father has two such horses, twins in fact. I daresay you won't find anything unequal about them. They're so alike even Jimkins has trouble telling them apart. The race will consist of your horsemanship and skill against mine."

"And you think to win?" The charming little vixen had very cunningly put his pride on the line.

"I *will* win," Catherine said confidently.

"Very well, I accept the wager," Granby said just as confidently. "Where and when is this duel of talents to take place?"

"Tomorrow morning. I'll meet you in the meadow just after dawn."

Catherine smiled. Step one of her plan was underway. Now, all she had to do was convince her father to become step two without making him suspicious.

"Since your first dance of the evening will be taken by whomever retrieves your bonnet, may I ask for the last dance?" Granby asked, surprising her.

"The last dance, then," she agreed absently. She looked around for her father. She needed to find him before the earl did. "You understand, of course, that our race must be kept secret. Father would never allow it otherwise."

"I'd already concluded as much," he said. "Don't worry, I'll not make my offer to Sir Hardwick until after our little riding duel. In the interim, may I suggest that you accommodate yourself to the loss of the stallion."

"I shan't lose any sleep over it, my lord," she replied smugly. "Now, if you'll excuse me, I really should join Felicity."

With that she was gone, leaving the earl to think about a victory kiss once he'd proven himself the better rider.

Catherine found her father a short time later. He had just paid for a tankard of ale. She slipped her arm through his, leading him away for a few minutes of private conversation.

"Don't waste a festival day keeping me company," Sir Hardwick said, as they sat down on one of the benches that had been removed from the church rectory and placed under a sprawling elm for the benefit of those who preferred watching the activities to participating in them.

"I want a word with you away from Aunt Felicity's ears," Catherine confessed.

"Up to no good, are you?"

"You know I don't want to go to London."

"Aye, I know. But Felicity has helped me to see the error of my ways. It isn't right for me to keep you bridled here in the country. Just being selfish. I was away for so many years."

Catherine leaned over and gave him a kiss on the

cheek. "You haven't bridled me. There's no place I'd rather be than Stonebridge."

They were interrupted by Reverend Marlowe who asked Sir Hardwick if he'd do the honors of starting the pole race. Catherine's father accepted, then turned back to her, having lost the thread of their conversation. "What is it you wanted to talk to me about, lass?"

"Storm Dancer," she said, getting to the point before anyone else could interrupt them. "Are you going to sell him because you need the money to dress me fashionably enough for London?'

"Don't be worrying your pretty head about money. You'll have a nice dowry when the time comes. We've never spoken of it before, but your mother left you a tidy sum and a nice piece of land that came to her through her family. You'll not go empty-handed to the altar."

"You're set on me going to London then?"

"I am. Made Felicity a promise. I won't be going back on it."

"Then give Storm Dancer to me."

"What!"

"Give him to me," Catherine said. "I can't bear the thought of you selling him to anyone. If you don't need the money to send me to London, then I'll go willingly. I'll attend every ball, dance every dance, smile at all the eligible young lords, I'll even try to find someone to fall in love with, just don't sell Storm Dancer."

Her father turned to her as if she'd just announced that she was going to marry the Prince of Wales. "What's this? Are you really that attached to the beast?"

"I'm afraid so," Catherine said. "I know he isn't a pet, but, well . . . I just think you'd be making a mistake to sell him. Stonebridge will pass to me one day, and I want to make sure Storm Dancer's bloodline passes with it."

She glanced quickly toward the heavens, just to make sure a thunderbolt wasn't waiting to claim her. She wasn't lying, not entirely. She was attached to the stallion, and the colts he sired would carry the future of Stonebridge in their blood. The only thing she was omitting was her determination to teach Lord Granby a lesson. If he won, and it was a big if, then he couldn't possibly buy Storm Dancer from her father because the stallion would belong to her, and she'd never sell him.

"The last time you asked me for anything, you were eight years old and you'd just found a litter of kittens in the barn," Hardwick said, looking at her as if he was seeing that same little girl. "You begged me not to let the grooms drown them in the creek. We had more than enough mousers about the place, but I couldn't say no to you then, anymore than I can now. Very well. Storm Dancer is yours, but that doesn't mean you can go galloping off any time you take the notion to. He's to be put to stud after the local races. I'll be telling Jimkins the same thing, so don't think otherwise."

Catherine was all smiles as she threw her arms around her father and hugged him tight. "I love you."

"It's settled then. No more pouting or arguing about London."

"No more pouting or arguing, I promise," she said, meaning it.

Knowing the earl couldn't get his hands on Storm Dancer was worth the misery of a few weeks in London. As for being underhanded, it served his high-and-mighty lordship right. He'd done nothing but tease and taunt her since he'd ridden into Winchcombe. Come morning, she'd get the last laugh.

Granby wasn't surprised by the outcome of the race. As expected, David Malbane, Catherine's local admirer, came riding into the square brandishing her bonnet. His win was accompanied by cheers and whistles, and a chaste kiss on the cheek from the bonnet's owner.

The earl watched the whole event, knowing full well that Catherine was trying to make him jealous again. The problem was, she was succeeding.

He wasn't sure which one of the two young people he wanted to inflict pain upon first. Malbane for being so bloody cheerful about winning the bonnet, or Catherine for smiling so triumphantly when it came time for her admirer to claim the first dance of the evening.

The more Granby thought about it, the more he wanted to paddle the young lady's backside. Unfortunately, he couldn't. What he could do was have another ale.

It was easy to see that the dancing was the lively climax of an eventful day. Lady Forbes-Hammond looked on from a seat near the gazebo, while Catherine's father and the Dents conversed with Reverend Marlowe.

The dancers were mostly young, though a few older couples could be seen among them. Granby paid for his ale, then strolled aimlessly across the green. He settled onto a bench, content to watch the activities and think of the next day. Having witnessed how adeptly Catherine had handled the stallion that day in the lane, he wouldn't allow himself to underestimate her riding abilities. Still confident that he could win, he found himself watching her as she danced.

The sun had set, and the moon hung low in the evening sky. The Chinese lanterns that lit the dance floor bobbed slightly in the breeze. Granby watched as the glancing light played over Catherine's hair, changing the color from golden red to deep rust and back. She laughed at something her partner was saying, and Granby bristled with jealousy again.

How many more dances before he could claim her? He'd bribed the lead musician, making sure the last dance would be a waltz. He wanted to hold her again, to feel the vitality of her young body under his hands, to look into those magnificent catlike eyes, and with his gaze remind her of all the times he'd kissed her before, and in the reminding make her want to be kissed again.

It was a game he'd played often enough in the past, but this time it was more than the chase. It was the principle of the thing. If he was doomed to a restless night, then it was only right that she have a few fitful dreams of her own.

Catherine sighed with relief when the music ended and Timothy Thurber stopped stepping on her toes. She was breathless from having danced every dance since the musicians had begun playing.

As was her custom, Sadie had left her shop open so the ladies could avail themselves of its facilities. There was plenty of moonlight to guide her steps as Catherine made her way across the village square. If the earl had forgotten their dance, all the better. She was having a surprisingly good time, considering that most of the young men in Winchcombe had two left feet. And she was going to have an even better time in the morning, when she bested the earl at his own game.

"Have you forgotten our dance?" the voice came at her out of the shadows.

Catherine stopped in her tracks, while her heart started racing. The Earl of Granby was suddenly standing in front of her, looking devilishly handsome in the moonlight.

They were well beyond the sight of the people who had remained for the dance. The rest of the festival attendees had either already returned to their homes or were busy in one of the taverns. The street was empty, except for the two of them, and the music floating on the air.

Knowing she shouldn't, but wanting at least the memory of one dance to go along with all the other memories the earl had supplied since his arrival, Catherine accepted his hand. The warmth of his fingers as they closed around hers—he wasn't wearing gloves—sent a shudder of excitement flickering across her nerve endings.

He led her away from the street, into the narrow alley between Sadie's shop and the neighboring haberdashery run by Chester Wynne, a thin-faced old man who rarely attended anything but his shop and Sunday services.

"Are you always this daring?" she asked, knowing the answer.

"No more daring than you, Miss Hardwick," he whispered as his hand slipped to her waist.

Dancing in the dark with the handsome Lord Granby was not something Catherine was likely to forget. He moved as gracefully as a cat, even on the uneven cobblestones of the alley, his body matching the rhythm of the music with effortless ease. When the music ended, his fingers brushed her cheek, then ever so gently he tilted her chin up and kissed her.

The kiss was long and deep and leisurely, as if the night had been created just for them.

Catherine felt the warm, hard length of him as his arms tightened around her. She breathed in the scent of the summer night, and tasted the ale he'd been drinking as his tongue swept inside her mouth. Before she knew what she was doing, she was up on her tiptoes, arms around his neck, kissing him back. Nothing felt as good as this, her body pressed against his, his strong arms around her.

She heard voices and laughter and the sound of the musicians putting away their instruments. She felt the brush of the summer breeze and the coolness of the shadows. She smelled the cigar smoke clinging to his shirt and the expensive cologne on his skin. The power of her senses were magnified, as if by some magical power of the moon, but most of all she *felt* the wonder of his kiss.

For a moment Catherine regretted how she planned to repay him, but the smugness of his voice when he told her good night wiped the remorse from her mind.

"Until tomorrow," he said, before walking past her and into the night.

Ten

Dawn was a misty ghost slipping over the meadow as Granby reined in his gelding. He'd dressed and slipped away from Sudeley without disturbing so much as a footman, although he had awakened one of the stable lads when he'd led Lieutenant from his stall. He'd dispatched the boy back to his bed in the loft above the mews, insisting that he could see to his own horse.

Peck had been given his instructions last night. The coach was to be readied and on its way south to Reading no later than ten this morning. Regardless of the outcome of the wager, Granby would be leaving Winchcombe. He'd meet up with his coach and valet at the Didbrook Inn this evening. Another two days' travel, weather permitting, and he'd be home.

It was time that he applied himself to his own business—the running of his estate in Berkshire. He hadn't been home in months, not caring to spend time in a cavernous old house with no one but servants for company, but now that summer had arrived there would be plenty to keep him busy until autumn heralded in the hunting season.

Unlike most of his peers, Granby didn't hunt for

hunting's sake, but he did enjoy the crispness of an autumn morning and a rousing ride through the woods. It had been his father's favorite season, as well, and the time of year when they'd shared each other's company more as friends than father and son.

He missed the old gent.

The melancholy thought came with the first rays of light, catching Granby by surprise. He supposed it was the setting. The meadow was reminiscent of one of his father's favorite glens near Foxleigh, the grand estate which now belong to him. His memories of the place were pleasant ones; it was a childhood growing up with horses and hunting hounds, and the knowledge that one day he'd take over the reins of an earldom.

Thoughts of family and home kept him occupied until the sound of another horse and rider broke the stillness of the hour. His pulse quickened in anticipation of the upcoming meeting.

Lost in the morning's spell, Granby smiled as he watched Catherine ride across the mist-shrouded meadow. Her face lit up at the sight of him, softening for a few seconds the resoluteness that was always present in her expression. She was a strong-willed young woman, and it showed.

The man watching her didn't mind her willfulness anymore than he minded her cinnamon-colored hair or the hazel eyes that sparkled with fire whenever she looked at him. On the contrary, it made her all the more appealing.

Catherine felt the anticipation too. It vibrated inside her as she rode across the meadow. The mare snorted restlessly, as if sensing her rider's change of mood.

Reminding herself that she was here to race, to prove not only to the earl but to herself that she could and would chart her own course in life, Catherine tried to stop her errant thoughts. But the moment their gazes met, she was instantly taken back in time, to a waltz in the moonlight and a kiss that had filled her night with dreams.

"Good morning," he said to her.

"Good morning." She reached into her jacket and pulled out a small flask. After uncorking the top, she passed it to him. "Mrs. Gibson had a pot of coffee brewing in the kitchen. I thought you might like some."

"Thank you." He took the flask from her hand, then turned it up for a drink. The coffee was strong and hot, and finished the job the chilly morning had begun; he came fully awake. He took a second drink before passing the flask back to her.

He watched as she drank in turn. It was a simple thing, and yet he felt as though they'd exchanged another intimacy—her lips were where his had been. Another thought followed. In all his years, never once had he felt this close to a woman, not physically, but in spirit.

It was an absurd thought, but Granby couldn't shake it. Sitting in a summer meadow at sunrise, sharing hot coffee, each intent on winning an unorthodox race that neither really needed to win. Why? Because he'd dared to demand a kiss? Or because they were both pridefully stubborn, and the stallion had become the symbol of that stubbornness?

Regardless of the reason, they were here.

"The horses?"

"In a pasture not far from here," she told him. "Follow me."

They rode into the woods, which curved around the open field like an embracing arm. It was reverently quiet, as if they'd entered a church. They went some distance, saying nothing until they reached another opening in the trees, a fenced pasture where half a dozen horses were munching on the dew-covered grass.

Catherine dismounted before he could offer his assistance, sliding her leg over the saddlebow and jumping down from the horse. He'd never seen a lady dismount like that, but then he'd never gone riding with a woman who wore breeches just as beautifully as she worn silk and satin. These breeches were a deep walnut brown, tucked into knee-high riding boots, and hugging her round bottom ever so nicely.

Granby wanted to get his hands on that bottom, to caress it, to cup it in his palms, raising her hips to receive him. He dismounted, knowing he needed to concentrate on something else. He had a race to win. Even though it would be considered the gentlemanly thing to let *her* win, he knew he'd do his best to beat her. His nature was a competitive one, be it cards, women, or racing.

When Catherine began to unsaddle her mare, Granby stepped forward. "I'll do that."

"You forget, I was literally raised in a stable," she said, refusing to step aside and relinquish the duty. "While my friends were playing with kites and dolls, I was working alongside the grooms. The only thing Jimkins won't let me do is help when the mares are being serviced."

"I should hope not."

"Why?" She looked over her shoulder, her hazel eyes surveying him thoughtfully. "I'm not like the young ladies you've met in London. Stonebridge is a breeding stable. I know what happens, even if I've never seen it. We have three mares ready to foal. I like being there when the new ones are born."

Granby wasn't sure what to say. He'd witnessed several mares giving birth, and each time he'd thanked the Almighty for being born a male of the species.

He unsaddled his gelding, trying not to think of what it would be like to stand idly by while a woman brought one of his children into the world. Sterling had managed well enough, though his friend had admitted to draining at least one brandy decanter during the long night.

Despite his resolve to concentrate on something else, Granby couldn't stop the image from forming in his mind—Catherine sitting in a rocker in front of the fire, her breast bared while she nursed a child.

It came to him with a rush, a strong urgency he hadn't experienced in years. He wanted to keep this woman in his life. The physical need of it hit him like a wave, washing over his senses, tightening his muscles, bringing a sheen of perspiration to his forehead.

"I'll get Cain and Abel," Catherine said, unaware that she was pulling him away from a most surprising thought.

"Twin horses," he said, placing his saddle on the ground next to hers. "Did the mare survive the birth?"

"Yes. In fact, she's foaled twice since then. Her name is Romola. She's a beautiful roan mare with a white blaze. Can you pick out her twins?"

It wasn't a difficult task. The two young stallions had inherited their mother's markings. Granby judged both horses to be fifteen hands high with thick chests and strong flanks. Their configuration was excellent, but that didn't surprise him. Stonebridge had proven its ability to produce a fine horse in Storm Dancer.

"Father bred Romola to a Russian Kabardin. The breed is a strong mountain horse. The troops in the Crimea used them for cavalry mounts. They have stamina and endurance. Romola has an Arabian bloodline."

"They're strong and fast," Granby said.

"Exactly." She whistled then, and all but one of the horses in the meadow came trotting their way. "That's Irish Lad. Father's the only one who can get him to answer a whistle. He's stubborn."

"Most things Irish are," Granby said, holding onto his gelding's bridle. Lieutenant was normally well behaved, but finding four young stallions and two sleek mares so close at hand could upset even the best-trained horse.

"Which will it be, Cain or Abel?" Catherine asked as

she slipped the bridle off the mare and gave her flank a soft slap to get her moving.

Granby carefully appraised the two stallions. The horses were as perfectly matched as the gold-mounted carnelian cuff links his father had given him on his sixteenth birthday.

He examined each animal, finding no fault with either one. "It makes little difference, since I can't tell one from the other."

With that, he saddled both horses, leaving his gelding to graze along with the mare. "What course do you have in mind? Open country or a hunting run?"

"A little of both," Catherine replied, mounting the horse she thought was Abel, but could just as easily be Cain. "The starting line will be the north end of this pasture, just beyond the gate. From there we go east. The trail will take us into part of Sudeley's old parklands. There are several natural hurdles, a crumbling stone wall and a narrow ribbon of a creek. The finish line will be the turnoff to the lane that takes us to Sudeley itself. It's the old road; no one uses it now but the gamekeeper."

"And the distance?" He asked, taking up the reins of his own mount. The young stallion snorted and shook his head, sensing something was about to happen.

"Four furlongs, give or take a few yards."

"Shall we reiterate the terms of the wager," he said. "If you win, I will dispatch myself from Winchcombe without making an offer for Storm Dancer."

"And if you win," Catherine said, "you can offer my father whatever sum you wish."

Granby smiled, his first real smile of the day. "Ah, but you've forgotten the most important part. My winning will also require that you avail yourself of a full London Season."

"I haven't forgotten," she said, having spent most of the morning thinking of just that thing.

If she went to London, she'd be sure to see Lord Granby again. The idea shouldn't be appealing, but it was. Despite his arrogance, her senses still went chaotic whenever she looked into those silver blue eyes. And when he smiled at her, the way he was smiling now . . .

"Shall we make our way to the starting line?"

Once they were outside the pasture, and the gate had been latched behind them, Granby brought his mount in line with Catherine's. He nodded, silently signaling that she should start the race.

Remembering that she'd ridden the planned course hundreds of times, and that she very much wanted to win, Catherine began a short count.

Three seconds later they were off. The calm silence of the morning was broken by the sound of pounding hooves as both horses jumped forward, instinctively sensing that their individual abilities were being tested.

Catherine leaned low over her mount's neck, streamlining her body the way Jimkins had taught her to, as she encouraged Abel to stretch out his long legs and eat up the ground. The earl kept pace with her, and for a brief moment she feared the race might end in a dead heat.

The trees went by in a blur of greens and browns, the wind whipping at her face, as Catherine urged her horse on. She loved to ride, the faster the better. It was exhilarating, and the excitement made her laugh out loud. She couldn't be sure, but she thought she heard the earl laughing too.

They'd covered half the course when the stone wall came into view. It was a good four feet high, dipping in places where the rocks had fallen away, but still a challenging hurdle. Both horses took it effortlessly, their hooves digging into the moist ground as they landed smoothly, then ran on.

Damn! If she didn't gain the lead as soon as they crossed the stream, the race would end up being nothing more than a daring ride with no discernable winner.

They raced on, side by side for another quarter mile, the two huge horses tearing up the ground, their thundering hooves the only sound to be heard. The creek was only a few hundred yards ahead of them now. The water gleamed in the early morning light. Catherine looked to her right. The earl was abreast of her, the two horses matching each other stride for powerful stride.

The creek was jumped as easily as the stone wall had been, with barely a drop of water being splashed.

They were on the last quarter of the race when Catherine saw the doe leap from the woods. Instead of running away from them, the animal turned and darted back across the old road, directly into their path.

"Watch out!" Granby shouted at her.

The next few seconds were nightmarish.

Catherine was able to veer her mount to the left, but there was no place for the earl to go. He was between her and a thick row of birch trees, with a now frightened and paralyzed deer directly in his way.

She reined in her horse, slowing him down just enough for Granby to turn his mount to the path hers would have taken, missing the doe by inches. The animal, now startled into movement, leaped to safety, its hind hooves hitting the stallion in the lower chest.

Both horse and rider went down.

By the time Catherine had her mount under control, the second stallion was on its feet. The animal didn't appear to be injured, but its rider was her first concern. She jumped from the saddle and hit the ground running, skidding to a stop next to the earl, who was lying on his side, his face hidden from her.

"Are you all right?" she asked breathlessly.

"My shoulder," he moaned, then cursed. "Bloody hell!"

"Don't move," she said. "I'll get help."

He rolled over then, or tried to, and she saw that his face was scratched and bleeding. "Are you all right?" he asked, his voice strained.

"I'm fine. The doe kicked out as she sprinted for cover and caught your horse in the chest." Tears blurred her vision, so she wiped them away. "Please, don't move. I'll get Jimkins. He'll know what to do."

"Where's my horse?"

"He's fine," Catherine reassured him. "Let me help you to sit up."

"Ouch, dammit!"

"I'm sorry."

"I can manage," Granby said, determined to get to his feet. He gritted his teeth. His shoulder was dislocated, his left arm dangling at an awkward, painful angle. "Get my horse. I can ride."

"No. Stay here. I'll go for help."

"Get the damn horse," he growled.

Catherine did as he asked, shaking so badly it took her two tries before she gripped the reins and led the stallion to where the earl was leaning against a tree. His head was down, and she knew he was trying to stay focused. The pain had to be horrendous. One of the grooms had dislocated his shoulder once and fainted dead away.

"Are you sure you can ride?" she asked, fearful of more injuries if he fell from his horse a second time.

"Once I'm in the saddle, I'll stay on until we get to Sudeley," he said. He paused to take a deep breath, fighting back a wave of nausea. He was not going to vomit in front of a woman. Two deep breaths later, he asked weakly. "Which is closer, Stonebridge or Sudeley?"

"Stonebridge," Catherine replied, easing the stallion close. "Put your foot in the stirrup, I'll help you up."

It took two tries, but Granby managed to get on the horse.

Catherine gathered the reins, then walked to where her own horse was waiting. Once she was in the saddle, she looked at the earl. "Hang on."

Granby bit back a curse when the animal started moving. Every step the horse took jarred his shoulder anew, but there was no helping it, so he knotted his hand in the horse's mane and hung on.

As soon as Stonebridge was in sight, Catherine started shouting. Jimkins came running out of the stable, followed by several grooms. One of the men was immediately dispatched to the village to bring back the physician.

"Easy, milord," Jimkins said, as he helped Granby to dismount. "Let's get you into the cottage."

Catherine moved ahead of them, opening the door. Once they were inside, she tried not to get in the way. Jimkins poured the earl a drink.

"Sip on this," he said, putting it into the earl's good hand.

Granby sipped the whiskey, knowing that if he gulped it down it would be coming right back up. His left hand was beginning to swell. He tried not to think about what the physician was going to have to do to get the shoulder back into place. It was going to hurt like hell.

Jimkins told the groom to take care of the horses, before turning to Catherine. "What happened?"

"We were riding and a doe darted in front of Lord Granby's horse. He missed running over the animal, but the doe kicked Cain in the chest and they went down."

The stablemaster gave her a dubious look. "You'd best get up to the house and warn Mrs. Gibson we're on our way with an injured man."

Catherine looked at the earl. His head was resting against the back of the chair and his eyes were closed. He looked pale.

"Go on," Jimkins urged her. "Davey and me will see to his lordship."

Catherine left the cottage and ran up the hill toward the house. What was she going to tell her father?

"I was able to get the shoulder back into place," Dr. Hawkins announced as he stepped into the morning room, where Catherine was waiting with her father and Felicity. "I've given him some laudanum to ease the pain. He should sleep for several hours."

"What can we do?" Felicity asked. Breakfast had been interrupted by the news of the earl's injury, but Mrs. Gibson had brought fresh tea and cakes for Catherine, who had left the house without eating.

"I've wrapped the shoulder and arm," the physician replied. "I don't suspect we'll have to worry about fever in this case. Nevertheless, send for me if he shows any signs of distress. Keep him as quiet as possible for the first few days. Other than that, I recommend rest and lots of Mrs. Gibson's good, strong tea. He should be up and around in three or four days, but the arm will have to remain immobilized for a good two weeks."

Very little had been said since the earl had been carried into the house and placed in the second-floor guest suite, across the hall from the set of rooms Felicity was occupying. Dr. Hawkins had arrived a short time later.

Catherine couldn't speak at all. Fear had knotted in her stomach hours ago and it was still there, lying as cold and hard as a lump of winter coal. Everyone was looking at her as if she'd committed some deadly sin, and she almost had. Granby could have been killed.

"All his needs will be met," Sir Hardwick announced in a firm voice that didn't bode well for his daughter. "Thank you, Dr. Hawkins."

The physician, a kindly man in his late fifties who knew everyone in Winchcombe by name, gave Catherine a sympathetic glance as he exited the room. No one had yet asked for an explanation of the accident, but it was apparent that Catherine and the earl had been riding pell-mell down the old Sudeley road while everyone else in the parish was still tucked tight in their beds.

Taking his leave, after being assured that the cook had a nice breakfast waiting for him in the kitchen, the portly physician closed the door behind him.

"I think we should have a cup of tea and compose ourselves," Felicity suggested. She was still in her dressing gown, her silver hair hastily wrapped up in a blue turban.

Catherine shuddered on the inside. She wanted to rush to her room and burst into tears, but she knew her father was expecting an explanation. The problem was that when he heard it, things were only going to get worse.

"Have your tea," Sir Hardwick said. "Catherine and I will be in the library."

"You mustn't lose your temper with the girl, Warren. Anyone can see that she's already regretting her actions."

"Not half as much as she's going to regret them," he announced as he marched out of the room, expecting his daughter to follow.

"Oh, dear," Felicity said, as she patted Catherine's trembling hands.

"It's all my fault," Catherine confessed shakily. She turned to face her aunt, her eyes brimming with tears. "I'm sorry."

"Perhaps I should come to the library with you," Felicity said. "I can't recall every seeing Warren this angry before."

Any other time Felicity would have been far more inquisitive and considerably more persistent, but Sir Hardwick was waiting and it went without question that his daughter needed to get herself to the library with all due haste, lest his anger increase.

"It was an accident," Catherine said, giving Felicity the only explanation she could in the time allotted to her. Of course, she hadn't told anyone but Jimkins about the doe. No one else had asked. They had all been too busy seeing to the earl.

Catherine was relieved to know that he'd recover, but that didn't ease her conscience about what had happened, nor her fear for what was about to happen when she faced her father. Even worse, she was going to have to face Granby sooner or later.

The best thing would be for the floor to open and swallow her whole, but Catherine didn't hold out much hope for that easy an escape. She walked out of the morning room and down the hall to her father's library.

It was one of Catherine's favorite rooms. She associated it with her father, and the time she had spent on his knee as a child. Whenever he had been home, which hadn't been often, they had divided their shared time between the library and the stables.

It was a functional room, with a broad desk inlaid with burgundy leather, the chair behind it well padded and comfortable. The walls displayed a number of pastoral scenes, mostly horses and hunting. The sword that had been part of her father's dress uniform now hung over the mantelpiece. There was a stub of a cigar in the quartz ashtray, left over from the previous evening. With all the commotion, Agnes hadn't had time to give the room its usual daily cleaning.

Her father was standing in front of the windows, his hands folded behind his back, his feet braced slightly apart in a military stance. It wasn't a good sign.

Catherine grew increasingly uncomfortable as she closed the door and waited for her father to acknowledge her.

"I would like to believe that you have a reasonable explanation for this morning's events," he said irritably. "I think it's time you shared it with me."

Catherine took a deep breath, licked her lips, and . . . and couldn't find the words.

"Well?" her father prompted angrily. He wasn't a temperamental man, but he did have his limits.

"The earl and I were riding. A deer darted out of the woods and frightened his horse."

"I'll have the whole story," he said impatiently.

There was no avoiding it. Disaster was at hand.

"I challenged the earl to a race."

"You what!"

"A race." Thinking quickly, she gave her father as many of the facts as she dared. "He criticized me for riding Storm Dancer, so I challenged him to a race to prove which of us was the better rider."

"Of all the bloody idiotic things to do!" her father ranted. "A man could have been killed today because of your foolish pride. I didn't think you were that childish."

Catherine couldn't defend herself without admitting that she'd tricked her father into giving her Storm Dancer, and that she'd meant to trick the earl if he won the race. Even worse, she couldn't justify her actions by telling anyone that the earl had done more than criticize her—he'd kissed her. If she'd been insulted by the impropriety, she should have spoken up days ago. Instead, she'd allowed the kisses to go on—nay, she'd encouraged them.

Her father was right. She'd been foolish and childish, and now a man was hurt, badly hurt and in pain.

"I'm sorry."

"As you should be," her father snapped. "The problem now being how to rectify your earlier stupidity. I'm tempted to give you the thrashing you deserve."

"It was an accident," Catherine said fearfully.

"Felicity is right," he said with conviction. "It's time you realized the responsibilities of being a young woman."

"What are you going to do?"

"You will install yourself in your room for the remainder of the day," he told her, his voice colder and harder than she could remember ever hearing it before. "Beginning tomorrow you will keep to the house. If I see you anywhere near the stables or a horse, you will sorely regret it. As for proper punishment, I'm not sure such a thing exists for this particular infraction. I shall have to do some thinking on the matter. In the interim, you will do as I've said. And stay away from the earl. You've done the man enough harm."

Eleven

At sunset, after a long day of solitude in which Catherine had tried to sort through a mass of conflicting emotions, including a heavy dose of guilt, she slumped down on her bed more confused than she'd been when she'd entered the room that morning.

The circumstances alone were enough to keep her nerves quivering, but knowing the earl was just down the hall added to her misery. She needed to talk to him, to let him know that she was genuinely sorry that he'd been hurt.

She owed the man an apology.

Agnes had been a blessed messenger of information when she'd brought up Catherine's luncheon tray. Lord Granby's valet had arrived, having been summoned from Sudeley to attend his injured employer. Peck had thanked Mrs. Gibson for her efforts and assured the housekeeper that his lordship was resting comfortably.

But that had been hours ago, and the minutes were ticking by like rain dripping off a leaf, one drop at a time.

There was a knock on the door. Catherine answered, and both Agnes and Felicity stepped across the threshold. Agnes gave her a small smile, then put down her dinner tray.

Felicity took a more somber approach. She waited until Agnes had returned to her duties in the kitchen before beginning the interrogation she'd had to postpone that morning.

"Am I to understand that you *invited* the Earl of Granby to race at an hour so early in the morning it required you to leave the house before dawn? If so, I cannot begin to express my concern, Catherine. A young lady does not—"

"I know what I did and what I shouldn't have done," Catherine said impatiently. "Please don't lecture me about it now, Aunt Felicity. I've been in this room for hours. The boredom and worry have become unbearable. How is the earl?"

"His man assures me that he is resting comfortably. Your father said it can be a most painful injury, one frequently associated with a fall from a horse."

Catherine found it difficult to subdue her curiosity. "Has Father spoken to the earl?"

"Not as yet, though I suspect he will as soon as Granby is up to the conversation. I will not lecture you, since you seem remorseful, though the regret is belated and the damage done. You must know that you've put your father in a very awkward situation. Lord Granby is a man of substantial influence."

"I'm the one he will be upset with, not Father."

"Regardless, it is time you realized that your actions have consequences that go beyond being confined to your room. Your reputation is at stake."

Catherine poured tea and passed a cup to her aunt. "No one could think any worse of me at this moment than I think of myself," she said. "As for my reputation, I can't say that I'm greatly concerned about what people in London may think of me, having never met them."

"But you are concerned about Lord Granby's opinion."

Catherine caught the nuance of Felicity's tone. "I do not want him to hate me."

"I don't think that need be a concern," her aunt replied, helping herself to a piece of ginger cake. "Were I asked, I would venture to say that Lord Granby is taken with you."

"He thinks I'm a spoiled child with nothing better to do than gallop about the countryside in breeches."

"I have seen the way he looks at you, my dear, and his admiration is not that of a man who finds you unacceptable. But I must say your recent actions could change his mind. Wounded pride is no excuse to incite gossip by asking a man to meet you at dawn for a devil-may-care race through the woods. Really, Catherine, whatever were you thinking?"

"Apparently, I wasn't thinking at all."

Blessedly, Felicity let it rest with that. She visited with Catherine for another half hour, then wished her a good night's sleep. "I'm sure your father will be more amicable come morning. As for the earl, that will be up to you."

Catherine wasn't entirely sure what Felicity meant by the parting remark, nor did she care. She couldn't abide the idleness much longer. The summer days were lengthy, and she'd been behind closed doors for over ten hours. Dare she try to see the earl tonight? She could speculate as to his welfare, but nothing short of seeing him with her own eyes would satisfy the need to know that he was truly all right.

Just a short visit. She wouldn't be able to sleep until she had the apology out of the way.

"Damn bloody nuisance this is going to be," Granby complained for the hundredth time in the hour since he'd awakened from a laudanum-induced nap that had lasted all day.

Peck was sitting in an overstuffed chair by the bed. "Try to rest, milord."

"I don't want to rest. I want a drink. No, don't look at the bloody teapot. Go downstairs and fetch me a bottle of port. Better yet, make it whiskey," Granby growled in a belligerent voice.

He lay staring at the ceiling, trying to remember the last time he'd felt this miserable. His body was a mass of bruises, his left arm and shoulder were encased in bandages, his hand was swollen to twice its normal size, and he was worried about Catherine.

"I would like to see Miss Hardwick," he announced, trying to sound casual, as if the request had nothing to do with the lady herself.

Peck ignored his employer's words, picked up a book and began reading.

"Did you hear me?"

"Yes, milord, but I wouldn't think it a good idea for a strange servant, one who is in the household by the courtesy of her father, to go traipsing about the hallways, knocking on closed doors, searching for the young lady."

"Then find her maid."

"Her maid's name is Agnes, and the young lady has been confined to her room until her father deems otherwise," Peck informed him with bland practicality. "It seems her conduct is in question."

"It was an accident. And put that bloody book away. You're here to see to my needs, and I need to know what's going on in this house."

Peck gave him a look not unlike the kind a father would give a misbehaving child. "Miss Hardwick had a tray delivered to her room less than an hour ago. Your personal belongings have been brought from Sudeley, accompanied by heartfelt condolences from Mr. and Mrs. Dent. When you feel up to it, I will give you a shave, though I think we should let the scratches heal first. Dr.

Hawkins will return tomorrow morning to check on your progress. What else would you like to know, milord?"

"Nothing," the earl said, realizing Peck was reading him as easily as the book he'd borrowed from the Hardwick library. "I'm going back to sleep."

"Good night, milord."

Granby closed his eyes, then opened them at the sound of someone knocking ever so lightly on the door.

Peck put aside his book and answered the door.

"Yes, miss?"

"His lordship," Granby heard Catherine whisper, "Is he resting?"

"Let her in," Granby ordered, grimacing as he tried to raise himself into a sitting position without Peck's helping hands. He was covered to the waist by a sheet and a summer blanket, but under the linens he was completely naked.

Catherine stepped into the room. Her heart ached when she saw the bruises on his left arm and shoulder. His face was scraped and bruised, as well.

She tried not to look at his bare chest, but it was impossible. His skin glowed golden in the dim light, and she could see the thick dusting of crisp hair on his chest where the bandage didn't cover him. Even injured, he was a handsome man.

"I didn't expect to see you this evening," he said.

"I had to know if you were in pain."

The smile he offered spoke to Catherine more loudly than any words. In the charged silence of the room, she returned his smile.

It was happening again, that strange sense of falling headlong under his spell. What sort of man was this lord, that he could bring about such changes in her? What had happened to the contented young woman she had been only a few days ago?

Suddenly self-conscious because she'd been staring at him, Catherine looked down at her feet. This was not the time to let her imagination run away with her. She'd come to apologize, not gawk.

"I just wanted to check on you," she said shyly. "Are you hungry? Do you need anything?"

"Peck has seen to all my needs, except one." He gave the old fossil a hard look. "Something stronger than tea, wasn't it?"

"Yes, milord," the servant said. Reluctantly he went in search of the requested beverage, but not before giving his employer a fierce scowl that said if Sir Hardwick found his daughter at the earl's bedside there'd be hell to pay.

"I'm so very sorry," Catherine said once they were alone.

The words didn't come close to what she really wanted to say, but they were all she could manage without crying. Her father was right. She'd been stupid and foolish. Today was undoubtedly the worst day of her life. She'd had hours to think about what she'd done, and why'd she done it. The reasons seemed so childish now.

"I will speak to your father in the morning," he told her. "The blame rests on my shoulders. I shouldn't have agreed to the race.

"No. The blame is mine," Catherine insisted. "And I am sorry. Father has every right to be angry with me. Challenging you to a race was a foolish thing to do. You could have been killed."

Granby motioned her toward the chair.

It was odd, but he felt better now that he'd seen her. The sight of her was enough to eclipse the pain in his shoulder. She was wearing a blue dress, and her hair was pulled back and tied with a blue ribbon. He could see the curtain of auburn curls falling down her back. Her face was pale, and he couldn't be sure, but it looked as if she'd been crying.

He wanted to comfort her, to pull her into his arms

and tell her not to worry, but he wasn't in any condition to do more than talk.

He'd spent his entire adult life thinking he was in control of his emotions. Now that control had been taken away from him. There had been times in the last week when he'd awakened in the middle of the night aching with desire for an innocent young woman whom he should be avoiding at all cost. And yet, he hadn't avoided her. He'd sought her out at every turn, encouraged her with kisses, and taunted her into acting recklessly.

Catherine was nervous, not knowing what the earl was thinking, but she didn't want to leave. "Are you sure there's nothing I can do to make you more comfortable? Some task, no matter how small, would at least allow me to feel useful."

"You could kiss me."

Catherine drew in her breath. The mere thought of kissing him sent a ripple of shocking need through her body. For a moment her common sense was blinded by that need, but the long hours she'd spent confined to her room because of a similar impulsiveness kept her rooted to the chair.

Kissing him again would be courting disaster. Summoning her resistance, she met his gaze.

"All of this started with a kiss, and look where it's ended."

His mouth softened into a smile. "On the contrary, all of this started when you nearly rode me into the ground. A kiss was my reward then, why not now? This time I did end up in the dirt."

"And you don't hate me for it?"

He turned his head on the pillow, so he could look more fully at her. The amber light from the gasolier glinted off her auburn hair, making it even more fiery in color. The glow limned her profile like a halo, the high cheekbones and curves of her jaw, the fullness of her mouth.

He remembered what that mouth tasted like, the sweetness of her innocence combined with a feminine strength he'd witnessed in few women her age. The recollection inspired a need his injured body shouldn't be able to feel, but did.

He held out his hand. "Just one kiss."

The room became uncomfortably quiet as Catherine wondered what he was thinking. Were this man's thoughts ever serious, or was his request meant to be just one more reminder that up until now she'd failed to resist him? He was a charming rake, a man who thrived on bringing women to their knees. She knew it as well as she knew her own mind, and yet . . .

Did his mind ever venture into the same realm as hers, to the feelings kindled by the kisses they had shared? If so, she should leave immediately, for no good would come of it.

Despite her thoughts, Catherine left the chair and walked to the side of the bed. She looked down at his bruised face, shadowed by a day's growth of beard. It was a fascinating face, all hard angles and intense eyes, with a firm mouth that was still slightly curved into a smile.

When he took her hand, clasping it in his larger, stronger one, Catherine felt the impact of his touch all the way to her bones. "Just one kiss," she whispered. "Our last kiss."

Granby didn't say a word.

She leaned down, only intending to give him a light kiss but the magic came back full force as she found herself drowning in his gaze. Deep and mesmerizing, it drew her forward.

Their breath mingled as she lightly brushed her lips against his with genuine tenderness. He was hurt, and she wanted to soothe his pain.

His hand held her in place, but she wasn't going anywhere. This was exactly where she wanted to be.

Somehow she ended up sitting on the side of the
bed, one hand resting on the pillow above his left shoulder. The other, suddenly freed from his grasp, came to
rest on his right shoulder. His skin felt wonderfully warm.

Granby continued to kiss her, as his good arm slid
across the small of her back and slowly pressed her
closer. He licked at her upper lips and she made a soft,
gasping sound that ended as he took her mouth in a
full, complete kiss that had nothing to do with saying
good-bye and everything to do with satisfying his raven-
ing hunger. She tasted like tea and ginger cakes and
warm summer nights.

His tongue filled her mouth, searching and retreat-
ing in a sensual parry that made Catherine's resolve go
flying. Her heart pounded in her chest, and she felt
flushed, but she didn't pull away. The feeling of his
tongue filling her mouth, of his lips pressing so intimately against her own, of his arm holding her firmly in
place was too wonderful to forsake.

His hand found its way into her hair, and he buried
his fingers in it while he continued kissing her, long and
deep, his tongue stroking until she was resting limply
against his right side. He freed her hair of the blue ribbon, letting the thick curls pool around her face and
shoulders. She had lovely hair, long and thick and wavy,
the kind of hair a man enjoyed playing with.

Hesitantly, Catherine slid the palm of her hand over
the naked flesh of his right shoulder, her fingers kneading as she learned what a man felt like when his body
wasn't hidden under lawn shirts and riding jackets.
With the barest of touches, she let her hand trail down
to his collarbone. She could feel the springy hair that
covered his chest.

Her blood quickened, rushing through her veins along
with the knowledge that what she was doing—*they* were

doing—was forbidden. She should go back to her room, but all she could do was continue kissing him.

When he finally pulled away, Catherine gave an unconscious little cry of complaint. Her eyes drifted open, and she saw that his steely gaze had softened to the color of a summer dawn. With his eyes still fixed on her face, she smiled, then lowered her mouth to the bare skin of his bruised shoulder.

Granby sucked in his breath and held it as her lips pressed a feathering caress against his flesh. He gritted his teeth as her mouth skimmed along the plane of his shoulder and collarbone. God, did the chit have any idea what she was doing to him? He was already hard and aching, a constant affliction whenever she was around.

Without thinking, only knowing that he couldn't let her go, his hand cupped the back of her head and held her against his chest. He breathed in deeply, trying to still the effect she was having on his body, but it was in vain. He wanted her to the point of obsession.

Catherine closed her eyes as she pressed another kiss against his throat. Then, slowly, ever so lightly, she kissed a path back to his mouth. Just one more kiss, she promised herself. It had only begun when someone knocked on the door.

"Peck," Granby growled low in his throat. "Damn the man."

Catherine pulled back, embarrassed that she'd been so bold, so wanton, yet not regretting it. She stood up, about to answer the door, when the person on the other side announced himself.

"Lord Granby, it's Hardwick. I'd like a word with you."

Her father!

"The dressing room," the earl said. "Close the door, and for God's sake don't make a sound."

Heart pounding, her mouth dry with fear, Catherine eased the door closed behind her and waited.

"Come in," she heard Granby call out.

The sound of a door opening and closing confirmed that her father was now with the earl. She pushed back her hair and panicked anew—her ribbon! The earl had pulled it out of her hair. Was it lying on the floor where her father might see it? If he did, she was doomed.

"How are you feeling?" Hardwick asked.

"I've felt better," Granby replied. "The swelling will go away in a few days. Until then, I appreciate your hospitality."

"It's the least I can do," her father replied. "It was my daughter's foolishness that brought this on. For that, I ask your forgiveness."

"None is necessary. I agreed to the race. As a gentleman, it is I who should be apologizing."

Catherine could hear the sound of her father's footsteps as he moved around the room. "I must admit some confusion over Catherine's actions," her father said. "I've never known her to act so recklessly."

Granby realized that Catherine hadn't told her father everything. If she had, Hardwick wouldn't be nearly this congenial. Unsure of what to say, he let the older man lead the conversation.

"She's proud," Hardwick told him. "Unfortunately, I can't blame the trait on her mother. Lucinda was an amicable woman, always willing to please. Felicity warned me that it was time to take Catherine in hand; that I've been overly indulgent. I should have sent her to London three years ago. A husband would serve her better than an indulgent parent. My fault, not hers."

"Let's put aside all fault," Granby replied. "It was an unfortunate accident, nothing more. My shoulder will heal, and I will return to my own estate—without the stallion, as much as it pains me."

"I would gladly gift you with Storm Dancer as a means of restitution for your inconvenience and suffering, were he still mine to give," Hardwick said. "I gave him to Catherine only yesterday. Another fatherly indulgence."

Hidden from sight, Catherine flinched from guilt.

The earl clinched his swollen hand, sending an arrow of pain up his arm and into his shoulder. It served him right. Catherine had fooled him again, the little vixen. If he had won the race, the victory would have been an empty one, and she knew it. She had planned to stand back and gloat, regardless of the outcome.

Hell, she'd just been kissing him, and doing a bloody good job of it, too!

For a scant second, Granby considered calling her out of the dressing room and forcing her to confront her father, but he knew the outcome wouldn't be the one he wanted. The convincing little piece of baggage needed more than a few days in her room. She needed a good thrashing.

With his pride hurting almost as much as his bruised body, Granby vowed to teach the girl a lesson she'd never forget.

"I shall take my leave and let you rest," Hardwick said, unaware his houseguest was plotting his daughter's downfall. "Good night, my lord."

"Good night."

The outer door to the bedroom closed a brief second before the dressing room door opened. Catherine walked out, meeting the earl's gaze because she'd promised herself to face up to what she'd done.

If the man hated her, so be it. She'd be better off if he didn't want any more of her kisses. He could recover, then return to his own estate, while she found the contentment of her former life once again. Hate would be better than the steamy, uncontrollable emotions she'd been dealing with ever since the earl had found his way to Stonebridge.

"You are a minx who enjoys stirring up trouble," he said in a voice that was as husky as it was menacing.

Catherine was trapped, as thoroughly as if he had her pinned in place. She could run from the room, but her pride—a problem she'd deal with later—wouldn't let her.

"You allowed it to happen, my lord. Had you not flaunted your conceit by telling me that my father would not be able to resist your next offer for Storm Dancer, had you not kissed me so boldly that morning on the lane, had you not set out to seduce me in order to teach me a lesson, I would not have been forced to resort to similar means. I am sorry that you were injured, but I am not sorry that Storm Dancer belongs to me."

"I can see that you have little remorse," Granby replied. An edge came to his voice as he withdrew his right hand from beneath the covers. Her ribbon dangled from his fingertips. "I wonder, should I tell your father the *entire* story."

"You wouldn't dare," she said, taking a step toward the bed. "And even if you did, you would be the one at fault. A gentleman does not seduce an innocent, and you did set out to seduce me. Admit it."

"Yes, that's me. A ne'er-do-well rascal of the worst sort. Then again, a young lady of pristine reputation does not visit a gentleman in his room late at night, especially when that gentleman is as naked as the day he was born under flimsy covers. Nor does she kiss him." He waved the ribbon through the air. "I'm sure your father could find a suitable punishment for such a breach of good upbringing. Perhaps the spanking you deserve. Should we call him back and ask?"

Pride gave way to anger. Catherine stomped across the room, intending to retrieve her ribbon, then return to her room. The earl was bluffing. He had to be.

But he wasn't, at least not about teaching her a lesson. The moment she reached out for the ribbon, he dropped it to floor, catching her wrist. He pulled her down on the bed beside him. "I will have one more kiss from you, Miss Hardwick. Our *last* one."

"No!"

The word was lost as his mouth came down hard on hers.

There was no seduction in this kiss, no enticement. It was hard and domineering, punishing her, but Catherine didn't feel punished. As always, she felt drawn to the strength of the man, the compelling promise he made with his mouth—the promise that there were even more wonderful things to be found in his arms.

The intimacy of his tongue sweeping into her mouth dissolved most of her anger, but her pride was still there, and badly wounded. She knew she had been in the wrong, and she was willing to admit it, even apologize for it, but not this way. Her body pulsed with the realization of how easily this man could have his way with her. It was more than embarrassing, it was shameful.

Granby was having an equally difficult time holding on to his temper. He told himself, as he continued to ravish her mouth, that he was acting out of the need to show her that he wasn't a man to be trifled with. He wasn't David Malbane, or the other village lads who worshipped at her feet, thinking a simple dance some divine gift to be treasured.

He kept thinking that as he pulled her tightly against him, ignoring the pain in his shoulder, intent only on making their last kiss one that would haunt her for years to come. No woman, innocent or experienced, had ever been able to ignite his temper so easily.

When he finally released her, Catherine stumbled to her feet. Their gazes locked, riveted together, as she fought to regain her breath and her composure. If the man wasn't already hurting, she'd slap his face.

"I will be sure not to disturb you again," she said with a calm she didn't feel. "I wish you a good night's sleep and a fast recovery."

The man had the audacity to laugh. "And a hasty trip back to whence I came."

"Yes."

Before he could respond, Catherine turned and walked out of the room, closing the door firmly behind her.

Wincing at the discomfort, Granby leaned over the side of the bed and picked up the forgotten ribbon. Smiling, he tucked it under his pillow.

Twelve

Boredom dogged Catherine as she sat in the morning room. Her father was slowly forgetting his annoyance with her; breakfast with him and Felicity had been almost pleasant. Still, she longed to venture beyond the house, to walk down to the stables, but she didn't dare upset the fragile peace that had settled over the household.

It had been five days since the earl's injury, and she was still seething that she'd played into his hands with that last kiss. Damn the man for being so irresistible. No doubt he'd reveled in her acquiescence, gloating over his victory after she'd fled the room.

If only she felt as glorious about her own victory. Storm Dancer belonged to her, but she was forbidden to ride him. Forbidden to do more than work on the household accounts or read or sit for endless hours while the days passed by with summer warmth and sunshine.

So what was she to do with herself? If the last few days were an example of how a proper young lady existed, then she had no wish to be proper.

One thought led to another, and soon Catherine

found herself thinking of the Earl of Granby. The man should be up and about in another day or so, and gone from underneath their roof. In the meantime, she had made a point to avoid any contact with him or his valet.

She might have the stallion, but the earl had her attention, and Catherine didn't like it.

Disgusted with herself, she closed the book she couldn't find any interest in reading, and walked to the window. At the sound of someone entering the room, she turned around.

"Excuse me, miss," the earl's valet said. "I was looking for Mr. Gabs."

"He went into town with Mrs. Gibson. It's market day," she told him, biting back the need to ask if his lordship was feeling better today. "Is there something I can do for you?"

"Horse liniment," Peck said. "His lordship is complaining of some discomfort, and Dr. Hawkins recommended a good rubbing with liniment."

"There's a bottle in the pantry," she told him. "My father uses it for the same thing. I'll fetch it for you."

"Thank you," Peck said, his expression unreadable. "His lordship is sure to appreciate it. He hopes to be able to join the family for dinner."

Catherine hid her alarm. "The pantry is this way."

Once they reached the large cupboard in the hallway just beyond the kitchen, she gave the crusty old servant the dark amber bottle. "Warming the liniment may be helpful," she told him. "My father says it's more soothing that way."

"Then I shall warm it. Thank you."

"Do you know when his lordship plans on leaving?" she asked, hoping to sound concerned rather than curious.

"Of that I am not sure, miss. His lordship did mention something about the day after tomorrow, but that will depend on Dr. Hawkins giving him leave to travel."

"Yes, of course."

The valet nodded respectively before returning to the second floor and his awaiting employer. Catherine stood in the hallway for a moment, unsure if she should return to the morning room and her book, or take herself upstairs.

She could visit with Felicity. Her aunt was in her sitting room, responding to the various letters that had arrived by post that morning. The idea passed quickly. She wasn't in the mood for a conversation centered around who was doing what until the Season resumed.

Catherine thought of returning to the morning room to write her own letters. It had been several weeks since she'd corresponded with either Sarah or Veronica. Unfortunately, that idea didn't appeal to her, either. It would be impossible to give an accounting of her life since their last letter without mentioning the earl, and she couldn't mention the earl without hinting that she was, or had been, infatuated with the man.

The infatuation had ended, of course. All she felt for the man now was an increasingly hearty wish that he recover and be on his way.

Deciding that her room was as good a place to be bored as any, Catherine went upstairs. She met Peck in the hallway.

"His lordship is out of cigars and insists that I go into the village immediately and buy him more."

"My father has cigars," she said. "In the humidor in the library."

"The earl was most adamant that I not infringe on Sir Hardwick's hospitality by pilfering. I am to take myself to Winchcombe forthwith."

Catherine smiled for the first time in days. "You've been with the earl for a long time, haven't you?"

"I was in service to his father. The current lord was a child in the nursery when I found a post at Foxleigh. That was a good many years ago."

Catherine didn't want to think about the earl's child-hood. She didn't want to think about the man at all. Resigning herself to that, she said, "I'm sure you'll find what you need at the Malbane tobacco shop. It's just down the street from the White Lion Inn, near St. Paul's green."

"Thank you," Peck said, before disappearing down the staircase.

Catherine continued down the hall. She stopped at the sound of cursing from the earl's room.

"Blasted, bloody bandages," he was grumbling.

She hesitated, thinking he might need assistance, but unsure if she should be the one to offer it. The last time she'd gone into his room she'd left feeling emotionally bruised and guilty.

More curses, these not so benign, brought her hand to the doorknob. She tapped lightly, then opened the door to find Granby sitting on the side of the bed, en-tangled in the bandages he had been trying to remove.

"Here, let me," she said. "Stop waving your arm, you're only making matters worse."

"I doubt they could get worse," he snapped impa-tiently. "No offense to your father's hospitality, but I'm bloody tired of this room."

"No offense taken," she said. "Hold still. I'm going to need some scissors. You've made a mess of things; the knot has only gotten tighter."

Granby watched as Catherine went to the dresser, bringing back a pair of scissors and a fresh roll of clean bandages. She was wearing green today, and looking very pretty. Her hair was pulled back and loosely braided beginning at the nape of her neck. It fell to her hips, swaying gently with each movement she made.

Smiling to himself, Granby wondered if he'd be lucky enough to add a green ribbon to his collection. The blue one was now in the same box as his cuff links, a memento of his strange visit to Stonebridge Stables.

"You've been avoiding me," he said.

"Did you expect otherwise?" Catherine replied as she turned, scissors in hand. "I have a perfectly good reason. You're angry because I own Storm Dancer, thus putting him beyond your financial reach."

"You tricked me."

"Yes. Yes, I did, and I am sorry for that. I realize it wasn't very well done of me, but it seemed like the right thing to do at the time."

The sun was shining, and outside the window the birds were twittering melodically. It was a lovely day.

"You should sit in front of the window. The sunlight will soothe your aches and pains."

The only thing that was going to soothe Granby was the last thing he needed—Catherine back in his arms. He'd had five long, boring days in which to do nothing but think about her and all the reasons he should strangle her instead of kissing her.

The time had given him an opportunity to plot his revenge, but he hadn't decided on a specific plan. Not yet. If the right moment didn't present itself before he left, there was always the upcoming Season. He was sure to encounter the lady in London.

With that thought in mind, the earl tried to ignore the quickening of his pulse as she moved toward the bed. The woman was a maddening invitation to a man who hadn't indulged himself in a sexual feast for more than three weeks.

He wasn't used to abstinence or confinement. The combination had him in a foul mood, and the impudent little vixen had found her way into his dreams. She'd come to him in the dark, opening her arms, eagerly seeking his kisses. He'd envisioned her mass of ginger-colored curls spread across his pillow, her hazel eyes bright with passion, her body bare to his touch.

"Why were you taking off the bandage?"

"To rub in the liniment," he said, looking toward the

bedside table. The small amber bottle was sitting in a basin of warm water. "Peck was going to do it, but I wanted a cigar, so I sent him into the village."

"Sit still," she warned him, scissors in hand. "I'll cut away the bandage."

Granby sat still.

He was dressed in trousers and socks, no shoes, and no shirt. Catherine tried not to notice that he looked rakishly handsome, but it was impossible. The swelling in his left hand had lessened and the bruises were beginning to fade. His improving health made it even more dangerous for her to be in his room. In his present state of undress, he was a tempting image of a man, and she'd already proven that the temptation was one she found hard to refuse. Still, he needed help.

She cut the bandage just below the unruly knot, then being careful not to touch him, pulled it way and tossed it into a small basket next to the bed. In the bright light coming through the window, she could see that the hair on his chest was several shades darker than the hair on his head. She could also see two flat male nipples. His lower stomach was firm and corded with muscles. When she looked up, she saw the nasty mass of bruises that covered his left shoulder. The skin was discolored, ranging from an angry purple to a pale yellow-green hue.

"I'm sorry," she said, truly meaning it this time.

He rolled his shoulder slightly, then raised his arm and flexed his fingers. "It's feeling better."

"The liniment should help."

"Let's have a go at it then," he said.

He wanted her to take Peck's place, to rub the liniment into his shoulder and arm.

She hesitated. The emotional residue of all that had passed between them was still with her.

"Well, get on with it," he said. "I wouldn't need a dousing in horse liniment if you hadn't tricked me into a useless race."

"You don't have to snap at me. I'm well aware that I'm to blame for your current discomfort."

"I'm in pain," he said, turning to the side, so she could reach his shoulder. "Since the sooner my recovery progresses to the point of being free to take my leave, the sooner I will be gone, I would think that you would be more cooperative. Unless I'm incorrect in my assumption that you're eager to be rid of me."

"Most eager," Catherine said with a touch of tartness.

"Then we're in full agreement." He turned even more, presenting her with his back and shoulders.

Catherine was tempted to uncork the bottle and pour the foul-smelling liniment over his lordship's handsome head, but she was wise enough to know that her present edginess was due to the fact that she was actually looking forward to touching him again.

Why did this man appeal to her so? Was it because underneath his aristocratic veneer and good looks, there was a real person she longed to know better?

Uncorking the bottle, she wrinkled her nose at the smell. Mrs. Gibson's added herbs did soften the odor, but nothing could completely do away with the pungent smell. She poured a small amount into the center of her palm, then moved toward the bed.

"I'll try not to hurt you," she said softly.

"The whole purpose of a rubdown is to rub the pain away, to stimulate the aching muscles, not pamper them," Granby said. "Don't be afraid to be thorough."

Thorough. The word brought a range of shameful images to mind, but Catherine pushed them aside.

She'd handled injured horses all her life. Looking at the earl's naked shoulders, she tried to see nothing but the muscle and skin, just another animal in need of a vigorous rubdown. Spreading the liniment evenly between her palms, she took a quick breath, then laid her hands on the earl's bare back.

Nothing was said as she rubbed, kneading the bruised

muscles of his left shoulder and upper arm. She ran her hands over and around the discolored skin, the slope of his shoulder and neck, using the friction to increase the heat. The strong scent of the liniment filled the room.

"That feels good," Granby groaned, leaning into her hands.

The desire to cast aside the charade of their former arguments was overpowering as Catherine continued massaging his shoulder and upper back. With a need that bordered on desperation, she tried to think of anything but the warm male skin under her hands.

The sight of him sitting so near to her, naked from the waist up, was stimulating enough. The feel of him under her hands was the most erotic thing she'd ever experienced. In many ways, it was far more intimate than a kiss. Catherine was glad that he was facing away from her; he couldn't see her reaction. It was small consolation, but it was better than reaffirming his belief that she found him irresistible.

Knowing she needed to get the massage over and done with, so she could escape the feelings that were building with every stroke of her fingers on his skin, Catherine increased the pressure of her hands. Her thumbs dug into the tendons on either side of his neck, and he groaned with pleasure. She rubbed harder, unable to deny the simple fact that she enjoyed touching him, giving him pleasure even if in this strange way.

Granby tried not to groan again. Her hands were wonderful, and the pain she was easing away was quickly being replaced by another stiffness, this one affecting the lower part of his body. A fire rose in his loins, and common sense told him to ask her to leave. He didn't. Instead, he sat there, letting his former thoughts of revenge be eased away by her gentle hands.

Catherine kneaded back and forth until her arms began to ache. Finally, she stopped and lifted her hands.

Without looking at him, she used the warm water to wash the remaining liniment away.

"Thank you," he said, his voice husky. "Could I impose on you to help me with the confounded bandage. I dislike being wrapped up like a mummy, but it does help to keep the arm immobilized."

"Of course." She reached for the roll of bandages. "Fold you arm across your chest."

When she moved, so did the earl. Before she could take a breath, he pulled her down beside him. He kissed her then, his tongue easing between her lips, parted in a sound of surprise. He captured her soft gasp merging their mouths.

Granby knew he'd lost his mind. He should be opening the door and tossing the vixen out into the hall, not keeping her at his side, but five days of not seeing her, of being confined to this blasted room with no one for company but a pompous valet who treated him as if he were still in the nursery, had him running short of common sense. He'd done little but think about the young lady. Having her this close was the final salvo—his control shattered.

"You shouldn't," Catherine said as he raised his head and looked at her. "This is wrong."

"Is it?" he asked, easing her back so she was lying on the bed and he was looming over her. He rubbed his thumb back and forth over the luscious curve of her lower lip. "Then why do I want to kiss you again?"

"You only want to embarrass me again," she said shakily. "You're angry that you can't take Storm Dancer with you when you leave."

"Believe me, sweetheart, the last thing I am is angry. Don't you like my kisses?" His fingers moved from her mouth to the neckline of her dress in persuasive little circles that teased and tickled.

She put her hands on his shoulders, wanting to push him away, but reluctant to hurt him. "Please, let me go."

He leaned down to kiss her again, but Catherine turned her head to the side. His lips found her cheek, then moved to her temple. His hands found their way into her hair so he could hold her in place while he rained light kisses over her face. A heady pleasure raced through Granby's blood as he found the pulse beating at the base of her throat and kissed it.

Unconsciously she helped him by angling her head back and giving him better access. He took his time, licking and nibbling at her throat, until she was straining against him, silently begging for more. He gave it to her. The kiss was deep and possessive, totally dominating.

Catherine found herself unable to think—all she could do was feel, and the feelings were wonderful.

When the kiss ended, she was breathless. Mystified, she let him remove the ribbon from her hair, then comb his fingers through the thick curls.

"I like your hair. It reminds me of autumn leaves, red and brown and a dozen shades in-between. It's the first thing I noticed about you."

"Not the stallion I was riding?" Catherine teased, surprised that she could speak at all.

He chuckled. "That was the second thing. And this was the third."

His gaze locked with her, as his right hand moved to her breast in a bold caress that made Catherine catch her breath.

He watched her reaction, his eyes gleaming with desire—a desire he was making her all too aware of as his thumb brushed across the crown of her breast. Her nipple hardened under his exquisite handling.

"You like it," he breathed. "Admit it, Miss Hardwick. You like me."

"I hate you."

It was a lie, and they both knew it.

She closed her eyes to keep from seeing his smug smile.

There were more kisses, along her jaw and throat, the corner of her mouth, her ear, and all the while his hand moved over her breast, his thumb stroking the nipple. She wasn't wearing a corset, and there was only the muslin of her day dress and the sheer cloth of her chemise between them. Raw need surged through her body, and Catherine was helpless against it.

The things his mouth and hands were doing to her were wild, creating even more scandalous thoughts. Hands that had been pressed against him to push him away now moved with the opposite intention. They encircled his neck to bring him closer.

Giving in to his body's desperate urging, Granby pressed her into the cradle of his thighs, letting her feel the strength of his arousal.

He kissed her with all his expertise, wooing her gently, holding his desire in check though he longed to crush her beneath him, to end the aching need in his groin.

Catherine shivered as her resistance faded kiss by kiss. Her small moans of defeat were music to Granby's ears. She parted her lips, and their tongues met and mated. They lay pressed hip to hip, thigh to thigh.

The scent of liniment mixed with the fragrance of freshly washed bed linens and the soap she had used to wash her hands. The heat of his body merged with the heat of her own. The ensuing sensations drove the last objection from Catherine's mind. The only thing left was the urgent need that arched her body against him. She wanted more of his touch, not less.

Again the earl accommodated her. Since her dress buttoned down the back there was no easy way to get to the breasts he was caressing, so he lowered his mouth and suckled her through the cloth, drawing the crown into his mouth. His good hand inched slowly, seductively, down the length of her thigh. He bunched up the fabric of her skirt until he found the hem, then expertly ventured beneath it.

A cotton petticoat, a stocking-clad calf, a lacy garter, then bare skin. He'd been here before, that day in the parlor at Sudeley Castle, but this was different. He'd been playing with her then; now his efforts were in earnest. He wanted more than a few kisses this time. He wanted to touch the hot, wet center of her, to feel her respond, to savor the sweet victory of having her climax in his arms.

To Catherine's shame, she was enjoying what the earl was doing to her. His kisses, the slow, deplorable way he was drawing on her breast, the warm glide of his hand over her thigh.

His fingers roamed higher and higher, past the lacy hem of her drawers to the center slit. Then his fingers brushed against the soft curls that shielded her most womanly secrets.

"You feel good," he whispered into her ear. "Better than I remember."

The intimate caresses were almost too much to bear, but Catherine didn't want it to stop. She clutched at his hair, straining to pull him closer, to raise herself higher. He made her feel wild—wilder than any stallion ride, wilder than she'd ever imagined she could feel.

He moved, leveling himself up on one knee as his hand continued on its path, higher and higher, until he was there—the very center of her.

All resistance drained away as his fingers found the most intimate part of her, the part that was aching for his touch.

Granby groaned low in his chest. He knew she'd be hot, but he'd never imagined how good it would feel to touch that heat, to dip his finger into the very core of her.

"You don't know how many times I've imagined doing

this," he said, as he continued sliding his finger in and out of her. "No, don't close your eyes. Look at me. Tell me that you like what I'm doing."

She couldn't, it was too shameful, too wicked—too wonderful. She buried her face in the curve of his neck as he continued rubbing those skilled fingers against her in small, endless circles. An unnamed instinct was roused deep within her, and Catherine raised her hips to meet his hand, pushing herself urgently against him. The sensation that followed was so keen it brought a soft cry from her throat.

The world began to shimmer, the sunlight turning to a golden mist around her, and Catherine reveled in it all—in the sinful sensations that the earl was inducing, in the heat of his kisses and the small, startling bites he made at her covered breasts.

Catherine dared to open her eyes and meet his gaze. A spark flared in his eyes, a blue-white light that burned away the last of her control. He touched the place he had only been teasing before, and she shuddered from the inside out, her body convulsing in tiny shivers of ecstasy.

The sweet violence frightened her, but he saw that, and stopped her fear with a kiss while his hand stroked the inside of her thigh, calming her. He whispered her name and she answered with an incoherent sound as she wrapped her arms around him and held on tight. She trembled, but it was a contented shiver, an aftershock of what he'd made her feel.

Granby smiled. He'd pleased her, and in doing so had pleased himself. At least to some degree. His own body was in a terrible state. He was hard and aching, and if he allowed himself to reach for the buttons on his trousers, he'd be taking a virgin. He wanted to. Oh, God, how he wanted it. But something stopped him.

Perhaps it was the way she was whispering his name, or the trust she'd put in him when her first climax began to simmer inside her and she hadn't recognized what was happening. Or maybe it was his conscience, though it couldn't have chosen a more inconvenient time to tap him on the shoulder.

"Granby," she said weakly, emotions flooding through her as she looked at him.

His eyes were still hard with desire, but he was smiling, and Catherine found herself smiling, too. She was more knowledgeable of sex than most young women, having grown up around a breeding stable, but she'd never imagined having a man touch her so intimately could be so wonderful.

"My name is Norton," he whispered, then smiled. "I think you've earned the right to use it."

Earned!

Without a sound, Catherine wrenched herself away from him. It took a moment since his hand was still up her skirt.

Much too late, she realized what she'd allowed to happen. And she *had* allowed it. Her heart froze for an awful instant. The magic that she'd felt while in his arms shredded into fragments of disgust and self-loathing.

Catherine look at him then, at the way he was lying back on the bed, his features intense, his gaze questioning, his body fully aroused. There was no mistaking the bulge in his trousers, or the fact that he could easily have taken even more liberties with her.

She'd been a fool to think she could waltz into his room like some ministering angel of mercy, then waltz out again with only the smell of liniment on her hands.

Granby saw the self-doubt in her eyes, and knew what she was thinking, and why she was thinking it. Damn, but he hadn't planned on things happening this way. He'd only meant to kiss her, to force her to declare him the victor in their unorthodox little war.

"Don't," he said, reaching for her.

Ashamed to the point of tears, Catherine yanked at

her skirt and turned way from the bed. But again, it was too late.

Felicity was standing in the doorway.

"Wait for me in your room," Felicity said, her tone as solid as the mahogany posters of the bed upon which the earl was still sprawled, bare chested and looking very much like a man who had just had his way with a woman.

Granby came to his feet the instant he heard Felicity's voice. It was clear—from the flushed look on Catherine's face; from the tangle of curls falling about her shoulders; from his state of undress—that something illicit had just taken place.

Furthermore, it went against all propriety for a man of his station to have the daughter of his host in his bedroom, no matter the circumstances. Since there was no excuse, he offered no explanation as he moved to stand beside Catherine.

"Lady Forbes-Hammond," he said, as politely as if they were meeting in the downstairs parlor.

Catherine didn't realize what he was doing, but her aunt did. By taking his place at her side, the earl was taking responsibility for her actions along with his own.

He turned to look at Catherine. She was still flushed, but the pallor of shock was quickly stripping away her color. He tipped up her chin, his gaze focusing on hers. "Go to you room and wait as your aunt has requested. Don't worry, I'll take care of everything."

Catherine stared back at him, her eyes wide with the aftermath of passion and the stinging fear that had accompanied her aunt into the room. Her hands were trembling as he took them into his own. His touch was tender. Had the circumstances not been so disastrous, she might interpret his actions as those of a man who cared.

"Go on, sweetheart," he said, his voice soft with concern. "We'll talk again soon, but first I must speak to your aunt."

Catherine wasn't sure she could move. The ramifications of what had just happened were making her knees wobbly. He kissed her then; not a passionate kiss, but a soft reassuring kiss on the cheek.

When she still didn't move, he put his arm around her waist and walked her toward the door. Felicity had stepped inside the room to stand in front of the dresser, directly opposite the bed, with its wrinkled coverlet.

"But I . . . I need to . . ." She couldn't even speak. God, what a mess! Horrified to be caught doing what she'd been doing, by *Felicity* of all people, Catherine felt tears stinging her eyes. "You have to make her understand."

"Shhh, I'll make the necessary explanations," Granby said, realizing what he had to do and finding the prospect surprisingly pleasing. "Ring for Agnes and have her bring you a nice cup of tea. Felicity will be along soon."

He waited in the doorway, watching until she reached the door to her own room. Once she'd stepped inside, Granby turned to face the formidable matron, Lady Felicity Forbes-Hammond.

Dressed in black, her expression was unreadable, but the earl knew exactly what she was thinking. He walked to the armoire and withdrew a shirt. Grimacing slightly, he slid the sleeve over his injured arm and shoulder. Once the shirt was buttoned, he turned around. He smiled, but received no smile in return. Not that he'd expected one.

"Forgive my appearance," he said.

"You have greatest sins to atone for, my lord," she remarked with her eyebrows raised. Her voice was as frosty as her pale eyes. "I am a woman of considerable years, but I have not been rendered witless by their passing. What has just taken place here needs no further explanation. Yet, I feel the need to remind you that this is Sir Hardwick's home, a place in which he assumes his daughter is safe."

Granby chose his words carefully, wanting no shame to fall on Catherine. "I will address Sir Hardwick this evening after dinner."

"Is there a need for a hasty wedding?"

"No."

An awkward silence ensued, during which Granby was reminded of just how close he had come to taking complete advantage of Catherine. It wasn't something of which to be proud, yet he found no apology to offer Lady Forbes-Hammond.

"May I assume that her father will accept my suit?"

"Both you and I know this marriage would be everything I had hoped to accomplish by giving Catherine a Season. I could hardly find a more eligible candidate than yourself, though I hadn't planned on the proposal being so unconventional."

"Convincing the bride will be the hard part," Granby said, realizing he had an ally of sorts. "She'll refuse to marry me, but then you already know that."

Felicity eyed him thoroughly. "I am not without an opinion as to why things have happened as they have. I'm sure your sensitivity to the situation will prevent you from informing Sir Hardwick of this afternoon's events. As for Catherine herself, I know she can be unreasonably stubborn at times, but I'm confident your powers of persuasion go beyond the bedroom. That being the case, I see no reason why your engagement cannot be announced at Waltham's regatta party, followed by an introduction to society on the arm of her husband, and all will be well."

Granby wondered if he shouldn't suggest a more hasty schedule, regardless of the fact that Catherine was still a virgin. He had the nagging suspicion that she'd use the time to scheme her way out of the engagement.

"Do I note some reluctance on your part?"

Granby knew he should be reluctant. The very thought of marriage should produce a panic, but it didn't.

"I have no reluctance. In fact, I find myself amazingly eager to take a bride. It's Catherine's willingness that gives me pause. If I may be candid, it is impossible to speculate what she may do, especially since she hasn't shown any consistency in her actions thus far."

"A female prerogative, but common sense will prevail. I shall see to it," Felicity declared. She moved to leave the room, hesitating at the door. "As delighted as I may be at the prospect of my beloved Catherine marrying a man of rank and privilege, I am not so callous as to disregard the less formal issues of marriage. Am I correct that you have feelings for her? That you will see to her happiness?"

"I will do everything within my power to see that Catherine does not regret this marriage," Granby replied with all honesty.

Felicity gave him a long, searching gaze. A small smile curved her mouth before she replied. "Yes, I think you will. In fact, I'm beginning to think that everything will work out just fine."

Thirteen

Catherine sat in her room, gazing blankly out the window. The gentle ticking of a porcelain-paneled clock measured the time. Outside there was a fine sprinkling of rain, and banners of dull gray clouds where the sun had been shining less than an hour before.

The change in weather suited Catherine's mood. Try as she might to banish the man from her mind, her thoughts were sharpened by the intimate knowledge she had gained of him, and he of her.

Disliking the difficulty she was having in forgetting that what had passed between them had been nothing more than outrageous behavior on his part and untamed curiosity on hers, or so she rationalized, Catherine deliberately concentrated on the random pattern of raindrops splattering the window. Unbidden, the image of his steel blue eyes came to mind.

"No," she declared aloud. "I will not be done in by you again."

She began to pace the room, swept up in emotions—too many emotions. Catherine shook them off. The facts were more important than the feelings, and the fact was that she'd let Granby make a fool of her again.

Her turmoil was interrupted by a knock. Hoping it was Agnes with her tea, but fearing it was Felicity, Catherine opened the door.

"If you would prefer to rest before we speak, I will leave you to a nap," Felicity said, remaining in the hall.

"No. Come in."

She was given a small reprieve when Agnes tapped on the door a second later. A tea caddy was pushed into the room. While the maid saw to the pouring of two cups, Catherine tried to gather her thoughts.

The moment they were alone, Felicity set aside her teacup. There was no time for Catherine to prepare a defense; her aunt was intent that she listen, and listen carefully.

"Lord Granby will speak to your father this evening, immediately following dinner."

"Speak with Father! But why? Does he think to blame the entire folly on me?"

"Now is not the time for blame," Felicity replied sternly, "but a time for accountability. Lord Granby is taking that responsibility upon himself. He intends to make his intentions clear."

"His intentions?" Catherine shook her head. "Whatever are you talking about?"

"Marriage, of course. A situation such as this calls for only one remedy."

"Marriage!" Catherine jumped up from the bed, almost spilling her tea. She managed to get the cup and saucer back to the caddy before losing her temper completely. "I won't marry him! The idea is absurd."

She looked at Felicity only to find a blank expression, one of total incomprehension as to why any young lady in her right mind would think to refuse the offer of an advantageous marriage.

"Lord Granby will speak to your father and offer his suit. Since there is no necessity for haste, your engagement can be properly announced, a wedding date set, and—"

"There will be no engagement," Catherine said frantically. "How can you possibly think that I want to marry the man? He's a scoundrel! A charming, sophisticated rake who has a higher opinion of himself than I will ever have!"

"Are you saying that he forced his intentions upon you?"

Catherine's hesitation was her condemnation. "There is no need for us to marry."

"I disagree," Felicity said, with a gesture that dismissed any such youthful foolishness. "Although you have lacked the presence of a mother in your upbringing, you do not lack common sense. I am not privy to all that happened between you and the earl, but I am wise enough to know that today's actions speak of far more than girlish infatuation."

Catherine moved to the window, keeping her back to the room. How could she explain to Felicity what she didn't understand herself? Even explaining what she did understand would only sway her aunt more fully toward the idea that a marriage between herself and Granby was the most prudent course of action.

As much as she loathed the idea of marriage to a man of society, Catherine couldn't dismiss the tide of emotions that accompanied each and every thought of the earl.

The problem being that the emotions were hers, not the earl's.

"The time for candor is now," Felicity told her. "Do you love him?"

"How can I possibly love him when I know nothing about him?" Catherine said desperately. "I admit my foolishness of today as readily as I admitted it the day he was injured, but that is no reason to condemn me by insisting we marry. Surely Father would not be that cold-hearted."

"Your father wants nothing but your happiness. Granby is a man of significant standing, and well respected among his peers. I have his assurance that he will say nothing to your father beyond what is necessary to convince him that a marriage between you will be an affable one."

"Affable!" Catherine scoffed. "Disastrous would be a better word."

The older woman's jaw clamped into a hard line. "I have yet to hear you explain why. It is obvious that you are enamored of the man. Your recent actions speak to that, and more. Once again, I must caution you as to your reputation."

"I am still a virgin," Catherine said, swirling away from the window. "A few kisses have not ruined me for marriage to a more suitable man."

Felicity stood up, sending the full force of her gaze across the room.

A sudden, inexplicable sense of doom overtook Catherine. She felt as if she'd stepped into a prison more inescapable than anything built of stone.

"Really, Catherine, you are being unreasonably stubborn about things. Knowing you as I do, I cannot entertain the idea that your relationship with Lord Granby is a minor affair. Had I not intervened this afternoon—"

"I was leaving the room," Catherine blurted out. "Nothing more would have happened. I came to my senses in time."

"Not soon enough," Felicity retorted without solicitation. "Your exuberant spirit has taken you beyond normal flirtation. Your participation cannot be overlooked or excused."

"I will speak to the earl," Catherine said, searching for an escape. "He does not really want to marry me, I'm sure of it. His offer is presented out of duty and obligation—surely you can see that. Neither will bring me happiness."

"If the man is so repugnant, why were you in his room?"

Catherine didn't want to recite the whys and wherefores.

"He doesn't love me," she said. It was a blunt statement, but one she needed to verbalize in order to accept it herself. "I'm nothing but a country diversion. Even you referred to him as a rascal."

Felicity resumed her seat, her expression softening as she reached for her teacup. "Let me tell you a secret about rascals, my dear. They all pretend to think marriage an end to be avoided. They claim to love their freedom, yet once wed they are the most devoted of husbands. I have seen it more than once, and am confident I shall see it again, once your wedding to the rascal Granby takes place."

Catherine looked at her own teacup, wishing it held whiskey. She could feel a headache coming on. Nay, it was here. For the first time in her life she understood the phrase "between a rock and a hard place." It seemed that Felicity and Lord Granby had joined forces.

The honor of a gentleman simply didn't suit the man, not after the way he'd acted. Still, she couldn't go to her father without admitting that she had disobeyed him by entering the earl's room. As for what had happened afterward, it didn't bear thinking about.

She had been raised with a great deal more freedom than most young ladies, but her father was still of a conservative mind. If he found out about the day's indiscretion, he'd not only agree to Lord Granby's suit, he'd insist that they marry immediately.

No matter what she did, she was doomed. Unless she could convince the earl to leave Stonebridge *without* speaking to her father. If he withdrew his offer, Felicity would be furious, but better ferocity on her aunt's part than disaster on her own. Once Granby was out of reach, so to speak, she could reason with her aunt, and if necessary, her father.

"The earl will join us for dinner this evening," Felicity said. "I expect you to be on your best behavior."

Catherine nodded, but her expression was noncommittal.

"A woman is not always consulting wisely when she listens to her own heart, but that is my advice to you. Put aside your pride and think of your future happiness," Felicity said. "I cannot imagine a man capturing your attention so strongly were he not worthy of it."

"I don't love him," she said, refusing to admit the possibility.

"Love is not what it may seem at first glance," Felicity replied. "Give yourself time to think on the matter. There has been enough spontaneity for one day."

As soon as Felicity took her leave, Catherine hurried to the small desk in the corner of her room and penned a note. A hard jerk on the bell cord summoned Agnes to act as messenger.

"Slip this note to the earl's valet," she said, "and be discreet about it."

Agnes accepted the assignment with little more than a curious glance at the paper that had been folded and sealed.

Catherine breathed a sigh of relief, then prepared herself for what she hoped would be her last encounter with the charming Earl of Granby.

"No bandages tonight," Granby told Peck. "I refuse to present myself as an invalid."

The windows, which had been opened to eliminate the lingering odor of liniment, were now closed against the dampness of the evening air. The earl walked from the dressing room, wearing only his trousers. Peck assisted him with his shirt. The valet didn't speak until an onyx cuff link had been inserted into the starched cuff of the left sleeve.

"You seem to be looking forward to the evening, milord."

"That's an understatement," Granby replied. "You may as well know, it's no ordinary evening. I intend to ask for Miss Hardwick's hand."

Peck accepted the news in his usual mundane way, which meant he reacted as if his employer had remarked on nothing more unusual than the weather. He did, however, inquire as to why the earl had decided upon Miss Hardwick.

"Why Miss Hardwick?" he mused aloud. Had it only been last week that he'd declared himself uninterested in marriage?

Peck would think him besotted, and to some degree he was. But his attraction wasn't one of the heart. Marriage was not a necessity, but it could be in the very near future. He couldn't keep his hands to himself where the young lady was concerned, which meant today had simply happened sooner rather than later. Besides, marriage would gain him what he wanted—Catherine in his bed.

In answering, Granby kept his voice casual. "Why not? She's the daughter of a man knighted for courage, she's young and pretty, and strong enough to bear children without serious consequence. I am obliged to produce an heir, am I not?"

Peck gave the shoulders of the earl's jacket a light brushing. His expression said he was waiting for the real reason.

The real reason: Catherine was sunshine and excitement and all the things Granby had forgotten he enjoyed about life.

"I haven't been bored since I met her, except for the days I've been confined alone in this room, " he confessed gruffly. "Is that reason enough?"

The earl waited for some comment, but none was forthcoming. So Peck approved, did he?

A light tapping at the door was promptly answered by the valet. After a whispered word, the door was closed and the earl was handed a note. He didn't have to break the seal to know that his bride-to-be was already trying to wiggle out of their engagement.

Well, no matter. When it came to females, he could appreciate and accommodate them if it suited him to do so. He had yet to fail when it came to winning a lady's favor, and Miss Catherine Hardwick was just another woman, even if a good deal more inventive than most.

Still, they needed to talk, and it would serve his purpose to have the conversation out of the way before he confronted her father.

Ten minutes later, Granby stepped inside the small second-floor parlor. A button back sociable upholstered in green silk damask with long tasseled fringe faced the hearth, neighbored by two armchairs and a low pedestal table. The room presented a comfortable setting, but nothing could have been less comfortable than the look Catherine gave him as she turned away from the rain-splattered window. Her eyes were glittering with anger, the pupils wide and dark in the dim light.

"You wished to speak to me?" he asked, stopping midway into the room. His gaze did not waver, and there was a smile in his eyes, as if he were glad to see her under any circumstances.

"Felicity told me that you feel obligated to speak with my father. It isn't necessary. Regardless of what happened, you are not *required* to offer marriage."

"My actions say otherwise."

"If Felicity hadn't discovered us, would you feel obliged to speak to my father? I think not."

"It is pointless to assume what I would or wouldn't do," he answered her. "Your aunt *did* discover us together, and I *do* intend to speak with your father. I am not without honor."

"And I wasn't compromised," she said firmly.

"Not completely," he reminded her, "but our relationship has not been a platonic one."

Catherine blushed in spite of herself. She didn't need to be reminded of the intimacy she'd shared with the earl. Damn and blast the man for not acting like a typical scoundrel and fleeing the scene as soon as he could.

"The issue is not what happened, but what *will* happen if we marry."

"And that would be what?" he urged, taking a step closer.

"Misery," she retorted. "Neither of us wants to marry. Why pretend otherwise? Because social propriety demands it of us? Because all young ladies are supposed to be naturally inclined toward marriage and children? Because an earl needs an heir, and thus a wife? The reasons are as ridiculous as the idea of us, you and I, spending the rest of our lives together."

Granby wasn't the least offended by Catherine's anger. In fact, he'd be surprised if she weren't angry. She was a passionate, impulsive, headstrong young woman, and truth be known, he wouldn't have her any other way. These qualities, while in need of some tempering for harmony's sake, were a great part of her appeal.

The problem wasn't her attitude, it was his newly discovered feelings—feelings that still had him wrestling with himself.

The explanation that he'd given Peck wasn't far from

the mark. Catherine had inherited her father's courage and spirit. She was beautiful, and her body had been made for childbearing. He'd also been truthful about the ennui that evaporated the moment she walked into a room.

Although it was true that his decision had been made in haste, Granby didn't find himself regretting it. His marriage, an inevitable state since he was expected to produce an heir, might as well be an enjoyable one. And he certainly enjoyed Catherine—or at least as much of her as he'd had so far, which wasn't nearly enough.

Catherine wasn't encouraged by his silence. She walked to the opposite end of the room, stopping at a teakwood game table to finger the ivory and jade chess pieces her father had brought back after his service in India. She had asked Granby to meet her intending to reason with him, believing he'd jump at the chance to end things here and now, yet he didn't seem to think himself trapped. It was a puzzlement, but in retrospect, nothing that had happened in the last two weeks made any sense.

"You wish me to think you noble," she said, swinging around to look at him. He was dressed for dinner and looking quite handsome, but Catherine refused to allow the distraction. "You wish for me to think of you as a man who would sacrifice his cherished freedom because my innocence has been tarnished."

"I wish you to think of me as a man who finds you extremely desirable," he replied, moving toward her with a slow predatory stride that sent her sauntering back toward the window. "Is that so incomprehensible?"

He watched as she moved away from him, her tempting body bathed in soft twilight. He was quickly losing his mood for conversation.

"Desire is a word that comes much too easily to you, my lord," she countered smoothly. "But again, you avoid the real issue. I have no wish to marry. And if I did, it would not be to a man who has confessed that he prefers his life as it is. That being the case, your proposal lacks enthusiasm."

"I don't recall either one of us lacking enthusiasm this afternoon," he said. His gaze trailed over her. "In fact, I recall just the opposite."

"If you were the gentleman you claim to be, you wouldn't remind me," she snapped. "Which only serves to prove my point. Marriage would soon become an obstacle for you, unless you are seeking a wife who will tolerate indiscretion. If that's the case, then you will have to look elsewhere. I will not allow myself to be turned into a docile, submissive wife."

"I have no desire for a docile, submissive wife," he told her.

"Then what do you want?" she demanded, somewhat desperately. "For me to beg? To plead my case with frantic tears and hysterical sobs? Would that satisfy your vanity?"

"We seem at cross-purposes," he said, realizing that her stubbornness was simply a shield to hide something else.

He looked into her angry eyes, at the stubborn set of her chin, and knew that it wasn't going to be easy to convince her to marry him. She was a temperamental bit of news, and a very tempting woman. He wanted her, and he was going to have her—one way or the other.

Softening his approach, because he'd rather kiss her than argue with her, he said, "I thought, or at least I assumed, that you held some affection for me. Am I wrong?"

"Infatuation is not affection," she said adamantly. "Just as desire is not love."

He acquiesced with a slight shrug. "Love. I have seen it, in the marriages of two of my closest friends. At least they call it love."

"You sound skeptical."

"Do you love me?"

The question took Catherine completely by surprise. Her mouth parted to speak, but no words came out.

"What? You expect me to confess heartfelt emotions while you lack them yourself," Granby said, deciding it was time to take the offensive. "Love may or may not be a reality. I've yet to make the determination because I've yet to feel the emotion, but I am not without a heart, Miss Hardwick. Nor am I without feelings. I desire you, but I also like you. That's not to say that you don't fire my temper, but I think that's to be expected when two people find themselves in a passionate relationship. In fact, it's to be expected. Passion is a fiery emotion."

Catherine wasn't sure what to say. The earl was making it sound as if marriage had been his idea, not Felicity's. But that couldn't be true. He said he wanted her, but he could have any woman—why her? Because she challenged him in some way? Storm Dancer came to mind, but Catherine told herself no man would propose marriage just to get his hands on a horse.

On the other hand, he might be persuaded *not* to propose for that reason.

Granby used Catherine's silence to his advantage. He moved toward her, not stopping until she was within reach. "If you want the truth, I think we will do well together, given the proper encouragement."

"What kind of encouragement?"

"Our obvious attraction for one another," he said candidly.

"I'm afraid that isn't enough. Why should I forfeit control of my life for a few minutes' pleasure? The exchange is hardly an equitable one."

Granby laughed. "You do have a way of making a man feel insecure."

"You, insecure?"

"Very well, I want you in my bed. Does that make me an ogre?"

"It certainly doesn't make you a good marriage risk."

He backed away for a moment, realizing it was going to take more than a few teasing remarks to gain her compliance. "Why are you so set against marriage? I have the impression that your father and mother had a satisfying relationship."

"My father seems to think so," Catherine agreed. "I don't remember my mother."

"Then why? John and Emma Dent. Are they not a contented couple?"

"They seem to be," she replied.

"Something has soured you into thinking marriage is a circumstance to be avoided at all cost. Will you tell me why?"

Catherine shifted her gaze around the room, unsure what his strategy was. Deciding there was no reason not to be candid, she looked at him. "Two of my dearest friends recently married. Both are miserable. Sarah married a *gentleman* who turned into a tyrant the moment the honeymoon was over. She can scarcely breathe without her beloved husband belittling her for taking too long about it. And he has a fierce temper, a trait she was not allowed to witness until after the wedding. She has written me of times she has hidden behind locked doors, fearing that he might do her physical harm. Another friend married an equally charming *gentleman,* only to discover that he prefers parlor maids to his wife."

The derision in her voice sliced away Granby's suspicion that she was simply being stubborn. He knew of similar marriages. Almost everyone he knew who was married came close to fitting the description of Catherine's friends, with the exception of Sterling and Waltham.

"I cannot speak for anyone but myself," he replied. "I would never hurt a woman intentionally. As for dictatorial attitudes, I suspect I have a few, but none that would cause a wife misery."

Why was he being so understanding, and why did she want to believe him? Frantic that her resolve was lessening the longer they conversed, Catherine stiffened her shoulders. "One cannot emulate love or offer a substitute, my lord. It either exists or it doesn't."

"So it's either love or scandal," Granby responded. "Which do you think your father would prefer?"

"Don't threaten me." Her rebellious streak surfaced, along with her temper. "I won't be bullied to the altar."

"I'm not forcing you."

She glared at him. "No. You'll tell my father, and he'll do the forcing."

"I have no intention of telling your father anything that will cause you embarrassment. But I do have every intention of marrying you."

Catherine couldn't believe he was being so pigheaded. Knowing she was expected to present herself downstairs in less than an hour, she decided it was time to get to the heart of the matter. "There's no point in discussing this any further. I will continue to refuse your offer."

"I can make you change your mind."

His confidence annoyed her no end. "I won't marry you," she said, her tolerance slipping even more. "And no amount of persuasion will change my mind."

"Perhaps," he said, in a casual tone that only served to irritate her. "Then again, perhaps not."

They stared at each other for a tension-fraught moment, and Catherine felt a current of excitement pass through her. She stood motionless, trapped in a web of her own making. If only she hadn't been so foolish as to enter his room this afternoon.

"I can see that we've come to an impasse," he finally said, moving toward her until he'd literally backed her into a corner. "Either you agree to our engagement, or I'll be forced to compromise you completely."

"You wouldn't dare!"

She could scream, but by the time someone reached

the parlor Catherine was certain Granby would make it look as if she'd cried out in pleasure instead of fright. She might be able to talk her way out of one encounter, but two—not bloody likely.

"Oh, but I would," he replied, the tone ominous. He reached out and touched her cheek. "Right here, right now."

"I'm not afraid of you," she said, summoning her courage.

"You should be. I can be a very dangerous man when I want something, and I want you very much."

His fingertip found her mouth this time, outlining the lower lip with a feather-light touch that sent a bolt of panic through Catherine's body. She felt like a country mouse trapped by a very large, very cunning alley cat. Her insides filled with fury, and just enough fear to keep her in place.

She gave him a contemptuous glance, but he only kept smiling. If she had any doubts that he'd make a complete job of her seduction this time, one look into those steely blue eyes told her otherwise.

Catherine wanted to push him away, to run from the room, but at the same time she wanted him to kiss her. There was no logic to her feelings, only a deep nameless melancholy that crept into her heart. Granby was a solicitous charmer, but there was no depth to his feelings—he wasn't interested in giving her the kind of affection she needed. Passion, yes. Lust, most certainly. Games of love were his specialty, and he was a skilled player, but he never risked his heart.

She'd be risking all if she married him. There'd be no going back, no undoing of their wedding vows. She'd be trapped, just as Sarah and Veronica were trapped—forever joined to a man who didn't love her.

Granby saw the shades of sadness that darkened her eyes, and vowed that he'd not let the situation get out of hand. When in doubt, distraction often served to confuse the enemy. He lowered his head to kiss her, but she turned her face to the side.

"I'll give you Storm Dancer," she said desperately.

"What?"

"Storm Dancer. That is what you want, isn't it? You came to Stonebridge to acquire horses for your stable. You took one look at the stallion and decided you'd have him no matter the price. The price is my freedom, and your promise to leave this house *without* speaking to my father."

Granby couldn't have been more surprised if she'd doubled up her fist and knocked him on his arse. The shock quickly turned to anger. "You think to bribe me!"

"Call it what you will," Catherine replied curtly. He had stepped back when she'd made the offer, and she used the space to escape him, moving to the center of the room. "Storm Dancer in exchange for putting an end to this farce of a proposal."

Granby drew himself to his full height. Never in his life had he been more tempted to bend a woman over his knee. He considered it for an uncontrollable second, knowing it couldn't possibly make matters worse.

Catherine watched as his eyes darkened to the shade of a winter blizzard. A slow, insolent smile formed on his face.

He took a step toward her, and she instinctively knew what he was thinking. Even worse, he was arrogant enough to do it. Despite his injured shoulder and the advantage it gave her should she have to struggle against his greater strength, Catherine moved closer to the door. If she'd learned anything, it was not to underestimate this man.

"I've never had my honor measured in horseflesh before," he said in a bristling tone. "Tell me, just how much is your freedom worth? What if I want more than one horse? Can you swindle your father out of three good breeding mares, as well? I did take note of a strawberry roan the other day. If serviced properly, I'm sure she'd produce a champion foal."

Catherine's heart thumped hard inside her chest, but she forced herself to meet his gaze. "Your honor measured against a lifetime of misery," she said, ignoring his cutting reply. "Mine, as well as yours. Surely honor can afford to take second place in such a contest."

"Why take second place when I can have first in both contests," he said, all too confidently and much too coldly. "Marriage will get me both you *and* the stallion."

It wasn't something Catherine had considered, mainly because she'd been expecting him to jump at a way out of the situation. Seeing that he wasn't nearly as eager to flee as she had assumed gave her pause. What did the man expect to accomplish by marrying her, other than gaining the wife he had previously confessed to not wanting?

"We are expected downstairs soon," he said, his tone suddenly congenial, though there was a faint warning in his eyes. "As much as I'd like to continue this conversation, you need to dress."

"You can't be serious?"

"But I am serious. My answer is no."

He kissed her then, mastering her with a simple touch, instantly luring her closer. He kissed her gently at first, savoring the faint tremor that went through her body as he drew her into the circle of his arms.

A dreamlike quality took hold of Catherine the moment Granby claimed her mouth. If only her rebellious heart would agree with her head, she might be able to convince herself that she hated the man. She did hate him, or at least she hated the idea of marrying him without a glimpse of his true feelings.

Finally remembering that she was supposed to be discouraging him, not encouraging him, Catherine pulled away.

Granby smiled. He'd achieved his objective, dishing

out a dose of humility to an otherwise brash young woman. Now it was time to remind her that as her husband he would demand her respect. His eyes darkened, flashing dangerously, as he raised her chin, forcing her to meet his gaze.

"If you ever question my honor again, you *will* sorely regret it."

"What honor is there in forcing this marriage upon me?" she demanded. "You will gain nothing but an uncooperative wife."

"Oh, I assure you, I'll gain more than that." His tone was humorous, but his gaze was still dark and intense.

With a quick peck on the cheek, and not another word, he left Catherine to wonder what else fate could possibly have in store for her.

Fourteen

Catherine returned to her room, shaken and angry. The earl was actually going to ask her father for her hand in marriage. It was unbelievable. She told herself he was merely toying with her, that he'd join her father in the library only to discuss racing or politics, that her current anxiety was meant to be another hard-learned lesson. It was a game, a pretense that would soon end.

Catherine told herself that, but she didn't believe it.

Should any other young woman find herself in a similar dilemma, marriage would be the solution. Unfortunately, it seemed she was no exception to that rule. She had capitulated to the cravings of the flesh, to yearnings that no decent young woman should entertain outside the bonds of marriage. Or at least that was the way everyone else saw the situation. The fact that she didn't concur with their assumptions would do her little good.

Reluctantly, she dressed for dinner. If only she had more time to reconcile her feelings, time in which to think of an alternative to marriage. But time was running out. She was expected to present herself downstairs in a few minutes, to behave in a decorous fashion, to smile and converse as if her whole life wasn't being torn asunder.

By the time Catherine descended the staircase, she was certain that giving in to the earl's offer of marriage would be akin to willingly walking into a prison cell. A prison in which her heart would be held captive while "his lordship" was free to do as he pleased.

It was the way of aristocratic marriages. The man did his duty by giving his name and financial security, and the woman did hers by playing hostess and producing children.

Catherine paused midway down the staircase, her hand resting on the polished balustrade as she took a long, deep breath to calm herself. She could do one of two things: submit to the circumstances, or do everything within her power to make the earl change his mind before the wedding vows were spoken. There was still time.

With that in mind, she decided to endure the evening as best she could. Little would be served by throwing a tantrum, especially since her father was still acting standoffish over her challenging the earl to a race. No, her purpose would be better served if she pretended to be agreeable. Just because her father was likely to accept the earl's suit didn't mean she had to actually marry the man. Engagements could be broken.

Catherine entered the parlor, feeling somewhat confident that her cause wasn't completely lost. Felicity was seated in front of the hearth, where a small fire had been lit to ward off the chill that had descended with the rain. Her father had yet to come downstairs, but the earl was there, standing in front of the mantelpiece, drink in hand, smiling at something Felicity had just said.

Catherine lost her optimism the moment Granby turned to look at her. Suddenly at a loss, she grappled with something akin to astonishment that this man had such an impact on her heart and mind and body.

He stepped forward to greet her, taking her hand and bowing over it. "You look lovely," he said. Then, lowering his voice, he added, "Lovely enough to kiss."

Appalled that the man's impertinence came so close to her own thoughts, Catherine pulled her hand away.

"Good evening," she commented casually, moving toward her aunt, who offered some degree of safety.

Felicity was sipping her customary sherry and looking very pleased with herself. Catherine kissed her on the cheek before sitting down in a neighboring chair. She said nothing directly to the earl, but managed a smile that was convincing enough for the occasion.

"You do look lovely," Felicity agreed, then skillfully turned the conversation away from the impending doom that awaited Catherine later in the evening.

Granby leaned an elbow on the mantelpiece and stared at the woman he planned to marry. She looked feminine and totally bewitching in a gown of bottle green silk that showed the frothy lace of several petticoats beneath it. Her auburn hair was arranged in wavy tendrils about her face, with a small green feather added for accent. Two delicate strands of pearls were interwoven and worn as a choker around her slender neck.

He looked at her unadorned hands and decided an emerald engagement ring would do nicely, followed by a matching necklace and earrings as a bride's gift.

Over the years he had learned what jewels looked best on what woman, and Catherine's coloring definitely demanded emeralds.

He knew a lot about women; what put them on guard, what turned interest into anticipation, what soothed, and what stimulated. He knew what they liked in bed, where and how to touch them, what kept their passion simmering, and what pushed them over the edge. He had learned how to suppress his own desires long enough to make sure his partner was thoroughly satisfied. Now those desires were giving him fits.

He was still simmering over Catherine's insults, but at the same time, he had to admit to enjoying the "chase."

His inability to predict what she was going to do next kept him on his toes. Excluding the dislocated shoulder, he was having a very good time.

The basis for their marriage no longer mattered. He wanted her, and he'd soon have her. She would be his wife, his to cherish and protect. The realization eliminated any lingering traces of guilt that seducing her might have left lurking in his mind.

He smiled at the thought of how differently the day was going to end, considering the way it had begun. This morning he had awakened with a stiff shoulder, alone in bed with nothing but self-pity to keep him company. This evening, the pain had lessened and he was about to solicit Sir Hardwick for his daughter's hand in marriage. All in all, a most eventful day.

"Sorry to keep you waiting," Warren Hardwick said as he strolled into the parlor a few minutes later. He kissed Catherine, then Felicity, finally turning to offer his hand to the earl. "You're looking fit," he said, accepting the drink Granby had, poured and waiting.

They talked of minor things until the footmen called them into the dining room. Once there, Catherine couldn't escape the fact that the Earl of Granby was a force to be reckoned with, especially when he offered her a wicked smile to go along with the first course.

The moment the smile brightened his face, Catherine could see why he was so confident—those haunting eyes and that rakish smile had conquered dozens of women.

Not her.

She wouldn't be this man's legal plaything, a wife to be shown about town like a trophy, then forgotten once the nursery had its required occupants. The more Catherine thought about marriage, the more she remembered the reasons both Sarah and Veronica regretted it, and the angrier she got. By the time dessert was served, she was looking toward the night-darkened windows and craving a walk in the garden, even if she had to get wet to enjoy the fresh air.

Fortunately her father kept the dinner conversation moving briskly, with Felicity supplying an occasional anecdote that allowed the meal to progress much more smoothly than Catherine had thought possible.

In the privacy of her own thoughts, she tried to imagine herself at another table in another house, the home she would be expected to share with Lord Granby if she married him.

Surprisingly, it wasn't a difficult vision to conjure up. She had never thought of having a home other than Stonebridge, and the idea upset her.

"You'll need a proper dress for Waltham's annual party."

"What party?" Catherine asked, embarrassed that she'd been so preoccupied with thoughts of the earl she'd lost the direction of the conversation.

"Lord Waltham's annual regatta party," Felicity said. "I have a standing invitation. You'll accompany me."

Catherine looked at her father, who gave her a short nod to confirm that Felicity had already presented the idea and that it met with his approval. Having previously been informed by her aunt that Lord Granby and the Marquis of Waltham were close friends, she knew her aunt was aiding the earl's plans for them to marry.

Being seen on Granby's arm in a social environment would pave the way for their engagement to be officially announced in the London papers.

"I've never been to a regatta party," she said, holding to the casual attitude she'd assumed for the evening. "But then, I've never been sailing."

"It's a racing event, limited to members of the yacht

club," Granby said. "Waltham took the trophy last year. But I'd be glad to take you sailing, if you like."

"It will be good for her to see there's more to life than stables and village fairs," her father said, giving her a stern look that said he hadn't forgotten her promise to accept a London Season without complaint.

Of course, he wasn't aware that a proposal of marriage was forthcoming.

Catherine pushed her dessert around on her plate until her father stood, calling an end to the meal. The moment was at hand. She stared across the table, meeting the earl's gaze, only to find it as unwavering as his resolve. His expression said he hadn't changed his mind, so she had better change hers.

"Come along, Catherine," Felicity said. "We shall leave the men to their cigars and brandy and take ourselves into the drawing room."

Catherine hesitated, looking at her father. She thought to ask him for a moment of his time, to express her feelings before the earl could present his offer, but how could she explain without inciting questions she had no wish to answer? Feeling a twinge of guilt, she joined her aunt. She had no one to blame but herself for the ways things had turned out.

Sir Hardwick clipped the end of his cigar, stopping in the act of lighting it as Granby announced his intentions in a calm, firm voice.

"Take Catherine to wife?" he said a stunned moment later. "You want to marry my daughter!"

"Yes, sir," Granby replied, understanding the older man's surprise. "As soon as possible, though I understand that young women have certain ideas as to how weddings should take place, thus lengthening the process considerably. A fall ceremony, I would think. If you agree, of course."

Hardwick put aside his unlit cigar and reached for his brandy. He took a drink, looking at the earl over the rim of the glass. "Why?" he finally asked.

Granby smiled. "She suits me," he replied candidly. "She's also beautiful, intelligent, and—"

"And as stubborn as the day is long," Hardwick finished for him. After a pensive look, he continued. "Have you expressed yourself to Catherine?"

"Yes, and I must tell you she isn't all that enthusiastic about becoming my wife."

A pause ensued and the cigar was finally lit. "Does this sudden proposal have anything to do with what happened last week?"

"In what way?" Granby responded, helping himself to a brandy and walking to the fireplace before turning to look at his host again.

"That damnable race, of course. A meeting at dawn, your shoulder, my daughter acting as if she'd forgotten the good sense she was born with."

"I think I'm the one who's forgotten his good sense. If I may be blunt, Sir Hardwick, I find your daughter to be a very exciting young woman. I think she'll do well as my wife, once I've convinced her that the marriage can benefit us both."

Hardwick laughed. "So that's the way of it. I thought as much. Makes a man wonder why women are called the weaker sex."

"It does indeed," Granby replied with a smile.

"Had to do a bit of convincing myself when I decided to marry Lucinda. She didn't like the idea of having a soldier for a husband. But persistence won out. It usually does."

"Can I take your remark to mean that you have no objection to my suit?"

"I'd be a fool to object to my daughter making such a marriage, and I'm no fool. I am, however, well versed in just how stubborn Catherine can be when she puts her mind to it."

"She already has. Put her mind to it, that is. She offered to give me Storm Dancer if I packed my bags and left Stonebridge before morning's first light."

"Can't say I'm surprised. She's as brassy as a military band when her temper's riled. It won't be easy to keep her on a tight rein."

"No, I suppose it won't. But I admit to liking the idea."

Hardwick gave it some thought, not being as impulsive as his daughter. After a second brandy was poured, he nodded. "Very well, my lord. I'll endorse the marriage. Not that my word will settle the matter. Catherine's got a mind of her own."

"Your consent is all I require."

Fifteen

Catherine watched the sun rise over the wooded hills. Try as she might, she couldn't think charitably toward the earl. Not after what he had done, not after the gloating smile he had given her last night when he'd entered the drawing room behind her father.

It was settled. Or so it seemed to everyone but her. The marriage would take place in late September.

Marriage!

How she hated the thought of it, knowing that the earl didn't love her, that there was little hope of him ever coming to care for her as deeply as she cared for him. And she did care.

She had come of age in a few short weeks. Never again would she be the same country lass who thought to spend her days among horses and wild meadows. Marriage would change all that. She would be expected to be a lady—a countess.

Sunlight was dancing over the lawn, the house still quiet, as she went downstairs. Mrs. Gibson was in the kitchen when Catherine entered, wearing breeches and a faded jacket.

Her father had lifted his restrictions last night. The

only limitation still intact was that she not ride Storm Dancer again.

Eager for the freedom only a ride could give her, she asked the cook for a small helping of eggs and bacon and a single muffin, then ate quickly, and quit the house before her insufferable fiancé could come downstairs and ruin her morning.

Another part of her wanted to get beyond the reach of everything that was proper and expected, the rules and expectations that prevented her from taking charge of her own life.

It seemed inconceivable that she'd accepted her father's congratulations so easily, that she'd met the earl's gaze and said nothing, that no protest had crossed her lips. And yet she had done just that. Why? Because she had been raised to accept the consequences of her actions, or because somewhere deep inside her heart she wanted to become the earl's wife.

She'd struggled with the mingled emotions all night, but she was no closer to understanding them than she'd been yesterday when she'd submitted to his advances, and in doing so caused the very event she so dreaded.

Despite her desire to ride as fast as she could, Catherine waited patiently while one of the grooms saddled her mare. She set out for Sudeley and the private meadow where she always went to be alone.

The soft ground yielded to her horse's hooves as she nudged the mare into a canter. The sunlight was growing warmer and stronger, slowly steaming away the dampness of the previous night's rain. Of all the seasons, she loved summer the best. The vibrant colors and thick grass; the familiar fragrance of growing things that hung over the pasture, blending with the scent of horses.

The country was where she belonged, not London or Bath or one of the other dozen cities that were considered fashionable.

She knew this place—the woodlands and streams,

Sudeley Castle, the village with its quaint shops and villagers, who had called Winchcombe their home for generation upon generation. Everything was familiar here, yet nothing was the same—not now.

Catherine stopped when she reached the meadow. Framed in rays of golden sunshine, the field looked like a patchwork quilt of wildflowers and deep green grass. Tethering the mare, she walked to the stream and sat on top of the flat rock where she'd once carved her initials. She rubbed her hands over the lettering, thinking again of all the reasons she didn't want to leave Stonebridge.

"You're up early," a voice behind her remarked.

Flinching, she turned to find the earl, his posture suggesting that of a military man. His eyes were bright this morning, devoid of the pain that had plagued him for the last several days, his gaze as blue as the water that bubbled at her feet.

"Go away."

He laughed. "Is that any way for a young lady to greet the man she's going to marry?"

"My father's endorsement doesn't guarantee a wedding, my lord."

Despite the waspishness of her reply, Granby wasn't to be denied. He left his mount to graze on the rain-sweet grass, then walked toward her until he was beside the small boulder she had turned into a morning chair.

"I will be leaving this afternoon," he announced. "We will not see each other again until the regatta party."

"Good-bye."

Granby set his jaw. He had hoped their parting could be an amicable one. Realizing that was not to be the case, he decided now was as good a time as any to let Catherine know that he was not going to be ignored. Not now, and certainly not in the future.

"You may make whatever preparations you like regarding the ceremony. St. Peter's Church will suit, if you wish to marry here in Winchcombe. My guest list will be short; mostly close friends. I have no immediate family."

"The guest list may be shorter than you think. The church could lack a bride," Catherine said, climbing down from the boulder, as her peaceful morning was now a thing of the past.

He met her challenge with one of his famous smiles. "If you think to test my patience any further, be warned that it is close to an end. I have had enough of your schemes and insults. We will be married."

She stared at him, guilt and worry seeping into her as she realized she couldn't blame him for seducing her. She'd been a willing partner. Catherine moved to leave, but a firm hand on her arm stayed her.

"We will finish this conversation," he said. "Here and now. Things will be settled between us before I leave."

"There is nothing to settle," she said, her voice rising with each word. "You have my father's blessings, and Felicity's, but you don't have mine. Nor will you, until I know that I won't be a wife who finds no solace in marriage but wealth and position, which mean nothing to me."

The ensuing silence carried the weight of a war cannon. It hung heavily between them as the earl met her hostile gaze with one equally determined. Part of Catherine quailed at what she saw in those steel blue eyes, while another part of her wanted to soothe his anger.

"You are right," he said, relaxing his grip but not releasing her. "I am acting like a domineering ass. You have every right to expect better of me."

"You're changing tactics again," she accused him. "It won't work. I won't be seduced with gentlemanly words and gestures."

Granby laughed in spite of himself. "God, but you're a stubborn woman. And a reckless one. What must I do, lock you away until I can procure a special license, then wed you before week's end to make sure you don't take to sea during my absence, hiding away on a freighter bound for some faraway port?"

"I'm not running away," she said, insulted that he'd think such a thing. "I'm staying right here in Winchcombe, where I belong."

He was furious with her, but he couldn't help but be delighted that she wasn't cowed. One thing was for certain—their children would be spirited and strong. He looked at her, his gaze moving from her scuffed boots to the lovely mouth he wanted to kiss one more time.

In his mind, he imagined her swollen with his child, and the picture pleased him. It also aroused him.

"After our wedding, my family estate in Reading will be our home, and you will live there as my countess."

Catherine stood motionless, except for the wild racing of her heart. She looked away for a brief moment, hoping to compose herself, wanting to make him understand. But why should he? He was getting what he wanted, what society expected him to want, a wife to bear his heir and grace his home.

"Is it so impossible to believe that we can make a good marriage?" he asked of her. "We have more in common than you think," he added, exercising great effort because what he really wanted to do was carry her down to the grass and end the argument once and for all. "I am not the Londoner you think me to be. I enjoy the country life, just as you do."

"I don't want to leave Stonebridge," she said, hating the quivering quality of her voice but unable to undo it. She was trembling on the inside. He always had that effect on her.

He turned her to face him and saw the shimmer of tears in her eyes. They were his undoing.

"Don't," he whispered fervently. "Don't fight me."

His hand touched her cheek, wiping away the one tear she had been unable to contain. Her skin felt smooth and silky and warm to the touch. He lowered his head and kissed her cheek, then the corner of her mouth, and Catherine moaned deep in her throat.

"Oh, God, please don't."

Granby ignored her. He was finally past her defenses, and he couldn't stop now. He had to make her realize that she belonged to him, that she had stepped into his domain that morning on the lane, and he couldn't— wouldn't—let her escape.

"Why?" she said in a shaky whisper. "Why?"

The question demanded an answer Granby wasn't ready to give. One he couldn't give, not without revealing more of himself than he'd ever disclosed to a woman before. The rule he had lived by since reaching adulthood had been to keep women at a distance, to enjoy them without committing more than his body. Old habits were hard to break.

Still, something was happening to him. Feelings he didn't completely understand. Why—with a full life, with the demands of his properties and title, with the company of friends, both male and female, should he suddenly find his life lacking and lonely? He knew himself well enough, understood his own motivations, knew his own limitations, and yet his self-discipline, a trait that had never given him trouble until recently, seemed impaired whenever this woman was within reach.

Catherine started to speak, but didn't. He was pressing his lips against her temple, her cheek, her forehead—light, feathery kisses that made her heart race with longing. Her hands curled into fists as she fought the need to touch him in return.

"I don't want to marry you to make you unhappy," he whispered. "I want to take care of you."

If he hadn't said it so gently, so sincerely, Catherine might have been able to rebuke him, but his voice was as tender as his touch. She struggled to keep more tears from falling.

Remembering that she didn't want to marry this man, at least not for the reason everyone wanted her to marry him, she gathered her emotions and pulled them back inside.

Granby saw the change as much as he felt it. Her body stiffened for a moment, as if she were about to spring away from him. He brushed his mouth ever so lightly across her forehead, then smiled. "What must I do to convince you that my proposal is sincere?"

Catherine found her voice. "Your sincerity was triggered by necessity, my lord. If Felicity hadn't found me in your room, we wouldn't be having this conversation."

"I wouldn't be so sure of that. Sooner or later what we feel for each other would have brought about similar circumstances."

"You don't feel anything for me. Nor I for you." It was a lie, but she'd stopped counting her sins since that day on the lane. Would one more matter all that much?

"On the contrary, I feel very strongly," Granby said, keeping his hands on her shoulders because he was afraid she'd bolt the moment he let go. "And although you want to deny it, I know you feel something for me. The name we give it may be different, but the results are the same."

The smooth glide of his mouth over her temple only added to Catherine's dilemma. How did you tell a man to go away when all you wanted was for him to get closer?

"I'd like to kiss you goodbye," he said.

"You're already kissing me."

"Not the way I want to kiss you. Not the way you want to be kissed."

The truth of the matter increased Catherine's uneasiness, but before she could stop herself, she was lifting her face so he could give her the kiss they both wanted.

It wasn't the ravenous kiss she'd expected.

Not at first.

His mouth moved slowly over hers, softly but expertly, until she shivered and parted her lips, inviting him inside.

A bolt of passion tore through Granby, but he refused to let it control him. Instead he concentrated on making the kiss the best he and Catherine had ever shared—slow and sweet and sensual. He wanted to prove to her that he could give as well as take, and in doing so reassure her that marrying him wouldn't be the colossal mistake she had convinced herself it would be.

It wasn't easy.

The tiny, sexy sound she made when he deepened the kiss went through him like lightning through a rainy sky, deep and hot and piercing. His hands moved from her shoulders, down her arms, then around to her back. He held her snugly against him, but not too tightly. He could feel the heat of her body through her blouse.

The controlled but sensual joining of their mouths began to unravel Catherine's resolve. Each soft caress of Granby's tongue sent a current of need through her body.

"Norton."

The soft, almost soundless, whisper fanned the flames that Granby was desperately trying to keep under control. He had to take his time. Somehow he had to find the self-control not to rush her into something she didn't want.

He lifted his head and looked into her eyes; they were liquid with passion, gleaming green-gold in the morning sunlight. Uncertain, her gaze wavered for a moment before returning to meet his.

"I like it when you kiss me."

His smile was reply enough, as his hands moved over her, down the graceful line of her spine, the indentation of her waist, the flare of her hips, then around to the soft curve of her bottom to tuck her closer.

The uncertainty in her eyes vanished, as she rose on tiptoe to take his mouth this time, becoming the aggressor.

His hands tightened for a moment, then relaxed, as he decided to let her take the lead. Her fingers slid up the center of his chest, then underneath the lapels of his jacket and onto his shoulders. Granby matched the caress with one of his own, allowing his hands to lightly knead the softness of her trouser-clad bottom.

Her hands moved around his neck, her fingers sliding into his hair. His moved up to her waist, then around to gently cup her breasts.

The kiss continued.

Catherine only knew that she was enjoying it, reveling in the heat of his body, and in the touch of his hands. Even as she realized that she was taking the opposite direction of the one she had promised herself, she couldn't force him to release her. The elemental power he personified was even more tempting than it had been the previous day.

Catherine felt it, clung to it, as he continued kissing her.

She wanted it. Craved it as she longed for nothing else in her life.

It felt wonderful to be with him like this, standing in the meadow with nothing but sunlight and fresh morning air. Crisp and bright, like the feelings he created inside her. Suddenly free of all constraints, she kissed him more passionately. She ran her hands over him, over his shoulders and down his chest, then up again, wanting to touch as much of him as she could.

Granby sucked in his breath and held it as Catherine began exploring on her own, kissing the hollow of his neck, then edging her way into the open collar of his shirt to kiss the ridge of his collarbone. He tried to remember that—although she wasn't completely innocent of the things that happened between a man and a woman, thanks to their brief lovemaking yesterday—she was still very much a virgin.

She deserved patience and gentleness. The problem was, if she kept licking and kissing his neck, he was going to lose control and take her right here in the meadow.

He'd followed her with the intention of settling things between them, of gaining her promise that she wouldn't do anything rash or impulsive, that she'd give their engagement a chance.

What was he doing instead?

Kissing her, holding her much too closely, and soon he'd be doing more than that—unless one of them regained their sanity.

He thought about praying for strength, but seeking divine intervention at a time like this was blasphemy. He knew what he wanted, knew what he had to have— Catherine.

"I want to make love to you," he said. "I want to lay you down in the wildflowers and . . . Let me show you, teach you."

Catherine's breath rushed out with a soft sigh. She blinked back the tears that wanted to fall. She could fight it—this attraction that came so close to love she was sure it was the real thing—or she could surrender to it, and to be brutally honest with herself, she wanted to surrender. To give herself over to the havoc and uncertainty, to experience what his kisses had been promising from the first day they'd met.

His thumb rubbed over the crown of her breast and the simple caress was enough to unravel her.

"Yes," she whispered.

He released her long enough to take his jacket off, then knelt to spread it on the ground. When he looked up at her, he smiled. "Are you sure?"

She slipped her own riding jacket off, letting it fall to join his. Her fingers went to the buttons on her blouse and one by one they came open, revealing a white muslin camisole.

Granby unbuttoned his shirt, then pulled it free of his trousers. He sat down, then held out his hand, breathing a sigh of relief when Catherine accepted it. A gentle tug brought her to a kneeling position.

They looked at each other, their private thoughts showing on their faces.

"Say you'll marry me."

Catherine caught her lower lip between her teeth.

"Say it," he said hoarsely. "Tell me that you'll be my wife."

Catherine looked at the passion burning in his eyes, and felt an answering passion coiled deep in the heart of her. She was straightforward in her thinking most of the time, but there was no such thing where this man was concerned. She wished she could still the yearning in her heart and body, but there was no remedy except the man looking at her as if she were something rare and beautiful, something to be cherished and treasured.

Could she make this moment last—nourish it until it grew into something more than passion? Was this man capable of loving the right woman? Felicity thought he was, and so did her father, or he wouldn't have agreed to their engagement.

Granby saw the doubt in her eyes. "Trust me to take care of you," he said, his voice low and soft. "Trust me."

Did she dare? If she was wrong, if her trust was misplaced, she'd lose more than her virginity—she'd lose her heart.

A deep, plundering kiss fogged her thinking processes.

"I . . . I'll marry you."

The words came out in a frantic rush of breath, before her common sense could stop them.

Catherine watched his expression, expecting triumph, but all she saw was a slow smile that said he was glad to have the arguing over.

His hand reached out to touch her cheek, then moved slowly downward to the lace of her camisole. His fingers played along the lace, touching but not touching her. "The sunlight suits you."

They weren't the words she'd expected, but they brought a smile to her face anyway. She wanted to say something, a compliment in return for the one he'd just given her, but nothing came to mind except the silly words of a young woman in love—words he didn't want to hear.

Unsure what to say, she said nothing.

He began to undress her, his hands intent but gentle. She'd never been bare-breasted in front of anyone before. Catherine knew she was blushing, but she didn't stop him. The sun felt warm as her camisole was unlaced and pushed aside, exposing more of her to his gaze.

Granby couldn't take his eyes off her. Her breasts were full and firm, not voluptuous or oversized, but in proportion to the rest of her, with dark coral tips that pearled into hard kernels the moment he exposed them to the air.

The sight of her naked skin thrilled him, and he could feel the heat in his groin grow even hotter. He had to taste her—know the satin and velvet textures of her.

He pulled her close, then lowered his head.

Catherine knew what he was going to do, and she allowed it willingly, cradling his head in her hands as he drew the tip of one breast into his mouth. The burning desire intensified as he sucked at her, his tongue swirling in tiny circles around her nipple.

Granby dragged his mouth from one breast to the other, all the while struggling to keep his passion under control. He continued feasting on her, drawing her deep into his mouth, licking and nibbling at her until she was shaking and off balance.

Catherine felt his hands at her belt, felt the slight tugging and the gradual relaxing of the leather, then his hands unbuttoning her breeches. But his mouth kept her focused, centered on the delicious sensations that were warming her belly and making her whole body tingle.

"Sit down. I need to take off our boots."

She sank to the ground, and he had her boots and socks off in no time. All the while, she couldn't take her eyes off him, off the gleam of sunlight in his hair. He was still wearing his shirt, but it was open. More hair gleamed there, crisp and curly against his chest, swirling down the center of his body, narrowing at his navel, then disappearing beneath the waistband of his trousers.

She wiggled her toes when he pulled her socks off. Granby chuckled deep in his chest. He should have known she'd react this way, confident once the decision had been made. Virgin or not, she wasn't a shy woman.

He leaned back, resting on his knees with his legs doubled under him. He undid his trousers, but he didn't take them off. He was aching to get inside of her, to ease the aroused state he'd been in for the last two weeks, but caution ruled, and he smiled at the tempting picture she made, naked from the waist up with the sunlight on her flushed skin.

He cupped her breasts in his hands, kneading them, then squeezing the nipples until she arched her back.

The heat of her body was an addiction, one he wanted to end at the same time he wanted it to last forever. He played with her, kissing her mouth, her throat, the swell of her breasts, as he gradually lowered her to the ground. His shoulder ached, but he ignored the pain.

Once she was lying on her back, he pulled at her trousers and drawers. Catherine lifted her hips, and off they came. She was completely naked.

Granby looked at her, at the graceful lines of her body, the soft curves and valleys. Instinctively, his gaze was drawn to the russet curls between her legs.

Catherine lay in the sunshine, feeling wantonly wonderful and wicked in a way that had nothing to do with propriety, and everything to do with wishing the earl's trousers would disappear next.

He lowered himself over her, sparing her the bulk of his weight. When he flinched with pain, she moved to the side and sat up, her hair falling in thick ringlets over her shoulders. "I forgot about your shoulder."

"It doesn't hurt that much."

There was no way he was going to stop now that she was naked and within reach. He sat up and jerked at his boots and socks. Once they were out of the way, he stretched out on his back.

"Come here," he said, reaching for her.

Catherine let herself be pulled into place next to him, then over him. He moved her until she was half-covering his body, her hair curtaining their faces as he took her mouth in a hot, hungry kiss that said they'd come too far to stop now.

She gasped as his hands slid from her breasts to her belly, measuring her hips, then down again, to slide between her legs. He urged them to spread, and then he was touching her in that private, special place.

He moved her again, so she was straddling his hips, his hands on the back of her thighs, his fingers pressing into the soft skin, then sliding down to her knees and up again, learning her, teaching her, arousing them both.

She moaned, then arched her back as his fingers returned to ply their magic on that special place. He left her just long enough to open his trousers.

She felt his kisses on her neck, felt him stroke her again, his fingers sliding easily through her wetness, gently opening her, then probing. Each slow movement of his hand brought a surge of pleasure. He found the sensitive nub and rubbed it, circling it the same way his tongue was circling her nipple, creating a rhythm that sang through her blood.

Slowly, the sensation changed, growing more urgent, more needful with each caress of his fingers. The feeling was fluid, hot and liquidizing. Her eyes drifted closed, and she moved to the rhythm, the silent beat of pleasure that was coursing through her body. One hand stayed between her legs as the other moved to her hip, guiding her.

"That's it," he whispered, as a second finger pushed inside her. "Relax and move with me."

He said something else, but Catherine couldn't make out the words. She was lost in sensations; the heat of the morning sun, the breeze moving over her naked skin, the pressure of his fingers as they moved deep only to withdraw, and with each retreat to caress her so intimately it brought tears to her eyes.

Then she felt his sex, pushing against her, into her.

Catherine tensed.

"It's all right," he told her. "Relax, sweetheart. Give yourself to me."

Putting both hands on her hips, Granby lifted her, then arched his hips high, forcing his way past the internal barrier and her clenching muscles until he was buried inside her hot channel.

Catherine felt a sharp pain, but it didn't last for long. The fullness didn't go away as easily. The sensation of being stretched and filled was completely new, and she tensed again.

He kissed her, telling her it was all right and she began to relax. He was inside her, possessing her. She could feel him move, feel the hard length of him rubbing against her. It felt strange, but not unpleasant.

"Touch me," Granby groaned, thinking he'd be lucky to last more than a few strokes, she was so hot and tight, and he'd wanted her for so long.

Her hands were tentative as first. She brushed her fingers down his chest, her fingernails scraping over a nipple. He'd thought of her riding him since that morning in the lane, and now that she was it was almost more than he could take. Each time he pushed into her, she clenched those muscles around him, and he had to grit his teeth to keep from climaxing. He kissed her, stroking her breasts, as much of her body as he could reach, for as long as he could bear it.

He talked to her, focusing on the words, telling her how beautiful she was, how much he wanted her, would keep wanting her. He forced himself to take his time, to love her slowly, luxuriously, as though the urgency didn't exist.

He cupped her breasts and used his teeth and tongue on them, sucking them, flicking his tongue over and around the tight little nipples. He gripped her hips more firmly and moved his own in a circular motion that left her gasping.

Catherine pressed down each time he pushed high into her. She ran her fingers through the curly hair on his chest. She called out his name as he pushed high again, going deeper, possessing more of her, stealing her senses until everything blurred into a foggy, golden haze of sunlight.

Granby could feel the softness of her flesh, the inside of her thighs pressing against his hips, and the sultry softness surrounding his cock. He pushed deeper and deeper, spinning out of control toward a climax that was coming . . . coming. He fought it, but his senses screamed that the peak had to be reached—the ultimate pleasure found.

Catherine felt the change, the nameless need that rose like a fire inside her. It was strange and frightening. She stiffened, and he pushed high into her.

"Yes," he urged. "Now, sweetheart. Let it happen. *Now!*"

She came in hard little spasms that shredded the last

of his control. The sweet shuddering tremors seemed to come from the very core of her. She pushed down and twisted her hips against him until the fire burst like a shooting star, engulfing her in wave after molten wave of pleasure.

A few minutes later, Catherine felt feathery kisses against her mouth and face, her eyelashes and temple. She couldn't stop a smile from forming. So this was what it was all about, giving yourself to a man. She'd never imagined it could be so powerful, so utterly overwhelming.

She opened her eyes as Granby threaded his fingers through hers and pressed their clasped hands against his chest. The simple gesture sent a flood of warmth into her confused heart. She had never known a man like this man, an earl with assurance, intelligence, and wit. And she'd certainly never expected to be engaged to him.

There was no going back now, and Catherine knew it. She'd known it the moment she reached for the buttons on her blouse, and despite everything, she couldn't regret it.

Granby pulled her close, and she felt happy and lazy, like a cat that had just found the coziest corner of the kitchen. He smoothed back wisps of damp hair from her face, then kissed her forehead.

"You're beautiful."

"Mmm-hmm," she sighed. "It was wonderful."

"Yes, it was," he agreed.

God, but he felt weak—weak and completely satisfied. He smiled, and the smile went all the way through him, down deep where he couldn't remember a smile ever reaching before. It was the oddest thing, but he did care for her. It wasn't just her beauty or her spirited nature that had caused him to promise to take care of her—it was simply her: Catherine.

Sixteen

Foxleigh was a beautiful estate several miles north of Reading, set in a wooded landscape amidst an amphitheatre of rolling hills that changed from season to season in a symphony of colors and scents. The manor house faced the long slope of the most westerly hills, its lawns a carpet of emerald green, the front gardens a maze of purples and golds and reds.

As the carriage slowed, a particularly strong hope upon which Granby had allowed his mind to dwell these last two days rose up within him. Soon Foxleigh would have a mistress, and he would have a wife.

Exiting the carriage, he was promptly greeted by Briggs, his butler. Briggs had closed the bachelor residence on Belgrave Square and headed into the country to oversee Foxleigh, now that his lordship would be in residence.

"Milord," Briggs said, his voice as deep and staunch as a British musket. "Welcome home."

"It's good to be home," Granby said, meaning it.

He thought of the old house with its gleaming brasses and polished oak, with curtains opened to let in the summer sun or closed during winter to keep out the chill, of fires red on the hearth while winter winds blew over the hills, rattling the glass windowpanes. He hoped Catherine liked it.

It was a good place to raise children.

She could already be with his child. He'd taken no precautions when he'd made love to her—their encounter more surprise than seduction. He would write her and tactfully inquire as to her health. If she was pregnant, they would marry sooner than the now-planned September wedding.

Their second parting, the one in front of her father and Felicity, had been polite and unadorned. He'd voiced his intentions to see her again at the regatta party, she'd smiled wordlessly in reply. A chaste kiss on the cheek, and that had been that.

But he hadn't been able to get her out of his mind these last two days. The trip home had been uneventful except for his thoughts. He had never been inclined to daydream, and yet that was exactly what he'd done. Catherine's habitation of his mind was a novelty he was still accustoming himself to, an indefatigable interest that had kept him occupied for hour upon hour.

Entering the house, Granby knew there was work enough to keep him occupied for the next two months. He would set himself to it now that his future had a definite path, that of a wife and family.

After a hot bath and a change of clothes, he made his way to the library. The summer day was still lingering, and he'd asked for a light supper to be served on a tray while he tackled the stack of correspondence on his desk. He came downstairs only to be stopped on the second floor landing by one of the maids and congratulated on his upcoming marriage.

"Peck told Briggs, milord," she said with a shy smile. "Briggs isn't one to gossip, of course, but the footman overheard, and he told Cook, who told me. It will be so nice to have a mistress again. We all miss your mother so."

"Thank you," Granby replied. Louisa had been his mother's lady's maid, and he knew she expected to return to the post once he installed his wife. "I'm sure the staff will find themselves as enthralled with Miss Hardwick as I am."

He continued downstairs to find Briggs in the library, filling the liquor decanters. The butler, who wasn't one to express his personal feelings even when asked—a trait Granby wished would rub off on Peck—congratulated him in turn.

"The house is abuzz with the news, milord. I daresay the old place will liven up a bit with a lady in residence."

"Considering the lady, I can guarantee it," Granby said with a smile. "She's a country lass who prefers breeches to petticoats and rides better than most men."

Briggs chuckled. "Breeches."

"Breeches. I'm going to have my hands full."

The butler didn't reply, but words weren't necessary. His expression said he was well pleased that Foxleigh would soon have a countess under its roof again.

Several weeks passed in which Granby reacquainted himself with the life of a country gentleman. The awkwardness he had first experienced at having Catherine occupy so much of his mind soon became a longing to see her. He had written—an uncomfortable task in itself, since he had never written a letter to a woman before—but there had been no reply by post.

As he sat behind his desk, leafing through the pile of estate reports that he would soon meet with his steward to discuss, he had to admit a certain disappointment that she hadn't answered his letter. Logic told him that she must be dueling with her own feelings. She wasn't excited about their upcoming marriage, though he suspected her feelings were stronger than she was willing to admit. Still, he didn't like the uneasiness of thinking she might change her mind.

Catherine wasn't like other young women, and he was beginning to find the differences both a blessing and a curse. It wasn't the embarrassment of the wedding being cancelled that concerned him as much as the idea that he was actually looking forward to speaking the vows.

The thought lingered as he went over an estimate for some estate improvements: repairs to the gamekeeper's cottage and stables, and a new cookstove for the kitchen. He took a moment to look around the room, always liking the dark tones of the library.

The desk was dark oak with thick legs and a marquetry-inlaid top. The bookshelves were well stocked, and the sofa comfortable for both sitting and sleeping. A large Act of Parliament clock hung on the wall over a low satinwood bookcase. The Parliament clock was similar to the ones that could be seen in inns and taverns throughout the English countryside, taking its name from the 1797 legislative act that had taxed all clocks in Britain, thus encouraging many of its residents to rely on publicly displayed timepieces. The law had been repealed shortly thereafter, as it had come close to putting many English clockmakers out of business.

Granby decided Catherine could test her hand redecorating other rooms if she wished. He was content with the way his father had left the library.

The earl was in deep conversation with his steward when Briggs announced Viscount Rathbone. Granby promptly told his steward, a serious-faced, middle-aged man by the name of Samuel Corbett, that their meeting would be resumed in the morning, then stood to greet his best friend.

Rathbone strolled into the library. He was casually

dressed, but it was easy to see that his London tailor was one of the best. His usual relaxed smile was in place as he greeted his friend.

"Stopped by to see if you wanted to take a short jaunt with me. Bath, if you're in the mood for a little fun."

Knowing the viscount's definition of fun, Granby smiled. "I've only just returned to Foxleigh, so I'll have to decline the invitation."

"Bollocks!" Rathbone said, helping himself to a drink. "You must be as tired of the country life as I am. Bath," he said lusciously, "Ramsbury is having a house party."

Granby shook his head. Willard Ramsbury was a young lord with perverted tastes. He enjoyed filling his ancestral home with expensive prostitutes and having orgies. Unlike some men, Ramsbury had no aversion to paying for sex, and there were plenty of tarts to accommodate him.

"Just think of it," Rathbone said, sitting down in the chair the steward had vacated minutes earlier. "Pretty young ladies with firm tits and tight little cunnies, all yours for the asking. Blonde or brunette, Ramsbury always has a nice selection."

"No thank you." Granby smiled as he poured himself a drink.

"Don't tell me that you've given up women," Rathbone countered with a wicked smile. "Fucking keeps a man young."

"You're going to wear your cock down to a nub," Granby said laughingly. "What about the lovely Lady Kendrick? Have you tired of her forbidden fruit so quickly?"

"A month of bedding the same woman," the viscount replied with a shrug of his well-tailored shoulders. It was all the explanation that anyone who knew him needed. When it came to life's variety, Rathbone was a connoisseur.

"So if one of Ramsbury's parties doesn't interest you, what does?"

Granby braced himself for the explosion that was sure to follow his announcement. "I've decided to marry."

Silence filled the room for several tense seconds. The viscount lowered his glass, looking at his friend as if Granby had just announced the abdication of his title in favor of joining a monastery.

"Marriage as in the taking of vows, of pledging fidelity until you turn up your toes?"

"Yes."

The drink was finished and another one poured before Rathbone looked at Granby again. "Bloody hell, you can't go and get married on me. It's an absurd idea. And don't even think about asking me to stand for you, because I won't. I'm having nothing to do with wedding ceremonies. Watching Waltham give up his freedom with a smile on his face was enough to make my stomach sour. Marriage"—he shuddered as if the whiskey he took the time to swallow tasted like castor oil—"I get chills just thinking about it."

The earl sat behind his desk, waiting for the truth of the matter to settle into the viscount's reluctant brain.

"Bollocks! You're bloody well going to do it, aren't you?"

"September," Granby replied matter-of-factly. "And I expect you at the wedding. Morland will stand for me, if the task is too distasteful for you."

"Who is she?" Rathbone demanded.

"Miss Catherine Hardwick of Winchcombe. Her father owns a stable, and a very good one. I brought back two mares with me, and wait until you see the stallion that comes with the bride. He's magnificent."

"Sounds like you're more excited about her father's livestock that you are about taking a wife."

"It's a long story," Granby replied. "You might say the stallion acted as matchmaker."

"Matchmaker? You'd better tell me the whole story. Have you compromised the chit? That's it, isn't it? You, who warned me about getting caught with my pants down, were the one to get caught. Where was it? The hayloft? No better way to spend an afternoon than a good tumble in the hay."

"It wasn't a hayloft," Granby said, knowing he was going to have to admit to some of the sordid details. "It was a bedroom in her father's house. Lady Felicity Forbes-Hammond interrupted us. And I didn't compromise her, not completely."

It wasn't the whole truth, but it was enough to satisfy his friend. A marriage forced upon a gentleman by propriety was not a willing one, thus Granby was relieved of the burden of having been assumed to have lost his mind.

Rathbone laughed until tears ran down his face. He was still laughing when he refilled both his glass and the one sitting on the earl's desk. A wicked glint appeared in his eyes as he resumed his seat. "Is she pretty?"

"Very."

"How pretty?"

"Her hair is a nice shade of auburn, her eyes are hazel, and she wears breeches when she rides."

"Breeches! She sounds enchanting. I can't wait to meet the lady."

"Just remember that she's *my* lady."

"Sorry, old boy," Rathbone said, looking properly chastened. "It's hard to think of you settling into married life without a fight. The *ton* thinks I'm a blue-blooded hellion, but you're not any better. I remember the night we went to Madame Ranere's. We had a wager, remember? Which one of us could mount the most women in one night. You won. Six, wasn't it?"

"I was twenty-two. Mounting women was a way of life then."

"Hardwick. Can't say I recognize the name."

"Her father is Sir Warren Hardwick. He was knighted

for service after Crimea. Knows Fitch, by the way. They both served in the Eighth Hussars."

A long pause followed the short recital of Catherine's lineage. Granby knew Rathbone was trying to think of a way to congratulate him without making it sound like a death sentence. To the viscount's way of thinking, there were two kinds of women in the world. The kind you took to bed and the kind you took to wife—he preferred the first.

"You'll meet her at Waltham's regatta party. She's accompanying Lady Forbes-Hammond."

"That's not for another month. Until then you're a free man. Why not take advantage of it and come to Bath with me?"

Granby wondered how he could explain that he wasn't interested in bedding another woman without admitting that his feelings for Catherine went deeper than the viscount suspected. Having been caught in a compromising situation, duty demanded marriage. His friend could accept that duty, could equate it to the honorable thing to do, thus marriage. But not wanting to bed another woman? That was too close to actually being in love, and according to Rathbone's book of rules that was a man's ultimate downfall.

Granby didn't like contemplating the idea that a woman had rearranged his thinking for him, that a free-spirited female with the body of a goddess and the temper of a shrew had turned his life upside down. It certainly wasn't something he could admit to Rathbone.

"You're going to have to manage without me," he said. "I've work to do here."

"Work?" his friend said skeptically. "Are you sure? Sounds more like a retreat. Don't tell me you're actually enamored of the young lady. I've had enough shocks for one day."

*   *   *

While the earl was entertaining his friend at Foxleigh, his fiancée was having doubts. It was broad daylight and Catherine was sitting in her room, staring out the window.

She looked out at the world, at the green pastures and the lazy sway of the leaves, and wondered if she was seeing the image of her future life, a wife resigned to the country while her husband entertained himself elsewhere.

The last morning the earl had attended Stonebridge she had awakened with a resolve to put an end to the farce of their engagement, but instead she'd reaffirmed his claim by letting him make love to her in the meadow.

Instead of resisting him, she'd surrendered. And it had been wonderful. Then. Now, she wasn't so sure.

She wasn't so old-fashioned or limited in her thinking to demand marriage in exchange for her virginity. Both her father and Felicity would be shocked by her thoughts, but Catherine held firm to them. Enough time has passed for her to know pregnancy wasn't an issue. With that in mind, she reread the letter. *He* had written her, and although the majority of the words were benign, his inquiry into her health was a potent reminder that they had shared an intimacy meant only for wedlock.

Looking down at the crisp paper and the bold handwriting, Catherine suddenly felt an overpowering sense of loneliness.

She missed him.

Blast and damn the man for getting under her skin and into her heart. No matter how hard she tried to enjoy the remaining days of summer, he was always with her—lingering in the back of her mind, invading her dreams. The woman he had awakened in her was eager to repeat the experience, to once again know his touch, his embrace, and the searing pleasure that had left her lying exhausted in his arms. She missed his wicked smiles and the soft rumble of his laughter.

Catherine shut her eyes tightly, then opened them again. The world hadn't changed. The birds were still chirping, the trees still a green silhouette against a blue sky, the horses still grazing on sweet summer grass, and she was still lonely.

She considered taking a ride to Sudeley Castle, seeking out Emma Dent for an afternoon of conversation, but the idea held no real appeal. Felicity was in the downstairs parlor, but Catherine didn't want to spend the rest of the day discussing wedding plans or being scolded because she'd sent the seamstress away after a short fitting that would yield only three dresses, instead of six.

She wanted to free her mind, to be rid of doubtful thoughts and questioning shadows, but how? Knowing there would be no end to her hesitation until Granby looked her in the eye and stated his true feelings, Catherine left the windowseat and made her way downstairs. Perhaps some time in the stables would brighten her mood.

She was in the hallway when Gabs appeared at the top of the stairs.

"You have a caller," he informed her.

"Who?"

"Lady Dunvale."

"Sarah's here!" Excitement bubbled up inside her. It had been months since she'd seen her friend. "Have you shown her into the parlor?"

If Sarah was with Felicity, her aunt was sure to announce the engagement to Lord Granby, and Catherine wasn't sure she wanted anyone beyond Stonebridge to know just yet.

"I passed by the door and noticed that your aunt was dozing on the chaise. Not wanting to disturb her, I showed Lady Dunvale into the morning room."

"Excellent. Please have refreshments served."

Gabs nodded, then turned around and went back

downstairs. Catherine followed after taking a moment to compose herself. Once she reached the ground floor, she paused to look nervously in the mirror. It was silly to think that anyone could see a change in her. Felicity hadn't commented, and her aunt had eyes like a hawk.

Taking a deep breath and assuming a serene smile, Catherine opened the door to the morning room and stepped inside. The room was spacious and filled with summer light. Sarah was waiting, dressed in a smart blue suit and a cream-colored blouse that said the seamstress had been found in London, not in the small village of Farmcotte, where she now lived.

She left the sofa and hurried across the room to give Catherine a warm hug. "Oh, I've missed you."

"Why didn't you write and tell me you were coming?" Catherine asked, equally delighted to see her friend.

Sarah, a pretty brunette who had turned her share of heads during her London Season, took Catherine's hand and led her to the sofa.

"I didn't know until just a few days ago, and Silas's carriage moves faster than the post. He had business in Brockhampton and suggested that I might want to accompany him as far as Winchcombe, since he would be passing through the village. We arrived yesterday. He went on this morning, leaving me to visit with my parents until next week."

"It's good to see you. How are you getting along?"

"Better, I think." A tiny smile touched the corners of her mouth.

Before she could expand, Gabs rolled the tea caddy into the room. Once their cups were filled, and Sarah had selected a slice of lemon cake from the cart, Catherine urged her friend to tell her what had been happening in her life since their last visit.

"I am redecorating the house," Sarah announced proudly. There was a flush of color in her cheeks that

Catherine didn't understand at first. "Not all the rooms. I'm paying special attention to the nursery."

The hint was as subtle as a thunderstorm. Catherine laughed. "You're going to have a baby!"

"Yes. Near Christmas, I think. Silas is delighted, of course. He's hoping for a son, but I'm sure there will be other children if I disappoint him this time."

The required heir.

Apparently Sarah had either forgiven her husband's infidelity or chosen to ignore it. Catherine kept that thought to herself, not wanting to dampen her friend's mood. She did, however, allow herself the comment that a child shouldn't disappoint, no matter the gender.

"Yes, but I do so want to please him by giving him a son the first time," Sarah said, unconsciously allowing a hint of doubt to surface in her voice.

Catherine could tell Sarah believed that a child would bring about some miraculous change in her husband. Perhaps it would, though the odds were against it. Having already decided to pretend complete ignorance of the incident between Lord Dunvale and his parlor maid, Catherine kept a smile on her face, and congratulated Sarah on her upcoming motherhood.

"You can't imagine how different I feel, knowing there's going to be a baby. Mother was right in telling me that children are the true blessing of a marriage."

Catherine maintained her smile, all the while thinking that love should be the true blessing of a marriage. Sarah's attitude didn't surprise her. Her friend was merely doing what a lot of women did, accepting her lot in life.

"Have you heard from Veronica?" she asked. "I wrote, but there hasn't been a reply."

Sarah's smile faded. "Lord Curtley is as harsh as ever in his criticism, and poor Veronica is helpless to do anything about it. He even censors her mail. I called upon her last month, and she insists that she is adjusting. Her attention is focused on charity now. It's her one endeavor in which her husband hasn't found fault."

"I wish she could be happier," Catherine said, knowing she had no more control over Lord Curtley's heart than she did Lord Granby's.

She refused to compare herself to either of her friends, knowing she was stronger of mind than both of them.

Unfortunately, her mind hadn't been in control that day in the meadow. It had been her heart and her body, and both seemed inclined to forgot themselves when the earl was at hand.

"And what of you?" Sarah asked. "The village is abuzz with rumors about you and the Earl of Granby? Was he actually here at Stonebridge? I saw him in London during the winter. He's so dashingly handsome. I can't imagine having him sitting across the dinner table. I'd be all thumbs. How did you get on?"

"Well enough, I suppose," Catherine said with a slight smile. "We're engaged to be married."

"Married!" Sarah popped off the sofa as though she'd just sat on a pin cushion. "You're engaged to the Earl of Granby? Oh, my goodness. Do tell me all about it. How did he propose? On bended knee?"

Catherine had to laugh. "We met on the lane."

Sarah sat down, looking duly perplexed. "Don't tell me you met him while you were out riding. In your breeches!"

"I was wearing a riding habit," Catherine said. "At least I was the first time we met. And his lordship doesn't seem to mind my breeches. In fact, I think he likes them."

Sarah smiled a bit more openly. "Silas would have a fit were I to put on a pair of breeches. But then, I'm not as daring as you."

The question was just how much was she willing to dare? Could she risk her heart, and marry a man who had made no mention of love? And if she did, would she wake up one day to find herself in Veronica or Sarah's shoes? Dare she believe that two souls could be destined to meet, and with that meeting forge the foundations of love?

If not, then what had stirred between herself and Granby that morning in the meadow? Passion alone? Or a recognition that they did indeed *feel* something, one for another, something that encompassed their bodies and their hearts—something rare and beautiful and well worth the risk?

Seventeen

"You're brooding again," Felicity said as the coach rolled south along the coast road toward Ipswich.

"I'm not brooding, I'm thinking." Catherine's reply came with a smile, but it was a forced one. The closer she came to a reunion with her fiancé—her lover—the more apprehension seeped into her system.

He loves me. He loves me not.

The uncertainty was punishing.

"There's to be a ball tonight," Felicity informed her. "Lord Granby will officially announce your engagement."

"What if he doesn't?" Catherine asked much too eagerly. "What if he's changed his mind?"

"Gentlemen of Lord Granby's caliber do not *change* their minds about matters such as this. Your engagement will be announced, and you will dance the first waltz. May I suggest the gold gown. It really is lovely, and you should look your best."

For the first time since leaving Stonebridge, Catherine allowed her mask to drop, revealing her true concerns to Felicity's sharp eye. "I wish Father had come with us. Except for you, I shan't know a soul."

"You will make friends fast enough."

Catherine wasn't worried about making friends, she was worried about making the biggest mistake of her life—if she hadn't already made it by falling in love with one Norton Russell Foxhall.

By the time the coach stopped in front of Bedford Hall, Catherine's nerves had coiled so tightly she felt as though her entire body were made of knots. She told herself it was silly, there was no reason to be afraid of the earl, no reason to think that his feelings might have changed. And no reason to believe that she'd reconciled her own feelings. She was hopelessly in love with the man.

The footman opened the door of the coach. Felicity was handed down first. Catherine could hear well wishes and the customary greetings until it was her turn. Catherine was brought out of the coach to face a tall, dark-haired man with warm brown eyes.

She knew from the cut of his clothes and the confidence in his smile that she was looking at the Marquis of Waltham.

"Welcome to Bedford Hall, Miss Hardwick. May I introduce my wife, Lady Waltham."

The wife of the marquis was a lovely woman with light brown hair and blue eyes. Magnificently gowned in a rich blue satin day dress, she smiled at Catherine. "Welcome to our home, Miss Hardwick. I'm so pleased that you accepted our invitation."

"Thank you for inviting me." She looked up at the twin bell towers that fronted the east and west wings of the large manor house. "It's lovely."

"Come inside. I'm sure you're in need of some refreshments. The trip from Gloucestershire is not a short one."

"Two and a half days in a coach," Catherine said with a weary grimace. "I would very much like a cup of tea."

Felicity had told her that the majority of guests would

not be arriving until tomorrow. The festive week would
begin with a private ball, attended by family and close
friends of the marquis. The Earl of Granby was one of
those friends, which meant he had probably already arrived, or would be arriving within the next few hours.

He was nowhere in sight as Catherine followed her
aunt up the imposing steps of Bedford Hall and into
the manor house that sat snugly on the coastline of the
English Channel.

They were shown to their rooms; she and Felicity
would be sharing an adjoining suite, and Catherine
wondered if her aunt had tactfully requested the rooms
so as to prevent a reoccurrence of what she'd stumbled
upon that afternoon at Stonebridge.

The rest of the afternoon was spent unpacking—
Felicity's maid had traveled with them and would serve
as attendant to both ladies. Tea was served and baths
drawn. Felicity settled down for a nap, while Catherine
sat on a cushioned windowseat.

Wisely, the windows had not been shrouded with heavy
drapes, but with gauzy lace curtains that allowed the
natural beauty of the sea to fuse with the house, creating
a sedating influence upon the spirit that eased some of
Catherine's apprehension.

Beyond the open windows, incessant waves broke
onto the shore with foamy fingers that stretched high
onto the sandy beach only to retreat, then reach again.
The sound was as inspiring as the sight, as if God's own
hands were playing an instrument.

The symphony of sea and wind continued to soothe
Catherine's spirit. She found her mind drifting with the
current, moving from memories to the future, recalling
the last time she had seen Granby and looking forward,
with mixed feelings, to their next encounter.

As the afternoon progressed, the anticipation of seeing him grew. The sun moved closer to the horizon, but
it was hours away from setting, and still a strong force in

the sky, sending down rays of light and making the surface of the Channel glisten like topaz sateen. The soft colors of land and sea and sky invaded her senses, accented by the bright blues and gold that made up the room, and the muffled sounds of conversation from arriving guests and accommodating servants in the hallway.

Catherine heard each sound, saw each color, felt the brush of the wind upon her skin, and thought of the man she loved.

Soon, Felicity was awake and the bustle of preparing for the evening began. Mary was there, running between the two rooms in an efficient manner, demonstrating that the purpose of adjoining rooms had been practicality, and not chaperonage.

When both ladies were attired to the maid's satisfaction, Catherine linked her arm with Felicity's and began her tremulous trip downstairs. The guests had gathered in a large parlor in the east wing, the room offering doors that opened onto a large stone terrace. With her gold satin skirts swishing softly about her legs, Catherine stepped over the threshold and chaos followed.

"My God, Granby, don't tell me this is the chit."

The announcement came from the man standing beside her fiancé. From a distance, he might have been a duplication of the earl, a brother perhaps. Both men were blond, both had blue-gray eyes, and both were extremely handsome.

Catherine paused, instantly trapped by the earl's expression. It said he was happy to see her. When he stepped forward to claim her, his smile brightened along with the glint in his eye.

"You look beautiful," he said.

"My lord." It was all she could think to say. He was staring at her as if he wanted nothing more than to take her into his arms that very moment.

Granby controlled his baser impulses, though it wasn't

easy. Dressed in gold satin and white lace, Catherine was the most beautiful woman in the room. He glanced down, admiring the way the gown fit snugly over her breasts, but thinking at the same time that he'd prefer more fabric. There was too much of her creamy skin showing—bared shoulders and the gentle swell of her breasts, which he now knew were crowned with delicious coral nipples. The full skirt flared over her slender hips, fluttering fashionably to the floor.

He took her gloved hand and placed it on his arm, then looked at Felicity. "Thank you for bringing her to me."

"You're welcome," her aunt replied with a triumphant smile. "Take good care of her, my lord."

"I shall," he promised. "The very best of care."

Without giving Catherine a moment in which to think, Granby turned to faced the room with her on his arm. His fingers came to rest lightly upon her hand, holding her in place at his side.

"May I present Miss Catherine Hardwick, the lady who has graciously agreed to become my wife."

The room came alive with sounds of astonishment. The women all smiled, while the men looked at Catherine for a pensive moment, each eventually smiling in turn, but for a different reason.

Granby escorted her around the room, making the necessary introductions and accepting well wishes in return.

Catherine fought to stay focused, to listen to the names and match them with faces: Lord and Lady Kniveton, the marquis's mother and her second husband: the viscount Sterling and his lovely wife, Lady Sterling, followed by the earl of Ackerman, a brown-eyed man with the most welcoming smile of all. The Earl of Lansdowne and his wife, Lady Winnifred, sister to the marquis. And last but not least, Viscount Rathbone, who gave her a bold wink before bowing over her hand.

"Lovely, indeed," he said, looking at the earl.

Granby countered the remark by saying, "I'll permit you one dance this evening, but nothing more, Rathbone, so shake that look off your face. Miss Hardwick belongs to me."

"Might have known he'd turn into the jealous type," the viscount said, his gaze returning to Catherine.

Rathbone was a charmer of the worse sort, and enjoyed every minute of it, Catherine decided. The smooth tone of his voice, while teasing, warned of even stronger currents hidden underneath the formal black of his evening clothes. Unconsciously, she tightened her hold on Granby's arm. He answered with a movement that brought her closer to his protecting body.

"I admit not wanting to share her with anyone," Granby announced. "So be warned, Rathbone, or an early morning duel on the beach may be in order."

"I'm the better shot," the viscount challenged good-naturedly.

Catherine relaxed; it was easy to see that the two men shared not only a similarity in appearance but a solid friendship, as well.

"I wouldn't be so sure of that," the earl of Ackerman said, joining the conversation. "I've seen Granby use a pistol more than once. He's no novice. Remember that and mind your manners."

"My manners are impeccable," Rathbone retorted without a hint of regret. "Though they have been known to fail me when I find myself in the company of a beautiful woman."

"Then I shall take this beautiful woman beyond your reach," Granby said just as smoothly.

He led her across the room to where Felicity was chatting with her real niece, Lady Rebecca Sterling. "I will return you to Lady Forbes-Hammond. She will keep the wolves at bay."

"If that were the case, we would not be engaged to be married," Catherine said, finally finding her voice.

"Touché," Granby replied with a wicked smile. "I would very much like to be a wolf this evening. That dress makes you the most tempting of morsels, and I find myself extremely hungry."

The remark was made in a whispered voice meant only for her ears, and Catherine felt the blush of color that rose to her face. She'd almost forgotten how daring the man could be.

"A gentleman must learn to control his appetites, my lord, least they make him into a glutton."

"I've a long way to go before I get my fill of you, so be warned, Miss Hardwick. I know Bedford Hall as well as I know my own estates, and there are countless places in which a man can quench his appetites."

Granby wasn't warning her, he was plainly stating his intentions. He wanted her again, and as soon as possible. Instead of being shocked, Catherine was excited.

She decided to return his boldness with one of her own. "I saw no sunlit meadows, my lord, only sandy beaches and miles of coastline."

The little vixen was heating his blood with every word, and she knew it, damn her beautiful hide. The delicate gold gown she was wearing was feminine yet seductive in its cut, missing the high neckline that usually hid a lady's charms. The skirt was full, but not overly so, and the insets of filmy white lace left little doubt as to the exquisite curves suggested by its regal design.

"Miles and miles of coastline," he said, his eyes growing darker with each word. "I can think of one particular stretch of sand where the Channel has hollowed out a small cove. A very isolated place, especially when the moon is shining."

"I shall enjoy seeing it," she said in a silky tone. "Perhaps before I return to Winchcombe."

"Of that, you can be guaranteed."

The smooth quality of his voice flowed over Catherine's skin like a lover's caress. She felt her nipples harden under the fabric of her silk chemise, and wondered if she'd be able to keep up the cat and mouse game for an entire week. The odds were against it.

Truth be told, she was just as hungry as the earl, just as eager for them to be alone, and just as ravenous for a kiss. Wanting to tease him as much as he was teasing her, she met his gaze and gently licked her lips.

"Back to Felicity with you," he said with a soft groan. "And behave yourself. I'm not made of stone."

He excused himself with a hot glance and a graceful bow before returning to the small cluster of men who had gathered near the mantelpiece, drinks in hand.

There was more casual conversation as Catherine became acquainted with the ladies in the room, each eager to hear of the upcoming wedding plans. She withstood the avalanche of good wishes with a smile, all the while conscious of the earl's gaze from across the room.

Things weren't turning out the way she'd expected. There was no gentlemanly attitude, no reserve of emotion. His actions and words were just as arousing in a room full of people as they'd been each and every day in Gloucestershire. It was going to be a long week.

A long, exciting week.

The bell for dinner was chimed by a stern-faced footman, and the ladies and gentlemen paired off. Catherine found herself being escorted into a huge dining room on the arm of the Earl of Ackerman. He was darker in coloring than his friends, but there was a banked heat in his gaze that said he was no less the rogue when it suited his purpose. Tonight, he was charming and good-natured and remarkably easy to talk to, considering they had only just met.

"My congratulations to both you and Granby," he

said. "Had I known there were such lovely ladies hiding in the quaint village of Winchcombe, I would have visited myself."

She was seated across the table from Viscount Sterling, with Lady Lansdowne to her left and Lord Kniveton to her right. The dinner conversation was lively and entertaining, and Catherine soon found herself relaxing and enjoying the food, which was some of the most delicious she'd ever tasted.

Dessert was being served when Rathbone tapped on the rim of his plate with the end of his dessert fork, then rose to his feet. Wineglass in hand, he looked first at the earl, then at Catherine. "May your marriage bring you happiness."

It wasn't the sort of toast she'd expected from the roguish viscount, but there had been sincerity in his voice, and Catherine found herself hoping it held a degree of prophecy, too.

Unbeknownst to the earl, he had a week to convince his fiancée that she was loved.

If not . . . Catherine would cross that bridge when she came to it. Until then, she'd enjoy herself and get to know the man she was engaged to marry. They had become lovers, but she knew little about him in the way of those casual, seemingly insignificant things that brought two people closer, the things that existed only in friendship and shared respect.

They had an entire week, but regardless of Granby's passionate plans, Catherine knew Felicity took her chaperonage very seriously. They'd find little time alone, if any.

After dinner, the men retired for cigars and brandy, while the ladies sought their refuge in the drawing room. The dancing would begin soon, in the large ballroom on the second floor.

"A September wedding—that's not very far away," Lady Kniveton commented as she poured Felicity a customary evening sherry. "It's been ages since I was in Gloucestershire."

"It's to be a small wedding, at Catherine's request," Felicity replied. "An ivory gown that will bring tears to the eye. Lovely. Absolutely lovely."

"I can't remember my wedding," Rebecca Sterling confessed with a bright smile. "I was so nervous I was sure I'd fall flat on my face before I reached the altar. Thank goodness for my father's strong arm. I'm sure you'll be far more surefooted, Miss Hardwick."

"Please, call me Catherine," she said, not wanting to think of a wedding that might not take place. No matter how easily Granby melted her physical resolve, her heart and mind were set on being loved.

"Then you must call me Rebecca in return. Come morning, I shall introduce you to my son, Morgan. He's an adorable toddler, who has inherited his father's good looks and sense of mischief."

"Miss Hardwick isn't the only one to have good news this evening," Lady Waltham said, reaching for her mother-in-law's hand. "I'm to have a child."

The room exploded with good wishes and teary congratulations as Lady Waltham sat on the settee, gowned in plum silk and glowing with happiness.

"I had to tell Marshall three times before he could comprehend it," she said laughingly. "He just kept staring at me as if I'd popped out of a colored bottle like a genie."

"He'll understand soon enough," Rebecca assured her. "I got so round I began to think people would mistake me for a ball."

"And your husband loved you all the more for it," Felicity said with her usual confidence. "Though I do believe he wore a hole in the carpet, pacing the room until he was told he had a son. Men have no patience for childbirth."

The conversation ended as the doors to the drawing room opened and the gentlemen joined them again.

Catherine drew in a quick breath as she met Granby's gaze. He strolled across the room and offered her his arm. "I have come to claim my waltz."

The way he said it led Catherine to believe that he was claiming much more. She glanced around to see the viscount Rathbone looking at them, his gaze unreadable.

"The music hasn't started yet," she said, keeping her voice low.

"It will, soon enough."

They made their way to the ballroom, where a small group of musicians had just finished tuning their instruments. It was a warm summer evening and the doors to the balcony were open, making the most of an offshore breeze.

At the first notes of the waltz, Granby drew her into his arms and whirled her away from the small crowd. He waltzed like he did everything else—confidently and gracefully. With his hand at her waist, Catherine felt his power. It grew as they circled the ballroom, his gaze intense as the music ebbed and flowed like the swelling tide beyond the open doors.

"I've missed you," he said, smiling down at her. "Did you bring your breeches?"

"No," she laughed, unable to resist the power of the moment—the potency of the man. "Felicity's maid packed my trunk. Breeches were strictly forbidden."

"A riding habit, then." He turned her expertly, and she flowed to match his movements, the skirt of her gown billowing out like a gold wave.

"Yes," she answered breathlessly, unaware that other dancers had joined them on the floor. All Catherine could see were the blue depths of Granby's mesmerizing eyes.

"Excellent. If memory serves, there is still a race to be run. Shall we say just before dawn? The tide will be out, and the sand makes an excellent course."

"Felicity won't like it," Catherine said, knowing she'd risk anything to find a way out of the house and onto the beach—back into the earl's arms.

"The servant's door in the east wing will take you outside and onto a path. Follow it to the beach," he said, then added, "I want to kiss you. Do you think Felicity will have my head if I do?"

"On a platter."

"Some things are worth the risk," he said, echoing her very thoughts. His voice dropped to a seductive whisper as he pulled her close for one last turn. "Before the night is over."

The music ended on the earl's wicked promise, leaving Catherine breathless and filled with anticipation. For a perilous moment it looked as if he might kiss her in front of the assembled guests. When he stepped back, sweeping her an elegant bow instead, Catherine breathed a sigh of relief.

She was quickly snatched up by Lord Waltham, using his rank as host to claim the next dance. One tall, handsome man was replaced by another and then another, until Catherine found herself dancing with the viscount Rathbone.

"I didn't believe it when Granby told me he was going to marry," he said, swirling her in perfect time to the music. "Then you walked into the room and I knew it was true. Are you certain you wouldn't rather marry me?"

"You! Do you think me mad?" Catherine bantered back at him, thoroughly enjoying herself.

"You wound me, Miss Hardwick," he said, his smile so charming Catherine could easily understand how he'd come by his reputation as one of London's most notorious rakes.

"Not as much as a well-aimed bullet would," she replied. "You were warned to behave yourself."

"Ah, so I was. My only excuse is that your beauty has muddled my mind."

She laughed and the sound of it make Granby's heart clench in his chest. He knew Rathbone was flirting, and he tried hard not to let his friend's natural inclinations cause trouble, but he didn't want Catherine smiling at another man, dancing with another man, laughing with another man.

She was his. Only his.

The obsession was as shocking to Granby as the realization that he may indeed have fallen victim to the elusive, inexplicable emotion of love.

He looked around the room. Waltham was dancing with his wife, as was Sterling. Both men looked content. No. More than content—genuinely happy with themselves and the ladies in their arms. He averted his glance to a nearby mirror and gave himself a quick look-see. Did he look at Catherine the same way as Waltham looked at Evelyn? As Sterling looked at his lovely Rebecca?

Was the evidence of his affection that unadorned, that obvious, written on his face for all the world to see?

And what of Catherine? Was that love glowing in her eyes when she looked at him, or only the desire he'd brought to the surface? Desire, and her own natural boldness.

But most of all he wondered, did he want to be loved?

"You look as if you could use this," Rathbone said, putting a champagne glass into his hand. "Turning a bit pale around the gills, if you ask me."

"I'm not asking," Granby said before taking a sturdy sip of champagne.

"I know what you're thinking."

"What?"

"It's a big house with lots of cozy hiding places. If only you could get Miss Hardwick out of the ballroom and into one."

"The thought crossed my mind."

"I knew it. Shall I help? Let's see, a short diversion for the aunt, then a quick getaway."

Granby laughed. "On occasion, we do think alike."

"Excellent, the next waltz then. Watch for my signal, then out the door with you. There's a nice stand of ferns at the end of the terrace should you care to use them to disguise your unsavory behavior."

"I'll be sure to return the favor one day," Granby said, handing his empty champagne glass to a passing footman.

When the moment arrived, Catherine's capture was expertly executed.

"But . . ."

Before she could form the next word, Granby was tugging her to the far end of the terrace, pulling her behind a stand of ferns, gently easing her back against the wall, and kissing her.

The kiss was every bit as hungry as Catherine expected it to be, and every bit as satisfying. The second his lips settled on hers, his tongue darted deep into her mouth to taste and tease and satisfy.

He moved against her, pinning her to the wall with the hard pressure of his hips. Catherine felt the beginnings of pleasure, the wave of intoxicating desire that came with each gentle thrust of his tongue. The kiss went on and on, his body moving against her in a suggestive dance that was far more erotic than any waltz.

"The moment Felicity is asleep, come downstairs. I'll be waiting on the beach. We'll take a moonlight ride," he said, before kissing her again.

Catherine didn't agree to the meeting. She didn't have to. Her eyes gleamed the answer at him as he pulled back, smiled, then took her hand and tugged her to the French doors. A second later, she was back in his arms, being swirled across the ballroom floor as if the kiss had never happened.

But it had.

The moment Felicity is asleep.

Catherine looked at her aunt, wide-eyed and well

rested from an afternoon nap. It would be hours before she'd be free to sneak downstairs for a moonlight ride on the beach.

While Catherine was plotting her escape from the house, Granby hoped she wouldn't shy away from the surprise he had planned for her. If he did what he'd been thinking of doing, had made preparations to do, that part of his worries would be in the past, leaving only the future with Catherine as his wife.

After relinquishing his fiancée to Lord Kniveton and a country reel, he walked across the ballroom to where the Earl of Ackerman and Viscount Sterling were in conversation. Patting the pocket of his jacket, Granby gave Fitch a look that said the daring plan had been set into motion.

Eighteen

A clock, hidden in the dark depths of the house, chimed twice. Two o'clock in the morning and she was reaching for the door, opening it, feeling the chill of the night air against her face. Catherine didn't stop to consider the consequences of her actions. It went without saying that she shouldn't be doing what she was doing, thinking what she was thinking, wanting what she was wanting.

She closed the door, holding her breath until the latch fell with a soft click. Looking around she saw nothing but the featureless darkness of the night, the glow of the moon silhouetting the trees of the eastern garden, and the white stones that led away from the house toward the beach.

When she reached the path that sloped down to the sea, she stopped and looked out over the Channel. The water that had been a breathtaking blue earlier in the day now rolled silver and gray onto the waiting shore. The roar of the waves seemed louder than before, closer, more dangerous, and Catherine knew she would embrace that danger.

In all the days that she'd had to think, to ponder her

feelings and to wonder at Granby's, she had never felt a moment's peace. Now, standing on the edge of the beach in a white summer dress meant for picnics and lawn games, she felt the peace she'd been searching for.

The moonlight washed down upon her, and she knew with a certainty of heart and mind that life wasn't a long journey, but small accumulating moments that combined to form the patterns of a person's life just as small droplets of water joined to create the vast oceans of the world.

The most eventful moments came when one least expected them, directing a person to turn left or right, to stand still with acceptance or forge ahead with adventure. The moments could be claimed or ignored, disastrous or wonderful, passionate or sorrowful, monumental or unnoticed; thus life seemed to pass one person by while turning another person's existence upside down.

The moment she had met the Earl of Granby had been such a moment, and it couldn't be erased.

The days she had spent worrying and thinking had not been spent on indecision, but had grown into now— this night.

The path wasn't steep, but long and sloping, the sand packed hard after years of use. Catherine stopped once to look back at Bedford Hall, its windows dark, its occupants in their beds, all but two—two lovers bound for a midnight ride.

She was standing at the water's edge, looking like some mythical creature cast from the sea by Poseidon's hand when Granby saw her. He stopped to savor the sight, thinking he'd never seen a more sensual woman. The wind tugged at her hair and clothing, molding the gauzy cloth to her body as the waves washed over her bare feet.

The sound of his approach was lost in the churning of the water, but Catherine sensed his presence, sensed it as surely as she sensed she belonged to this man—not legally, that was still to be determined, but emotionally and spiritually. She was his, and whether he knew it or not, he was hers.

Her first love. Her first lover.

"They're not twins, but they're evenly matched," he said, handing her a set of reins.

She looked at the horses he'd led down to the beach. One was a dark bay with a white star, the other a black gelding. She looked over each horse with a discerning eye, then smiled.

"Do you have a finish line in mind?" she asked as she stroked her hand down the length of the bay's wide muzzle.

"An outcropping of rocks that will block our path a mile or so down the beach," he told her. "Can you ride without boots?"

"All I need is a horse and a saddle."

"Then up you go."

He helped her to mount, thinking she was the most daring young woman he'd ever met. With her dress hitched up to accommodate riding astride, he could see a good portion of her long legs, but not nearly as much as he was going to see after the race. Running his hand from her heel to the bend of her knee, he smiled and said. "What shall we wager? And don't say Storm Dancer, or I will thrash you this time."

"What do I have that you want?" she asked innocently.

His fingers moved from her knee, trailing upward under the hem of her dress to gently massage her thigh.

"I'll think of something when the time comes."

"And what if I win, my lord? What will you forfeit?"

His hand moved higher to discover that she wasn't wearing anything under the white dress but a thin chemise. God help him, he'd be lucky to sit a saddle for a whole mile.

"Want do I have that interests you, Miss Hardwick?"

What Catherine wanted most was for this man to love her, but she couldn't capture his heart with a horse race. It had to be given freely. She could ask that their engagement be set aside, but again, she hesitated. Tonight wasn't about horsemanship or winning, it was one of those *moments,* and she dare not let it slip away.

"When the time comes, I'm sure I'll be able to think of something," she replied, not so innocently this time.

"To the victor goes the spoils," he said, slowly withdrawing his hand.

Granby's breathing was heavy with anticipation as he mounted the other horse and nudged him forward until the two animals were side by side. The warmth of the night mixed with the sound and scent of the sea to heighten each and every one of his senses.

He began to imagine what else the night would bring—victory, sweet and unhurried, a satisfaction he hadn't felt since the last time he'd made love to Catherine.

A simple count of three sent them racing down the beach, their horses' hooves kicking up clumps of wet sand. Catherine tried to concentrate on the animal moving beneath her, its long strides and straining muscles; she was a natural competitor no matter the circumstances, and she wanted to win.

Moonlight illuminated the sand like a silver sun. Water splashed as she sent her mount galloping through the surf.

The earl's horse matched hers stride for stride as they raced through the night. There were no trees or hurdles, nothing but open beach and the exhilaration of their own heartbeats.

"The rocks are just ahead," he called out to her. "Be ready."

Catherine saw them moments later, looming out of the darkness like a beached ship. She gauged the distance and urged her horse forward.

Granby's heart lodged in his throat when it appeared

as if Catherine was going to try to jump the rocks. He shouted, warning her to pull back, but she paid him no mind. He reined in his mount just short of the boulders, but not close enough to win. Catherine charged on, turning her horse at the last possible moment and sending him crashing into the surf.

Both horse and rider got a good drenching.

When his heart started beating again, Granby dismounted and ran toward the water. "My God, woman, are you completely mad! You could have been killed."

Catherine dismounted into the knee-deep surf. "I won!"

"You've turned my hair gray, that's what you've done," he shouted as he waded in after her. Realizing that threats were useless where this woman was concerned, he pulled her into his arms and kissed her until she was clinging to him.

"I should give you a thrashing," he threatened when the kiss ended. "You're as wild as a mink."

"I feel more like a fish," she said, looking down at her dress.

Granby did some looking of his own. After being soaked by the sea, she might as well be wearing nothing but the smile on her face. The wet fabric was clinging to every curve of her body, outlining bud-hard nipples and the soft indentation of her navel.

Taking her hand he pulled her from the water. "I know the perfect place to get dry."

Catherine looked around her. All she could see was water and sky, shimmering moonlight and churning waves.

"Waltham has a cottage just up the beach," he said, lifting her back into the saddle. "It's small and cozy."

They rode, neither saying a word. The time for words had passed. They both knew what they wanted.

When they reached the cottage, Granby dismounted, then helped Catherine to do the same. Once she was on the ground, he pulled her into his arms and gave her another rapacious kiss.

Still holding on to her, he said, "There are people in the cottage."

"Who?" She looked over her shoulder at the closed door. There was no sign of light or life.

"The Earl of Ackerman, Peck, my valet, and John Greenmore, a magistrate from Ipswich. I acquired a special license before I left Reading. Fitch and Peck will stand as our witnesses. We're going to be married tonight."

"Married! Tonight!" Catherine tried to back away, but he refused to let her go. "I can't marry you tonight. I'm soaking wet, and . . . and I'm not even wearing a petticoat. What will people think? And Felicity, she'll—"

"You agreed to marry me," he reminded her. "If you want a lavish wedding, we can repeat the ceremony in September."

"Why?" She finally managed to step away, but only because he let her.

"Why not?"

Catherine licked her lips and tasted sea salt. She looked down at her dress, then lower to her bare feet. Her toes were covered with sand and her hair was a mass of wind-tossed curls.

"I'm barefoot." It was the only thing she could think to say.

"You'll be wearing even less before too long," Granby said, taking her arm and shepparding her toward the door. "You've plagued me with your unconventionality since the moment I met you, why worry about it now?"

"Because I wasn't marrying you then," she said, dragging her feet. She stubbed her toe. "Ouch!"

Thinking it the perfect excuse, and knowing he wouldn't be carrying her over the threshold after the ceremony—they would spend their wedding night in the cottage—Granby picked her up and walked toward the door.

Fitch opened it and heralded them into the room with a perfectly executed bow.

"Welcome," he said, signaling for Peck to light the candles.

"Put me down," Catherine demanded.

Granby did, but not until they were across the room and both Fitch and Peck had taken up their posts in front of the door.

She was trapped.

"Mr. Greenmore, may I present the bride, Miss Catherine Hardwick."

Catherine turned around to find a tall man wearing his nightshirt under a coarse black coat. Under different circumstances the idea of a half-dressed, sleepy-eyed magistrate marrying a wet, barefoot bride to a peer of the realm would be laughable. But she wasn't laughing.

"Miss Hardwick," magistrate Greenmore said, then yawned. "My lord, if you'll present the license, I'll begin the ceremony."

Granby produced the required document from the pocket of his coat and handed it to the magistrate.

"I . . . I'd like to brush my hair first." She needed a moment to think. She'd been in a sensual haze since stepping out of the house, but this was reality, and a wedding was a very serious thing.

Suspecting his bride might climb out a window if given the chance, Granby told her she was beautiful wearing salt water and sand. He drew her to his side.

With Granby's arm securely around her waist, Catherine found herself facing the magistrate. He opened a small black leather-bound book and the wedding began.

Granby spoke his vows first, his voice deep, his words evenly paced. When it was her turn, Catherine took a quick breath and prayed that her heart wasn't leading her down the wrong path.

The Earl of Ackerman stepped forward to drop an emerald-and-diamond wedding ring into Granby's open palm. He slipped it on Catherine's finger.

The magistrate finished his duty with the words, "You may kiss your bride, my lord."

Catherine recovered from her trancelike state when Granby turned her to face him. Even though he'd kissed her on the terrace, and on the beach, and again just outside the cottage door, this would be their first kiss as man and wife.

It was neither chaste nor ravenous, but somewhere in between, just long enough to make her toes start to curl.

When it ended, Catherine blinked back tears.

She was a hopeless romantic, so much in love with this man she'd just put her life in his hands.

Managing a smile, she accepted the magistrate's congratulations, followed by Peck's. When the Earl of Ackerman stepped in front of her, Catherine tried to act as if she always went about with bare feet and a wet dress. Thankfully, the cottage was dimly lit, and the earl gentlemanly enough to pretend he didn't notice her untidy state.

"May I again wish you all happiness," Ackerman said, smiling at her. "I have to admit enjoying this wedding more than most. It isn't every night that I'm asked to roust a magistrate from his bed." He leaned down and kissed her on the cheek. "Be happy, my lady."

Unsure how to proceed, Catherine waited while her husband—it was going to take time to absorb that fact—said his good-byes to Mr. Greenmore, Peck, and his friend, Fitch.

He turned to her then, and Catherine immediately recognized the gleam in his eye. She knew that look, knew what it meant and what her husband had in mind—a wedding night.

Were they to spend it here, in the cottage?

"Peck isn't a lady's maid, but he has endeavored to anticipate your needs," her husband said. "I believe you will find a hot bath waiting just beyond that door. Shall I join you, or would you prefer some time to yourself?"

"I can manage."

She hesitated just long enough for Granby to take her in his arms. Shockingly aware that he was now her husband, Catherine tried to keep her wits about her as his mouth came down on hers.

There was nothing chaste about their second kiss as man and wife. He took his time, leisurely seducing her mouth with his tongue. His hands moved from her waist to her hips to pull her close.

"I really do want to brush my hair," she said, pulling back before he could begin their wedding night.

"Very well. I'll keep myself busy with a brandy." He released her and stepped back, but there was no mistaking the desire in his eyes or the impatience in his voice. He was her husband now, and he intended to act accordingly.

Once opened, the door revealed a bedroom with a large double bed and a thick rag rug centered on the dark wooden floor. Candlelight flickered, revealing that the coverlet had been turned down and the pillows fluffed. A large hip bath sat on the far side of the room, the water steaming. Catherine looked at the bed again and noticed that a white nightgown was neatly folded and waiting for her.

She walked around the room, stopping to open the closet door. The capable valet had also provided a change of clothes for the morning, one of her own dresses. How they had gotten to the cottage was the least of Catherine's problems.

She'd shut the bedroom door behind her, but it lacked a lock, which meant she'd have to hurry or Granby would find her in the tub. The thought gave Catherine a moment's pause at the same time it brought a blush to her face. What was wrong with her? It wasn't as if she were still a virgin. She knew what was going to happen when Granby walked through the door.

Or did she?

She crossed the floor to get the nightgown, and stopped in front of an oval cheval glass. Standing before the mirror, Catherine ran her fingers through her hair and let it fall to her shoulders. Her husband had told her she was beautiful. Am I? she wondered. All she saw was a woman who was unfashionably tall and too broad at the hips and shoulders, with a nose that wasn't nearly as small and pert as it should be, a mass of hair that wasn't soft and blond and flowing, but cinnamon red and tangled as if it hadn't seen a brush in days.

She unbuttoned her dress and let it fall to the floor. Her gaze fell to the ring the earl had slipped on her finger. It was a wide gold band, encrusted with emeralds and diamonds. The stones twinkled as if God had put a star inside each one.

It was tempting to imagine that her heart's desire would come to be as easily as their marriage had taken place, that her husband would walk through the door, look at her, and say the words she longed to hear. It was tempting to think that marriage begat love. It sounded simple, even logical, but Catherine was old enough to know that life and logic rarely shared the same bed.

Still, Granby had arranged the wedding. No one had forced him to procure a special license. And, despite the oddity, the ceremony had had its romantic side. That in itself was enough to give her hope.

* * *

She was in the tub, rubbing a soapy cloth up and down her arms, when the door opened. There was nothing to do but stare at the man who was now her legal husband. He'd shed his jacket, and unbuttoned his shirt until it gapped into a wide vee.

The bride felt awkward, and to her bewilderment, unsure what to say or do.

"You are beautiful." He spoke very quietly, as if any tone louder than a whisper might shatter their marriage vows.

He smiled then—a soft smile that was genuine and totally disarming. She had put that smile there and the realization of it made Catherine's heart leap with happiness.

He set the glass he held on the dresser, next to the brush she had used to smooth the tangles from her hair, before pinning it into a hasty knot to keep it from getting wet again when she bathed. Then he was kneeling beside the tub, his face level with hers.

She looked into his eyes, gentle in the dim candlelight. His gaze was as disarming as his smile had been. She could feel the tension of the moment, and the vitality. She inhaled and breathed in the subtle scent of him, dangerously male and potent.

Catherine shivered with delight when he reached out to cradle her breasts, cupping their weight, his thumbs lightly flickering against her nipples.

"Your skin is as soft as a rose petal," he told her. "And your nipples . . . I've never seen such beautiful nipples. I want to suckle them like a hungry babe."

It was an unusual compliment, and it brought an unusual blush to her face. Catherine closed her eyes against the effect it was having on her, and heard a soft laugh.

"I've never met anyone like you—a woman so passionate, so direct and honest, so completely without guile, and yet you're blushing from head to toe. You fascinate me. You intrigue me. I want to discover all your secrets."

"A naked woman doesn't have any secrets," she said, opening her eyes, then wishing she hadn't. His gaze had darkened and his expression had grown serious, as if he wished he hadn't confessed that she captivated him.

His fingers caressed her neck, from the slope of her damp shoulder to the lobe of her right ear. "I want you."

The words were simple and direct, filling her with fire.

Catherine watched him watching her, and felt another rush of uncertainty. She struggled against the knowledge that she was married to this man, that he could engulf her mind and body and heart with a single glance, that he could and would, from this night forward, be an irrevocable part of her life.

"Stand up," he said, moving back a step.

Slowly, Catherine stood up. Water sheeted off her skin, running down her smooth belly, over her hips, and down her ivory thighs. It gathered in moist pearls in the patch of hair between her legs, and Granby prayed he'd have the strength to wait until she was dry and fully aroused, that he wouldn't hoist her from the tub and make love to her on the wooden floor like an impatient lad who'd never had a woman.

"Look at you," he said before he could stop himself. "My God, you're lovely."

The power of his gaze was mesmerizing, and her own gaze averted, down to the water that covered only her feet and ankles now. Then he was there, touching her, wrapping her in a soft Turkish towel and lifting her free of the brass tub.

He began to dry her, the pressure of his hands gently

persuasive and expertly enticing, sending tremors throughout her body. Then she was on the bed, lying on her back, looking up at him, and his hands were everywhere—upon her shoulders and arms, her breasts and belly, sliding along her thighs. It was frightening and erotic . . . against the shadows of the room, against the muffled sound of the sea, neither right nor wrong, it added to the confusion of the night.

"Norton."

The sound of his name was all the encouragement Granby needed. He tossed the towel aside and looked down at her—his wife—lying naked on a cotton coverlet, her hair a tangled mass of cinnamon curls, her breasts tipped in coral, her belly flat and quivering as she tried to control the desire surging through her body. God, she was beautiful. Beautiful and wild and finally his, all his.

There was more to it than that, Granby was convinced, but now wasn't the time to contemplate the inner depths of his feelings. Right now, all he wanted to think about was having his wife—his *wife!* The word should form awkwardly in his mind, but it didn't. It flowed, the same way his desire was flowing, hot and heavy in his veins.

Catherine had been created for passion; her entire body was womanly perfection, sweetly lush, with wonderful, firm breasts, her legs long and shapely and strong enough to hold a man in place while he rode her.

A button popped from his shirt and skidded across the floor in his haste to be as naked as she was, to be completely free of all restraints. She watched as he shed each piece of clothing, watched with gleaming hazel eyes. When he was completely naked, she licked her lips, and he thought he'd lose control then and there.

He joined her on the bed, pulling her into his arms, crushing her to him. He kissed her deeply, her cheek, behind her ear, her throat. He cupped her breasts in the palms of his hand and suckled her nipples until she called out his name again.

"Please, stop." She needed to catch her breath, to gain some control over herself.

But he didn't stop. As the candles flickered, casting a soft glow over her skin, he kept on stroking her bare breasts, licking the erect nipples until they ached. Then he was stroking the rest of her, his fingers moving down the plane of her belly to the junction of her legs, combing through the curls he found there and touching that special place.

He was skilled. He knew just where to touch, how much pressure to use to make her feel weak with need. He pushed one finger and then another inside her, stroking her until her breath quickened, until she was writhing against him.

Entranced by desire, Catherine relished the all-consuming fire he had started inside her. She needed the friction of his skin against her, his touch inside her.

And then he took his hand away.

"No, don't stop," she protested, opening her eyes.

"Ssshh," he said, silencing her words with a kiss. Hard and aching, he slipped inside her, and her eyes drifted closed.

"No, look at me," he said. "Don't be afraid to see me, to see us."

Something warm and tingling caused her heart to skip a beat as the fervor of his words touched her. His eyes were dark and dusky, his face set hard. He pushed deeper into her body, and she arched up, taking him greedily.

"Yes. That's it. Slow and easy." His thumbs returned to her breasts, to rub lightly over her nipples. She flinched, inside and out. "God, yes. Use those lovely muscles to squeeze me, to keep me inside you. Don't let me go."

The words were whispered into her ear, then his mouth

was there, kissing, his tongue darting out to trace, and create new shivers. She moved with him in the ensuing silence, her hands upon his shoulders, her legs wrapped around his hips as he pushed and retreated, only to return in a smooth downward stroke that filled her completely.

Just as easily as he filled her, he left her. Her sound of protest was met with light laughter. "Don't be greedy," he said, smiling.

He dipped his head and kissed her, the tip of his tongue flicking over her parted lips. He played with her senses, spreading light kisses over her face, then her breasts, then her belly. When his tongue outlined her navel, she shivered with pleasure.

"Are you cold?" he asked, his voice laced with teasing mockery as he returned to the plane of her stomach and repeated the caress. "You don't feel cold," he breathed against her skin.

No, she wasn't cold. She was burning up, her body aching with need, and still he teased her. He stroked the length of her torso with his open hands, down to her waist and up again to cup her breasts, then down again. Hands under her hips, he lifted her high and she closed her eyes, flushing with embarrassment that he was looking at her so intimately. But that wasn't all he was doing. The first touch of his mouth made her gasp in surprise, and the second brought a soft moan.

Her fingers found the bedsheet and knotted into it. She tried not to think of what he was doing, tried not to be shocked that a man would touch a woman in such a way. Then she couldn't think at all. His tongue laved and probed, stroked and dipped inside her, making her burn anew.

He released her, but not until tiny waves of ecstasy had set her to floating, drifting in the wonder that a man's mouth could be so talented—so wickedly talented.

When she opened her eyes again, he was still there, hovering over her like a handsome shadow, his eyes dark with passion. "You taste like wild honey," he whispered. "Here, let me show you."

He kissed her deeply, and Catherine could taste the musky flavor of herself on his lips and tongue. He crawled over her and thrust deep, joining them once again. She shuddered when the power of his body enveloped hers. Fierce. Wonderful. Primitive. He moved like a tempest, coming into her. Nothing was slow now— his thrusts were deep and powerful, meant to dominate, to claim, to conquer.

Catherine matched the pace, wanting the same thing he wanted, needing it until her body glistened with sweat and her hair lay damply against her temples.

On and on the tempest raged.

They moved in unison, driving toward another crest of fulfillment. He would join her this time, take his pleasure as he pleased her.

Catherine wanted to cry out her love for him, but she bit into her lower lip and kept the words inside, suddenly afraid of the depth of her feelings, fearful that they would make her a slave to this man—her husband. She mustn't give all of herself; not yet, not until she knew he was willing to expand their marriage beyond the bedroom.

His threaded his fingers into her hair and pulled her head back, arching her against the pillow as his lips traveled downward to the pulse at her throat. He pushed hard and deep and she felt him at the mouth of her womb.

"Now," he said, the word little more than a grunt as the muscles in his body tightened and he filled her with honeyed warmth.

Their eyes met in that final moment, that melting of bodies and spirits that is the ultimate reward of passion.

A few minutes later, Catherine could still feel the

heat of his body, sleek and powerfully muscular, relaxed now as he wrapped an arm around her and pulled her close, her bottom pressing against his hips. He was as silent as she, his breathing deep and even, now that the tempest has passed.

She thought that he might be sleeping, but she wasn't certain. She turned slightly, and his arm tightened, his hand resting beneath her breast. She smiled, then snuggled closer.

"Catherine."

She responded with a groggy sound, almost asleep herself. A wedding night was an exhausting thing, she thought as her eyes finally closed.

They opened again two hours later. Confused at first, then remembering where she was and why, Catherine looked at the pale light pushing in through the closed shutters. It was dawn, rising slow and pinkish white over the Channel. She had fallen asleep in her husband's arms, soundly exhausted and comfortably secure. A short second later, she felt an even greater comfort, his arms coming around her and the soft pressure of his palms as they covered her bare breasts.

A whisper brushed against her ear. "Good morning, my lady."

"It's not yet dawn," she said, thinking she should dress and return to the house before Felicity awakened.

There was going to be hell to pay—the earl had cheated her aunt out of a grand wedding, and Lady Forbes-Hammond was not going to take that lightly.

As for the rest of the household, Catherine dared not think what everyone would be saying—a wedding in the middle of the night, the newlyweds cloistered in a tiny cottage at the edge of the beach. It was all highly improper, and just romantic enough to evoke all sorts of jaded comments.

"The time doesn't matter," he said, moving a hand over her buttocks, then between her thighs. The caress started out smooth and gentle, then deepened as their passion ignited.

Would it always be like this, this hunger between them? Right or wrong, Catherine couldn't deny it. Shivering, but from growing heat, not cold, she moved against him.

She wanted him, but Granby wanted her more. He craved the sweetness of her body, the soft moans he drew with each gentle probing of his fingers.

Catherine started to speak, but it turned into a gasp as he slipped into her from behind, his hard length filling her in one smooth, erotic stroke. She came fully awake.

"Easy," he whispered, but there was nothing easy about the sensations that erupted inside her.

The rasp of his tongue against the sensitive skin at the back of her neck sent a bolt of desire through her, tightening her core, and producing a spasm in her womb.

"You're a fast learner," he said, rolling her onto her stomach. "Raise your hips. That's right. Perfect. Don't move."

He leaned into her, pressing her knees apart with his legs, filling her more deeply than Catherine thought possible. His hands came around her and lifted the fullness of her breasts, kneading them with his palms and then pinching the pebbled tips with his fingers.

Granby could feel the tension building at the base of his spine. It was going to be fast and furious if he didn't gain some control. Then Catherine pushed back against him, wiggling her sweet little butt against his groin, and control was a thing of the past.

He pressed into her again and again, burying himself in her velvet heat, straining to get as close as he could, as deep as her body would allow.

Thunder exploded inside Catherine, rumbling down the length of every nerve ending, through every extremity, until she was too weak to support herself, and Granby had to wrap an arm around her waist to keep her from collapsing against the pillows. And still he pounded into her, taking her in the most primal way possible, pushing her toward that moment of blinding bliss when every muscle in her body contracted in exquisite release.

Granby pushed deep one last time, his fingers digging into the flesh of her hips. With a hoarse sound of triumph, he climaxed powerfully, surging deep inside her, depositing his seed at the mouth of her womb.

After a long, long time, when breath and consciousness returned to them, Catherine lay spent at his side, her hair curtaining her face. He brushed it aside, kissing her tenderly. "Did I hurt you?"

"No," she answered, drowsy and sated. "I'm just too tired to move."

He laughed. "So am I. Go back to sleep."

"What about—"

"We're married, and no one but Peck will have the audacity to knock on the door. When he does, it will be with a tray of hot tea and buttered scones."

"Felicity isn't going to be happy."

"Are you?" he asked, studying her so closely Catherine knew she didn't dare lie.

"I'm not sure," she told him. "I haven't been married long enough to get over the shock of seeing a wedding ring on my finger."

He lifted her hand and kissed each knuckle. "There's a necklace and earrings to match. I want you to wear them this evening when I introduce you to the duke."

"A duke!" she sat upright, immediately rejuvenated.

"Morland isn't stomping through the door this very moment," he said, pulling her back into place, at his side where she belonged. "Sleep. I told Peck I'd have him drawn and quartered if he brought tea any earlier than nine."

It was her husband who slept, though. The deep sound of his breathing filled the small room that had become their world for these few short hours. But what of later?

A sudden lump of emotion clogged Catherine's throat as she turned to look at him. On impulse, she reached out and brushed a strand of hair away from his forehead.

It was a simple thing, touching him in such a wifely way, and yet tears came into her eyes. She told herself a woman in love was allowed a few moments of weakness, especially when the man she loved was keeping his own feelings to himself.

She didn't have any reason to think that Granby's desire for her was feigned. He had enjoyed her too thoroughly for her to suspect he had forced himself to perform. But at the same time he pleased her, the pleasure left Catherine feeling empty.

She wanted more than passion in his arms. She wanted a place in his heart, to be allowed past the charming veneer he painted on for the rest of the world. Would she ever know this man, truly know him? There was a hardness beneath his charm, a defensiveness that made her wonder if she'd ever be able to reach his heart. The only time she couldn't feel it was when they were making love, but there had to be more.

There had to be.

Easing herself from the bed so as not to wake her sleeping husband, Catherine moved quietly about the room. She found the cloth at the bottom of the tub and used the tepid water to bathe herself, then dressed. She was not at all surprised to find that the closet held not only a dress, but a chemise, petticoat, stockings and garters. Her shoes, the ones she'd worn during her journey from Winchcombe to Ipswich, were polished and waiting for her on the closet floor.

The clock in the manor's bell tower was chiming nine when a knock sounded on the cottage door. Catherine opened it, expecting Granby's meticulous valet, but she found the Viscount Rathbone instead, carrying a tray of tea and looking full of mischief.

"Ahh, the bride," he said, sauntering into the front room. He put the tray on the table, swishing away the covering cloth to reveal a tea service and a plate of hot scones. "And where will I find the groom? Still sleeping? Slumbering away after a night of—"

"I'm right here," Granby said. He was wearing his trousers, but nothing else. "What I want to know is what the bloody hell you think you're doing?"

"A mission of mercy," Rathbone announced. "I intercepted that valet of yours as he was leaving the kitchen. Had to wrest the tray from his hands. Devoted, I'll give him that, but I insisted. After all, I am your closest friend. The one you *forgot* to invite to your wedding."

"You told me weddings make you nauseous," Granby grumbled. He reached for the teapot, poured two cups, then handed one to Catherine.

"A friend is a friend," Rathbone told him. "I could have fetched the magistrate just as well as Fitch. Bloody boasting about it this morning, he was. Saying that he thoroughly enjoyed the little escapade."

"At least he brought me a real magistrate," Granby replied after a sip of tea. "Had I left the task up to you, God only knows what charlatan would have presided over my wedding."

Rathbone laughed. "Think what you will, but I won't be cheated out of the privilege of kissing the bride."

"You're too late. She stopped being a bride last night. Now, she's my wife, and I'll be doing all the kissing."

"I'm wounded," the viscount said, making a dramatic show of placing his hand over his heart. "I never knew you to be a selfish man. And after all the years we've been friends. Surely, one little kiss. I'm deserving of that, if nothing more."

"You're deserving of a good toss out of the door," the earl said. "And take your hands off my wife."

"One kiss," the viscount replied. "Or are you worried that the lady will cast aside your heart in favor of mine? I'm a much better kisser. Shall we put the theory to the test?"

Rathbone was a wicked tease, and it was all for her husband's benefit. Deciding a little jealousy could be a good thing, Catherine allowed the viscount to kiss her.

Once the kiss was over, her husband put a cup of tea into Rathbone's hand and pulled Catherine close. "So tell me, is Felicity polishing the muskets?"

Rathbone laughed. "She's out for blood, make no mistake about it. Seems a lovely ivory gown will go to waste."

"I should go up and see her," Catherine insisted.

"Not without me," Granby said, keeping his arm firmly anchored around her waist.

"Quite right," Rathbone said. "Can't wait to see the feathers fly." He turned and headed for the door, then paused and looked over his shoulder. "I'd lace that tea with some brandy if I were you. Morland's coach arrived an hour ago."

"Bloody hell," Granby cursed.

"You can be sure of it," the viscount replied. "The last time the old man blistered my ears, I felt as if he'd done the same thing to my arse. Nothing like a ducal dressing-down to make a chap feel as if he's still in short pants."

Nineteen

The moment Lord and Lady Granby stepped into the morning room, all conversation ceased. The group of people assembled there were the same ones Catherine had met at dinner the previous evening. The women were clustered in front of the window, sitting on a long settee and the nearby chairs, while the men were gathered on the opposite side of the room.

Granby noticed several sympathetic looks from his peers. The married gentlemen in the room understood the frustration that could come with a lengthy engagement, and thus his haste to marry. Having seen his fiancée, they would privately admit to being surprised that he hadn't married her before leaving Winchcombe.

In the corner of the room, near a small table bearing a silver tea service, sat his nemesis, Lady Forbes-Hammond. She rose magnificently to the occasion, coming to her feet with the aid of a cane which she used only when she wanted to emphasize her age and the risk of upsetting an elderly woman's fragile constitution.

Opposite the sofa, in a deep armchair with wings, sat the Viscount Rathbone, presenting the picture of a man intent on not missing a thing. A little withdrawn from the rest of the men, the Duke of Morland stood near a corner window.

"Granby," he said, handing off his teacup to Fitch, who placed it on a nearby table. "Good of you to join us. May I assume that this lovely young lady is your newly acquired wife?"

The way he accented the words "newly acquired" was enough to make Granby flinch on the inside. The duke was a stickler for propriety, and the earl had broken more than one rule in the last twenty-four hours.

"This is Catherine," he said. He escorted her across the room. "May I present the Duke of Morland, an old and valued friend of the family."

"Your Grace," Catherine said, dipping into a curtsy.

From the way Rathbone had spoken of the duke, she'd been expecting a dried-up old ogre with liver-spotted skin and an unforgiving disposition. What she saw was an immaculately dressed elderly man. Although he grasped an ebony walking stick, he did not seem to need it for support.

"She's lovely," Morland said, looking at Granby. "Seeing her makes it easier to understand how a man might slip his reins and do something foolish."

"Yes, Your Grace," he said, knowing it would do no good to argue. Morland meant for him to do a little squirming, and what the old man wanted, the old man got.

"As for your conduct," the duke said, "That requires a private conservation. If you will excuse us, Lady Granby."

With that, he stepped around the earl and moved toward the door. Catherine was instantly reminded of the morning of the nearly fatal race between Granby and herself, when she'd been summoned to her father's study. Looking at her husband, she suspected the same sour feeling was settling in his stomach. Catherine wanted to laugh, but she didn't dare.

"Are you all right?" Felicity asked, moving across the

room. She glared at Granby. His rank as an earl wasn't going to save him this time. "You scared the life out of me, young man. Stealing Catherine out from beneath my very nose."

"I thought you wanted us to marry?"

"I do. I did. But not in the middle of the night. That valet of yours told me all about it, and it took quite a few threats, I might add. A magistrate in a nightshirt. For shame."

Rathbone couldn't contain his laughter a moment longer. "A nightshirt! By Jove, I should have been there."

"Be quiet," Felicity reprimanded him. "Or I shall direct my resources to finding *you* a wife."

The threat was enough to turn the viscount into a mute.

"Morland isn't known for his patience," Lord Sterling said, stifling a smile. "Best not keep him waiting."

Granby's expression remained undaunted, but his friends knew he wasn't looking forward to the upcoming discussion. There wasn't a man in the room, excluding Lord Lansdowne, who hadn't experienced the wrath of the duke's capable tongue. Each and every one had been called to account for something in their lives, although Rathbone held the record.

"Shall I drop my trousers, bend over the desk, and take my punishment?" Granby asked once he was cloistered behind closed doors with Morland.

"I don't think anything that drastic is in order," the duke replied. "You've got a lot of apologizing to do, starting with Lady Forbes-Hammond. She wanted your head on a pole this morning."

"I'm sure she did."

"Insisted that you'd gone and ruined everything."

"A wedding is a wedding, as far as I'm concerned. Catherine is my wife now, and I'll soon have my heir."

"Felicity assured me there was no need for haste."

"There isn't, or rather, there wasn't."

The duke sat down, making himself comfortable while he waited for the earl's explanation.

"I didn't want Catherine to find a way to break off the engagement," Granby confessed after a brief silence. "She had reservations about marrying me."

"Reservations?"

"Seems several of her friends have married recently and found their dreams of matrimonial bliss shattered. Catherine was set against having a Season, and dead set against having a lord for a husband."

"She seemed willing enough last night, or so Fitch insisted."

"She was willing," Granby replied, unsure how long she'd stay that way once the shock wore off.

"What about her father? Never met the man, but Felicity told me he's an upstanding chap."

"Sir Hardwick . . . I like him. And he approved of the engagement. I don't anticipate any problems from that quarter."

"Your method was a bit unorthodox."

"Yes, but justified," Granby said. "Catherine's as strong-willed as she is beautiful. I had to strike while the iron was hot, so to speak."

"I'd recommend posting a letter to her father before Felicity has time to send one of her own."

"Good idea," Granby said. "I'll be returning to Foxleigh after the regatta. I'm confident that Catherine will settle into her wifely role, once she sees the place."

"And will you settle in, as well? I understand Lady Aldershaw is to arrive later today."

"Have I ever bedded a woman you don't know about?" Granby asked crisply. He wasn't concerned with Jane Aldershaw. There would be gentlemen aplenty to keep the lovely widow company, should she wish for more than the scheduled entertainment.

The duke gave him a half smile. "I promised your father that I'd keep an eye on you."

"Yes, well, now that I'm married and ready to begin a family, I trust that will end."

"Perhaps," the duke said, putting down his glass. "You may tell Rathbone that you were properly chastised. Don't want the young scamp to think I'm becoming complacent in my old age."

"Never fear, I'll sit on a cushion at dinner this evening. That should keep him on the right side of things."

"Truth be told, Rathbone isn't foremost in my mind at the moment. I'm concerned about Fitch."

"Fitch?"

"He seems . . . distant, though the word isn't exactly what I'm striving for. Has he mentioned anything to you, anything that may be weighing on his mind?"

"No. Nothing. Shall I make a discreet inquiry?"

The duke shook his head. "I'd rather you didn't. He's a levelheaded lad. Just an impression I got. I'm sure he can manage. If not, he knows who his friends are."

Catherine had anticipated returning to the room she had been assigned yesterday, adjacent to Felicity's, to enjoy a hot bath and a much-needed nap, but it seemed the events of the night were still dictating her actions. Upon climbing the stairs, she found Mary shuffling up and down the hallway, supervising the transfer of her personal belongings to a suite in the west wing of the massive manor house.

"Oh, there you are, miss—I mean, my lady," the maid said rather nervously. "It's a tizzy we're in this morning. If you'll follow me, I'll show you to the earl's suite."

Catherine followed, pausing en route to appreciate several family portraits. The Bedford family was a handsome lot.

"That's my great-grandfather," a young voice informed her.

Catherine turned to find a girl of ten or so, standing in the doorway of what appeared to be a music room.

"Hello. I'm Catherine," the girl announced with a bright smile. Dressed in a lavender dress with white ruffles, she bobbed into a curtsy. "You're the new Lady Granby. I heard Marshall talking about you this morning. Of course, I wasn't meant to hear what he said, but I'm an incurable eavesdropper."

"Are you?" Catherine replied, unable to resist smiling. "Then you must know that we have something in common. Our names. I'm also a Catherine."

"Do you like it? I don't. I'd much rather have a more sophisticated name. Dulcima, I think, or Saretta, though I'm partial to Laureen. What do you think?"

"I'm content being Catherine."

"You're very pretty. Marshall said that's why Lord Granby is acting like such a horse's butt."

Catherine laughed. "I'll let you in on a secret," she said, stepping closer and bending down so her words didn't carry. "Most men have something in common with a horse's posterior at one time or another."

The smaller Catherine giggled. "I like you. So does Evelyn, that's Marshall wife. I'm supposed to call her Lady Waltham when I'm speaking to someone outside the family, but Lord Granby is almost family, he's one of Marshall's best friends, so that makes you almost family, too. She's going to have a baby."

"Yes, I know. Are you excited about being an aunt?"

"Oh, yes. Then I won't be the littlest one in the house and people will stop treating me like a child." She glanced down the hallway to where Mary was waiting. "I'm keeping you from settling into your new room. We can talk again at the luncheon."

"I'd like that very much."

"Do you like seashells? We can walk on the beach and collect them. I have a piece of sea glass. It's blue and very pretty."

"I look forward to seeing it."

"Good-bye, then," the young girl said, stepping back inside the room, but not closing the door. Blond curls framed her face when she peered back around the edge of the door to say, "Lord Granby is a very nice man. I'm sure you're going to make him a very nice wife."

"I'm going to try," Catherine replied, wishing it were that easy.

When she reached the suite of rooms she'd be sharing with her husband, Catherine was startled by what she saw; a grand welcome had been arranged. There were large vases of fresh flowers on the table between the tall windows and on the bedside stand. Her toiletries were ready and waiting, and a robe was laid out for her to wear after her bath. A light meal was to be served, if she felt hungry, and tea had already been ordered. A maid would be bringing up a tray momentarily.

"Is there anything else, milady?" Mary asked as she opened Catherine's trunk and began transferring items to the armoire and matching walnut tallboy.

"No, you seem to have thought of everything."

"Let me help you with your buttons, then off with you to soak in a hot tub. I added those lilac bath salts you like."

"Thank you," Catherine replied rather numbly. A hot bath sounded wonderful, and she did need a nap. There had been none the previous afternoon, since she'd been too anxious about seeing the earl again, and last night had offered little sleep.

Her wedding night.

It had certainly been a night to remember.

Once she was alone, Catherine let out an audible sigh. So much had happened in so short a time. She took a moment to reflect on what had transpired, then looked about the room once again. It was large, and the rose tones were pleasing to the eye. She counted the doors. Three. The one through which she had entered, the one that led to the dressing room, and one that would open into her husband's bedroom. Was he there now, awaiting a bath and a few hours of repose before rejoining the festivities with a new wife on his arm?

She listened, but no sound penetrated the room, none but the rush of wind over and around the huge manor house.

This isn't the time to be daydreaming, Catherine told herself. Your bath is growing cold.

Once she had bathed, and shampooed her hair, Catherine opened the windows overlooking the west lawn. Sitting on a slender gilt chair, she tackled the mass of wet curls that would have to be tamed before she was presented to the balance of the guests.

Catherine pulled the brush through her hair. Each stroke of the brush brought her wedding ring into the sunlight, causing the emerald and diamond stones to shimmer and shine. The sound of a door being opened caused her to look up expectantly, but it wasn't the expected maid with a gown freshly pressed for the luncheon.

It was her husband.

Shocked, because she hadn't expected to see him for several more hours, Catherine scrambled to put down the brush and close the bodice of her robe. She was successful, but not quickly enough for her husband's keen eyes to miss what she was trying to hide.

His gaze moved over her, as if she were a temptation he had to resist or be forever damned.

"I wanted to make sure you were settled."

"All unpacked," she said, unsure if that's what he really meant. "It appears that you survived the duke's scolding."

"Yes." He smiled for the first time since entering the room. "And I've had a share of humble pie, thanks to

Lady Forbes-Hammond. The apology was accepted, but not until I'd been made to feel like a schoolboy."

"I know the feeling."

He walked to where she was sitting. "You have beautiful hair. When the sunlight is upon it, it seems more a dozen colors than one. Cinnamon and ginger with a touch of nutmeg."

"You sound as if you're describing a cake."

"A very sweet, very spicy cake," he said, leaning down to plant a kiss on her cheek. "I'm tempted to take a nap with you, but I fear we'd get little sleep."

There was a teasing quality to his voice, but there was also something else, a soft wistful note that caused a tingle to run up and down her spine.

"Will there be many guests?" she asked, wishing she had more time to herself—time to herd her feelings into order.

"Dozens," he replied. "But it won't last for long. We'll be leaving for Foxleigh at week's end. I'm sure you'll find the estate to your liking. If you want to travel, we can do that as well, and I'll leave it up to you where we will honeymoon."

"I need to go home," she said. "All my things are there, and Father . . . he has to be told that we've married."

"Whatever you want can be packed and brought to Foxleigh. As for your father, I'll write him before the day is over and extend an invitation for him to visit us as soon as possible."

"But—"

"You're my wife now. You belong with me."

"I belong at Stonebridge," Catherine said before she could think better of it. "It's my home."

"It *was* your home. As my wife, you will reside at Foxleigh in Reading. That is where we will live, and where our children will be born."

"The required heir," she said, disliking his tone.

"*All* our children."

Catherine tried to calm herself, knowing she shouldn't have spoken so hastily, knowing she put him on the defensive. "Please, try to understand. I didn't come to Ipswich with the intentions of marrying you, at least not now. I need more time."

"You had no misgivings about sharing a marital bed with me, why not a house as large as this one?"

"The wedding was to be in September. This is July."

"The calendar has nothing to do with the vows we've taken." His tone tore her excuse to shreds.

Feelings boiled up inside Catherine, but she dared not let them escape. He was right. She had willingly spoken her vows, and foolishly put her heart at risk. Frantically searching for a reply that would postpone an argument until she could organize her thoughts, she said, "I'm sure I'll find Foxleigh to my liking, my lord. I thought only that we might travel to Stonebridge together to inform my father that our wedding has already taken place. It seems a bit coldhearted to inform him by post."

Granby hesitated. It wasn't that he couldn't return to Stonebridge, it was his sense that Catherine was looking for an excuse to delay the solidification of their marriage.

"Your father is a reasonable man. I'm sure an invitation to visit will set the matter straight." His gaze softened to the one she knew so well. "I'm looking forward to installing you at Foxleigh. The estate has lacked a countess for some time."

His mouth was almost upon hers when Catherine lifted her head to end the journey. She needed to find an antidote against his charms, but since none was at hand . . .

Granby didn't hesitate to claim what he considered his. Although the kiss was mild compared to some he'd shared with her, it was no less potent. When he finally separated their mouths, his eyes were gleaming with need.

"Your nap," he said, his voice deep and dark.

The next instant she was being lifted from the chair and carried to the bed. Once she was spread out on the bed like a feast to be savored, he parted her robe, exposing her breasts.

"I want to look at you."

He was smiling again, that wicked, devil-may-care smile that always made her insides melt. Deliberately taking his time, he sat down on the side of the bed before bending his head to draw first one nipple, then the other, into his mouth.

Catherine lay there with her body aching as only he could make it ache, knowing he wasn't going to stop until he'd proven his point—she was his wife and he'd have her whenever he wanted.

She should be protesting, but the only sound that came from her was a soft moan when his teeth bit down ever so gently.

"You need to rest," he said a moment later. "I don't want you tired tonight."

He closed her robe, taking time to tie the ribbons. "Sleep well, sweetheart." Another kiss, this one on her forehead. "Tonight, you'll sleep with me."

Tonight.

That was hours away. She was aching now. Wanting him now. The man had toyed with her again, and she'd let him. When was she going to learn that his charms couldn't be trusted?

Disappointed but not defeated, Catherine closed her eyes, and began plotting her revenge.

Twenty

When Catherine made her appearance at the top of the stairs, both her husband and the Viscount Rathbone, with whom Granby had been sharing a private laugh, turned to stare at the stunning woman who was about to join them.

"My lady," Granby said, when she reached the foot of the wide staircase.

"My lovely lady, is more like it," Rathbone said, launching into an elaborate bow. "I find myself more envious of my friend each time I look upon his wife."

Catherine laughed. "Save your flattery for one of the other ladies, my lord. I'm content with the man I have."

Granby smiled inwardly at the compliment Catherine had just paid him, but he frowned at the viscount. Rathbone's eyes were popping out of his head, and with good reason. Catherine had never looked more beautiful. Her sea green Chinese silk dress suited her perfectly, the soft hue emphasizing her bold coloring.

As she moved from the bottom step, to place her hand on his arm, he glimpsed the heavy white satin underskirt, embroidered with yellow roses. Her shoulders were draped with a thin three-cornered shawl of delicate

Mechlin lace, tied in a loose knot over the bodice of her dress. The lace added just the right touch of softness and femininity. Unfortunately, rather than concealing what he concerned her best assets, the knotted shawl drew attention to the lushness of her breasts.

Before her husband could lead her away from his gawking friend, Rathbone extended his arm to Catherine. "I may just sit on the sidelines and watch as my peers faint dead away at the sight of your loveliness."

Granby held his tongue, knowing Rathbone was sputtering nonsense more for his sake than Catherine's. He trusted his friend, or at least he wanted to trust him. Unfortunately, Rathbone was currently undergoing a fascination with married women that kept the earl from being completely at ease with the situation. As a man who had vowed to remain a bachelor for as long as possible, and who now found himself married, Granby could attest to Catherine's ability to tempt a man beyond reason.

They proceeded outside to the front lawn where the guests were gathering. Catherine took a deep breath. The sky was a faultless blue, without a single cloud and radiant with summer sunshine.

Raising her hand to brush back a curl caught by the breeze, the ring on the third finger of her left hand flashed as the pristine light caught the stones. Its brilliance captured her attention for a moment. She would wear this ring until the day she died, and if she were blessed with a daughter, the ring would pass to her as part of her legacy.

But would it be a happy bequest, or would the ring simply become the symbol of an aristocratic marriage that held little affection once the passion had burned out?

Granby chose that moment to look at his wife, at the play of sunlight on her hair and the graceful lines of her face. She was staring past the lawn, focusing on something unseen by the rest of them. He sensed her distraction, as if she were trying to work something out in her head.

"Hungry?" he asked, giving Rathbone a quick scowl that said it was time the man dispatched himself.

"A little."

Her tone, while polite, had a hint of the distraction he had noted. He was not insensitive to what she must be feeling, unexpectedly married and surrounded by strangers, but Granby also knew he couldn't let those thoughts dominate her mind. He couldn't allow her to drive a wedge between them, cutting off their chance of making a new life together.

For a split second, he wondered why he couldn't accept what so many of his peers accepted without question: that taking a wife and begetting an heir did not require happiness, only a willingness to fulfill one's obligations in life.

He supposed, as they continued across the lawn to where Waltham and his family had gathered around a linen-covered table, that obligations could be just as easily met by a happy man as an unhappy one. And Catherine did make him happy—when she wasn't being stubborn, which was most of the time.

As for her happiness, he considered it his duty to see that her role as his wife didn't bring discontent. She was lovely when she smiled, and he felt duty-bound to keep her smiling into her dotage.

As they joined the others, both her husband's and Catherine's private thoughts were abandoned for the light conversation and formalities that accompanied lawn parties.

Lady Waltham, aided by her mother-in-law, Lady Kniveton, had soon introduced Catherine to most of the guests. The men stared, most discreetly, at the new Lady Granby, while the women congratulated her most heartily.

Catherine endeavored to remember all their names,

though she knew she'd need help before the day was out. Even more guests were to arrive to attend the ball that evening, and then the regatta, in two days hence.

She was sipping from a glass of lemonade when Catherine raised her eyes and met the gaze of another woman, one to whom she hadn't yet been formally introduced. Catherine was startled by the naked hatred etched into the woman's face. She instantly recognized a most dangerous enemy, though she hadn't the slightest idea why the woman should despise her so.

The female, wearing a magnificently cut rose silk dress, obviously a pricey piece of haute couture, had raven hair and piercing eyes. Whoever she was, she was a beauty, the sort of woman one could not think of except in regard to her appearance, which was classically beautiful and well refined.

The woman averted her gaze for a moment to search the crowd. Catherine let her eyes follow, only to discover that the woman was looking at Granby. He caught the glance, immediately looking away, and in that brief instant, Catherine knew who the woman was. Or *what* she was—one of her husband's former lovers.

An involuntary shiver went through Catherine as she was forced to admit that she should have expected it. Granby was no monk, nor had he pretended to be. Still, it was unnerving to encounter one of his sexual enthusiasms on what could literally be called their wedding day.

Unable to stop herself, Catherine continued staring at the woman until their gazes met again. They regarded each other alertly, each wondering which one of them would make the next move. Neither did.

It wasn't acceptable for either one of them to acknowledge that, while they might not know each other's names they did indeed have something in common—the Earl of Granby.

For a moment, Catherine considered seeking out

her husband, placing her hand on his arm, then leaning close to give him a kiss. That would give Lady Whoever-the-Hell-She-Might-Be something to think about. It's what any other woman—*wife*—would do, but Catherine wasn't any woman. She was proud, and at the moment, she was seething with anger.

An image of Granby making love to the raven-haired woman formed in Catherine's mind. Something died inside her as the vision clarified—Granby smiling that wicked smile as the woman opened her arms and summoned him to join her on the bed.

Catherine tried to direct her energy into listening to what Lady Sterling and Felicity were saying, but all she could hear was the muffled sound of sexual laughter as the imagined couple rolled about on a red velvet coverlet.

"Catherine, are you feeling ill?"

The question came from Felicity, whose sharp eyes missed little.

"I'm fine," she said, forcing a normalcy she didn't feel into her voice. "Just more hungry than I first thought. I think I'll make myself a plate and find some shade."

"I'll join you," Rebecca Sterling said. "Then, if you're up to it and Morgan is awake, I'll introduce you to my son."

"I'm looking forward to it," Catherine replied, turning her back on the woman's intermittent glances, which were meant to be subtle, but weren't.

Once she was seated next to Rebecca, they were joined by Lady Eugenia Hammershaw, a round-faced woman in her mid-thirties, married to a man almost twice her age, who had been a business associate of the former Marquis of Waltham. Lady Hammershaw was known as a bore. She enjoyed telling pointless stories about people with whom no one was acquainted, speaking in a high-pitched voice that irritated her audience at the same time it trapped them into listening.

Within moments of her introduction to Catherine, the lady immediately began reciting the details of her latest trip to Scotland, to visit an aging aunt. The account took the better part of an hour, Lady Hammershaw dishing out the details in dribs and drabs between bites of food.

Catherine managed to hide her impatience, wanting nothing more than to leave the lawn, visit young Morgan in the nursery, then take to her room.

If the woman in the rose silk dress looked her way one more time, Catherine knew she would do something that wasn't the least bit ladylike—something guaranteed to make their wedding day one her husband would never forget.

Lady Hammershaw, after exhausting her supply of gossip, moved on to another victim, making room for Felicity to join Catherine and Rebecca.

"I've never seen you looking lovelier," she said, settling onto the bench, which has been cushioned for the day's gathering and therefore quite comfortable for a lengthy chat. "As for Granby, the scoundrel, I've forgiven him, of course."

"Of course. He's a forgivable scoundrel," Catherine replied. *Unless you're his wife, and an old lover comes to roost.*

After a few moments, Catherine's curiosity got the best of her. "Refresh my memory," she said, indicating a young lady who had stopped to exchange words with the mysterious rose-clad woman. "I've forgotten that young lady's name."

"Which young lady?" Rebecca asked, searching the crowd in the general direction Catherine had indicated.

"The one wearing the bonnet with the blue scarf."

"That's Louisa Kott. Her father sits on the board of the Royal Academy."

"Sweetly pretty and not an ounce of sense to her," Felicity said with a wave of her hand. "As for the other, that's Lady Jane Aldershaw, recently widowed, and sur-prisingly happy about it."

"Felicity!" Rebecca responded in a scolding tone. "You're being rude."

"I'm being truthful. Can't say that I blame her. Alder-shaw wasn't what one would call an impressive man, un-less you were counting his money."

Lady Aldershaw was beautiful and sophisticated. As a financially secure, experienced female, she made the perfect bed partner. The more Catherine watched the *widow*, watching Granby, the more certain she was that the two were intimately acquainted.

"Would you like to meet Morgan now?" Rebecca asked.

Catherine smiled, thankful that she could escape the party for the house and some much-needed privacy.

As she and Rebecca crossed the lawn, Granby sepa-rated himself from a group of men, joining his wife be-fore she could make good her escape.

"I understand we're scheduled for a shell-collecting expedition," he said, seemingly undaunted by Lady Aldershaw's appearance. "Young Catherine has her bas-ket waiting."

"I'll bring Morgan down to the beach," Rebecca said with a smile. "He loves watching the water."

"Excellent," Granby said. He offered Catherine his arm.

Catherine accepted it, smiling in spite of the pain that was searing her heart.

For a short time, she'd allowed herself to believe that her husband could come to love her, but seeing the in-difference he was showing to another woman—one he'd probably bedded more times than he'd bedded his wife—it was difficult to hold on to the hope that love would eventually find its way into their marriage.

At some point during the night, she'd decided to win Granby's heart, if not immediately, then gradually, one day, one night at a time, until he realized that their relationship was fueled by more than passion. Suspecting that her husband and Lady Aldershaw had been lovers cast a shadow on that decision. Her doubts were back.

Rebecca went into the house, leaving the newlyweds to make their way to the beach. Catherine cast a surreptitious glance at her husband's face, only to find him doing the same. For an instant their gazes met. Neither spoke, as each assessed the other's frame of mind.

"Waltham would accept my excuse, should you like to leave for Reading this afternoon," Granby said as they reached the sloping path that separated the manicured lawn from the sandy beach. "As newlyweds, our departure would be understandable."

Did he want to be alone with her, or did he want to be away from Lady Aldershaw? Catherine was tempted to pose the question, but she held back. It was hard to keep emotion out of her voice as she replied, "The regatta is only two days away. We have the rest of our lives together."

The rest of their lives. Granby had been thinking the same thing all morning. His patience had been tested all morning, wanting to be rid of a houseful of people, wanting to be alone with his wife. *His wife.* The phrase was going to take some getting used to, but he was pleased with the sound of it. His obsession had increased with each passing hour, but she was right, they would have the rest of their lives together, hours and days that would stretch into months and years.

He helped her down the slope, struggling to decide if she was more beautiful in sunlight or in moonlight. Both suited her far too well to make the decision an easy one. He thought of the night ahead. Would she come as willingly into his arms as she had last night in the cottage? Or would she, with the descent of the sun, regress to the noncompliant young woman from Winchcombe, full of skepticism and doubts?

"I was hoping you hadn't forgotten," the younger of

the two Catherines called out. She was at the water's
edge while a serious-faced footman, assigned the task of
keeping her out of the surf, looked on from a distance
that kept his shoes dry. "Come look at the shell I just
found. Do you suppose it could have come across the
Channel from France?"

After a close inspection of the pearly pink shell that
filled the young girl's palm, Granby decided that it
could indeed have made its way from the continent to
grace England's saintly shores.

They walked then, pretending to search the sand so
as not to hurt the young girl's feelings, while they were
both actually consumed with private thoughts of each
other.

Granby held Catherine's hand. It was impossible to
walk beside her and not think of the way she had looked
last night, gloriously naked except for the wedding ring
he had put on her finger.

They stopped to inspect a small shell. Catherine looked
at him, her eyes wide and curious as she scanned his
face.

Granby smiled. There was so much in her gaze, things
he didn't understand, things he was almost afraid to
consider. The complexities of their relationship were
too vast, too compelling, for him to think that marriage
would not have permanent consequences for his life.

It was already affecting him.

"I like the sound of the water," Catherine said, trying
to find a topic that would distract from the sexual tension she felt each time her husband was near. "It's very
relaxing."

"Yes," her husband agreed, "but I like it best when a
storm is approaching. The wind moans and the water
crashes against the shore. It's an intimidating display of
God's power."

"You, intimidated?"

Granby laughed. "Only by God, and the Duke of Morland."

Suddenly they were both smiling.

He reached out and touched her cheek. Even in casual afternoon dress with the wind in his hair, the Earl of Granby was the epitome of a virile man. The sound of the water and the brush of the wind added to that virility.

Polished gentleman or not, he was a physically strong man with a personality to match, and Catherine felt that strength. It called to her on the most primitive level imaginable.

She flushed, recalling the way he'd made love to her this morning. There was no doubt that they were compatible in their desire for one another. The hope that in time he might truly come to care for her still reigned supreme in her heart.

"There will be another ball this evening, a grand affair with all the trimmings," he told her when they began walking again. "I enjoyed dancing with you last night."

Blessedly the wind had put enough color in her cheeks for Catherine to blush and not look embarrassed by the remark. Her husband's tone said he was thinking of more than a simple waltz in the ballroom.

They strolled on, arm in arm, while young Catherine used a small shovel to dig into the soft sand, hunting for shells. The next hour passed quietly but enjoyably, and Catherine found herself wondering if she hadn't overreacted to Lady Aldershaw.

A few minutes later, Lord and Lady Sterling joined the shell-collecting expedition. The viscount carried his son, a cherubic dark-haired toddler, in his arms. The little boy was all smiles, pointing at the lapping waves, and squirming to get down and enjoy them.

Little Catherine hurried to take him in hand, insisting that she was big enough to keep the Sterling heir from drowning should he decide to test the churning surf, and needing the practice anyway. She would be expected to keep her nephew occupied once he learned to walk.

"He's a handsome boy," Granby said, as the two couples watched Morgan waddle toward the waves, then hurry back when they got too close for comfort. "Looks like his mother."

"Yes, he does," Sterling agreed with a smile. "Though, I've been told he has his father's disposition."

"Only when he's getting into mischief," Rebecca replied, lacing her arm through her husband's as she turned to watch their son playing on the beach. "Of course, the only time he isn't getting into mischief is when he's sleeping."

Catherine looked at Granby. He was smiling again, and she wondered how he would react when their love-making finally produced a child. The thought brought another in its wake. How would *she* react to motherhood? The prospect was a little frightening, but she assumed she'd manage the same way Rebecca Sterling was managing. Would their first child be a son? Funny, but she suddenly shared Sarah's desire not to disappoint her husband by making him wait for his heir. She wanted to give Granby a strong little boy who would grow up to be an equally strong man.

The afternoon gradually gave way to a peaceful evening. The guests retired as they were disposed to: the ladies to rest before dinner and a night of dancing, the men disappearing into the library and game rooms to relax and discuss the upcoming race pitting the members of the Harwick Yacht Club against their rival, the Royal Yacht Club.

Only the servants were busy, rushing up and down the stairs with clothing that had been pressed free of wrinkles, freshly polished shoes, and the inevitable trays of tea and sweetcakes requested to fortify the cloistered guests until it was time to enter the formal dining room and partake of a ten-course meal.

Catherine used the time to reflect on the night ahead. Another night of pleasure, another night of doubt.

No matter how hard she tried to put the image of Lady Aldershaw from her mind, the idea refused to be dismissed. By the time Mary appeared to help her dress, Catherine was a bundle of nerves. Determined to present herself as fashionably as possible, she chose a daringly low-cut evening gown that was the height of sophistication, or so the seamstress had insisted.

She was in the process of deciding what jewels would best complement the emerald green satin when Mary answered a light knock on the door that connected Catherine's room to her husband's.

"Milord," Mary said, stepping back as the earl advanced into the room.

Catherine had prepared herself for the possibility of an interruption. She was wearing a robe, securely fastened this time, but there were no locks on her heart, and it fluttered when she turned to face her husband. He stood just inside the connecting doorway, looking very much like the polished, titled gentleman he was. Dressed in impeccable black, as good taste demanded, he smiled at her.

She searched his face, looking for a sign of his true feelings. He stared at her mouth for a long moment, and she knew he was thinking about kissing her.

Mary had discreetly exited the room, leaving them alone. The emerald gown lay on the bed.

Granby looked at it before closing the distance between them.

Catherine held her breath. For the first time since speaking her vows, she truly felt like a wife. There would be more moments like this one; countless moments

when she would find herself alone with her husband—
a lifetime of moments.

"Your bride gift," he said, holding out a velvet box.
"Seeing your gown, I'm glad I decided to give it to you
tonight."

Catherine took the oblong box from his hand and
opened it. All she could do was stare. The velvet case
held a diamond-and-emerald necklace, a bracelet de-
signed in the same matching stones, and earrings. The
settings were of silver, the clasp a tiny silver mermaid.

"They're beautiful."

"Not as beautiful as my wife."

Catherine looked from the magnificent, teardrop
diamond-and-emerald jewelry into the face of the man
who had so generously presented the gift.

"May I?" he asked, taking the box from her hand.
"The first night I saw you dressed for dinner, I knew I
wanted to give you emeralds."

She recalled that night, and the way she had dreaded
it. So much had happened since then—so very much.

Catherine turned to look into the vanity mirror, allowing Granby to drape the necklace around her throat
and fasten the clasp. The silver felt momentarily cold
against her skin, but it warmed within seconds. Lifting
her hand to touch the diamond-encrusted emeralds,
Catherine unconsciously added her wedding ring to
the expensive display of jewels.

"I have to kiss you," her husband said. "Stand up and
turn around."

Catherine did as he asked, wanting the kiss as much,
if not more, than her husband.

A second later she was in his arms, his tongue hun-
grily parting her lips to burrow deep into her mouth in
that wicked, captivating way he managed so easily.
Catherine tried to control her response, but it was useless.

Several kisses later, he was warning her that if he didn't

get back to his own room, there'd be two less guests at the supper table. "You're addicting," he said. "Deliciously addicting."

"Am I?"

"More than you realize." His expression changed with the words, as if he regretted speaking them. "It's almost time to go downstairs."

He left her then, without so much as a backward glance, and Catherine prayed he hadn't given her the jewels because it was expected, but because he truly thought they suited her.

Only time would tell.

Twenty-one

Catherine entered the ballroom on the arm of her husband and immediately drew looks from everyone. As expected, when the Walthams gave a ball, they gave it thoroughly. The room was washed in light from a huge overhead chandelier that recalled the day's bright sunshine. A wall of mirrored glass reflected the guests, dressed in their summer best; the ladies in pale pastels and crisp satin, the men in evening black. The music was just as delightful, a soft melody that would soon turn into the swirling beat that made waltzing so popular.

Although she had met most of the people now in attendance at the lawn party, Catherine knew this was her *formal* introduction as the Countess of Granby. Looking radiant on her husband's arm, she smiled as the Duke of Morland made his way across the room to greet them.

She took a moment to look at her husband, noting that he seemed very pleased with himself. Catherine found a small shred of confidence in his expression, thinking she had managed to marry this man when so many other women had failed to hold his attention. The thought was shattered when she saw Lady Aldershaw.

The dark-haired widow was wearing a provocative dress of vibrant blue silk and looking like a cat on the prowl. She was talking to Rathbone, emphasizing her words with a gesture of a feathered fan. Once again, Catherine caught her gaze and held it, letting her chin rise just a tad in the process. She was Granby's wife; it was high time Lady Aldershaw realized whatever she had shared with the earl was a thing of the past.

"Oh, to be young and able to waltz again," the duke said. Taking Catherine's gloved hand, he raised it to his mouth. "You are indeed beautiful, Lady Granby."

"Thank you, Your Grace."

"Fortunately, I am young enough to waltz," her husband said, slipping his arm around her waist and gently urging her toward the dance floor. "If you'll excuse us, Your Grace."

The first waltz began, and Catherine quickly found herself in her husband's arms, being turned and swirled about the floor.

It was a crush, but she was enjoying it, despite the curious glances she drew from guests who were still puzzling over the sudden, almost scandalous, marriage of an unknown country lass to the handsome Earl of Granby. They made an eye-catching couple; her bold coloring, accentuated by sparkling jewels, combined with the deceptively angelic appearance of her blond, blue-eyed husband.

The differences in their appearance reminded Catherine of their other differences. Granby expected her to become a contented wife, who, in time, would present him with an heir.

Unfortunately, she wasn't content, nor would she be, until she knew she was loved.

"I'm the envy of every man in the room," her husband said as his hand tightened at her waist. "I'm seriously thinking about waltzing you out onto the veranda again. It's a beautiful night."

"Yes, it is," she replied, breathless from the dance and the intensity of his gaze.

She stared into those blue eyes as the music swelled around them. Each turn brought more pressure from his hand, forcing her closer and closer until their bodies touched completely. The emeralds at her throat caught the light, twinkling as they made the last turn.

When the music ceased, they stopped dancing, but neither released their hold. They stood for a long moment, gazes locked, forgetting the world and the crush of people that surrounded them. In that intoxicating moment, Catherine knew beyond a shadow of a doubt that she had to win this man's heart or be forever incomplete.

Granby was battling with similar emotions. He wanted to say to hell with propriety and good manners, and order that his coach be readied immediately. He wanted to take her to Foxleigh, to take her away from any and all distractions, to spend the rest of the summer luxuriating in the warmth of her arms, the velvet heat of her body. It was overpowering need that engulfed him, drawing him down like the ocean pulled a drowning man into its depths.

Three months ago, the very thought of a woman having such power over him would have been laughable.

He glanced around the room as the bell announced dinner, and his gaze fell on Lady Jane Aldershaw. She was clinging to Rathbone's arm, smiling and plying her undeniable charms. Odd that he didn't feel the slightest twinge of jealousy. Even odder that he couldn't imagine himself with any woman but the one he had married in an impromptu ceremony less than twenty-four hours ago.

Catherine turned, as surely as if he'd spoken her name aloud, to look at him.

"It's going to be a long night," he said, wishing again

that they could make their escape and enjoy a private honeymoon at Foxleigh.

Instead of answering, she licked her lips, then smiled. It wasn't the revenge he was due for arousing her, then leaving her to try and nap this morning, but it was better than nothing.

Dinner was the expected affair of too much food and gossip. Used to affairs of this nature, Granby exchanged the expected conversation with the people sitting nearby. The seating arrangements called for his wife to be across and slightly down the table, between the Viscount Ackerman and a young lady whom Granby recognized from previous social events, but whose name evaded him. She had medium brown hair and brown eyes, a mouse of a young woman compared to the fiery-haired goddess sitting beside her.

It was an hour and a half later, while his wife danced with Lord Ackerman, that Granby stepped outside to enjoy a breath of fresh air and a cigar. The evening was pleasantly warm, the wind blowing off the Channel in cooling gusts. He stood near the veranda's balustrade, thinking of the night to come.

"You could at least speak to me," a female voice chided him.

Recognizing it, the earl turned to find Lady Aldershaw standing a few feet away. The look she gave him was part scowl, part pout.

"Good evening."

"Good evening yourself, my lord," she said just as curtly. "Imagine my surprise when I arrived and was told by a housemaid, of all people, that the notorious Lord Granby had taken a wife."

"Her name is Catherine."

There was an edge to his voice that warned the lovely

widow to tread carefully. But Lady Aldershaw wasn't in a careful mood. She was furious. Madly jealous and unbelievably angry that some country bumpkin, pretty though she may be, had succeeded in holding the earl's attention when she had failed.

Recalling the stinging way Granby had set her aside in Cheltenham, ending their affair as though it had never happened, Jane Aldershaw decided she was due an ounce or two of revenge. The method came to mind a moment later when she looked past the earl to see his lovely new bride making her way onto the terrace.

Never one to dally when an opportunity presented itself, Lady Aldershaw moved closer to Granby.

"I'm going to miss you," she said, softening her voice. "I'm certain there are a number of men who would be more than willing to appreciate your charms as much as I did."

"Perhaps. But none of them could appreciate me as skillfully as you have."

She smiled then, a soft, beguiling smile, that might have worked a few short months ago, but which now had lost its appeal.

The only problem was Catherine had no idea that her husband wasn't appreciating Lady Aldershaw's smile. She had no idea that he was no more interested in the widow than he was the empty champagne glass he'd set aside only moments earlier.

All she knew was that she'd finished dancing with the Earl of Ackerman, only to realize that her husband wasn't in the ballroom. She'd come looking for him, hoping that they might share a kiss in the moonlight.

Finding him standing within arm's reach of a provocative female who clearly had seduction on her mind was enough to send Catherine's suspicions and temper running rampant.

She had enjoyed the evening up until now, dancing under the glittering chandelier, but none of it held the same magic as her husband's arms. She wanted to dance with him, to be with him.

"I suppose I should congratulate you," Lady Aldershaw said, keeping her voice low, so it wouldn't carry.

Catherine froze in the shadows just beyond the opened veranda doors, straining to hear what Lady Aldershaw was saying to Granby, hoping against hope that her husband hadn't already tired of her, that he wasn't indulging himself with a former lover while his bride was still getting used to the wedding ring on her finger.

The couple spoke again, but their voices were too low for Catherine to hear more than a muffled blend of words. Lady Aldershaw was smiling, and Granby looked interested in that smile.

Then the widow kissed him, full on the mouth.

Catherine clenched her fists, suddenly aware that she was seeing what Sarah had seen—her husband with another woman.

Her stomach knotted until the pain threatened to break her in half. Here, before her very eyes, was the nightmare she'd dreaded—finding herself married to a man who didn't love her, who cared for nothing more than the pleasure a woman's body could give him, a man who had married her because he needed a young, healthy woman to provide him with children.

The night faded into a bitter blackness as Catherine stepped back, not into the ballroom, but deeper into the shadows at the end of the veranda. She'd been foolish to think that she could win Granby's heart—he didn't have one.

She'd been duped by his charms, his devil-may-care smile and teasing ways. Fooled into forfeiting not only her body, but her life. They were legally married, the union irrevocably sealed. Like Sarah and Veronica, she was trapped.

Catherine leaned against the wall and took a deep breath. Seeing Granby with another woman drove home the realization that she'd fallen in love with the wrong man. Another deep breath lessened the tightness in her chest, but did nothing for the pain stabbing at her heart. Her gaze drifted back to the other end of the veranda to where her husband now stood alone. Had he arranged to meet Lady Aldershaw in a more discreet place, to resume their affair?

Standing in the dark, Catherine felt empty and alone.

It seemed as if an eternity had passed before Catherine gathered the strength to return to the ballroom, although she knew it had been only a matter of minutes. Another *moment* that held the power to change the course of a person's life.

She wasn't sure what she would do, but she would do something. If not tonight, then soon, very soon, before her husband could take her to Foxleigh and install her at his country estate, while he continued his flirtatious lifestyle in London.

Amazingly, she found herself dancing as if nothing out of the ordinary had taken place. Lord Kniveton was partnering her when her husband returned to the ballroom. Catherine glanced his way, then averted her gaze, not wanting him to see the wrong emotion in her eyes.

No, she thought. I can't let anyone see how badly he has hurt me. I shan't give him, or Lady Aldershaw, another victory.

He had turned to another woman, after all they had shared.

Scandalous or not, Catherine had no intention of continuing their farce of a marriage. A plan formed in her mind—not an elaborate plot of revenge, but a method of escape. She needed the familiar right now, the place and people that made her feel loved and wanted and of some significant value. She wanted, *needed,* to go home to Stonebridge, the place she should never have left.

Blessedly she was able to make her way upstairs without drawing her husband's attention. As soon as she was alone, in the privacy of her room, Catherine set her plan into action. She changed, struggling out of the elegant evening gown and tossing it on the floor. Next came the jewels she had so proudly worn. What would Granby think when he came looking for her, only to find her gone? Would he panic with concern, or fume with indignation? Why should she care?

He was a womanizer. His reputation had preceded him; even Felicity had commented upon it, though she was confident that marriage would be his redemption. Some redemption. Their vows weren't even cold and he was kissing another woman.

Catherine didn't want to believe that her husband was so callous, so uncaring, but her eyes had seen the truth, and with that truth, she'd felt pain, an excruciating awareness that she'd lost something wonderful before she'd ever really been able to call it her own.

She wasn't like Sarah or Veronica, even if her current circumstances put her in the same kettle of soup as her friends. She wasn't complacent or submissive or tolerant. She was furious. At her husband, and at herself.

How could she have forgotten the very reason she'd been reluctant to marry him in the first place? She'd let him charm her onto the beach, then into the cottage, and then into marriage. Her own senses, her own sensuality, had trapped her as much as his smile. Her own actions had caused this chaos, this pandemonium, and there was naught she could do but weather the storm. And she would weather it, but not at the earl's side. She was going home to Stonebridge, where she belonged.

Catherine was in the process of turning the doorknob when she remembered Felicity. She couldn't leave Bedford Hall without telling her aunt where she was going.

There was no writing desk in her room, no paper, no ink. With only a small valise in tow, Catherine made her way to the second-floor library. Blessedly, it was empty. She wrote a hasty note to Felicity, saying that she had taken an instant dislike to marriage, and from this day forth could be found residing in Winchcombe.

The note was left where a maid could find it, then Catherine went downstairs, using the narrow staircase reserved for servants. Encountering a surprised footman along the way, she insisted that he keep the sighting to himself, before leaving the house the same way she'd left it the previous night. Only this time she wasn't meeting her love. She was running away from him.

It wasn't yet midnight, so it was easy enough to find the driver, who grumbled about taking to the roads so late. The new Lady Granby put an end to the argument with a few well-chosen words, informing the man that she'd drive the blasted carriage herself if necessary. Knowing a determined woman when he saw one, the man did what he was told, not nearly as reluctant once Catherine promised him an extra gold coin for his trouble.

Thus, Lady Granby made her escape.

Twenty-two

"Misplace something?" Waltham asked as his friend opened the door to a small, first-floor parlor and looked inside.

"My wife," Granby told him. "The last time I saw her, she was dancing with Lord Kniveton."

The two men continued searching, opening doors to a multitude of rooms, only to find them empty. "Perhaps she decided to retire early," the marquis suggested. "If you don't return to the ballroom, I'll know you've found her."

Granby smiled, but his heart wasn't in it. His instincts were warning him that something was amiss. He had returned from the veranda, and his not-so-pleasing encounter with Jane Aldershaw, intending to invite his wife to waltz one last time before making their way upstairs and into a bedroom with a sturdy lock on the door.

"Whom are we trying to find?" Rathbone asked, strolling down the hallway toward them. He was carrying two champagne glasses. After handing one to the marquis, he lifted a fringed tablecloth and peered under it. "No one here."

"Lady Granby is too tall to fit under a table," Waltham replied in the most serious of voices. A short second later he began to laugh.

"He's lost the bride," Rathbone chuckled. "Not at all the proper thing for a husband to do, don't you agree, Waltham?"

"Absolutely. One of the first rules of being a good husband is not to lose the woman to whom you have pledged your troth."

Granby's glare did nothing to lessen his friend's mirth. He was in the process of marching up the wide staircase, hoping to find that Catherine had indeed retired for the evening, when a footman appeared. The servant gave the marquis a beseeching look.

"Yes, Grange, what is it?"

"Something may be amiss, milord," the footman replied. "A lad from the stables just informed me that Lady Granby has taken her leave."

"Taken her leave? What the devil are you talking about?" Granby demanded. "Where is my wife?"

"On her way to . . . I'm not sure, milord. Only that she has left Bedford Hall."

Granby raced up the stairs, taking them two at a time. When he reached Catherine's room, he opened the door and stopped in his tracks. The gown she'd been wearing was lying on the floor, next to a pile of petticoats. He looked in the dressing room to find the same thing, clothing scattered hither and yon, as if she'd been in a panic to find something.

The instant he saw the necklace, Granby knew that Catherine had indeed left him. The costly jewels had not been returned to their box, but tossed haphazardly on the vanity tray, left behind as if they were nothing more than glass trinkets. He studied the tray—the necklace and bracelet and earrings were all there, but not her wedding ring. She must still be wearing it.

The thought gave him hope that he could get her back. But why had she left in the first place?

Only one reason came to mind. Catherine had somehow witnessed Lady Aldershaw's good-bye kiss.

Granby's fist clenched around the necklace, unsure which woman he wanted to thrash the most—his lovely wife, who apparently didn't trust him farther than she could see him in a dark room, or the scheming widow who had caused all this.

"I say, what's amiss?" Rathbone asked from just beyond the open door. "Trouble?"

Granby didn't answer him. Couldn't answer him.

Necklace in hand, he stood looking at the brilliant diamonds, the perfectly cut emeralds, and all he could feel was a bone-deep ache, a violent internal confrontation with his deepest, most heartfelt emotions. He had heretofore acknowledged only the most superficial of those emotions—he desired Catherine, wanted her, but now, knowing she was gone, he was forced to admit that he loved her.

Love.

It hadn't announced itself, but had waited until he was looking the other way, then pounced, knocking him off his feet.

He *loved* Catherine. But more than that, he wanted her to love him, to be as consumed by the emotion as he was at this very moment. Totally, uncontrollably consumed.

But she was gone—she'd left him, and in leaving she'd unknowingly stolen his heart.

Waltham had joined Rathbone by the time Granby turned around to face the viscount's question. "Trouble. Yes, I have trouble. But not for long. Waltham, may I borrow one of your horses, the faster the better?"

"You're going after her?"

"Yes."

"Good. I let Evelyn get away once. Had a miserable time of things until I got her back."

Granby headed for the door that connected Catherine's abandoned room with his own bedroom. Once inside, followed by Rathbone, who wasn't about to leave without knowing all the sordid details, the earl repeated his wife's actions. He began shedding his clothes as fast as possible.

Peck miraculously appeared, no doubt summoned by the footman who had delivered the news of Lady Granby's mysterious midnight flight from Bedford Hall. The valet came into the room with Granby's riding breeches draped over his arm, and carrying his riding boots, freshly polished and ready for wear.

"You'll be wanting these, milord."

Nothing more was said until Granby was clothed to make a mad dash into the night. He then informed Peck to begin packing for their return to Foxleigh. "Lady Granby and I will meet you there," he said.

"Don't suppose you want any company?" Rathbone asked as he followed his friend downstairs.

"No."

"Thought as much."

Waltham was waiting near the western doors that would take them to the stables. "My fastest horse is saddled and ready. The lanes should be clear this time of night. May I suggest a shortcut, east of the dovecote. There's enough moonlight to make the ride without incident, and it will bring you out on the main road in good time."

"Thank you. I'll see that the horse is returned." Granby shook his hand. "Please make my apologies to Lady Waltham."

"No apology necessary. Just be happy."

"I intend to, once I've found my *misplaced* wife."

Rathbone edged his way into things again. "What I'd like to know is why the lady misplaced herself. Strange bit of goings-on, if I do say so, Granby. Marry the chit one day, lose her the next."

Granby didn't answer him. Whether the reason was, as he suspected, Lady Aldershaw, or something else, it made little difference. Catherine was his wife. He loved her, and she loved him, or at least he hoped she loved him. Either love or pride or both had caused her to run away. It was up to him to set things right. And when he did . . .

Deciding to cross that bridge when he came to it, he bid his friends goodbye and left the house, making his way to the stables. As promised, a thoroughbred stallion was saddled and waiting.

He was in the saddle and ready to ride when Rathbone materialized out of the night. Smiling, he handed Granby a flask of brandy. "Never know when it might come in handy," he said. "Take care, old friend, and don't give up the chase."

"I won't. She's worth the trouble, and more."

"Oh, I'm sure there's more. Always is where a woman is concerned."

A gust of wind rushed over the open lawn that separated the stables from the ocean. The scent of salt air reminded Granby of the previous night, of the woman who had ridden so bravely down the beach, of the passionate, unorthodox lady he'd taken to wife.

"Ride safe," Rathbone said, stepping back. "And give the lady a kiss for me."

"Before or after I give her the thrashing of her life?"

"Before, I should think. A good kiss can solve a world of woes."

"I'll keep that in mind," Granby said, before leaving Bedford Hall at a full gallop.

Catherine stared out the window of the carriage, saw the dark silhouette of trees against the moonlit sky, and felt nothing. She was numb, inside and out. Her fury had diminished with the distance being put between herself and her husband.

A wife for less than a day, and she was miserable. All she'd gotten for her dreams was a broken heart.

She had dared to love the man, dared to dream that he could love her in return. And that dream had been shattered, torn apart by one kiss—a kiss he'd shared with another woman.

It was a painful thing to accept, and she had no one to blame but herself.

Had anyone noticed her disappearance as yet? Catherine hoped not. She needed more time. Time to reach the sanctuary only Stonebridge and her father could offer.

She'd acted impulsively again, but what other choice did she have? To remain at Bedford Hall, to pretend she hadn't seen what she'd seen, to allow Granby into her bed, into her body again would be more humiliation than she could bear. If he cared for her, even the least bit, he wouldn't have kissed another woman.

Did he care?

She'd agonized over the question for weeks, but the only one who could answer it was her husband. He had married her, though it hadn't been necessary, and his insistence on that marriage had given her hope. Now that hope was gone.

The woods began to thin as they neared the turnoff that would take them to the main thoroughfare connecting Ipswich to the Kedington Road and points east. Catherine tried to find some beauty in the night, some soothing quality in the moonbeams that illuminated the road, but all she could see was endless days of unhappiness, a lifetime spent loving a man who didn't love her in return.

A tear slipped down her cheek, falling on the lap of

the blue dress she'd hastily pulled from the closet and over her head. A lightweight cloak was about her shoulders, the night having a chill even though it was midsummer. She wiped the tear away, determined not to cry, knowing that if she started she might not stop.

The carriage slowed, the harness creaking and moaning as the horses made the turn. Then the carriage stopped.

Opening the door, Catherine leaned out far enough to be heard by the driver. "What's wrong? Why are you stopping?"

When the driver didn't answer, Catherine pushed the door wide and climbed out of the carriage.

"Get back inside, milady. It could be a highwayman."

"A highwayman in this quaint neck of the woods?" she scoffed. Peering down the road ahead of them, all Catherine could see was the shadowy form of a man atop a horse.

The rider nudged his mount forward and Catherine's heart jumped into her throat. Granby!

"You, get down from there," he said, speaking to the driver. "Lord Waltham loaned me this horse. He is an excellent steed. I would have you return him to Bedford Hall."

"Yes, milord," the driver said, without question.

"No." Catherine shouted. "Stay where you are. This carriage is going to Winchcombe."

The driver, not wanting to get caught in a confrontation between an angry lord and his wayward wife, ignored the second order. Once he was on the ground, he walked to where the earl was still seated atop the stallion.

Granby dismounted and handed him the reins. "He's had a good run. Take him back with less haste."

"Yes, milord."

Catherine wasn't sure what her husband had in mind,

but she knew he had no intention of letting her return to Stonebridge. His posture was stiff, his tone too polite. He was furious, and she was the object of that fury.

It was just as well, she decided. She might as well say what she had to say and get it over with. By the time she was done telling the handsome Lord Granby what she thought of him, he'd be glad to be rid of her.

Once the driver had made his exit, much too enthusiastically from Catherine's point of view, she stood her ground.

"Get back inside," her husband ordered in a tone she had never heard him use before. "I will drive the carriage."

"I'm not going back," she said, so angry she had to clench her fists to keep her hands from shaking. "I'm going home."

"Very well, I shall see that you arrive safely."

He held the carriage door open.

Catherine hesitated. He was angry. He had to be angry. But he wasn't acting angry. His tone was cold, not heated, his expression bland, giving no hint of his real feelings. She supposed she shouldn't be surprised. A man had to care to get angry, and her husband didn't care. He'd come after her because his pride had suffered, not his heart.

Granby saw the confusion on her face, and smiled to himself. A little worry would do the lady good. The only thing that was keeping him from turning her over his knee was his relief at finding her safe. That relief was her salvation—for the time being.

"Get inside," he said. There was an undercurrent to his words, one that warned Catherine that she could get into the carriage of her own volition or be put inside.

Once she resumed her seat, without the aid of her husband's offered hand, the door was shut with a firm, resounding click of the latch.

It had been years since Granby had driven a carriage, but he didn't hesitate to climb up into the seat and take the reins in hand. Winchcombe was a good two days' journey; Reading an equal distance, but southeast, not due east. He wondered how long it would take his astute wife to realize that the home to which she was being taken wasn't Stonebridge.

It didn't matter. He'd lock her in the carriage if necessary. Once they reach Foxleigh he'd face what had to be faced, but on his own ground, under his own roof. His adorable wife had had the advantage for too long.

Giving the reins a quick flick, Granby set the horses to moving again. As the miles slid by, and the night gradually gave way to dawn, he started humming to himself.

Rathbone was right. A good kiss could sooth a world of woes, and the next time he kissed Catherine, he wasn't going to stop until she admitted that she loved him. Then, he'd do the same, and all would be well.

All was well until shortly before noon. Catherine had fallen asleep, lulled into slumber by the constant rocking of the carriage. Upon awakening, she was immediately struck by the fact that her husband had not returned to Bedford Hall, as she had suspected he might, but was indeed taking her away from the coast and east toward Winchcombe. Once there, they'd be saying their formal and permanent goodbyes. Another fact was just as disturbing. She needed to get out of the carriage and see to a natural need that was fast becoming a necessity.

"Stop the carriage," she called out from the window.

Granby pulled back on the reins. After setting the brake, he climbed down and opened the door. "Good morning, my lady."

"What's so bloody good about it?" She ached from

head to toe, and her legs were cramped from the long hours in what had to be the most uncomfortable carriage in the Bedford mews.

Once she was standing, she smoothed her skirts, then looked around. There was nothing but trees and an empty dirt lane, stretching out in both directions. She had no idea where they were, or how much longer she'd have to suffer the carriage.

"Would you care to ride up top with me?" her husband asked. " 'Tis a beautiful morning."

"I need to . . . that is I, oh, never mind." She stomped off into the woods, her modesty replaced by anger at the flippant way he'd invited her to share the driver's seat.

As if she'd share anything with the insufferable man. The sooner she saw the last of him, the better.

Granby contained his laughter as she marched off, shoulders stiff, back straight, into the woods. He thought about following her, but decided against it. When he did make love to her, it wasn't going to be a quick tumble in the forest. It was going to be a long session in a featherbed with no one to disturb them. Hour upon hour of leisurely love was what he had in mind.

Once Catherine had seen to her personal needs, she took a few minutes to gather her thoughts. The woods were quiet, the summer silence broken only by the occasional chattering squirrel.

Granby was being much too cooperative for her liking; she was certain he was up to something. But what?

The crunch of leaves and twigs under booted feet alerted her that her husband had given her what he assumed was enough time to herself. Catherine bristled, then stepped forward to meet him.

There was no point in pretending that they were anything other than enemies now, and she'd not surrender, not this time.

"Where are we?" she demanded when he showed himself.

"A hour's ride from the Letchworth Inn, I believe," he told her. "I'll arrange for a change of horses and a good meal. Assuming you're hungry."

She didn't answer him, but gathered up her skirts and walked past him, back to the carriage.

Her husband followed, resuming his role as driver.

The carriage rolled on, and Catherine became more miserable with each passing mile. Her husband was acting as if they were strangers, as if he hadn't made love to her, hadn't put a ring on her finger, hadn't vowed to cherish her above all women.

Her only solace was that they would eventually reach Stonebridge, and once there, she would have an ally. She had no idea how her father would react to her returning home under such circumstances, but she was confident that he loved her enough to offer her the comfort of his arms. As for her husband, whatever excuse he planned to give—if any—would be words wasted. Being a military man, Warren Hardwick admired loyalty above all else. An unfaithful husband had no loyalty.

Granby guided the carriage into the yard of the Letchworth Inn, grateful for a reprieve from the hard seat. The morning coach, which carried passengers from the inn bound for London, had departed hours earlier, leaving the establishment vacant except for its proprietor, his wife, and a local lad who helped with the horses.

Once inside, Granby saw Catherine was seated at a table, and provided with a hearty meal and a pot of steaming tea. When he joined her, sitting down with a smile, she was grateful that the meal gave her something to do with her hands, lest she give way to an impulse to wrap them around her husband's charming throat.

"Another day should see you home," he said. "We

will stop for the night, of course. There's an inn along that way that will offer reasonable shelter."

"Let me be brief, and say merely that the sooner I am rid of you, the better," Catherine replied, keeping her voice as normal as the circumstances allowed.

"And why is that, my lady?"

Her fork came down with a clank, hitting the edge of her plate before dropping to the table. "Why, my lord? Because you are a coldhearted womanizer, a man who cares for nothing but his own pleasures, his own comforts. Why bother escorting me at all? I'm sure you could hire a trustworthy driver to see me back to the bosom of my family. More time for you to enjoy beautiful widows."

She was jealous! Ragingly, beautifully jealous, and he couldn't be happier.

Perhaps Lady Aldershaw had done him a favor after all. They could have wasted weeks, even months, before arriving at this point in their marriage, the point where they had to admit their love for each other. If things worked out as planned, he would owe the promiscuous widow his gratitude.

"Eat your breakfast. We won't be stopping again for a good long while." Not until they reached the south road, the one that would take them to Reading.

Leaving a silent, stubborn Catherine with a second cup of tea, he checked on the horses, then informed his wife that they were ready to continue their journey.

And quite a journey it was. By the end of the day, Granby decided any and all drivers were worthy of a raise in pay. His ass was numb from sitting on the hard seat, and his spirits were beginning to bruise, as well.

It was one thing to think about forcing a confession of love from his lovely wife, and quite another to form the words she'd expect in reply.

"I love you," should be sufficient, but Granby doubted they would get the job done, not after Catherine discovered she was being kidnapped. Knowing his wife's temper, he'd have to spout all kinds of flowery nonsense. He loved her, he'd always love her, she made his heart happy.

The truth was, she did. For the first time in his adult life, he was enjoying every minute of every day. Since meeting Catherine he had come alive, fully alive. Life was more than duty and the obligations associated with his title; it was quiet moments with her in his arms, laughter, and arguments, and all the other things that made one day different from the next.

Now that she had touched his life, Granby couldn't imagine a future without her.

Hoping that one English lane looked very much like another, he made the turn south toward Reading. When no question or complaint came from his passenger, Granby decided she must be sleeping. He gauged the strength of the horses. They were holding up well, but he dared not push them all the way to Foxleigh. They would need to stop for the night.

A small inn, one he recognized from his more turbulent past, came into view. When he opened the carriage door it was to find his wife curled up on the seat, sleeping, her head resting on a tapestry valise.

"A room for the night," he told the innkeeper.

Wrinkled clothing or not, the innkeeper recognized a gentleman when he saw one, and when he heard one, and this man was a gentleman. When he lifted a woman out of the carriage, and marched toward the front door, the proprietor scurried forward to open it.

"Take the lady upstairs, milord. Second door on the left. I'll have my wife put a kettle on to boil."

The room was small but clean, with a brass bed and a mattress that provided far more comfort than a carriage seat. Catherine stirred as he put her down, but she didn't awaken. Thinking she looked beautiful with her hair hanging in unruly waves about her face, Granby leaned down and kissed her, not the way he wanted, but a chaste kiss on the forehead.

He needed something to eat, a tankard of the inn's best ale, and a bath. Once he'd seen to that, he'd do the same for his temperamental wife. Right now, sleep served her best.

When Catherine did come fully awake, the room was dark. She sat up with a start, then remembered what had preceded her falling asleep in the carriage. Now, alone in a strange room of an unknown inn, she wondered if the rest of her life would be plagued by the same dreams that had awakened her. Dreams, or rather regrets, of the life she would never have with the man she loved.

Wondering what time it was, she left the bed and opened the shutters that covered the window. There was nothing moving beyond the inn's yard but moonbeams and a breeze, stirring the treetops with a gentle force that brushed one leaf against the other. All was silence.

She left the room then, stepping out into the corridor. All the doors were closed. Tiptoeing to the top of the stairs, she looked over the railing and into the common room of the inn. Granby was there, sitting at a corner table with a tankard of ale in front of him. He was alone, staring out the window. Was he having similar regrets, or had he cataloged her reaction as that of a spoiled woman who selfishly wanted to monopolize his life?

"There you be, milady," a robust voice said from behind her. "I was just bringing up a tray for you."

She turned to find a woman in her late forties wearing a white apron over a crisply ironed brown dress. She was small, plump, and fair of color with bright, clear eyes and an extraordinary air of neatness and briskness about her. She informed Catherine that her name was Mrs. Shane.

"Is that tea?"

"Hot and spiced with a touch of cinnamon," the woman replied with a proud smile. "I've brought a partridge pie and biscuits, as well. His lordship said you'd be famished."

Catherine stomach rumbled the necessary reply.

"Come along, then" Mrs. Shane instructed her in a motherly voice. "Or would you be wanting to join your husband?"

"No. I'd rather have the tray in my room. Then a hot bath, if that's possible?"

"I've got Willy heating the kettles. The bathing room is at the end of the hall. Nothing fancy, mind you, but a big brass tub and soft, clean towels."

Catherine felt much better after a meal and a bath. Not wanting a confrontation with her husband until she'd decided exactly what she would say, she returned to the room he had rented and latched the door.

The rest of the night was spent wondering if she hadn't acted a bit too impulsively. As tears seeped from her eyes, she gave herself up to the emotions she'd been holding in, recognizing that she couldn't keep them bottled up forever. Clutching the pillow, she buried her face in it and began to sob. All the pain and sorrow she had suppressed since seeing her husband in the arms of another woman rose to the surface, overflowing.

As she wept bitter tears, Catherine began to experience a measure of ease, a genuine relief from the searing heartache that had engulfed her since leaving Bedford Hall. When she had no more tears to shed, she lay quietly on the bed, her body limp and exhausted, her eyes red and swollen, wide open and staring at the ceiling.

Slowly, she began to sort out her muddled thoughts, sifting through the painful moments to examine her true feelings with a new objective in mind.

By early morning, she knew she'd made a mistake. Instead of running away, she should have scratched out Lady Aldershaw's eyes.

She'd done the very thing she hadn't wanted to do—she'd been weak; weak and frightened. Scared of losing the one thing she wanted most—a future with the man she loved.

Well, no longer. She was going to march downstairs and demand that Granby explain himself. Then she was going to give him an ear-blistering he wouldn't soon forget. What happened next was entirely up to her husband.

She descended the staircase, but instead of finding her husband, she found only the innkeeper and his wife.

Breakfast was a porridge, stewed apples, and a strong cup of steaming tea, guaranteed to put any traveler to rights. Catherine was thanking Mrs. Shane, the innkeeper's wife, for her hospitality, when her husband the earl came through the door.

Dressed in the same clothes he'd been wearing since stopping the carriage, he was still the handsomest man she'd ever seen.

"Your coach awaits, my lady," he said, sweeping into a formal bow. "You shall be home by midday."

Catherine looked into his eyes. They were bright with amusement, and she supposed he was laughing at the stubborn way she'd been acting. Well, he could keep laughing. She wasn't about to argue with him in front of strangers. What she had to say was meant for his ears only.

"Home sounds wonderful to me," she replied with a smile. It wouldn't do the man any harm to think she was still furious with him.

He helped her into the carriage, and this time Catherine allowed the courtesy. "Thank you," she said.

"You're most welcome," he replied, with a twinkle in his eye. She was looking very pretty this morning, but he wasn't yet ready to spring his trap.

"I can see that you're as eager to be rid of me as I am

of you," Catherine said, testing the waters. "Good riddance, then."

Granby refused to take the bait.

"Enjoy your lonely carriage," he replied before shutting the door.

As the carriage rolled out of the yard, Catherine stiffened. The morning was not progressing as she had planned. To make matters worst, her husband was singing—and not all that well.

After twenty minutes of a risqué little tune that she was certain he'd learned in a brothel, Catherine thumped on the roof of the carriage, demanding that he stop before she developed a headache. He replied by singing louder.

It was too much. He was being deliberately rude and insensitive. She shouted for him to stop the carriage, but instead of slowing down, it gained speed.

With each turn of the carriage wheels, her temper rose, until she felt as if she were trying to contain a volcano.

"Enough," she called out to him. "Stop! Let me out immediately."

This time there was no response at all.

Another ten minutes had her testing the door.

It opened, and Granby shouted down for her to stop acting like a spoiled child. She wanted to go home, so that was where he was taking her.

It was well past midday when Catherine noticed a sign at one of the many road junctions they had passed since leaving the inn. Maidenhead was not a hamlet with which she was familiar, and it certainly wasn't one she and Felicity had passed through on their way to Ipswich. The name was too memorable.

There was the possibility that her husband was taking a different route, but she suspected he was being his customary underhanded self and had an entirely different destination in mind.

It was another hour before Granby saw the rooftop of Foxleigh Manor. He breathed an audible sigh of relief as he guided the carriage onto the gravel drive. Home. How sweet it was. Or at least how sweet it would be, once he'd tackled his wife's temper and had her contently purring again.

The moment the carriage stopped, Catherine leapt from its confines. She didn't have to ask where she was. She'd already figured that out. Foxleigh. The family home of the Earl of Granby.

Her husband was just as nimble, coming down from the driver's seat and catching her by the arm. "Where do you think to run to this time, my lady?"

"Away from you," Catherine said, determined to get a decent apology out of the man.

She writhed to get free, but his hold was too firm.

"Easy, my love, you're tired from the journey and in need of something to refresh you. Cook brews a fine cup of tea."

Catherine opened her mouth, deciding it was finally time to speak her mind, when the front door of the impressive manor house opened and a butler came trotting down the steps.

"Briggs, may I introduce my countess. She can meet the rest of the staff later. Have a tray sent up to my room. We'll have a late dinner."

"I'm only a temporary countess," Catherine told the servant. "I'll take my tray in one of the guest rooms. Any room is fine, as long as it isn't his lordship's."

"She's overly tired," Granby explained as the butler looked on, his eyes going wide as Catherine flailed to be free of her husband. "A long nap should restore her."

With that, Catherine found herself lifted and tossed over her husband's shoulder with no more care than he'd give a sack of flour.

"Put me down!"

"Now, now, darling. It's traditional for a husband to carry his wife over the threshold."

He marched up the stairs and into the house.

She pounded his back with her fists, calling him several colorful names. When his hand came down on her backside in a stinging slap, Catherine stopped squirming.

"Let me go. I won't stay here. I won't."

"You will stay where I wish you to stay," her husband replied, much too calmly for her to think he was jesting. "This is the house where you will live out your days. Accept it, and I may be persuaded not to sting that pretty bottom again."

Two flights of stairs were mounted and a long, carpeted corridor strolled down before Catherine was taken through a door and dumped unceremoniously in the middle of a large bed.

She came up sputtering more obscenities, but her husband ignored them. Before she could climb off the bed, he was on top of her, holding her and laughing.

Laughing!

It was the last straw. She wiggled and squirmed to be free, but it did not work.

"Enough," he finally said. "Calm yourself."

"You kissed *her,*" Catherine shouted at him. "I saw you on the veranda. I saw her in your arms."

"She wasn't in my arms," Granby said, hoping to clarify the issue. "I didn't touch her, she touched me."

Catherine made a disgusted sound.

"Lady Aldershaw means nothing to me. A man interested in philandering doesn't procure a special license and send his friend out in the middle of the night to wake up the magistrate. I married you because it's *you* I want."

Catherine turned her head and closed her eyes. The situation called for a lot more groveling on her husband's part.

Granby took a deep breath, then blurted the words before he lost his courage. "I love you."

He was surprised at how easy they were to say when you meant them.

Catherine didn't move, nor did she look at him.

"I love you. From that first day on the lane, I knew I was falling, and I was. I was falling in love with you, completely in love. I have no interest in any other woman. There will be no more kisses, unless it's your mouth. No more lovemaking, unless it's your body."

Slowly, she turned her head and looked up at him—into those incredible blue eyes. What she saw satisfied her heart. There was love there, shining out at her, no longer concealed or trapped by pride, but strong and true.

"Promise."

"I promise," he said. "I love you, Katie."

She grimaced at the nickname.

He laughed. "I've been wanting to call you that ever since the morning you hissed at me like the she-cat you are, but I knew you wouldn't like it."

"I don't. And if you call me Katie again, I will do more than hiss."

"Mmmm, sounds interesting."

He looked knowingly and lovingly into her eyes, then smiled that charming roguish smile that always set her heart to pounding.

Their mouths met, each instantly warming to the touch of the other, lips parting, tongues dipping. He moved onto his back, his left hand holding the nape of her neck, his right smoothing down her back to curve around her hip. Her hands moved into his hair, strong and firm on his scalp, then caressing, as they combed through the blond locks.

Granby kissed her with passion and force, his mouth demanding that she give and keep giving, his tongue thrusting, their breath mingling. His hand moved to her breast, stroking the nipple until it pushed hard against his fingers.

They separated at last, but only long enough to shed their clothing, undressing rapidly, tossing garments here and there as they laughed at each other's urgency.

They came together again, their bodies touching, and it was heaven. He kissed her long and hard, then eased her onto her back, wanting to look at her, amazed that this beautiful woman actually belonged to him, only to him.

Catherine lay there naked and let him look his fill, every inch of her exposed, waiting for his touch.

When his hands began to explore, to glide over her breasts, down her belly, then her inner thighs, she moaned with pleasure. He caressed and touched every part of her, until his hand came to rest in the soft nest of curls between her thighs. Then his fingers began to ply their magic, gently seeking, probing, learning her as if it were the first time. And finally, when she thought she could take no more of his enchanting touch, his mouth joined his fingers, and she moaned again.

Resting against the pillows, eyes closed, her body on fire, Catherine let him do as he wished with her. She reveled in his expertise, in the skill he used to excite her, and she opened to him, spreading her legs and inviting him into her body.

She quivered as he entered her in a long, smooth stroke that joined them completely. The scorching heat of her arousal melted around him, and it was her husband's turn to moan.

Knowing he'd climax much too soon if he didn't concentrate, Granby used the little willpower he had left to intensify her pleasure. He lifted himself up, then pushed down, counting the strokes in his mind, focusing on the physical act and not the emotional bonding, but his concentration lacked the power of his love for this wife, and soon he was thrusting into her as deeply as he could, forcing her to climb the summit with him. When her body began to quiver, to spasm, to demand the same of him, he gave in to the need to go beyond physical possession.

He finally understood the power of love as he looked down into her eyes. They were open now, watching him as he pushed deep, one last time. As he felt his life's essence flow from his body into her womb, he whispered, "I love you, Katie."

Several hours later, they lay in the bed, naked and snuggled in each other arms. Her husband had astonished Catherine with his stamina, his lack of inhibition, and his willingness to both give and receive pleasure.

Their lovemaking had been different this time, so emotional she had cried all three times. They belonged to each other now, more completely than any words could bind them.

"I'm waiting," he said sleepily.

"For what?" She propped herself on one elbow and looked down at him. "Very well," she mumbled, her fingers combing lightly through the hair on his chest. "You may have Storm Dancer as a wedding present, but only if I am allowed to ride him from time to time."

She laughed when he sat up, rolled her onto her back, then began tickling her.

"That stallion will be the end of you," he said, finding a particularly sensitive spot behind her knee. "Now, tell me."

"I love you," she called out, half laughing, half crying.

"Forever," he urged, reaching for her other knee.

"Forever and always," she relented, with a smile that warmed his heart. "I vow to be the most wonderful of wives, to pamper you and care for you, to give you an heir, and a lifetime of happiness."

"Promise."

"I promise," she said, knowing she'd never spoken anything more true.

"And I vow to spend my life making you happy, loving you until you're too exhausted to leave my bed, at least as long as my strength holds out. You're a greedy wench."

Catherine slapped at his hand as it moved over her breast. "You're the greedy one, my lord."

"Forever and always," he said, before sealing her mouth with a kiss that promised that and much more.

"I suppose I'll have to apologize again," Granby said as they walked downstairs to greet their guests.

The coach carrying both Lady Felicity Forbes-Hammond and the Duke of Morland had just arrived at Foxleigh.

"You practiced on my father yesterday," Catherine said, taking his arm. "And most eloquently, I must say."

"Your father is an understanding man. If only Felicity exhibits similar good nature, this day may end well."

"It will end as it usually does," she said, smiling. "With me promising to love you forever and always."

"In that case, I shall be at my eloquent best," her husband promised. He stopped on the landing long enough to give her a hearty kiss, then insisted that she stop distracting him—they had guests to meet.

The day did go well. Felicity didn't require nearly as much groveling as Granby had expected, and the duke only chastised him for ten minutes. All in all, it was a good day.

But the night was better.

For it was that night, during a long session of gentle lovemaking, that the Granby heir was conceived.

DO YOU HAVE THE
HOHL COLLECTION?

Discover the Thrill of
Romance With

Kat Martin

__Hot Rain
0-8217-6935-9   **$6.99**US/**$8.99**CAN

Allie Parker is in the wrong place—at the worst possible time . . . Her only ally is mysterious Jake Dawson, who warns her that she must play the role of his reluctant bedmate . . . if she wants to stay alive. Now, as Alice places her trust—and herself—in the hands of a total stranger, she wonders if this desperate gamble will be her last . . .

__The Secret
0-8217-6798-4   **$6.99**US/**$8.99**CAN

Kat Rollins moved to Montana looking to change her life, not find another man like Chance McLain, with a sexy smile of empty heart. Chance can't ignore the desire he feels for her—or the suspicion that somebody wants her to leave Lost Peak . . .

__The Dream
0-8217-6568-X   **$6.99**US/**$8.50**CAN

Genny Austin is convinced that her nightmares are visions of another life she lived long ago. Jack Brennan is having nightmares, too, but his are real. In the shadows of dreams lurks a terrible truth, and only by unlocking the past will Genny be free to love at last. . .

__Silent Rose
0-8217-6281-8   **$6.99**US/**$8.50**CAN

When best-selling author Devon James checks into a bed-and-breakfast in Connecticut, she only hopes to put the spark back into her relationship with her fiancé. But what she experiences at the Stafford Inn changes her life forever . . .

Available Wherever Books Are Sold!

Visit our website at **www.kensingtonbooks.com**.

Discover the Thrill of
Romance with
Lisa Plumley

__Making Over Mike

0-8217-7110-8 $5.99US/$7.99CAN

Amanda Connor is a life coach—not a magician! Granted, as a
publicity stunt for her new business, the savvy entrepreneur has
promised to transform some poor slob into a perfectly balanced
example of modern manhood. But Mike Cavaco gives "raw material"
new meaning.

__Falling for April

0-8217-7111-6 $5.99US/$7.99CAN

Her hometown gourmet catering company may be in a slump, but
April Finnegan isn't about to begin again. Determined to save her
business, she sets out to win some local sponsors, unaware she's not
the only one with that idea. Turns out wealthy department store mogul
Ryan Forrester is one step—and thousands of dollars—ahead of her.

__Reconsidering Riley

0-8217-7340-2 $5.99US/$7.99CAN

Jayne Murphy's best-selling relationship manual *Heartbreak 101* was
inspired by her all-too-personal experience with gorgeous, capable . . .
outdoorsy . . . Riley Davis, who stole her heart—and promptly skipped
town with it. Now, Jayne's organized a workshop for dumpees. But it
becomes hell on her heart when the leader for her group's week-long
nature jaunt turns out to be none other than a certain . . .

*Availabl**e Everywhere Books a**re Sold!*

Visit our w**ebsite at www.kensington**books.com.